COLBERT

Louis XIV and his ministers, from an almanac for the year 1682. *(Photo. Bibl. nat. Paris.)*

COLBERT

By Inès Murat

TRANSLATED BY

Robert Francis Cook &

Jeannie Van Asselt

University Press of Virginia

Charlottesville

Library of Congress Cataloging in Publication Data

Murat, Inès.
   Colbert.

   Translation of: Colbert.
   Bibliography: p.
   Includes index.
   1. Colbert, Jean Baptiste, 1619–1683.   2. France—
History—Luis XIV, 1643–1715.   3. Statesmen—France—
Biography.   I. Title.
DC130.C6M8713 1984   944′.033′0924 [B]   84–2194

Printed in the United States of America

CONTENTS

Preface   vii

PART I

THE ASCENT

1   *A Family's Itinerary*   1

2   *The Fronde*   11

3   *Mazarin's Agent*   21

4   *A Political Duel*   35

5   *The Fall of Fouquet*   57

PART II

KING & STATE [1661–72]

6   *The Minister, the King, and France*   73

7   *The Court*   83

8   *The State as Dispenser of Justice*   91

9   *Paris and Versailles*   107

10   *The Arts and History*   113

CONTENTS

PART III

THE ECONOMIC WAR {1661–72}

11 *Mercantilism and War*   129

12 *"Colbertism" and the French*   151

13 *The Sea*   171

PART IV

GLORY & BITTERNESS {1662–83}

14 *The Sun-King's War*   197

15 *The Minister's Glory*   219

16 *Bitterness*   231

17 *The Affaire des Poisons*   253

18 *The Age of Colbert*   267

    Bibliography   281

    Index   289

PREFACE

THE IDEA FOR THIS BOOK was suggested to me by the large number of documents preserved by my family, descendants of Jean-Baptiste Colbert's eldest daughter, Jeanne-Marie-Thérèse Colbert, duchesse de Chevreuse. These archives consist essentially of Colbert's personal papers concerning the great events of his day. His political lifetime was unusually long: it began under the ministry of Richelieu and did not end until the height of Louis XIV's reign.

I have tried to present a general survey of the man and his work. The variety and the importance of the archives to which I have had access have encouraged this manner of presentation. Only Pierre Clément, Colbert's greatest historian, has had access to the collection and that was in the nineteenth century. Many of the documents it contains have never been published. The study of drafts written by a man whose political role was decisive can often shed unexpected light on critical events.

The collection includes several files:

—*The Mazarin dossier.* Colbert was the agent and the confidant of Mazarin. He kept in his personal archives the autograph drafts of the many letters he sent the cardinal. The family archives include about one hundred of these drafts, mostly unpublished. My grandfather, Honoré de Luynes, was prevented by his premature death from publishing the very important study he had undertaken to make of this file and of Colbert's activities during this period. I am fortunate in having been able to draw on his work, which has helped me considerably in studying this part of Colbert's life.

—*The Fouquet affair.* Colbert was the moving force behind the superintendant's fall. This file includes both the final and the early drafts that Colbert wrote in his own hand. The planning of Fouquet's arrest was also, as these documents show, the planning of a genuine coup d'état.

—*The king's letters.* Colbert was Louis XIV's minister for twenty-two years. When he wrote to the king, he used only half the width of the sheet, so that the king could write his replies himself on the same sheets. Moreover, the king wrote regularly to his chief minister while on his frequent campaigns.

PREFACE

Pierre Clément has published, in part, the correspondence preserved in the family archives. Some documents have been incorrectly published. Several memoranda and autograph letters of great importance have never been published, especially for the period of the war with the Netherlands.

The file also includes copies made of original documents some of which are in the Bibliothèque Nationale. It appears that several of these have never been published.

—*Memoranda addressed to Seignelay*. Colbert made his eldest son, the marquis de Seignelay, his principal aide for maritime affairs. None of these documents has been published except for one memorandum that appears in Clément.

—*The "Affaire des poisons."* This is Colbert's private file concerning an affair of exceptional delicacy for the regime. Some of the autographs in it are unpublished.

Various other files contain the minister's major reports on finances, industry, and trade in final autograph draft; reports on foreign powers capable of entering into trade agreements with France; and reports on work carried out at the Louvre and at Versailles, which was Colbert's responsibility as superintendant of buildings. There are also drafts that prove Colbert participated in the writings of Louis XIV's *Mémoires*.

I would like to give special thanks to my brother Thomas de Luynes, who gave me very efficient assistance in the organization and analysis of a set of documents that was fascinating, but often difficult, to study.

Note to the translated edition. Notes preceded by an arabic numeral have been reproduced from the original edition. Others have been added by the translators.

COLBERT

PART I

THE ASCENT

CHAPTER 1

A Family's Itinerary

THE TOWN

NEAR THE END OF THE MIDDLE AGES, a plowman looked toward the ramparts of the town. The soil seemed frozen; the rhythm of the seasons was immutable; existence was dissolved in an anonymous, undifferentiated universe without past or future. There, behind the ramparts, was variety, the activity of fairs, new construction—the confused, but powerful feeling of a future. Towns valued their privileged status, their uniqueness. Our plowman wanted to be involved in the urban world without having to leave the rural one. The city needed materials for fortifications, for buildings. It was, perhaps, with a simple team of oxen that the ancestor of Louis XIV's great minister brought to the city of Rheims a load of stone.

By the end of the fifteenth century, his descendants were at the head of a genuine business firm. They owned quarries, sold rough-cut stone, and directed the workers charged with extracting and transporting gravel, earth, and debris.

THE ASCENT

There were many Colberts around Rheims, but the name was especially prevalent in Champagne.[1] The minister's ancestors settled in the suburb of Porte-Cabres, or Porte-Chacre, to the northeast of Rheims. After two centuries of ruin and destruction, Rheims was starting to rebuild. Construction sites were everywhere, and Jehan Colbert II carried on a flourishing business. An educated and talented man, Jehan was a mason primarily, but also worked as an architect. It was probably he who designed a Renaissance chapel in the Church of Saint Jacques. The Colbert family had carved out a place in the town. It now had the capital necessary to contemplate wider horizons: the movement of goods along the great commercial route that ran from Italy to Flanders, passing through Rheims.

MERCHANDISE

By about 1510, the first Gérard Colbert had become a leading citizen of Rheims. An alderman, a councilman, and a tax farmer,* he made the most of Rheims's exceptionally valuable geographic position in the context of the economy of the age. Most commercial exchanges at that time between Italy and the Low Countries followed overland routes. Rheims appeared, after Lyons, as a sort of stopping place between the Midi and Northern Europe.

Champagne's commercial fairs were still famous. Oudard Colbert I (1520–73), the famous statesman's great-grandfather, allied himself to the best commercial bourgeoisie of Rheims when he wed Marie Coquebert. He bought, for 6,500 livres tournois (about 1.5 million French francs), a large house in the rue de Porte-Chacre, with a monumental porte cochere. He named his business venture Long Vestu,† after a house of the same name that he had earlier rented from his father-in-law.

What line of business did Long Vestu pursue? Despite what has often been written, Oudard Colbert was not a draper but a *mercier,* a type of wholesaler. The term *mercerie* refers to all the goods and products of long-distance trade. Nothing is more absurd than the legend that his was a modest family shop retailing pieces

[1]See Jean-Louis Bourgeon's very interesting *Les Colbert avant Colbert.* The family name surely derives from the Latin *collibertus,* used in the Middle Ages to mean a liberated serf.

*The taxes under the monarchy were farmed out to local noblemen called tax farmers, who had the job of collecting them for a percentage of the revenues.

†The name *Long Vestu* is the rough equivalent of the English "At the Sign of the Tabard" and refers to one of the painted signs by which all houses (not only taverns) were identified in the period.

of cloth. The *merciers* were a privileged class of merchants, allowed by law to deal wholesale in any kind of merchandise, without restriction. If they wished, they could also sell at retail, even though retailers were forbidden to engage in wholesale trade. Thus, the *merciers* were free from the narrow rigidity of the guild regulations of the ancien régime. Large-scale international trade implies adventure and freedom. Once again, the family Colbert chose a path open to risk, but also to an ambitious future. The company called Long Vestu brought together a vast commercial network that covered a broad geographical area including Lyons, Dijon, Paris, Troyes, Rouen, and Amiens. Most of Oudard's trade was in linens, velvets, and other fabrics.

The increased stocks of precious metals after the great discovery of the American continent had given a tremendous impetus to nascent capitalism. Europe was already the scene of financial dealings on a large scale. Letters of credit were used; speculation and scheming were common; means of payment and compensation were organized. The money market was then closely linked to commerce, perhaps particularly in France. The great wholesale merchants were the first to seize the opportunity to buy and sell letters of credit; little by little, they became "merchant bankers." Long-distance business dealings were slow and uncertain: and thus implied a system of loans. Advances in high finance led to a concentration of capital in certain places along the major commercial routes. In 1533, the first large stockmarket in Europe was founded at Antwerp. It was open "to traders of all languages and of all nations." Italian banks, responsible for collecting papal tithes throughout Europe, appeared to be considerable financial powers. Drawn by commercial fairs, the Italian bankers set up branches in Lyons, which became an enormous reservoir of capital. Milan, Lyons, Antwerp, the great financial marketplaces of Europe, were on the trade route of the company called Long Vestu. Men bought, sold, speculated on prices from market to market. They conspired to fix prices and they trafficked in large sums of money. Commercial capitalism and banking capitalism were inseparable.

When Oudard died, his widow had one of the greatest fortunes of all Rheims. For his three sons, the transfer of capital was as significant as the transport of goods. The Colbert brothers traveled widely. The youngest, Oudard II, left for Troyes. The eldest, Gérard III, often went to Paris or Amiens. Jehan V, the statesman's grandfather, went to Italy yearly to sound out the market and to seek raw materials, thus bypassing the many Italian middlemen in Lyons. He made his home with his mother in Rheims, and was head of the business from 1585 onward. Jehan dealt in goods of every sort, as the wholesalers were legally allowed to do: cloth, of course, but also herring (one cask of them to Rouen in 1595),[2]

[2]Ibid.

]3[

and salted fish, grain, wine, and salt. He was also a public official, inspector-general for the collection of the salt tax in the province of Burgundy. From 1589 to 1594, the struggle between the Ligue and the Royalists had interrupted trade in Rheims somewhat. The city had cast its lot with the Catholic confederacy. It was cut off from Lyons, but the Colbert brothers were powerful enough to operate outside the troubled areas. They made Milan the southern bridgehead for Long Vestu. Amiens and Paris, along with Troyes, became their new primary places of business.

Jehan died young, in 1596. His widow, Marie Bachelier, raised five children in the old family house. She did not dare continue the enterprising, even venturesome, policies of her husband. There is no large-scale international trade without risks. Long Vestu vegetated and seems to have gone into a slow decline.

On the other hand, the successes of Jehan's younger brother Oudard II (the minister's great-uncle) were exemplary. He had foreseen Lyons's decline to the benefit of Flanders and had chosen Troyes as his principal place of business. He was the very image of the grand capitalist in the early seventeenth century. Manufacturer, merchant, and international banker, he had the backing of Henri IV (whom he probably knew personally). Through him, the Colbert family made its entry into court circles, the seat of power. Oudard visited Paris and occupied a château at Villacerf, where he gave dazzling parties. His daughters married into the old *noblesse de robe*.* His sons, the lords of Saint-Pouange and of Villacerf, bore the titles he had bought.

Jean-Baptiste Colbert, Lord Saint-Pouange, was to marry Claude Le Tellier, sister of Michel Le Tellier,† future war minister and father of Louvois. The origins of the Le Tellier family were like those of the Colbert family. Rich wholesale merchants from Champagne, they had worked their way into the corridors of the monarchy in the same fashion. The families contemplated alliance by marriage, with no notion of the bitter rivalries that were to split the two clans under Louis XIV.

But let us return to Rheims, to the house Long Vestu, home of Jehan's widow. For her two elder sons, Jehan VI and Nicolas, formal schooling ended at about the age of fifteen. She sent them to Lyons for a time, to learn business techniques. In 1615, Nicolas, father of the great Colbert, married Marie Pussort, from a family of merchants. Three years later he joined forces with his brother and one of his Bachelier cousins, a banker in Lyons. As the local agents for the

*According to French law, only the first son could inherit his father's wealth and lands. Younger sons generally went into the military (*noblesse d'épée*), the priesthood, or the judiciary (*noblesse de robe*).

†Le Tellier was the man who was to be Colbert's patron and then his rival.

Parisian and Lyonnese firm of Mascramy and Lumagne, the two brothers seem to have spent more time as financiers than as wholesalers, without, however, abandoning that trade. Their uncle Oudard entrusted the management of the funds to them. They pursued the trade between Italy and Amiens, but never came near the great volume handled by Long Vestu at its zenith. The export of local wines to Flanders constituted a noteworthy share of their business.

Jean-Baptiste Colbert, eldest son of Nicolas, was born on August 29, 1619. He may have been born at his grandmother's, at the sign of the Long Vestu, as contemporary accounts would have it, but that is not certain. It was just about the time of his birth that his parents left the family home and successively occupied two other houses in the rue de Porte-Cerre. Nicolas and his family moved into the house of Gérard Colbert II in 1622, when Jean-Baptiste was three. His early childhood was spent in the home of the leading members of the Colbert merchants. Nicolas's social standing improved steadily. He was an alderman in Rheims; he received the fief of Vandières as a legacy from his wife's uncle. But "Milord de Vandières" seemed extremely worried. His business was stagnating, and his trade was in jeopardy. He could not, or would not, detach himself from the powerful attraction of Lyons in time. Lyons, however, had been going slowly downhill for some fifty years. The religious wars, the many loans to the French crown, and the poverty due to the long civil wars were incentives for Lyonnese bankers to transfer large capital sums to Antwerp. Spain's hegemony was suffocating high finance in Italy. Antwerp, in its turn, was ravaged by war, and yielded to Spanish vindictiveness. The Low Countries had defeated the heirs of Emperor Charles V, and the Dutch began to attract the monetary reserves formerly at Antwerp. Amsterdam was beginning to dazzle Europe. Now the Rhine route replaced in importance the great route via Lyons and Rheims. Champagne was progressively isolated from the mainstream of intra-European trade. The rapid deterioration of the economic situation at Rheims is shown by the large number of bankruptcies. Inflation, brought on by the influx of precious metals from the New World, a decline in the interest rate, the threat of war: the early seventeenth century saw the end of that exceptional expansion of credit that had so enriched the Renaissance capitalists. The financial decline of the Italy-Flanders axis was accompanied by its commercial decline. The development of navigation was a fatal blow to Continental traders. Lyons remained an important city in spite of everything, but it was no longer the arbiter of monetary exchanges. Its role as intermediary between north and south Europe was thoroughly eclipsed by seagoing vessels. The city's relative decline and, in a broader sense, the reasons for that decline had direct repercussions on the business operated by Jehan and Nicolas Colbert. It is likely that its failure had a strong influence on the latter's economic convictions. Lyons was a symbol for economic theorists: It meant free trade, a certain conception of the right to work, mistrust of guild regulations, and a strong distaste for protectionism. Colbert was to stand for everything Lyons was not, just as his idol Richelieu had done after taking power in 1624. In the meantime, Nicolas passed his time aimlessly in the house of the merchant pioneer. Economic difficulties, lethal epidemics in Italy and in Lyons, the beginnings of the Thirty Years War, all seemed to mean a dead end for the family. In 1629, Nicolas left Rheims and moved to Paris, the financiers' paradise.

HIGH FINANCE

Paris was flooded with money traffickers. The charging of interest was still forbidden by canon law, but there were plenty of devices and hypocrisies to circumvent the old law. The financiers came from everywhere, from every social class. Italians, Germans, Protestant bankers, mere advisors* of modest origins, merchant and banking bourgeoisie from the provinces: the realm of money was vast, diverse, and powerful enough to be hated by the population and to command the government's respect—"a leech sucking the people," and indispensable to the king. The royal treasury was always empty. The war economy was a heavy burden for France, and Richelieu openly admitted ignorance in financial matters. What a windfall for businessmen! They formed associations (*partis*) that lent the king the money he needed for enormous and urgent state expenses. Before long, they were farming the public revenues out, thus greatly reimbursing themselves at the taxpayers' expense. *Partisans* and tax farmers reigned supreme in France. Nicholas knew Paris well when he decided to move there. He had gone to the city often on business. He did not fail to visit his uncle Oudard or his cousins Saint-Pouange and Villacerf. The world of Parisian high finance held out hope of a more plentiful and more brilliant future.

The childhood of Jean-Baptiste remains obscure. It appears, however, that the future minister did not accompany his parents to Paris. The boy, ten years old, was probably sent to board at the Jesuit school in Rheims, which he would have left in 1634, at fifteen. As his father had done at the same age, he spent some time as a financier's apprentice in Lyons. There he was for a time in the employ of the banker Mascramy. Before long, he was reunited with his family in Paris, where his father placed him as a sort of intern in various offices and functions in order to complete his business training. The young Colbert worked in the offices of two lawyers, Chapelain, the *notaire,* then Béterne, the prosecutor of the court of the Châtelet. Later he held the title of junior clerk, or *commis subalterne,* to Sabatier, a treasurer of the loans made by special associations, or *partis.*

*If the advice they gave in matters of taxation was good, they might hope to receive part of the new revenue their ideas had generated.

What of Nicolas's Parisian career during this period? The large Colbert family lived in the part of town that businessmen preferred, in the rue Grenier-Saint-Lazare, near the church of Saint-Nicolas-des-Champs. Mme. Colbert gave birth to eighteen children, nine of whom lived. Nicolas became an independent banker and handled several private fortunes successfully. His uncle Oudard once again gave him some of his capital to manage. His clientele was made up basically of a number of provincial nobles, primarily from Champagne. He frequented the "cour du Palais," seat of the Paris exchange, with regularity. The lucrative schemes of the tax farmers attracted him. In 1632 he bought an office titled *receveur général et payeur des anciennes rentes de la ville de Paris assignées sur les aides.** Nicolas Colbert had entered the world of the *partisans*. At that time the management of state revenues facilitated personal speculation. Fouquet was to be living proof of that.[3] Jean-Baptiste's father did not fail to be swept down the slope of financial unscrupulousness. The profession of tax farmer implied huge risks, since it meant advancing enormous sums whose reimbursement was sometimes delayed. In 1634, late payments from the tax farmers brought Nicolas near disaster. The bureau of the city of Paris, to which the *rentes* were owed, declared him to be "in debt to the People by over 300,000 francs." His situation appeared hopeless, and he sold his office. When he bought it back the following year, his fortune seems to have been remade. Thanks to how many fraudulent statements and through what financial acrobatics, one will perhaps never know. Until his death in 1661, Nicolas continued to carry on his financial dealings, sometimes cleverly, often at some risk, and nearly always in close connection with the intelligent and profit-minded circles of Parisian high finance. He lived comfortably and honorably, without being able, nevertheless, to attain the splendid status his cousins enjoyed.

Thanks to his father's activity, Jean-Baptiste observed the world of the tax farmers. Was it at this time that he conceived his hatred towards this special group of moneyed men? Did he dream already of dragging them before a court of justice and of shaping the whole financial edifice?

Jean-Baptiste turned twenty-one in 1640; it was time to establish him in a situation. Nicolas had always remained close to his cousin Colbert de Saint-Pouange, an official of the war department under Sublet de Noyers. Richelieu's

---

[3]Nicolas Fouquet signed his name *Foucquet,* a spelling adopted by some historians (notably Georges Mongrédien and Georges Bordonove). But Colbert wrote *Fouquet,* as did many of his contemporaries. We have chosen the spelling found in Colbert's papers.

*Like nearly all such positions, Nicolas Colbert's was rather more important for its unofficial attributes than for its nominal functions. His formal title has no close equivalent in English or in modern French. Broadly speaking, it seems he handled the payment of interest on old public debts (the *rentes*) and drew the required funds from collection of one of the contemporary indirect taxes (the *aides*).

energy had lent government service new respectability. With Saint-Pouange's valuable support, Nicolas bought his son the post of *commissaire ordinaire des guerres.* Colbert chose to serve the state. Thanks to him, his family was to gain a new kind of power: political might.

THE STATE

A *commissaire des guerres* was expected to travel widely throughout France, inspecting garrisons, counting troops, overseeing equipment and materials. Even as a beginner under Richelieu, Colbert showed a strict temperament, precursor of his later righteous zeal. Sublet de Noyers noticed it; he wrote to Colbert on April 21, 1640: "Commissaire Colbert, having learning of the disobedience and rebellion of the inhabitants of my city of Dreux through your report, I have resolved to give them an exemplary punishment. I am giving my lord Bussy-Rabutin the orders contained in the enclosed letter; he is to give at once the best training he can to the companies of your regiment."[4] Colbert held the job for several years. He had a firm, precise, and assiduous turn of mind. He waited for the time when he could consider a higher position. He traveled through France. In 1640, he was in charge of troops in the region of Nevers; the next year he was given the regiment of Tavannes.

We may imagine that the news of Richelieu's death on December 4, 1642, made a profound impression on the young *commissaire,* and probably caused him some distress. Colbert was twenty-three. Richelieu's powerful rigor had mesmerized him. He himself was naturally dry in manner and stiff in character, but he warmed to the point of lyricism when he spoke of the cardinal. Richelieu had given the concept of government an emotional component. His great design for the nation, his political will, associated itself with a patriotic feeling. There would be blemishes in Colbert's life. He would lack neither cupidity nor cynicism. But his passion for the state was like a lasting excitement.

Louis XIII died on May 14, 1643, after having made Mazarin—of whom Richelieu had already taken note—his prime minister. A few days before his death, he had chosen the new cardinal as godfather to the dauphin, age four.

In April 1643, Michel Le Tellier, Saint-Pouange's brother-in-law, replaced Sublet de Noyers at the war ministry. He had impressed Mazarin, earlier, as an army inspector in the Piedmont (a posting Saint-Pouange had probably helped arrange). Le Tellier named his brother-in-law under-secretary. Young Colbert pursued his career as *commissaire.* Le Tellier was aware of his abilities and seems even to have liked him. In 1644, Jean-Baptiste sent him a letter expressing his

[4]Pierre Clément, *Lettres, instructions, et mémoires de Colbert,* 7:11.

regrets at the death of Le Tellier's sister, Saint-Pouange's wife. Le Tellier replied: "I thank you with all my heart, and beg that your love for me will continue."[5]

In 1645, Le Tellier decided to attach the *commissaire* to his own staff, and Colbert became the minister's agent. His worldly fortune soon matched his political advantage. In 1647, one of his Pussort uncles went over to the enemy. Acting (we may surmise) at Le Tellier's request, the king confiscated his estates and made a gift of them to Colbert. On December 13, 1648, Jean-Baptiste, "residing in Paris, rue de Montmartre, parish of Saint-Eustache," married a rich heiress, Marie Charron, daughter of a "member of King's council." Her dowry was 100,000 livres tournois. The marriage contract also mentions Colbert's 50,000 livres "deriving from his profession." It was an enormous sum for a mere *commissaire*. Did it include bonuses? Was he speculating? From his youth on, Colbert applied himself, with an undeniable genius to building his personal fortune. Michel Le Tellier was a witness to the marriage contract, and also procured him an appointment as a state councilor, which sanctioned his position as a high-level public servant.

In 1648, the rebellion of the Fronde broke out. The serious disorders that resulted were to bring Colbert exceptional and unexpected career opportunities. His prodigiously rapid rise to power would furnish, for the bourgeoisie from which he came, a kind of legend.

[5]Ibid., vol. 3.

CHAPTER 2

The Fronde

THE YEARS 1648–52 were black years for France, shamefully tragic. Her people, ravaged by foreign enemies and rent asunder by civil war, lived in a state of suffering without parallel. Revolts broke out against the administrative machinery that Richelieu had begun to assemble. An insurrection was the response of the privileged classes to the new centralism, with its overtones of strict justice. Improbable alliances gathered gleefully around a French state in the throes of death. Anne of Austria, still pushing, against all hope, for further progress toward absolute monarchy, found her political path blocked.

Let us recall briefly the principal events of the Fronde. In 1648, the Parlement of Paris had the audacity to request abolition of the office of intendant, an essential stone in the edifice of centralized government.* The parlement further required a royal vow that no new tax or public office would be created without its approval. The queen had the *parlementaire* Broussel arrested. An uprising of the Paris populace brought about Broussel's release and the abolition of the intendants. During 1649 and 1650, the queen fled Paris for Saint-Germain, taking with her the child Louis XIV and Mazarin, and Paris was blockaded by Condé, who was by then plotting to seize power himself. His supporters made pacts with foreign powers and stirred several provinces to revolt, which the royal troops struggled to put down, one by one. In 1651, the parlement and the disaffected great lords joined forces. By the beginning of 1653, France was bled dry, pillaged, and worn out, and was ready to sacrifice freedom to gain peace. The Fronde had died out. Louis XIV, and then Mazarin, were cheered as they entered Paris. Mazarin, naturalized as a French subject after 1638, was the detested Italian. Twice, in 1651 and in 1652, he had had to go into exile. From his refuge he had continued to counsel the queen and to guide the rebuilding of the government.

*The parlements of the ancien régime were high courts of justice, not merely legislative bodies. The intendants were royal agents (inspectors general of sorts) in the provinces.

The Ascent

During these terrible years, royal troops fought the Spanish and the Fronde simultaneously. War Minister Le Tellier took a leading role, entrusting ever more important and sensitive missions to his agent.

The Messenger

Colbert quickly became the intermediary between the court, as it moved about in the provinces, and Le Tellier, who was working to coordinate the war effort. His presence soon became a familiar one to the queen and the young king. Colbert did not like Mazarin. He was haunted by memories of Richelieu, and the very different personality of the prime minister offended him. As Colbert gave Le Tellier information on the military and political situation, he reported Mazarin's endless criticisms and his complaint that he "was not at ease." Le Tellier shared his agent's low opinion of the cardinal. "His Eminence," wrote Colbert to his superior in February 1650, "has still not varied from the principle to which I have heard you refer several times: that any accommodation was easy for him, provided it brought him money."[1]

According to Mazarin's own statements, he wished to be as gentle and accommodating as possible. He may have thought that attitude necessary to reconcile the French, then at each other's throats. But Colbert's energetic and firm temperament was revolted by the cardinal's approach. In April, he wrote to Le Tellier, expressing all his anger against the cardinal. "Irresolution is a quality the man possesses to a supreme degree. I wonder if it doesn't come from the fact that his mind has not room for two matters at once, and that when one is a bit urgent, it erases the other; and whatever his memory may do from time to time to find room for it, the place is filled, and it barely sets foot on the threshold before being driven out again." And Colbert did not fail to report to Le Tellier "those bitter words describing you." Further on, there are references to the distaste that, in Colbert's estimation, Mazarin aroused in his generals.

In June, Le Tellier ordered Colbert to obtain from Mazarin an abbey promised to someone else. Colbert used strong words. He could not hide his dislike for the cardinal. Mazarin wrote to Le Tellier in a fury:

Further, I am obliged to complain of the actions of said Colbert, who obliged me to become angry with him after I had been more patient with him than I should have, for though I had made known to him my displeasure with the state of the matter, he answered me back thrice, with such heat, and in terms so ill suited to his rank and mine, that I could not refrain from anger,

[1]Pierre Clément, *Lettres, instructions, et mémoires de Colbert,* vol. 1.

and told him that on no account would you have dreamt of saying the hundredth part of what he was saying, adding that I was convinced you would be the first to abandon him when you learned he was disrespectful to me.

Le Tellier gave his agent a reprimand and sent him to see Mazarin again. The cardinal made an appointment for Colbert at six in the morning but received him at noon for fifteen minutes. There was another interview the same evening, which Colbert described to Le Tellier: "My Lord, I went to His Eminence again yesterday evening, and he received me as he had done in the morning, turning his back on me and denying me a chance to come near, which led me to believe that he no longer wished to have dealings with me." And Colbert unhesitatingly went on to say: "Had it not been for the total obedience I owe you, I would have withdrawn, being unable to bring myself to bear such treatment without much pain and repugnance, especially from a man for whom I have no esteem."

Le Tellier tried to calm Mazarin, and Colbert "found at last that monsieur le cardinal is softening a little."

The royal family's situation never seemed so critical as in that month of August 1650. The great lords were treasonous; Guyenne was in revolt. Colbert saw the queen and Mazarin for long interviews almost daily, informing them of the situation from the coded reports he deciphered, then transmitting their instructions to Le Tellier. "At the reading of the first report," he wrote, "the queen manifested much bitterness at the conduct of Mme de Chevreuse, whom she accuses of too obviously playing both sides at once."

In that same month of August, Colbert was sent on a mission to Libourne, where Nicolas Fouquet had been sent by Mazarin. The two men met for the first time. Colbert was thirty-one, Fouquet thirty-five. Colbert's enthusiasm was aroused. The future superintendent was one day to be famous for his charm, but does that explain the infatuation? We should, rather, attempt to fathom Colbert's political sentiments (or emotions) at that particular time. Barely two months before, he had had his violent conflict with Mazarin. Their characters were incompatible, but from Colbert's point of view, their ethics were also different. He had not lost his nostalgic longing for Richelieu. As he was to say in later years, speaking as a minister: *"le grand cardinal"* would have said thus and so, *"le grand cardinal"* would have done thus and so. And Fouquet represented Richelieu's world. His father had been one of the *grand cardinal's* confidants, and his chief advisor in maritime and colonial affairs. Colbert's newfound friend was a *maître des requêtes** and former intendant, thus belonging to Richelieu's elite civilian corps in the service of centralized government. He had even taken up the defense of the populace

Maîtres des requêtes were officials under the control of the chancellor and attached to the royal council (see also note 1 to chapter 8).

against the tax farmers. On the eve of the Fronde, he had assumed the highly sensitive post of intendant of Paris. Fouquet's conduct during the disturbances had been above reproach: He had remained constantly amidst the troops faithful to the king, arranging the delivery of provisions to Paris with no thought for the parlement, which had revoked his commission.

According to statute, the king's representative to the parlement was the attorney general. In the first years of the Fronde, the easygoing Méliand had played that role quite inadequately. Mazarin managed to obtain Méliand's resignation and convinced Fouquet to take the risk of replacing him. Everything seemed to be working out according to the cardinal's desires. But it was also necessary to get the authorization of Gaston d'Orleans, younger brother of Louis XIII, to whom the title of regent had been given. The inconstant Gaston hated Mazarin and distrusted Fouquet, whom he thought too faithful to the prime minister. He refused to approve him. How could he be swayed? The regent thought well of Le Tellier; perhaps the war minister's influences would help Fouquet. Fouquet put all of his charm to work on Le Tellier's agent, and Colbert was won over to his enterprise. He wrote Le Tellier a letter of startling warmth, considering the ferocious intensity of his later attacks on Fouquet. It is worth quoting extensively:

Fouquet, here at His Eminence's order, has made clear to me on three different occasions that he most passionaely desires to be counted among your special servants and friends, thanks to the very special esteem he has for your merits, and also that he has no particular bond with any other person that could prevent his receiving such an honor, having shared his thoughts on many of the details touching the public impression that there is some disagreement between Servien and Lionne and yourself, though he has no especial knowledge of the matter, and though I am rather distant from it myself, yet I found that he spoke as a true man of honor. I thought it quite proper, since he is a man of good birth and especial merits, capable of taking on very high office one day, for me to make some suggestions that you shared his inclination, since it cannot be a burdensome commitment for you, but only a matter of receiving him favorably and of showing signs of friendship when you meet in public. If you agree with my feelings in the matter, I beg you will so inform me in the next letter with which you honor me, for I cannot refrain from telling you, with all due respect, that I could not imagine that I could repay a part of all I owe you in better coin than the winning of a hundred friends of his stripe, if only I were so estimable a man as to succeed in it.

Le Tellier was not convinced. He even suspected Fouquet of conniving with the enemy. Once again Colbert pleaded his friend's cause at length and explained the problems Gaston d'Orleans was causing.

Le Tellier intervened with Gaston d'Orleans. The king's uncle held out briefly, then accepted. On November 26, 1650, Nicolas Fouquet was named attorney general, and carried out his duties most faithfully and intelligently.

The city of Paris had thrown in its lot with the seditious princes. Mazarin felt forced to free the princes of Condé and Conti, as well as the duc de Longueville, whom he had imprisoned a year before. The three men were received with such enthusiasm in Paris that Mazarin left town precipitously for a place of exile in Germany. He settled in the castle of Brühl, in the territory of the Elector of Cologne. Le Tellier, still in Paris, was ordered by the queen to maintain contact with the cardinal. Colbert seemed designated as the man of the hour. His presence was now familiar to the cardinal. He knew state secrets, was in the habit of corresponding in code, and above all he inspired unmixed confidence. The latter trait was to be of great use in his brilliant career. Le Tellier's confidence in him was total, as was Mazarin's afterwards and, later, the king's. Colbert never neglected his own interests, any more than most of his contemporaries did; but one divines, one senses, in him a man of only one path, and that is rare. His perseverance in the application of a single policy shows the impression to be well founded. Fouquet instinctively inspired the opposite reaction. Nervous, clever, gifted, brilliant, his personality appears multiple, fascinating. It was attractive, but provoked doubt. Le Tellier did not trust Fouquet, however ireproachable he was during the Fronde, but readily confided the most serious secrets to Colbert.

Colbert was totally, almost savagely, devoted to his masters, but he was jealous where their trust was concerned. We shall see what passionate scenes that caused between Louis XIV and his minister.

Mazarin, in exile, turned to Colbert at once, despite the serious differences they had had less than a year before. Mazarin knew Le Tellier's agent to be able and suspected his capacity for loyalty. Colbert had observed the cardinal's sly intelligence, and had perhaps even grasped his genuine fidelity to the greatness of the state. But each hesitated. Mazarin had left behind not only his palace with its magnificent art collections, but the most tangled affairs one could imagine. The choice of a man to handle them seemed both weighty and difficult. As for Colbert, would he leave a minister in office to enter into the service of an exile?

Prudently, Mazarin first asked Colbert to suggest someone, without asking him directly. Colbert replied that the chosen agent must receive a clear power of attorney and His Eminence's full accreditation with those in power, so that "he may speak up, and also have enough judgment not to bother the queen with any but matters of consequence." The conditions had been laid down; and although Colbert did not name himself, who knew better than he, Colbert, what the queen should hear on the cardinal's behalf? Colbert assured Mazarin of his "zeal and passion," but insisted, in return, upon being the cardinal's only representative both in the management of his affairs and in his relations with the government. These sharp and abrupt demands rather upset Mazarin, but he slowly came around, and gave Colbert the blind trust he requested. In June, Colbert, though still assigned to the War Department, found himself "detached" and in the service of Mazarin. He was to defend the exile's interests with unflagging devotion and a sense of money worthy of the great merchant bankers of Rheims.

IN THE EXILE'S SERVICE

Colbert's first preoccupation was to be rid of all the assistants, secretaries, and servants who had been looking after the cardinal's interests. All those people "confused his mind instead of enlightening it." La Vieuville, who then held the office of superintendent, did not see things that way. He was on bad terms with Le Tellier, and feared that Colbert, becoming a single, all-powerful representative of Mazarin's, might try to undermine him as a service to Le Tellier. Mazarin replied without any sign of hesitation: "I say Colbert is my man and would drown those he loves for my sake, not excepting Le Tellier." Once again the firm, clear-cut, methodical strength that flowed from Colbert's personality swept away all doubts and relaxed all suspicious surveillance.

Let us observe the tactics that permitted Mazarin's man to consolidate this sort of pacifying authority. Colbert's capacity for work was almost abnormally large. He managed, quite cleverly, to point it out: "I would be most obliged to you," he wrote the cardinal, "if you would give me difficult tasks to occupy my mind, for their difficulty increases the pleasure it takes in carrying them forward." He alone was master of the whole situation: "Whatever understanding God has given me is now applied to disinterring, so to speak, knowledge about your affairs, with no assistance from anyone." Above all, he did not hesitate to speak in a frank manner that disconcerted and could charm in that age of courtiers and traitors. He reprimanded, then immediately presented a solution, which had its effect on a character as irresolute as Mazarin's. Colbert revealed himself to Mazarin as a superman striking down the demon of confusion. He wrote boldly:

I frankly admit that if you had handed your affairs over to me at the beginning or in the course of your ministry, you would scarcely have suffered my involvement for long, for I could not possibly have borne the horrible dissipation you have made of your fortune, through the gifts you have made of your best livings, or the creation of large pensions paid from what was left, or the loans you have taken out everywhere on the king's behalf, which have brought you to your present awkward state.

Colbert learned, as he studied Mazarin's situation, that a man can give his fortune to the king and to the state as easily as he can steal public resources. Soon Colbert was to make an open attack on that traditional confusion between the finances of the state and the private finances of those who governed it.

Colbert's frank statement of the facts shook the exile somewhat, and it established Colbert's authority at the outset. Colbert suggested that Mazarin should give him a trial for two or three months. His Eminence should "know me to the bottom of my heart before engaging his trust." But "once the trial is made," Colbert added, "I feel my spirit is incapable of bearing any division of confidence where your affairs are concerned." And, he went on, "That cannot be hidden from any degree of scrutiny." The implications are clear. And Colbert further threatened that if the cardinal continued to "dissipate" his fortune, he would request to be relieved of responsibility for his affairs.

Thenceforth Mazarin was to be unable to get along without his agent; the day would come when he judged him indispensable to the king and to France. Had Colbert's feelings about the exiled minister really changed? He proved his loyalty, but his irritation may be guessed at. The tone of his letters often seem imperious and even brutal, quite far from the respectful style he would employ upon Mazarin's triumphant return. The cardinal was sometimes scolded like a child: "I hope you will resolve to behave in a different fashion in the future." After these reproaches on the management of a private fortune, there came warnings addressed to the statesman: "The defects in the finances will destroy the state if Your Eminence does not work to determine its basic cause and to correct it, such as it may be." Colbert may have gone too far: "I beg Your Eminence's pardon if I have let myself slip while writing this. I realize my ignorance when reasoning upon matters of such import." This sort of remorse never lasted long, and Colbert had trouble hiding his hunger for political action. He confessed to Le Tellier, on January 4, 1652, his irritation with Mazarin, who (Colbert claimed) was influenced by his Italian entourage: "Further, our man is not still the same as he was; he's worse: he never used to think of tomorrow; now he can't see ahead from morning to noontime, and his reasoning is always based on false premises."

The royal army was gaining ground. It was time to strike fast, and energetically. Exasperated by the cardinal's lack of resolve, Colbert wrote to him angrily: "For God's sake, send me a proclamation to be printed, and give orders for it to be sent to all the attorney generals of the parlements."

We should note that Colbert did not refrain from harassing Mazarin in his own or his family's interest. His younger brother Edouard-François, barely seventeen, had already been given command of the first company in the regiment of Navarre. Another brother, Abbé Nicolas, future bishop of Auxerre, was granted vacant ecclesiastical offices: The abbey of Notre-Dame-la-Grande of Poitiers brought him 1,800 livres a year in income. The assignment without fee of an expensive public office (to be resold later) was a form of bonus to which Colbert was especially partial. He received, as a magnificent gift, the post of household officer to the "queen-to-be." But his essential occupation was still the perilous and complicated management of the absent cardinal's fortune. Colbert began to recover stolen objects, to patiently reconstitute the collections, to sell offices at the best possible price, to defend abbeys threatened by the armies, to make secure investments (such as woodlands), and to untangle the inextricably knotted speculations of the exile. But nothing of importance could be done until the parlement's distraint upon Mazarin's profits had been lifted. We must not forget that the *parlementaires* had expelled him, and remained highly excited where he was concerned. Nicolas Fouquet, as attorney general, bent his every effort to calming the parlement. His brother Basile shuttled back and forth between Brühl, Mazarin's refuge, and Paris. With the two brothers' help, Colbert saved what he could. He had furnishings shipped, and attempted to get raw diamonds of immense value out through the city gates, past the Fronde guards. A first shipment was successful in passing customs, but the second was too heavy, and it aroused the suspicions of the customs officers. The diamonds were sold, but Fouquet promised to have restitution made.

Out of jealousy of a man who, because of his position, participated in the cardinal's affairs; or out of a mistrust, aroused by a personality very different from his own; or out of a foreboding of ambitions that threatened to stifle his own political dreams—for whatever reason, Colbert saw Fouquet through new eyes. Little by little, he sowed doubt in Mazarin's mind. At first, the attorney general was not aware of Colbert's change in attitude.

But Nicolas and Basile were indignant at Mazarin's slowness in rewarding their fidelity. Again Nicolas asked Colbert to intervene on his behalf, complaining vehemently of the cardinal's attitude. Colbert hastened to pass Fouquet's letter on to Mazarin. The act has shocked historians. On Colbert's behalf, it seems just to note the overtones of blackmail that Fouquet included in his complaints: "It seems to me that even if the services rendered [Mazarin] up to now are of no interest to him, then what I can still accomplish here, positive or negative, should be of some weight." That sentence would leave forever a trace of suspicion in the cardinal's mind. Colbert advised Mazarin to accede to Fouquet's request, and still called the latter his friend. His game was becoming a double one—thanks to his ambition, certainly, and perhaps also in response to Fouquet's own curious personality. In any case, the fight was on, and Mazarin contemplated Colbert's remarks:

I am all the sorrier for you because the bad handling given your affairs has put us in such a state of want that you have need of all those people; and the more you have to have them, the more often they put a knife to your throat, demanding things that you have neither the right nor the power to give them.

He is a friend of mine, and I am obliged to say that he has served you very well ever since I have been in charge of your business. Yet I cannot avoid condemning his way of dealing, finding it most out of the ordinary.

In the last months of 1652, the Fronde collapsed for good, and in Paris, people began to speak of Mazarin's return. Colbert judged that the cardinal had nothing to fear by then and advised him to make his entry into the city: "I am having all the people Tubeuf had lodged in Your Eminence's palace removed, and having it thoroughly cleaned."[2] About that time, Superintendant La Vieuville died suddenly. Innocently, the queen asked Colbert whether any files that might compromise the cardinal should not be removed before a successor saw them. Colbert swore pompously that there were none in existence and reported all to Mazarin.

Who would replace La Vieuville? Colbert wished the post to go to M. de Bordeaux, an intendant of finances in good standing at court. When Fouquet's name came up, Colbert went on the offensive. On January 4, 1653, he wrote to the cardinal: "I cannot refrain from saying that Your Eminence should be aware of those whose inclination is to sacrifice and to give a great deal cheaply to the subordinates in order to betray the leader the more easily. That sums up the disorder of the past, which of all disorders can most harm your affairs and those of the state."

On February 3, the king, his mother, and Mazarin made a solemn entry into a wildly happy Paris. On February 7 two superintendants were named: Abel Servien, a former ambassador, was given responsibility for expenses, and Nicolas Fouquet was assigned the collection of income.

Mazarin was to govern France for eight years, until his death. Colbert's life would consist of the same two aspects we have already glimpsed, but with increased intensity. On the one hand, he would remain the cardinal's personal agent, the skillful businessman. And while managing that immense fortune, he would carry on one of the most ferocious and best-known political duels in French history.

---

[2]Jacques Tubeuf, usually called President Tubeuf, was president of the chamber of accounts of Paris, treasurer to the queen, Anne of Austria, and one of the richest financiers of the time. He owned a house in the rue Neuve-des-Petits-Champs that was bought by Mazarin for the construction of his palace and is now part of the Bibliothèque nationale.

CHAPTER 3

Mazarin's Agent

KEEPING THE MAN HE SERVED up-to-date, with great attention to detail and correctness, would turn out to be a permanent characteristic of Colbert's. The drafting of the letters and reports he sent Mazarin was the object of a laborious and meticulous attention. His handwriting was small, cramped, and very hard to read, so he had his rough drafts copied by paid clerks. Colbert wrote them on single sheets, without including the cardinal's title, with no margins or space between the lines. He scratched things out and added little slips of paper. He read through the clerks' copies with care, and sometimes made changes. On the final dispatch, he simply wrote "Monseigneur" and the formal salutation. Little by little, he forced himself to change his handwriting to make it more legible. It is relatively easy to read the letters he later sent Louis XIV.

Mazarin seemed worn out by the minute attention Colbert demanded of him. He said so clearly on October 16, 1653:

> It is well that you know once and for all, when you force me to attend to private business as I am now doing, that I am fifty years old; I have had greater needs than I now have; it has never been within my power to make any effort to put things in order. You must fill in where I fall short, and not insist on my giving a certain kind of attention that it is not possible for me to give to my own interests, which I have long preferred to neglect, both by inclination and by habit, in favor of public affairs.[1]

So there we have their roles laid out. Mazarin would do public service, and Colbert, private. It was a separation that could scarcely be observed, given the incredible confusion between the state's revenue and the cardinal's. Furthermore, Colbert was still obsessed by the shadow of Richelieu. He never abandoned his idol's political "grand design." But on the other hand, he carried out a sort of conspiracy of silence with respect to the late *grand cardinal*. Mazarin was an absolute ruler. The ascent of his agent and his family depended on the cardinal alone.

---

[1]Pierre Clément, *Lettres, instructions, et mémoires de Colbert*, vol. 1.

Political suggestions, timid at first, then fiery, would come in due time. For the moment Colbert acted to consolidate his position and to maintain absolutely the confidence Mazarin seemed to concede. Colbert's style was respectful. His gratitude seemed infinite. Yet in the agent's devotion and the cardinal's confidence there remain interesting, almost imperceptible, nuances. The letters Colbert sent to Mazarin filled only half the width of the sheet: "I beg Your Eminence to have replies written onto the margins of my letters if that seems easiest," he suggested in an unpublished letter of June 4, 1654. Did Mazarin suspect his agent of wanting to recover his own dispatches? Colbert's curious remark, a few days later, tends to confirm that hypothesis: "When I proposed that Your Eminence make reply in the margins of my letters, it was with the thought that it would be easier, as you saw during your previous trip; do as you please, and where my letters are concerned, I beg you to believe that I do not have any scruples about having them remain in your hands."[2] At times, Colbert's tone evokes fear of an always possible disgrace. He hastens to justify himself, "to respond to the small reproach" that His Eminence seems to give him. Why was the long letter of April 9, 1655, in which Colbert so intermingled thanks and flattery, first printed so luxuriously, then distributed in France and abroad? Did Colbert wish to drive home to his enemies the impressive list of the good deeds the cardinal had done on his account? Or, as Georges Mongrédien has suggested, could Mazarin have asked for the letter as a sort of guarantee, fearing Colbert's ambition? Enemies existed. Only two months after this strange publication, Colbert was complaining that he was being slandered before His Eminence. And yet, he added, "I have nothing to reproach myself with on the subject of any debauchery, amusement, excursion, or other affair."

Their reservations about each other, though deeply buried and never admitted, grew. But they should not mask the continued zeal of the agent, and the cardinal's genuine trust. For how could Mazarin's great and troubled fortune be reestablished without the zeal of the one and the trust of the other?

THE CARDINAL'S FORTUNE

Colbert had a passion for books. One of his priorities was the reconstitution of the cardinal's magnificent library. During the Fronde, the parlement had ordered the seizure and sale of Mazarin's possessions. The decree was to be carried out by some of its members, and they appropriated, or rather stole, a large number of books. Once Mazarin was back in France, Colbert hastened to seize the stolen

[2]Handwritten draft, June 14, 1654.

books, while at the same time giving orders for new and valuable acquisitions. By 1654, the library once more held between 25,000 and 30,000 volumes. This exceptional collection was eventually bequeathed to the Collège des Quatre-Nations and now belongs to the Bibliothèque Mazarine. Besides books, Colbert had to arrange the return of Mazarin's tapestries, chandeliers, furnitue, and various other objects that had been dispersed, sold, or stolen.

Aliases, clandestine operations, complex trafficking, risky speculation, sea prizes of doubtful legality, bribes: Mazarin, quite at ease in the haze of dishonesty, initiated Colbert into the extraordinary financial disorder of the times. The latter grew nervous at times, and gave timid warnings, but he found his way through the maze with aplomb, even giving impetus to a questionable operation himself on occasion.

The Fronde and the war with Austria had emptied the royal treasury. In 1653, the superintendants planned to carry out a revaluation of money owed on account, obviously to the creditors' advantage; and thus the king became, in effect, the kingdom's most important creditor, since he could collect taxes at the new rates. On the other hand, debtors stood to lose. Colbert hastened to "protect against loss due to decline in real value" the 150 or 200 livres in cash that Mazarin had in his possession.[3] He suggested to Mazarin that he make a loan to the king; that is to say, become a creditor himself. Mazarin agreed but insisted on using an assumed name. What happened if the price of wheat, which the cardinal furnished to the army, rose? Captured ships were counted on to procure that commodity at a good price. Or the sugar trade between Portugal and Italy was authorized. When prices dropped, there was still money to be made by producing baked goods. One way or another, speculation was always possible. The wheat was bought; then the cardinal resold it, at his price, using another name. How was it possible to avoid the innumerable local fees, tolls on the waterways, and custom duties of the ancien régime? Colbert suggested that letters from the king, ordering total exemption from all fees for the wheat, be sent to the intendants of Dauphiné and Languedoc. If need be, archers aboard the barges could clear a passage by force. Of course, those who received such fees rebelled. Monseigneur de Ventadour, archbishop of Bourges, and the duc de Damville detained the barges that fell into the hands of their men. Damville threatened to appeal to the royal court. With apparent satisfaction, Colbert announced that the claimants thought His Eminence had no part in the operation and attributed it to Colbert alone. In order to end the affair, he would have to pay 6,000 livres to release the barges, a payment important not only because of the sum but also because it set an

[3]Marc Bloch, *Esquísse d'une histoire monétaire de l'Europe,* p. 73.

important precedent.[4] And it was to be hoped that the cardinal would never have to explain himself to the duke.

The transportation of wheat by river meant other problems besides tolls. The barges were old, Colbert reported, and had attracted "an infinite number of insects," which ate the wheat even though it was "fresh and of extremely good quality." The cardinal's agent ordered that it be "stirred constantly, to drive out the vermin; but if that failed," he begged the cardinal's permission to "convert it all to flour."[5] Profiting by a decree of council authorizing the export of French wheat to foreign countries, Mazarin quickly stockpiled the wheat from the territory of La Rochelle, which he governed, for shipment via Mediterranean ports.

The trading of raw materials does not always seem to have been profitable. In 1655 Colbert sent the cardinal the accounts for salt sold in Holland, and the note of the price at which it was bought and sold, with these words: "These two papers will inform you that we lost 1,285 livres 15 sols 10 deniers on the deal, which is half the purchase price; it makes me think M. Chanut is right to tell me that every man should stick to his own profession."[6]

The war with Spain continued. The armies had to be supplied. The cardinal advanced the sum required for quartering the Soissonais troops by taking possession of vacant ecclesiastical livings and selling them to anyone who bribed him richly enough. Or else he speculated on the taking of prizes on the high seas, in order to demand steep ransoms from the outfitters of the captured ships. This latter means of raising money is illustrated by the expedition of the duc de Guise. Mazarin instigated this foray in order to come to the aid of Naples, then in revolt against the Spanish. He hoped to pay for the enterprise by the ransom demanded of the owners of the *Prophet Samuel,* which the French navy had captured. The ship was Portuguese, but unfortunately for it, the vessel was carrying wares belonging to Spanish subjects. The owners offered 100,000 livres; Mazarin demanded more. The Portuguese ambassador attempted to win the owners over. Colbert even wrote to Mazarin: "I have spoken with the Portuguese ambassador's confessor about Your Eminence's desires that the *Samuel*'s owners give satisfaction to the admiralty," and the confessor promised to do his best.[7] These rather special ways of balancing the books were a source of worry for Colbert. The superintendants must not learn of them. The *trésoriers de l'épargne* would have to ignore

[4]Unpublished document of May 18, 1657.

[5]October 20, 1657; this passage has never been published.

[6]Unpublished document of July 20, 1655.

[7]Handwritten draft of June 7, 1654.

them.[8] It was best to pass the money through the special war fund. "By that means," wrote Colbert, "the superintendants will be unaware of it, which is the essential thing here, and we will control its distribution, and can apply the usual financial terms." And a few days later, he begged the cardinal: "to consider what would happen if the 300,000 livres from Portugal became public knowledge, which cannot be avoided if the *épargne* handles them, while if we use the war fund we can manage so that only M. de Brienne, M. Le Tellier, and the fund's accountants know it, and the money from the ambassador will be at least as large and even larger."[9] Colbert had good reasons for wanting to hide expedients of this sort from the superintendants, especially Servien, who was one of the most honest men of finance of his time. While Mazarin was resorting to so many illicit or questionable means of meeting expenses that were indispensable for the defense of the state, he was also covering his enormous personal expenditures by transfers from the intendants' funds or by purely and simply withholding large sums from the revenues of the larger tax farms. Servien risked an occasional remonstrance. Colbert reported them to Mazarin. Ambassadors were dying of hunger; civil servants went ten years without receiving any salary; Field Marshall Fabert, so loyal a soldier, could not obtain payment of a four-year-old note. And at the same time, Mazarin was trying to appropriate the entire income from the *aides** collected in Normandy for his own use. Servien wanted half, communicating through Colbert the idea that "it would not be to Your Eminence's advantage for people to know that you had taken all the revenue."[10] These warnings did not trouble His Eminence greatly. Later he leased his livings and his abbeys at such a price that, according to Colbert, the farmers were reduced to ruin and bankruptcy.

Mazarin also received enormous bribes in connection with those public offices that were royal appointments. For example, Servien wished to receive the post of Chancellor of the Order of the Holy Ghost, which Abbé Rivière desired to relinquish. He needed the king's approval, or rather Mazarin's. On July 18, 1654, Colbert announced to the cardinal[11] that Servien had "knelt down and given thanks" to His Eminence, and was preparing the 60,000 livres for M. de la Rivière and

---

[8]Let us recall that under the ancien régime, the superintendants were executive officers answering to the king alone, and the *trésoriers de l'épargne* were accountants under the authority of the Court of Accounts.

[9]Unpublished documents of June 19 and 24, 1654.

[10]Unpublished document of June 24, 1654.

[11]Handwritten draft.

Aides were indirect taxes on such commodities as tobacco, drinks, iron, precious metals, and leather.

the 15,000 pistoles to be sent to His Eminence. In other words, Mazarin was to receive a higher sum than went to the holder of the office.

The agent's compliance in regard to the cardinal during the year 1655 is astonishing; it does not correspond to the "grand design" of Louis XIV's minister. Mazarin coveted a certain property in Auvergne. How were the funds to be procured? The usual expedients did not suffice. Then Colbert, who had nearly run out of ideas, suggested a solution: drawing on the queen's treasury. Anne of Austria could serve as a front, and could be paid back much later and in yearly installments. "Or if worst comes to worst," Colbert wrote, "and a counterdeed is required, the queen should sign it and assume ownership of the property, and in a year from now, we will find a way to have it put in Your Eminence's name."[12] Thus, the purchase was made in the queen's name from the Franche-Comté account.

Mazarin received income from a number of abbeys to which Colbert assumed management and, eventually, protection from the troops (or from their own neighbors). The reasons behind the poor returns from the abbey of La Chaise-Dieu seem strange today. According to Colbert, "the cause is that the gentlemen of the area enjoy, cheaply, under spurious peasant names, the abbey's prime lands."[13] Colbert suggested using the influence of the marquis d'Aligre, "whose authority over the province of Auvergne, and especially its gentlemen, is great."

Besides the properties acquired by the cardinal (such as La Fère), Colbert also had to administer immense domains under state ownership where Mazarin had awarded himself property rights, such as the Forest of Saint-Gobain or the wood and chateau of Vincennes.[14] The administration of property was new to Colbert. The many revisions and insertions in his earliest drafts concerning the domain of La Fère suggest a difficult adaptation to this sort of management. He ordered work to be carried out, and occupied himself with the animals and the vegetable garden at Vincennes. It was an apprenticeship for the man who would become superintendant of the royal buildings.

At Vincennes, he called for estimates from no fewer than fourteen competing enterprises. He established a menagerie and informed the cardinals about his Flemish cattle, sheep, and chickens. He even apprised him that "the little guinea pig has had six piglets, of whom three are dead, and the other three will have a hard time surviving, because she has no milk." The garden was soon full of "all

[12]Handwritten draft of May 20, 1655.

[13]Unpublished document of June 27, 1654.

[14]As "captain" of the château of Vincennes, Mazarin had more or less the same prerogatives he would have had if the château had been his personal property. It was Colbert, moreover, who gave Mazarin the idea of succeeding the preceding governor (1652).

sorts of vegetables." When the court drew near, Colbert hastened to send fruit, to have jams made for the queen, to dispatch a freshly caught sturgeon, with hopes that the king and his mother would find it to their taste. The tiniest of domestic details mingled in the same letter with the most serious problems. The duc de Guise was having trouble organizing his expedition intended to support the Neapolitan rebels against the Spanish foe.[15] And Colbert ended his letter as follows: "I don't think the calf at Vincennes will make good eating; he's too old, and can't be gotten from here to La Fère: it's too far."[16]

The work done at Vincennes was very burdensome. In 1657, it was time to construct the king's stables as well as the cardinal's. Colbert was of the opinion that "we should put off building the king's stables until next year," and settle for "building Your Eminence's stables this year."[17] Yet Louis XIV was already nineteen years old. We see here the supreme power vested in the cardinal who could build his own stables before those of the king.

The tapestries to be hung in the royal apartments were not long enough. Besides, added Colbert, "they belong to Your Eminence and it is not fair to furnish the king's and the queen's apartments with Your Eminence's furnishings."[18] It would be better to buy others.

Mazarin was more involved than ever in the most shady of affairs, such as the matter of bread for the armies of Catalonia and the Piedmont. He mingled his own interests and those of the state so naturally that one may be led to wonder whether he really was dishonest. During the Fronde, he raised troops in Germany at his own expense; they later accompanied him to France. Five years later he paid himself back at government expense. Colbert seems to have grown more and more disturbed at his master's financial practices. Mazarin acquired the duchy of Nevers, and Colbert tried to get him interested in the place. But unlike his agent, the cardinal disliked these large acquisitions that tied up his capital. He preferred holdings that he could get rid of quickly in order (as Colbert claimed, no doubt with some measure of truth) to meet urgent state needs. If only His Eminence "were capable of doing something you will never do, which is, not to share your

[15]The expedition had no success. The duc de Guise landed at Castellammare at the head of 7,000 men and ascertained that the Neopolitans did not seem inclined to revolt. Impelled by a lack of provisions, he returned to France, losing most of his fleet in a storm.

[16]Unpublished document, August 1654. The following year he announced that it was high time to eat two calves that were already too old and that he could also send "young turkeys and pheasants and some plump chickens" (July 17, 1655).

[17]Unpublished document of July 15, 1657.

[18]Unpublished document of October 16, 1657.

affections between the glory of the state and your domestic affairs, but only to reserve some small part of your affection for the latter"[19] The plea was fruitless. Colbert boasted of the château's impregnable site, of its glorious past. But the cardinal loved to wriggle into and out of the cloudiest of financial arrangements. Ostentatious, well-informed, Mazarin showed a passionate liking for works of art. He had agents in Italy, especially in Florence (such as Abbé Strozzi), who sent him rare furnishings, quality stones, and precious cloth. He set great store by richness in ornament, magnificence in materials, and the length of time spent on the work.

Since one of his jobs was to transmit the cardinal's orders and organize transportation of his objets d'art, Colbert learned his way about the art world. He could not have had a better master than the competent and gifted Mazarin. The cardinal's Italian leanings no doubt influenced the remarkable work Colbert carried on as minister of fine arts. He was to use the same network of agents on Louis XIV's account. Colbert seems to have been frightened by the enormous sums spent on the cardinal's collections, but Mazarin may have been right. The quality of the objects selected justified the expense. Later on, Colbert's timidity and insecurity led him to miss out on the purchase of certain articles that might have made welcome additions to the French heritage. The cardinal was on the lookout for good deals. He snapped up the tapestries that the duc de Guise had to sell before leaving for Naples. The jeweler Lescot was assigned exclusively to Mazarin's service. On July 16, 1655, Colbert asked if he could make use of a Turin banker, who would receive a commission, to effect the transfer of considerable sums to Rome so that the furnishings of the late Cardinal Montalte could be acquired for Mazarin. We may suppose that here the traditional relationships between the family Colbert and Italian banking circles were put to good use. The same letter mentions precious stones that had been redeemed from an Amsterdam moneylender on the cardinal's behalf. Should that not be seen a proof that Mazarin's financial problems were serious enough to force him to leave his jewelry as security against a foreign loan? Colbert remained in constant contact with Cantarini and Cenami, the cardinal's Italian bankers.

The cardinal's agent took great care of his master's person. He obtained lined dressing gowns and fur-lined boots for him. With regret, he supplied him two gold-embroidered doublets: In his opinion, money was being wasted, for one doublet was enough. Everywhere the cardinal went, Colbert sent him Portuguese oranges and premium wines and liqueurs. Once, en route to Lyons, Mazarin ran out of the wines he required. He lost his temper, and Colbert anxiously sent ten bottles of fine wine, carefully wrapped, by the first coach.

[19]October 26, 1659, in Clément, *Lettres,* vol. 1.

Mazarin's private interests also included those of his many relatives. Colbert took on the task of having the cardinal's entire family naturalized, even his father, Pierre Mazarini, who had died in Rome in 1654.[20] His nieces had to be married off (to Colbert's great irritation, they made off with their uncle's best chef whenever Mazarin was out of town). And Colbert begged His Eminence to stop raising the family's pensions all the time. One of the nieces, Laura Martinozzi, married the duc de Modena in 1655, who was to receive the sum of 710,000 livres. Colbert was ordered to pay the bride's travel expenses and the cost of her wardrobe. The cardinal further wished to make available to her the funds needed for her gifts and alms. Colbert admitted to his master that he found "these two classes of expenditure . . . rather surprising."[21]

In 1657, Colbert drew up the contract for the marriage of another niece, Olympia Mancini, with the comte de Soissons. Her brother Philippe was expected to appear at court. Colbert inquired whether His Eminence wished to give him any extra money beyond the usual clothing allowance of 100 écus a month.[22] Philippe was a disappointment to his uncle. He was very lazy, and ate meat on Holy Friday. Mazarin exiled him to Brisach, and Colbert was expected to keep an eye on him. Unfortunately, he seemed to show no improvement. Colbert advised the cardinal to bring his nephew home. As for "Monsieur Alphonse" Mancini, Colbert was of the opinion that his proper upbringing required a change of valets.[23] And the influence of the Soissons household on the young man seemed to displease both the cardinal and his agent. Olympia planned to take her brother away with her during his school vacation. Colbert warned their uncle of the plan, saying "Your Eminence should, I believe, prevent the execution of this plan, it being much better for said Lord Alphonse to go enjoy himself with the children of M. Le Tellier, as he did last year."[24]

In 1660 Colbert listed the many services he was rendering his master:

I'm not saying this to exaggerate my work to Your Eminence. On the contrary, I beg you believe, as a constant truth, that I have such a penchant for work that I realize daily, through self-examination, that it is impossible for my mind to bear idleness or moderate activity, so that, counting from the day such a misfortune mars my life, I shall not live six years more, which

[20]Under the laws of the ancien régime, naturalization was accomplished by "letters of naturalization" given under the Great Seal.

[21]June 19, 1655; unpublished passage.

[22]Clément, *Lettres,* vol. 1.

[23]Alphonse Mancini died accidentally in 1658 at the collège des Jésuites.

[24]June 11, 1657. (This passage does not appear in Clément's *Lettres.*)

makes me clearly aware that I owe Your Eminence my life, and a pleasant life it is, with all the kindnesses you have heaped upon me, both personally and through all my brothers.

Indeed, Colbert did not forget to increase his fortune at the same time as the cardinal's, and he took care of his own family while watching over his master's. Mazarin found that perfectly natural, and did not fail, given the opportunity, to let his agent know how totally satisfied he was with his service.

THE AGENT'S FORTUNE

When the Council of State was revived in 1654, Colbert remained a member, by reason of his "ability, adequacy, experience, probity, and good conduct," according to his new letter of appointment, copied from the old one. But the wages paid state councilors were far from adequate to the ambitions of Mazarin's agent. There was no help to be gotten from his father. The Fronde had so disturbed Nicolas Colbert's affairs that he was never able to pay his elder son the 60,000 livres promised him at the time of his marriage.

The agent constantly begged his master to grant him livings, priories, or offices. In 1652 he requested the vacant living of Saint-Ligeaire, a dependent of Saint-Médard of Soissons. On June 19, 1654, according to his unpublished draft, he wrote to Mazarin: "We have heard here the rumor that the bishop of Nantes has died, leaving two small abbeys and two priories, one attached to Annay, all together worth about 4,000 livres a year. I most humbly beg Your Eminence that, if the rumor is found to be true, or if a similar situation arises, you will gratify me with some living of about that same value." He did not fail to press the cardinal when he did not get an immediate reply. On June 24, he reminded Mazarin that "we are still hearing the rumor that the bishop of Nantes is dead, in which case I hope you will remember me."[25] This sort of request occurs often in his correspondence with Mazarin.

When Condé, in the service of Spain, defeated Turenne at Valenciennes in 1655, Colbert unhesitatingly drew 1000 gold louis from his own fortune and lent them to Mazarin to help His Eminence "to recover from such a troublesome accident," and further promised a forthcoming payment of 60,000 livres. Two years later the cardinal had not paid him back. Colbert did not fail to complain. "In all the time I have been serving Your Eminence, I have never been so short of money as I am now."[26] Consequently, he asked the cardinal to reimburse certain advances he had made him.

[25]Handwritten draft.

[26]Handwritten draft of May 27, 1657.

One of the largest personal profits Colbert realized under the cardinal's rule, and with his permission, was the 1660 sale of his office of secretary of the queen's household, for the enormous sum of half a million livres. Because the office was obtained without payment of fees, the sale was all net profit. Colbert had previously explained to His Eminence his desire to relinguish the office in these terms: "I am not naturally disposed to pay court to the ladies after a lifetime of almost continuous work."[27]

Colbert's brothers were gradually put into important posts where, in turn, they were of use to Jean-Baptiste's policies. Nicolas, nine years younger, was a priest. Mazarin granted him numerous priories and abbeys. In 1656 he was named king's librarian. Abbé Colbert was soon provided a living of seven to eight thousand livres a year. Colbert wanted to make him a bishop as well. Didn't the aged bishop of Luçon need a coadjutor? But Mazarin promised the position to another. When Colbert learned that, he let forth such cries of despair that the cardinal wound up giving the coadjutorship to the agent's brother. Abbé Nicolas became bishop of Luçon in 1661.

After having been an official of the duc de Guise's army, Charles Colbert* became intendant of Alsace in 1655, then First President of the province's sovereign council in 1658. Full of hope, Jean-Baptiste wrote to him: "I will admit I am most eager to see our family rise by paths of honor and virtue, and to hear everyone agree that we deserve our good fortune."[28] Colbert obtained many favors, but he also insisted upon doing work that was difficult and of the highest quality.

He had a special affection for his cousin Colbert du Terron, whom he had had appointed governor of Brouage, a military post belonging to Mazarin. Active, intelligent, a first class administrator, Colbert du Terron would be a valuable assistant to the future minister of Louis XIV.

Seventeenth-century France remained profoundly subjected to feudal rules. The possession of a noble estate consolidated one's situation and bore witness to a family's glory. Colbert recommended "solid investments in land" to his family, and himself began to put together what was to become in time a considerable domain. In 1657 he bought the barony of Seignelay, the most important in the *comté*, or county, of Auxerre. The château, built in Charles VII's time, stood on a ridge overlooking the Serain Valley. From the top of its towers one could see the cathedral of Sens. When Colbert bought it, the walls were in ruins and the fields abandoned. Jean-Baptiste took a passionate interest in the restoration of

---

[27]Clément, *Lettres,* vol. 1.

[28]Ibid.

*Charles Colbert de Saint-Marc, a cousin of Jean-Baptiste Colbert, was later dismissed from his position for bad conduct.

"his" castle and "his" ovens, and in the reestablishment of "his" gallows. He had the banks of "his" river built up. He filled "his" woodlands with game. The administration of his properties was to be one of his great amusements. The old walls must be made impregnable once again, the château quickly made ready to house him. François Le Vau, called the Younger, brother of Louis Le Vau, who built Vaux-le-Vicomte for Fouquet and later Versailles for Louis XIV, was called to direct the construction. Colbert kept close watch on him and overwhelmed him with precise directions. Le Vau wanted to lower the courtyard of the keep by two feet. Prudently, the master of the household asked the *bailiff* of Seignelay to dig first "a hole six feet in diameter and two feet deep, to find out what grace or ugliness it may exhibit."[29] Le Vau drew plans for the orchard. Colbert advised him to consider with care the spot where his chapel was to be built "and to make a little drawing of it, but especially to oblige the contractors to work most diligently."[30] And the architect was told precisely how he was to carry out the masonry and roofing.

Colbert openly exhibited the responsible paternalism of a seigneur. In 1658 he wrote the bailiff: "I beg you to tell M. le curé that I have gotten his letter, that no one has spoken ill of him to me, that he should do his duty well, and incite, as he should, my inhabitants to live proper lives, and see to it that the children receive good instruction, and that I will take care of him."[31] Let those who fished in the river of the seigneur beware! They risked "a flogging." And when Colbert visited his domain, it was necessary for his dependents to render him "faith and hommage."

At this date, Colbert was also seeking out rare books, an area in which he showed real competence. His library, of exceptional quality, came to be celebrated throughout Europe. To his brother Charles in Alsace he wrote "If you find, in any of the neighboring Huguenot towns, the works of John Huss and Jerome of Prague in large format, which is a pretty rare book, let me ask you to buy it for me."[32]

Between the cardinal's fortune and his own, had Colbert forgotten all preoccupation with politics? We should not be misled. To obtain for France the resources his policies required and to apply his policies with an uncompromising will, these were always Colbert's twin obsessions. But there was Mazarin, there

[29]Ibid., vol. 7.

[30]*Bulletin Charavay.*

[31]Clément, *Lettres,* vol. 7.

[32]May 2, 1659, ibid., vol. 1.

CHAPTER 4

A Political Duel

EXERCISING SIMULTANEOUSLY the responsibilities of superintendant of finances and attorney general of the Parlement of Paris, Fouquet seemed one of the most powerful men in the country. His lordly demeanor, the charms of his lively intelligence, his exceptional artistic sensitivity, his success with women, lent his entire personality a special brilliance. After the loss of his first wife, a rich heiress who had given him a daughter, he married Maria-Magdalena of Castille in 1651. While overseeing the superb work going on at his estate of Vaux-le-Vicomte, Fouquet lived in his lovely house at Saint-Mandé, bordering the woods of Vincennes, or in his Parisian town house behind Mazarin's palace. He dominated financial circles, commanded the respect of the *parlementaires,* and beguiled artists and writers.

When Mazarin returned to power, Colbert was not ready to attack Fouquet. And despite the reservations he expressed to the cardinal at the moment when the superintendancy went to Fouquet, had he considered it yet? Fouquet participated daily, and in many roles because of his numerous titles, in political life. Colbert's role under Mazarin was officially a private one. His first goal was to involve himself little by little in the affairs of state, while ensuring more and more each day his influence over the mind of the cardinal. But Mazarin's agent, who was in an excellent position to know the financial customs of the age (which were also those of the master he served), was to prepare slowly and thoroughly a plan to denounce and destroy them. Fouquet practiced with an extraordinary ease the "horrible intermingling" of state finances and his private fortune. Indeed, such confusion was tolerated, when it wasn't encouraged, by the monarchy. It seems to have been inherent in the ancien régime and was the result of a whole historical context. The Capetian monarchy had wanted, over the course of the centuries, to link its own grandeur with the power of the state. And yet, as Lucien Febvre has so clearly put it: "The state, from a financial point of view, did not exist. There was the monarch, who was a private individual . . . able to obtain credit only as an individual. It was not France who sought loans in 1530 but a prince, Francis I, who inspired more or less confidence in the lenders."[1] What a weakness! What a defect in the strong fortress of a great central administration! The king of a whole nation was but one lord among others. Here we touch upon the fundamental ambiguity of the relationship between king and state, an ambiguity that Colbert was to try to eliminate throughout his entire political life.

As an individual, the king was not rich. His lands brought in barely 80,000 livres a year. The head of state could not appeal directly to the moneylenders, who distrusted a king without credit, and who might well go bankrupt. Thus, the monarch was obliged to call upon the services of the bankers, manipulators of currency. Having become the intermediary between the king, or the state, on the one hand, and his own correspondents or friends on the other, the banker was now called a "man of finance or a financier." Naturally enough, our banker-financier wished, to be reimbursed—if possible with interest—for the money he had advanced to the king. The king, being poor, allowed him to deduct, in advance, in his own name, from one or more of the public revenues.* The "financier" attained, to a certain extent, the status of a civil servant. But it was a curious public servant indeed who used for his own affairs the powers vested in him by the state, with the king's blessing. Attaining the office of superintendent was the highest ambition to which these financial civil servants could aspire. The superintendent was not an accountant. No one could demand an accounting from him, not even the king. He "explained" his administration to the prince whenever his conscience or his whim required. Why, under these conditions, should he keep books?

Fouquet had the perfect personality for the job. Flexible, brilliant, showy, he attracted the businessmen that the upright Servien repulsed. And in addition, the superintendent was an important *parlementaire,* in a position to protect the financiers, if necessary, from any legal action against them by the parlement. Within financial circles, he had the credit the king lacked. The king became obligated to him. The temptation of blackmail was almost forced on the super-intendent, and the financiers in general. This helps explain the anger Colbert expressed to the cardinal when Fouquet, during the Fronde, rudely reminded him of the services he could render, in exchange for personal advantage. In substance Colbert was saying to his master: "You are forced to deal with those people, but the process is unacceptable and revolts me." Even while the concept of an absolute monarchy, a concept new to Europe, was becoming more definite, while the direct authority of the state was spreading and growing stronger, neither the king nor

[1]Quoted in Jean Bouvier and Henry Germain-Martin, *Finances et financiers de l'ancien régime.*

*That is to say, in return for a loan to the king, the banker-financier was given a note based on future revenues, taxes collectable two or three years hence.

the state had regular and secure means of applying a policy. This subjugation of the state by a group of private citizens seemed highly regrettable, but unavoidable. Richelieu himself had admitted it in his last testament: "The financiers and the *partisans* are a class apart, harmful to the state, yet still necessary." Nonetheless, he had denounced their "thievery," and even thought of establishing a chamber of justice, a special court of inquiry. But how could the system be replaced? Richelieu never hid his ignorance of financial matters. His genius, though vast and intuitive, seemed helpless in a situation beyond his grasp. It was not yet time to name the real obstacle, and it would still be too soon when Colbert would govern France. That obstacle was the feudal system, with its structures still in place, with its firmly established inequalities of taxation, its hierarchies of castes, and its contractual allegiances. The king wanted to affirm that he was head of state, but he remained and wished to remain a feudal king as well. The monarch reigned from the top of a succession of hierarchies that bitterly defended their privileges. The very essence of royal authority was feudal in nature. As Pierre Goubert has so rightly put it: "Royalty rested in fact on a series of contracts with the group of which France was composed: provinces, cities, ecclesiastical institutions, classes of society, and even economic groups such as trade guilds. All these contracts allowed each group its freedoms, its privileges, whose coexistence with the notion of submission to the king came as no shock to anyone."[2]

The great mass of the French peasantry, which bore the burden of taxation nearly alone, was taxed by all the large privileged groups, such as the ecclesiastical hierarchy and the local seigneur. Taxes due to the state in the name of the king did not supersede the others. When he approached the taxpayers, the king was competing with local lords. The people paid many times; they found themselves taxed by all in the most arbitrary fashion. The king thus appeared as just another privileged seigneur among the many to whom taxes were owed, in short, as an individual. Giving over to private concerns, such as the tax farmers or those who had purchased financial offices, the right to collect taxes on behalf of the king (who, despite all his majesty, was still an individual in the realm), seemed more normal.

The seventeenth was a watershed century. The nation-state that was to profit from future revolutions was growing up in a feudal context. From the moment that the king tried, in the name of the state, to control the totality of French finances directly, it meant attacking a régime sustained by a whole hierarchy of privileges. The parlement had joined the Fronde when Mazarin tried to impose certain fiscal measures on that privileged body. After the Fronde was defeated, a great historical evolution got under way. The times seemed divided in two. The

[2]Pierre Goubert, *Louis XIV et vingt millions de Français,* pp. 77–78.

structures of the state coexisted with feudal structures, and fidelity to the public good had to accommodate itself to private interests.

Mazarin is a marvelous example of the complexities of an age whose great transformations were not always obvious to him. He truly wished for the king and the state to have their due stature. His financial practices may astound us, but they appear less shocking when we are aware of his feeling that the state had no existence from a financial standpoint.

At first glance, Fouquet exhibited the same political feelings as the cardinal. He had proved that he could behave as a true statesman in critical circumstances. At the same time, his conception of public finance was identical to Mazarin's. He was a superior tax farmer. It was thanks to his personal guarantee that he furnished the state large sums; after all, the war with Spain was not yet over. How did he obtain reimbursement? That was his business. There was indeed someone called a registry clerk of funds who was expected to keep precise records and to exercise a sort of control over the superintendant; but those clerks were ordinarily appointed by the superintendant. It is true that Mazarin insisted upon the appointment of the Protestant Barthélemy Herwarth to the post. But what sort of control could the cardinal exercise over the superintendants when he himself treated the kingdom as his own domain? Fouquet allowed for Mazarin's strange doings more easily than his colleague Servien did. Servien had attempted to oppose the cardinal's furnishing the troops with wheat. Fouquet closed his eyes to the immense speculation deriving from those dealings. We may understand his indulgence when we learn of his own financial activities. Like Mazarin, Fouquet farmed taxes under assumed names. He possessed, among other things, the farming of customs dues and highway, river, and city tolls, and the taxes on sugar and wax from Rouen. He used these enormous sums to advance money to the state, still using aliases, which he then recouped with usurious interest charges. Furthermore, he drew sizeable incomes from other tax farms. The farmers of the *aides* (excise taxes on commodities) paid him 140,000 livres per year. Of course, the farmers reimbursed themselves afterwards by taxing the people more heavily. The king—always short of money, always seeking funds—ultimately became a sort of accomplice of the great moneylender, the superintendant. We may take as an example the manner in which the superintendant, as lender, got around the laws limiting interest, with the king's tacit approval. The nominal rate of interest was set at "one-in-eighteen," or 5.22 percent. To encourage the lender, or because he yielded to his blackmailer, the king allowed partial transfer of the borrowed capital, with the rest reverting to the lender. In this way, Fouquet could at times draw interest in the 15 to 18 percent range.

How can a state so shamelessly flouted ever gain respect? Yet the Italian cardinal's flexibility accommodated itself well to the contradiction. Fouquet seemed less sure of himself. His secretive, hasty, nervous character bordered on instability.

His enormous ambition seemed almost more feverish than calculated. And, little by little, the unscrupulous financier became a hatcher of plots.

Colbert opted for the state. He was revolted by the notion of arbitrary private control over public finances. He did not fail to contribute to the cardinal's questionable fortune, but he did so to gain the cardinal's confidence in order to eventually be able to propose his great plan of reform. Fouquet would write later, in his *Defenses*: "The said Lord Cardinal was himself governed by Colbert, his domestic servant, who while pretending to gather treasures for his master, had taken over his heart and mind, and was leading him to destroy me so as to enjoy my position." That is inaccurate. Colbert dreamed of directing French finances, but he wanted the office of superintendant abolished. That was the key point in the reform he suggested to the cardinal, without result. He thought, clearly and rightly, that the post itself was a symbol of the nonexistence of the state in the world of finances. In his view, the king, as head of state, had to fight for direct control of public money. He saw that feudalism was resisting the growing authority of centralized power. His feelings—one is tempted to say his political reflexes— prefigured the revolutionary Jacobinism that would triumph in the following century. He desired state domination in all public affairs because the state meant justice rather than what was arbitrary. Against those seigneurs nostalgic for the Fronde, he would proceed with a bloody violence foreshadowing the Revolution. Finally, he was haunted by Richelieu's ambitions for France. He understood that no great political plan can see the light of day without rudimentary budgeting and financial security. On this point he owed the late cardinal nothing. His economic policy was due entirely to Richelieu's inspiration, but his strictly financial policy was his own.

The three men—Mazarin, Fouquet, and Colbert—worked together on the same problems, met constantly, and dreamed, each according to his bent, of France's policies, even as the king's personality began to manifest itself. Fouquet thought the rivalry between himself and Colbert was personal in nature, but Colbert was later to claim it was political. We may observe the slow disintegration of their relationship within the shifting and difficult political context of those years of Mazarin's autocratic rule.

In 1653, Fouquet had just been named superintendant of finances. He ignored the letter Colbert had written Mazarin to express misgivings over his nomination. To all appearances, relations between the two men were cordial, even friendly. Colbert asked the new superintendent a favor on behalf of his father, whose business suffered during the Fronde. Fouquet agreed to help Nicolas Colbert divest himself of the registrar's office in Champagne.

In 1654, Louix XIV, age sixteen, was crowned at Rheims. His majority had been declared in 1651, but the young man, a bit backward by nature, had left all real power in the hands of his mother and the cardinal. Colbert and Fouquet joined forces to rebuild the cardinal's fortune. According to Colbert's correspondence, Fouquet was not always prompt enough to satisfy the cardinal's avarice: "The attorney general deserves a little reprimand," suggested Mazarin's agent.[3] Colbert served as an intermediary, passing on to the cardinal the sums Fouquet had collected. On June 25, he wrote: "I am sending Your Eminence through Monsieur Chappellin the 1000 gold louis that the attorney general had withdrawn from the farmers of the five large tax farms and given to me on the king's account."[4]

Colbert, like Fouquet, condemned the longings for the Fronde. The attorney general investigated and prosecuted the criminal cases with great severity, attempting to maintain the submission of the *parlementaires* to the politics of the cardinal. With the help of his brother, Abbé Basile—that curious police constable who was later to become his enemy—Fouquet kept an eye on the activities of the friends of two famous rebels: Condé, still in the service of Spain, and Cardinal de Retz, who had escaped from prison at Nantes. Colbert began, in 1654, to act as his master's interpreter in political affairs. He wrote to Mazarin: "I have told Abbé Fouquet what Your Eminence ordered by your letter of the nineteenth concerning negotiations with the party of Cardinal de Retz."[5]

On August 27, Colbert learned to his delight that the siege of Arras had been lifted. Stenay, a fort of Condé's in Picardy, had just fallen. Louis XIV received his baptism of fire in that campaign. The "malicious" were dumbfounded, he exclaimed. And, fearing the cardinal's tendency to compromise or hesitate, he added: "For God's sake, may Your Eminence remain firm in your resolve to chastise, and may you not yield to the reasoning of those many persons who—some more and some less, but all quite openly—don't want the king's authority to remain unrestrained and without being counterbalanced by illegitimate authorities such as that of the Parlement and others. I beg Your Eminence will pardon me this brief discourse, attributable to my zeal."[6] The cardinal responded: "I am comforted by the good sentiments you express."

Colbert also organized the visits of foreign envoys. He moved the privy councillor of Philip IV of Spain into Mazarin's palace. It was a highly important mission, possibly a forerunner of peace negotiations. A dinner with "divertissement by twenty-four violins" was carefully arranged.

By 1655, Colbert solidified more and more his position as informant and political counselor. That year, Mazarin had to deal with serious religious problems.

[3]Unpublished document of June 19, 1654.

[4]Unpublished document.

[5]Unpublished document of August 22, 1654.

[6]The word *illegitimate* may seem a bit strong applied to the parlement. We should remind ourselves, however, that the *parlementaires* were not elected, but purchased their offices.

Pope Alexander VII condemned Jansenism. Mazarin ordered the congregation of Port-Royal dispersed. He was about to commit a very imprudent act: He wished to have the condemnatory bull brought before the parlement and given legal status. Colbert foresaw the danger. Cardinal de Retz, who had fled to Rome, had many friends in Paris. The *parlementaires* poorly concealed their nostalgia for the Fronde and their sympathy for the Jansenists, now part of the opposition. Wouldn't Mazarin run the risk of bringing about an alliance between the *parlementaires,* the Jansenists, and Retz that could only lead to new disturbances? Mazarin agreed with his agent and put off the registration of the bull. Colbert, working with the Fouquet brothers, brought Mazarin information on Retz's contacts in Paris.

The Cluniac order was an example of those disorders and scandals. Richelieu had tried without success to bring about its reform. For the first time, Colbert suggested that Mazarin take over a particular project of the late cardinal's. He assembled a provisional council, which received Mazarin's authorization. Alas, it seemed very difficult to defeat an order in open rebellion against the cardinal.

Mazarin undertook seriously the political education of Louis XIV. Each day, the king went to the cardinal's chambers, where a secretary of state was called in. The young man heard their reports and then questioned Mazarin, who explained affairs of state to him. At the beginning of the year, Louis XIV himself registered new financial edicts with parlement by the process called *lit de justice* (which required his personal appearance at their reading).* But very soon afterward, the *parlementaires* claimed to have been unduly influenced by the king's presence during their deliberations and announced that they meant to revoke their decision. Louis XIV, mad with rage, left Vincennes in haste. He entered the great hall of the parlement in his hunting clothes, booted, spurred, whip in hand, and ordered the assembly to disband instantly. The *parlementaires* gave in to this strength of will, whose existence they had not suspected, but on the following day they were already thinking about reassembling. Mazarin seems to have been taken aback by the king's energy, and he sought as usual to proceed diplomatically.

With force and persuasion, Colbert encouraged the cardinal to show firmness. The *parlementaires* were claiming that the king owed them a formal apology, and they criticized Mazarin openly. Colbert wrote him: "All men of good will are horrified by those people's spitefulness, and are complaining rightly and justly that Your Eminence will not press your benevolence so far as to imprint the marks of fear on their minds, which is the only way to keep them in the path of duty." Colbert's character seems to match the king's better than it did Mazarin's.

Curiously enough, Louis attempted in the same year to turn Anne of Austria against Mazarin, whom he privately called "the Grand Turk." He pointed out to

---

*The *lit de justice* was a ceremony in which the king could personally enforce registration of edicts in the parlement or other sovereign courts.

his mother that Mazarin showed a lack of respect by not writing to her often enough. But the queen warned Mazarin of her son's intentions. When a courier brought Mazarin a letter from the king, the distracted cardinal thought that it contained news of his disgrace. But it did not, for despite certain irritations, Louis remained attached to Mazarin.

The poor state of the treasury was striking. "The superintendants," wrote Colbert, "speak of nothing but misery and the difficulties of obtaining money."[7] Nonetheless, Fouquet and Colbert were helping one another to increase Mazarin's fortune.

The cardinal's agent organized an official reception for the duke of Modena and one for the extravagant Queen Christina of Sweden, to whom he gave a tour of Mazarin's magnificent palace. He was responsible for the coloring of the silver-gilt work to be presented to the king of Sweden, and for having it marked with that monarch's coat of arms. How often Louis XIV would later entrust that sort of task to him!

In early 1656, the *parlementaires* were still up in arms. They wanted to meet, and even thought of stirring up a merchants' revolt in their behalf. There were also malcontent officers ready to support them. Colbert suggested exiling two members of each chamber. His advice was not taken. Meanwhile, the parlement was still seeking to severely limit royal power and that of the high public servants called *maîtres des requêtes*, who formed the real core of the national administration. The *maîtres des requêtes*, furious, sent a deputation to the king and to Anne of Austria that solemnly declared France would never have peace as long as the princes had their power, the Protestants their positions, and the parlements the right to speak. Both the king and the queen agreed with these men who, faithful to Richelieu's memory, would later support Colbert without flinching throughout his entire ministerial career. Anne of Austria, closer in spirit than Mazarin had been to the late Richelieu (who nonetheless had been her enemy), demanded an apology from the parlement.

Delighted by the trouble the *parlementaires* were stirring up, Cardinal de Retz left Italy and traveled under assumed names through France, hiding out in various hostelries. Fouquet and Colbert agreed that there should be no publicity if Retz's hiding-place were discovered, so as to avoid rekindling the Fronde. The two men busied themselves with searching for the elusive cardinal and watching his accomplices. Colbert put Mme de Pomereu, one of Retz's loyal followers, under the surveillance of a man "who is to follow her everywhere, who is to note all the lodgings she visits, how long she stays, and who enters next."[8] The duchesse

[7] Unpublished document of July 14, 1655.

[8] Pierre Clément, *Lettres, instructions, et mémoires de Colbert*, vol. 1.

de Chevreuse did not yet know which camp to choose: She began to give Colbert information while still sympathetic to Retz.

The year 1656 was a critical one for the kingdom and for Mazarin. Fouquet begged His Eminence "to believe that, having no enterprise that produces money, the least sums are gathered only with great effort."[9] To this distracting poverty, a true military catastrophe was added: Condé and Juan of Austria forced Turenne to raise the seige of Valenciennes. Despite his terrible difficulties in raising money, Fouquet, with the help of relatives and friends, managed to find the enormous sum of 90,000 livres in only four days.[10]

Mazarin was overflowing with enthusiasm and gratitude. He wrote to Fouquet: "I have spoken of it at length with Their Majesties, who are in agreement that you are full of a most positive zeal, and that one should prize a friend such as you."[11] Fouquet took on the image of a savior. His credit was at its zenith. The king and his mother went to visit him at Saint-Mandé. Surrounded by artists and writers, the superintendant imagined a dream palace that would bear witness to his glory. Working with the architect Louis de Vau, he made plans on a grand scale. The village of Vaux was razed, the property was enlarged, plans for the gardens were given to Le Nôtre. The work was clearly to be colossal from the beginning. Fouquet was going as deeply into debt on the state's behalf as he was for his château. The risks were immense. His feverish ambition struggled with difficulty to control the feelings of uneasiness that were growing in him.

Within a year, the outlines of the château de Vaux were already visible. The roof was being put on, and the installation of the fireplaces and the walls had begun. The queen was told 900 workmen were employed at the site. Fouquet lost his head and gave orders to have the doors closed to the public and to proceed with the work as quickly as possible "before the time of year when everyone goes to the country." What strange naiveté and what curious ambiguity in the personality of the superintendant! He wanted to hide the enormous undertaking, indecent in that period of such great poverty. At the same time, he wanted to show off his wealth and his power.

It was in 1657 that, quietly at first, the real duel between Colbert and Fouquet began. The superintendant had fired one of his subordinates, Delorme, for financial misconduct. Colbert (according to what he wrote Mazarin two years later) thought it "a favorable opportunity to make him change his

[9]June 10, 1656, *Bulletin Charavay*, no. 752.

[10]We should recall that Colbert handed over to Mazarin a sum drawn from his personal fortune at this time.

[11]Cited by Georges Mongrédien in *L'affaire Foucquet*.

ways."[12] Fouquet should place the blame for past lavishness on Delorme, and adopt new methods for himself. According to Colbert, Fouquet had promised to follow his advice, and the two men's friendship was "strongly rekindled." Alas, the superintendant fell "gradually deeper than ever into the same licenses," and "gradually" Colbert withdrew from the relationship.

Fouquet also dated the beginning of their rivalry to about the same time. Here is the superintendant's version as it stands in his *Défenses*:

He [Colbert] did me a thousand bad turns in secret, which I could not stop, before a suspicious, mistrustful man always disposed to believe the worst. . . . I was warned of it several times in 1657. I was convinced he meant to destroy me. . . . I tried to clear up the matter with Colbert and asked him sincerely and frankly why such an unjust process was underway, and why he had such a cold air about him, contrary to the friendship he had sworn, and to the pledge he had given me. . . . He admitted everything. . . . I tried to rekindle feeling in him as best I could.

These reciprocal "rekindlings" were of no use. The two men did not have the same conception either of public finances or of precisely what role the state was to take in that area. Fouquet continued to believe that his personal credit in business circles remained the best way to furnish money to the state. In Colbert's view, only a truly clear and orderly management of finances, under government control, could save the king and the country from such a regrettable situation. Mazarin began to look upon the very ostentatious superintendant with some distrust, but he still could conceive of only one sort of financial policy: the one Fouquet availed himself of.

To these clashes over public matters was added a serious private disagreement between Fouquet and Colbert. Hugues de Lionne, then a high official in the ministry of foreign affairs, brought suit against Colbert. This incident remains very obscure today, and is rarely referred to. Only Colbert's archives contain certain information on it, to be cited here because of its importance to the development of relations between Fouquet and Mazarin's agent.

According to Colbert, Lionne was backed by both superintendants, who prodded the judges into "prostituting their decision" by giving them money or by the promise of promotion. We may deduce from Colbert's indignant letters that what was involved was a large tax to be imposed on his very rich father-in-law, Charon—once a cooper and a wine broker, now a treasurer of the special war fund. Above and beyond that, Lionne seems to have tried to have Colbert sentenced to pay the 50,000 livres that his wife had received from Charon as her dowry.

[12]Clément, *Lettres,* vol. 1.

Fouquet tried to pack the courtroom with friends and to "instruct them in everything they are to say." Colbert, in a towering rage, asked Mazarin at least to prevent the giving of jobs to those who supported his adversaries. Mazarin intervened so decisively in his agent's favor that the affair was settled amicably, and Colbert's standing with the cardinal was given public confirmation.

Dislike and distrust were henceforth to dominate the two men's relationship. Fouquet attempted, in the same year, to breathe new life into commerce and industry, and submitted a report on the subject to Mazarin. In turn, Colbert hastened to propose his own projects for the nation. On July 8, 1657, he wrote in a draft: "I am sending Your Eminence a plan I have drawn up with respect to your grand design; I beg you most humbly to look it over at leisure, and to change or delete what you think proper, it being very important to weigh and consider such a great design thoroughly before undertaking it." And on July 21, he added: "Concerning the plan I have sent for the grand design, I am aware that there will be many changes and corrections; Your Eminence will please trouble to look it over at leisure in order to apply some part of your great knowledge to it, since it is a design that will bear your name in the coming centuries."[13] Colbert's correspondence does not spell out the project in detail.[14] Let us note that Colbert would willingly use the expression *grand design* in suggesting reforms to Louis XIV. The national scale of his ambition seems already evident in 1657.

Nervous and unsure of himself, Fouquet began to see enemies everywhere. For no apparent reason, he felt he was being watched by Barthélemy Herwarth, the registry clerk whom Mazarin was soon to name comptroller general. He was aware that Colbert was trying to destroy his standing with the cardinal. Mazarin had sent Fouquet a claim, in his own name, against the funds he had advanced for bread and munitions for Catalonia. The superintendant was slow to respond. Colbert did not miss the opportunity to insinuate that these delays were a result of "the attorney general's finances" being "diminished in the extreme."[15] Fouquet could not come up with cash. He proposed instead that Mazarin accept a share in an "extraordinary" deal that meant fabricating small coins with the help of the cardinal's Italian bankers. Colbert was quite hostile to this sort of operation. Mazarin agreed with his agent and called once again for reimbursement. Fouquet promised partial repayment; Mazarin replied that he wanted cash in hand and not promises. Irritated by this greedy insistence as much as by the malicious gossip to which the construction of Vaux-le-Vicomte was still giving rise, Fouquet sent

[13]Handwritten drafts.

[14]It is a matter, perhaps, of a memorandum concerning trade, of which only one (nonhandwritten) copy exists.

[15]Unpublished document of July 5, 1657.

Mazarin a letter in which, angrily and harshly, he reminded him that the state's other creditors were no better treated than Mazarin and that he himself was owed 300,000 livres more than at the first of the year. The letter was sent. Very quickly, however, the superintendant was overcome by panic and desperately regretted having written it. Fouquet was then at his estate of Saint-Mandé, which bordered Mazarin's Vincennes. He fell prey to horrible premonitions. Feverishly, with great care—as the numerous alterations show—he drew up the famous document known as the plan of Saint-Mandé, which was to make the statesman into a rebel.

THE PLAN OF SAINT-MANDÉ

Thus Fouquet—who had remained so faithful to the king during the long storm of the Fronde, and who as attorney general had been so hard on irreconcilable Frondeurs—was to reawaken the specter of rebellion and to adopt the plans of the most dangerous among the rebels. He tried to explain this insane attitude when he first set out to write his defense. A "distrustful and jealous" Mazarin, he claimed, would have stopped at nothing to destroy him. The proof? "The pleasure that he showed quite openly" in listening to Fouquet's enemies, to whom he gave "full access and full credence, without respect to their rank, the motives that drove them, and the harm he was doing to himself by discrediting a superintendent whose credit alone kept the state alive." Fouquet, sole support of the edifice of the state, its one and only savior, thought the state obliged to give him its approval, and to flatter him at need. The superintendent never understood that a state grown much stronger and a monarch careful of royal dignity would deny such unthinkable blackmail. At the time, he was preparing a plan to defend himself against the pitiless roguery of the cardinal and of his agent also, though the latter was not named. The plan would include two parts, that, in premonitory fashion, foreshadowed Fouquet's sad fate. In the first, the superintendent considered the possibility of imprisonment; in the second, he anticipated his being brought to trial.

The prisoner Fouquet should receive books; he should have a doctor. Attempts must be made to bribe his guards. His principal agents for the execution of his plan were two widows, both Breton like himself: his friend and great confidante the marquise du Plessis-Bellière, ten years older than he, and the marquise d'Assérac, whom he had earlier helped out of serious financial trouble.

It was from Brittany, the province of his origins,[16] that Fouquet gradually organized a network of loyal agents, took control of numerous coastal strongholds,

[16] A family of *parlementaires* from Nantes, the Fouquets came from Brittany. (*Fouquet* is the Breton word for "squirrel.")

and secretly obtained the submission of the Atlantic fleet. In other words, he acted to cut off France from the north and the west. Two ports would be his principal defensive bases, Concarneau, which Basile had bought with Nicolas's money, and Ham, which Mazarin had given Basile to reward him for undertaking a mission. Mme du Plessis-Bellière was to reach an immediate agreement with Deslandes, captain of Concarneau, and Mondejeu, governor of Arras and Ham, both men faithful friends to the superintendant. Deslandes "could quietly fortify his command with men and all sorts of munitions, call into port any ships he had at sea, and keep all things in readiness, buy horses and other things to be used at the right time."

Mme d'Assérac, proprietress of Ile-Dieu, was to fortify that place and to assemble vessels there "to lend their aid wherever needed." Soon Fouquet would buy several properties in Brittany in the marquise's name, including the duchy of Penthièvre. His daughter, the comtesse de Charost, could withdraw to Calais, where her father-in-law was governor. Charost was to prepare the city's defenses; the same recommendations were given to Bar, governor of Amiens, and Bellebrune, governor of Hesdin.

Fouquet was assured of the loyalty of Neuchèze, commander in chief of the dilapidated royal navy; bankrupted by a naval campaign in Crete against the Turks, he had accepted money from Fouquet to buy a vice-admiralty.

Fouquet drew up the list of his allies: Langlade, Gourville, his faithful clerk Pellisson, besides La Rochefoucald and Marsillac, who had been in the Fronde. They were to intervene on his behalf with the queen and Mazarin. Thus the plan was sketched out. Contrary to Fouquet's claims at his trial four years later, it was not a trifling folly, written in a moment of despair. From 1657 to 1661, the year of his arrest, we will see that the superintendant perfected his plan on paper as well as in fact.

The angry letter Fouquet sent Mazarin did not bring on any disgrace. The two men seemed to be reconciled; after all, the king would need money for the Flemish campaign. Colbert's influence was not diminished either. On the contrary, Mazarin thanked his faithful agent for his usefulness with such warmth that Colbert replied: "I must work for a lifetime if I am to deserve the terms that it has pleased Your Eminence to use in informing me that my little services are to your liking."[17] Mazarin recommended to Colbert that he and Fouquet work together to determine how antigovernment "libelmongers" could best be arrested and punished. Was the forever-elusive Retz hiding in Paris? He was surely the source of these "seditious writings."

[17]Unpublished document of October 24, 1657.

] 47 [

Louis XIV seemed pleased with the superintendant, whom he went to visit at Saint-Mandé. Colbert's correspondence reveals a curious incident that could suggest that Louis XIV may already have had some notion of governing alone. Colbert, certainly acting at Mazarin's request, had worked out a scheme to assign the offices of clerk of court for the province of Burgundy to the prince de Conti and to have his pension reduced in proportion. But a recent decree from the king disallowed it. The cardinal and his agent were very intrigued. How had the present owners of the Burgundy clerkship obtained the decree without Mazarin's knowing about it? Colbert promised to find out and to let His Eminence know."[18]

The monarchy had rarely seemed so threatened as it did in 1658. The war with Spain was bankrupting the country. Mazarin sought the support of Cromwell, who imposed stringent conditions in return for his alliance, notably the cession of Dunkirk. The nobility was in revolt nearly everywhere. The provincial parlements expressed opposition to new taxes. There were horrible riots by armed peasants. In June, Turenne rekindled hope with his victory over the troops of Condé and Juan of Austria in the battle of the Dunes. Alas, the following month Louis XIV fell gravely ill. A new Fronde seemed ready to break out, encouraged by the illness of the king. The parlement pardoned the countless libelists.

Colbert's sense of propaganda was already evident. He asked Mazarin for frequent news of the king. "If it is good, we will endeavor to make it public, and if it is bad, we will express it in the way we think it most advantageous for the king and for Your Eminence."[19] Colbert, extremely anxious, dropped everything for a week. At last, on June 12, word came that the king had been saved.

Colbert personally carried out specific inquiries into the activities of the nobility, then reported them to Mazarin. He carefully established a list of suspected gentlemen. The man who would later be the future unofficial minister of the interior served another apprenticeship. His responsibilities went far beyond the limits of the cardinal's private interests. Did Colbert's rise irritate Le Tellier? The exact reasons for the misunderstandings that poisoned the minister's whole career and that seem to have begun in 1658 are not known. Only the year before, Colbert had been full of praise for Le Tellier's eldest son, Louvois, his future rival, who appeared worthy of succeeding his father. Le Tellier now seemed to grow colder. Colbert pointed it out to him, with all the signs of real sadness. Le Tellier reassured him, but the rivalry had begun.

Fouquet, like Colbert, castigated the Frondeurs and declared that the nobles were "imperiling the monarchy." Despite great difficulties, he succeeded in raising the money Mazarin had demanded. He even applied part of his wife's fortune to

[18]Handwritten drafts of May 24 and June 2, 1657.

[19]Clément, *Lettres,* vol. 1.

the financing of the war. To all appearances, his loyalty was above reproach. And yet the plan of Saint-Mandé was being perfected, strange contracts of allegiance were signed, and secret purchases were pursued. The personality of the superintendant was truly a psychological enigma.

On June 2, Deslandes, governor of the port of Concarneau, gave Fouquet a written promise "never to belong to another besides him . . . to serve him generally against all sorts of persons, without exception, and to obey no other person but him." Even more serious is the document given him in September by Meridor, president of the Parlement of Brittany: "I promise the attorney general to remain at all times totally devoted to his interest, whatever may happen, without any reservation or distinction of persons, whatever rank or condition they may be, being resolved to execute his orders blindly in all matters that may arise and that involve him personally."[20] We may wonder whether Louis XIV would have dared demand such pledges even at the height of his powers.

Fouquet gradually increased, at his own expense, the patrimony of Mme d'Assérac, who in this manner became titular governor of Guérande, Le Croisic, and Mont-Saint-Michel. Shortly thereafter, in February of 1659, he had the marquise sign a promise to hand over those strongholds immediately upon request.

In August, Fouquet bought Belle-Ile in his own name, having first secured permission from Mazarin, who still knew nothing of the plan. That place had been put up for sale by the Retz family, and there was some risk that it would fall into the hands of the duc de Brissac, thought to be an adversary.

It was about that time that the dispute arose between Nicolas Fouquet and his brother, Abbé Basile. Fouquet replaced Ham, which belonged then to Basile, with Belle-Ile in his plan. One of Fouquet's mistresses, Mlle de Trécesson, was instructed to spy on the court. Toward the end of the same year, the doors and windows of the château de Vaux were installed. The chateau was already unusually splendid. La Fontaine was writing *Le Songe de Vaux*.

Fouquet fell ill, overcome with high fever. In December, exhausted by wearying toil, disheartened at the thought of having ruined his family and friends who had helped him lend money to the king, the superintendant gave Mazarin his resignation. Unfortunately for Fouquet, the cardinal refused to accept it.

On February 16, 1659, Fouquet's fellow superintendant, Servien, died. Colbert recommended that Mazarin replace him "either with someone who would outrank Fouquet, or with someone who was a subordinate." Mazarin considered taking Servien's title himself while leaving the actual duties of the office to Colbert. Fouquet would work directly with Mazarin, but it was to Colbert that the comptroller general, Herwarth, would submit dispatches for signature. Herwarth was

[20]See Georges Mongrédien, *L'affaire Foucquet.*

furious at being supplanted by Colbert. When Mazarin asked the comptroller general, who was also a banker, to advance him money, Herwarth refused, claiming that his credit was exhausted. As for Fouquet, he told Mazarin that he himself could not obtain any credit if he were not performing the duties of his office himself. Mazarin gave in, and Fouquet became sole superintendant of finances. After that miscalculation, Colbert was forced to wait some months before returning to the attack.

The king owed Fouquet more than five million livres. The court heaped compliments and favors upon Fouquet. Anne of Austria and her brother, the king of Spain, wanted to be reconciled. Mazarin left Paris in June for Saint-Jean-de-Luz, where he was to negotiate a peace as well as the marriage of Louis with the infanta, Maria Theresa. On his way, he stopped off at Vaux-le-Vicomte. On July 19, Louis XIV, his mother, and Gaston d'Orléans were received in turn at Fouquet's chateau. The superintendant may have felt safe from his enemies. If so, he was mistaken. Herwarth was again reconciled with Colbert, and on July 27, he complained to the cardinal of Fouquet's conduct: "Whenever he can, he prevents me from knowing anything, and mixes the past with the present, so that I cannot tell what is legitimately due from what is not, and so that no one can see clearly into the financial situation but him and his creatures."[21] On August 31, Colbert sent Mazarin a letter denouncing the arbitrariness and the bribes that were hampering scandalously the collection of taxes. Now that the war was drawing to a close, he wrote, it was time to correct the situation. And he added: "I cannot avoid telling Your Eminence something that you know much better than I—that finances in general badly need a severe and rigorous chamber of justice where the officials who compose it have no attachment, either by marriage or by interest, with the *partisans,* and you will not find that in Paris; and the provinces have great need of special hearings [*grand jours*] to punish all the uncalled-for harassment of the people."[22] Chambers of justice, *grand jours*—only later would Colbert convince the king of their need. Mazarin returned the letter, contenting himself with striking out the entire paragraph without responding.

Colbert went over the same ground on September 24: "The attorney general is almost always at Vaux. It would be well for Chancellor Séguier, who doesn't have enough to do, to hold a small council." Fouquet intercepted Colbert's correspondence for the first time, thanks to the intendant of the postal service, Nouveau, who owed him his position. Fearing the cardinal's fickleness, Fouquet left Paris in haste to rejoin him. A very worried Colbert decided to draw up a

[21]G. Depping, *Barthélemy Herwarth, contrôleur général des finances (1607–1676).*

[22]Clément, *Lettres,* vol. 1.

long report, of more than twenty pages—a merciless indictment of Fouquet and a summary of the great financial and judiciary reforms that were to mark the reign of Louis XIV. Colbert was forty. His plan was clear, well thought out, and imbued with an undeniable and sincere spirit of justice. It also embodied a great political design. Fouquet's obvious corrupt practices and his desire to make things so extremely complicated that he would be indispensable were pointed out in the harshest of terms. It was time to abolish the office of superintendant, to force the financiers to make restitution, to restore commerce, to work for a more powerful army and a greater navy, to fight against the proliferation of royal offices, which led so many subjects away from useful occupations.[23] Once again, Colbert suggested to Mazarin taking "sole and total control of the finances." Until he could return to Paris, however, the cardinal would still need Fouquet. It would be necessary to use "all sorts of flattery" on the superintendant, because that would be "a means of restraining his naturally active, restless, and scheming mind."

Colbert began his draft on September 28 and finished it the following day. He gave the report to his secretary-copyist Picon, whom he then closed up in a small office for two days. On the evening of October 1, he took the copy from Picon, signed it, and placed it in a packet that he sent to Mazarin on the second, the same day Fouquet reached Mazarin in Bordeaux. Nouveau intercepted Colbert's mail a second time. Fouquet had the report in his hands on the fifth. With the help of his faithful Gourville, Fouquet made a quick copy of it. Mazarin received Colbert's dispatch at Saint-Jean-de-Luz on October 15.

We may imagine Colbert's anxiety as he awaited Mazarin's reply. But the first letter from Mazarin spoke instead of a terrible blunder committed by his cousin Colbert du Terron. Louis XIV, then very much in love with Marie Mancini, Mazarin's niece, had been using Colbert and his cousin as go-betweens for letters between him and his beloved. Colbert and Mazarin had clearly agreed that the projected marriage with the Infanta Maria Theresa required that no more letters from her should be carried to the king. Yet Terron had continued to serve as courier. Mazarin was furious: Terron was making things highly complicated for him. It was perhaps "the most delicate" matter of his life. Colbert was overwhelmed. He could find no apologies humble enough. He expected his whole family to suffer disgrace; but he got off with a bad fright. The cardinal reassured him.

But what did Mazarin think of the famous report? Mazarin had read it before the arrival of Fouquet and responded to Colbert October 21: "I am quite pleased by the information I have gotten from it; and will take advantage of it as the

---

[23]The full text of the report can be found in volume 7 of Clément's *Lettres,* pp. 164 ff.

present situation allows." It was no more than a polite remark; Mazarin knew that to condemn Fouquet meant to condemn himself. He only seemed very surprised that Fouquet knew "from an unimpeachable source" that Colbert was working on a report concerning financial matters. He thought the two men should be reconciled, saying that Fouquet "wished fervently to get along" with Colbert. On October 22 Mazarin ordered his agent to meet with Fouquet when the latter reached Paris, and he repeated that he had full confidence in the superintendant. Colbert obeyed, but not without explaining to Mazarin how Fouquet was able to learn about his report, which seemed to disturb the cardinal a bit.

Fouquet was aware that Colbert's threats of retribution were not just words. He had seen the man pursue the plotting nobles of Normandy. During the disturbances of the Fronde, Anne of Austria and Gaston d'Orléans had promised the nobles a meeting of the Estates General. Once the danger was past, the court was eager to forget its promise. The nobles of Poitou, Anjou, and especially Normandy did not conceal their anger and seemed ready to stir up a new revolt. Colbert showed then that he was the unofficial head of Mazarin's police. With what tenaciousness he worked to have a certain Bonnesson arrested; and with what joy he announced to the cardinal the execution of that rebellious gentleman; with what attentiveness he sought to have the mutineers prosecuted by emergency courts and not by the parlement! Fouquet recognized how dangerous an enemy Colbert could be, and turned to Anne of Austria with his complaints. He was doing what he could to regain Colbert's confidence, he explained to the queen. He wanted to make "a full confession," to make a gift of Vaux to Mazarin. As for Belle Ile, he dreamed of living there in peaceful seclusion.

The queen knew nothing of the plan of Saint-Mandé, not to mention the insane additions Fouquet had made to it that very year. First, if he were arrested, there was to be an uprising of his own naval forces—which he intended to strengthen year by year—and also of the coastal strongholds he controlled. Fouquet was counting heavily on a sailor named Guinan: "M. Guinan, who has great knowledge of the sea, and whom I trust, must help to furnish all our strongholds with necessary supplies and with men who will be levied by order of Gourville or one of the people named above." And the royal navy? Neuchèze, its commander, was loyal; his role was to witness the uprising without making a move. Fouquet explained that very clearly: "Since the principal establishments on which I am relying are maritime—such as Belle-Ile, Concarneau, Le Havre, and Calais—there is no question that, since the vessels are under his command, he [Neuchèze] can be of great use to us by not doing anything." His supporters were not to use the mails—for obvious reasons; rather, they were to use special trustworthy agents. The attorney general, who gave every indication of being an enemy of the Fronde, asked his brothers Louis, bishop of Agde, and François, coadjutor of Narbonne, to incite the clergy to join the nobility in calling for the Estates General to meet. As an alternative he suggested that national councils be organized in places well removed from any military garrison: "and there, one might propose a thousand sensitive subjects." Next followed a dreadful suggestion: The brothers should not forget to mention "the aid that might be obtained from other kingdoms and states."

In the event that the king should wish to put him on trial, Fouquet foresaw another series of measures that leave us dumbfounded. His allies among the local governors were to seize the public funds and to cut off all communication between the central government and the provinces, using troops to block the roads. Captain Guinan would fit out every ship he could seize on the Seine between Rouen and Le Havre as a fire ship or a privateer. From Calais he could control the entrance to the Channel, and from Le Havre, the mouth of the Seine. Belle-Ile would be the central point from which ships could be sent in all directions. The nail that held all together, so to speak, was the kidnapping of Le Tellier, who would serve as a hostage. And since, at that point, a state of rebellion would have been reached, the recorder of the trial could also be kidnapped, from whom all the papers would be seized. And, of course, pamphlets were not to be neglected. Fouquet, who had been involved with Colbert in the prosecution of pamphleteers, knew how effective their writings could be. In fact, his crony Pelisson was one of the most skillful writers in that style. Finally, Fouquet counted on being judged by the parlement and not by a special court. He was himself a *parlementaire*. And didn't the First President owe him his job?

On January 6, 1660, Colbert went to Saint-Mandé, as Mazarin had ordered. Fouquet recounted the visit to Mazarin, saying that during their discussion Colbert "spoke most civilly." We may imagine Colbert's efforts to succeed in appearing amiable. Fouquet's position seemed unshakable, and once again Colbert was obliged to put off his attacks until later. In any case, he was totally engrossed in the preparations for the king's wedding. He had to send furniture, canopies, and portraits to Saint-Jean-de-Luz, as well as the crown for the future queen. Colbert chose materials for the infanta, sent down a carriage that turned out to be useless, became entangled in a thousand details. "I admit to Your Eminence that all this has me in such a daze that I no longer know what I'm doing." Next, he fell into despair at having sent the queen some bad oranges. Mazarin tried to calm him: "I am sorry that you are spending time on such trifles, as I am extremely satisfied with everything you do continuously in my behalf and for my advantage in all situations."[24] Grandiose ceremonies were arranged for the royal couple's entry into Paris. Mazarin, already ill, watched the parade from his window. Colbert had just sold the office of secretary of the queen's household to Bordeaux, but had not yet

[24]Clément, *Lettres,* vol. 1.

relinquished his duties. It was Colbert who, to the great resentment of M. de Bordeaux and despite his protest, had the honor of being placed behind the young queen's throne.

Colbert was also entrusted with another delicate mission. Condé, the Grand Prince,[25] recently reconciled with the government, had had studs placed on the cloth covering of his carriage, a privilege reserved solely for the male children of the kings. Gaston d'Orleans was furious. Colbert had to settle the matter. He went to see Condé at his formal levee on March 18, and the two men spoke of prerogatives and privileges in endless detail. Colbert did not want to offend the great Frondeur, who proved to be pleasant to the agent of the cardinal. Finally, the prince agreed that he would keep his studded cover only until he left Paris and then he promised never to use it again.

In the meantime, Fouquet had renegotiated at favorable terms the leases on the two major tax farms: the *aides* and the *gabelles*.* He had even gotten the Crown 100,000 ecus in *donatifs,* a polite term for bribery. On July 17, 1660, Louis, Maria Theresa, and the whole court visited Vaux. Fouquet, a year before the famous fête, arranged a sumptuous reception with a first-rate dinner for the king. His anxiety persisted. Again he tried to conceal the work going on at his chateau, where countless laborers were busy under the orders of Le Vau, Le Brun, and Le Nôtre.

He communicated his plan to his friend Gourville, who came to visit him at Saint-Mandé. In his *Mémoires,* Gourville claims he had persuaded Fouquet to burn the document, out of date on more than one point. Mme d'Assérac had sold the Ile-Dieu; Deslandes was no longer governor of Concarneau; Lamoignon could not be counted on, and Belle-Ile was still not in a defensible state. An inopportune visit forced Fouquet to hide the document hastily. Gourville said much later that he "had placed it behind his mirror, where he forgot it so completely that it was found in the same place after his arrest." Perhaps that is so. But then why did he continue to fortify Belle-Ile in secret? Why did he purchase vessels and cannon in Holland? The coast had to be blockaded, but provisions also had to be made for replenishing supplies through private colonial trade under Fouquet's control— of course, in secret. The office of viceroy of the two Americas, North and South, was created on behalf of Isaac de Pas, marquis of Feuquières. Then on September 15, 1660, Feuquières signed a document that he handed over to the superintendant, in which he recognized that "the office of viceroy of the Americas belongs to sieur Fouquet, who has paid 30,000 ecus for it."[26]

[25]Conde's title.

[26]See Charles de La Roncière, *La vrai crime du Surintendant Fouquet.*

*The *gabelle* was the tax on salt.

The king wanted to send a first governor to Newfoundland, and an old captain named Gargot was selected. Fortunately for Fouquet, he was poor. The superintendant took on all the expenses of getting him established, hoping in that way to gain control of the cod fisheries. Then, seeking to extend his hegemony, he became involved in the Canadian fur trade, bought the island of Saint Lucia, and made investments in Guadeloupe and Martinique. Should we not see here a parallel with the ambitious colonial policies Colbert later wanted to employ on behalf of the state?

By 1661 Mazarin was seriously ill. In January Fouquet gave a masked ball attended by the entire court, in his Parisian town house in the rue Neuve-des-Petits-Champs. Colbert was beginning to receive letters in which he was addressed as *Monsiegneur*. Mazarin died on March 9. Two days before his death he had affirmed in the presence of the king and Fouquet his full confidence in the superintendant's loyalty and competence. But in all likelihood he advised the king to have him watched by Colbert, who had recently been appointed intendant of finances.

In his will, Mazarin bequeathed "to Colbert the house in which he lives, without any obligation of accountability, on pain of disinheritance for anyone who requests such; and I ask the king to employ him, for he is trustworthy."

Fouquet and Colbert were among the executors. At Mazarin's request, however, the king entrusted Colbert with all of the cardinal's papers, both those concerning national affairs and those pertaining to Mazarin's private interests. Colbert was instructed to put them in order. Mazarin had bequeathed to the Crown the paintings from his library, and eighteen large "Mazarin diamonds," and various other objects and jewels as well. Because Mazarin's nieces and nephews were not interested in the arts, his former agent succeeded in buying the rest of his precious collections for the king at an excellent price. Now Colbert had become the king's man. Over the next six months he would prepare the fall of Fouquet.

CHAPTER 5

The Fall of Fouquet

MAZARIN DIED HOPING to see the king "govern on his own," using ministers "only to give advice." To facilitate the exercise of such personal government, the cardinal advised him to create a High Council, composed of the principal ministers of state to assist him on an equal footing. That meant a diminution of Anne of Austria's influence and the absence of a prime minister. Louis XIV, to the great astonishment of the court, announced that henceforth he would assume the supreme direction of the kingdom.

The secret High Council was to include only three ministers, who had been chosen for the king by Mazarin. They were Le Tellier, solid, experienced, and rather dull, but highly competent in matters of war and internal affairs; Hugues de Lionne, flexible and firm, who over the years had displayed his superiority in matters of diplomacy (the comte de Brienne, titular head of the department of foreign affairs, and his son, who had the right of succession to that office, were, in practice, overshadowed by Lionne); and Fouquet, in charge of finances, who was a very resourceful man, capable of rendering great services to the state, but a man who needed to be watched. Louis XIV respected Mazarin's political testament scrupulously, and Fouquet became one of the three.

From the very first council meetings, the king showed a very lively interest in foreign affairs. Very concerned about France's preeminence in Europe, he meant to conduct his government's foreign policy himself. The diplomatic service of the time was nothing like today's. Unorganized, lacking in numbers, it often made use of personal and temporary emissaries of the king. Fouquet had secretly been one such emissary under Mazarin, and served in such a capacity again during the first months of Louis XIV's personal reign. The king did not hesitate to entrust him with diplomatic missions of the greatest importance. Colbert's grand political plan primarily concerned domestic matters. Fouquet's secret role in foreign affairs risked establishing a sort of complicity between him and the king—one that seemed to exclude Colbert.

What basically were France's relations with the major European powers? France had been officially delivered from the grasp of the Hapsburgs, a grasp that had been a terrible nightmare for the two late cardinals. The Vienna Hapsburgs had ceased to fight after the Treaty of Westphalia (1648), and the Madrid Hapsburgs had recently signed the Peace of the Pyrenees (1659).

The king of Spain, Phillip IV, uncle and father-in-law to Louis XIV, was old and ill. His heir was a sickly child, unlikely to live long. Nonetheless, the French court remained obsessed with Spain—who continued to be a powerful threat on both the northern and southern borders of the kingdom. Let us recall that the "Spanish Netherlands" (roughly today's Belgium), a legacy of the Empire of Charles V, still belonged to the Spanish Crown. The United Provinces (of which the most important was Holland) revolted against Spanish domination and obtained their independence in 1648.

The provisions of the Peace of the Pyrenees contained the seeds of a future war. Phillip IV had officially excluded his daughter Maria Theresa, queen of France, from the succession, on the condition that he pay an enormous dowry—which he failed, in fact, to pay. The bad will of the Spanish king increased the distrust of the French. Louis XIV sought to secretly weaken Spain's power.

To the south, it was necessary to help Portugal, at war with Phillip IV for more than twenty years. To the North, an alliance with the United Provinces was prudently maintained, although the Dutch bourgeoisie in power in Amsterdam was beginning to irritate the great European nations by its growing economic hegemony.

France embarked upon a double diplomatic game all the more delicate and difficult because it had to remain secret. The king of England, Charles II, subsidized by Louis XIV, could be of use to France on two fronts.[1] In Holland he could encourage the House of Orange—who had been removed from real power by the businessmen of Amsterdam—more openly than Louis could. At the same time, Fouquet was making every effort to protect the interests of French commerce (and those of his own companies) against England as well as Holland. He carried out negotiations between France and Holland most ably and imposed a freight tax of fifty sous per ton on the shipowners of the United Provinces. In this case, the protectionist ideas of Fouquet joined those of Colbert.

Officially, Louis had promised the king of Spain that he would not support Portugal. Charles II could do that in his place. Fouquet was entrusted with the important mission of helping to arrange the marriage of the king of England with the infanta of Portugal. He succeeded brilliantly.[2] At the same time, he was promoting a treaty between Portugal and Holland.

---

[1] We should remember that Charles II came from the Stuart line, that his mother was the sister of Louis XIII, and that his sister, Henrietta Stuart, was married to Monsieur, Louis XIV's brother.

[2] The wedding took place in London on May 31, 1662.

In Vienna, the young Emperor Leopold of the Holy Roman Empire claimed that his "cousin and good brother" the king of France had no right to be treated as his equal. Louis XIV's indignation was immense—"bordering on the tragic," wrote Jean de Boislisle. The French diplomatic service busied itself with inconveniencing the Empire in various ways, and the superintendant again played a leading role. At first, he was entrusted with subsidizing the German princes, who chafed under the Austrian yoke. Pursuing Mazarin's policy, he sought to unite the Northern powers that could form a common front against the Empire. Fouquet succeeded in creating an alliance between France and Sweden. As for Poland, Louis XIV, like Mazarin, wanted to guarantee that Condé's eldest son, the duc d'Enghien, would succeed the incompetent King John Casimir. Together with the other two ministers of state, Fouquet actively involved himself in that matter— but without success.

Finally, the superintendant turned to easing the relations between Paris and the Papacy. Mazarin had gotten along very poorly with Pope Alexander VII, who had defended the prerogatives of Cardinal de Retz and had shown himself to have Spanish sympathies. Colbert's brother Colbert de Croissy was sent to Rome to request an amicable solution, but he failed. Once again the king turned to Fouquet, asking him to choose a secret envoy capable of overseeing the difficult negotiations with the pope.

Fouquet's services to French diplomacy were considerable. Did he not once again seem indispensable as before? Could Colbert finally defeat his enemy under circumstances that seemed favorable to the superintendant?

Fouquet was not lost. But Mazarin had communicated to the king his doubts about Fouquet and his confidence in Colbert. A few months would suffice for Mazarin's former agent to win Louis XIV over and arrange Fouquet's arrest.

THE SNARE

Colbert had recently become intendant of finances with Le Tellier's help. The minister of war disliked Fouquet and hoped to guide his former aide in the fight against the superintendant. Colbert now had access to the register of revenues and expenditures, although Herwarth continued to perform the office of comptroller general. Sometimes Colbert, modestly dressed, would bring that famous register to the after-dinner meetings of the Council of Three, carrying it in a small black-velvet pouch under his arm. The king asked Fouquet to give him an account of his administration daily. The superintendant committed the immense psychological error of believing that Louis would soon tire of business matters. He did not obey or, worse yet, attempted to conceal his financial falsehoods by means of further falsehoods—which Colbert revealed and explained to the young king night after night.

In the morning, Louis would press Fouquet for information on some particular expenditure of revenue, and the superintendant would become entangled in his own web of erroneous claims. Actually, the whole financial system was to blame. Fouquet was totally compromised by the system of tax farmers. His position itself, with its total lack of accountability, was outmoded. He lent to the king and reimbursed himself as he thought proper. Fouquet's was a divided nature: a true statesman, with the soul of a Frondeur. He seemed torn apart by his personal contradictions, contradictions that were those of the period as well. The lack of a sense of nationhood coexisted with the formation of a true nation. The incredible disorder of the ancien régime was on a collision course with the formidable need for reorganization characteristic of modern civilization. Fouquet went astray by sensing only half of the great transformations of the moment.

Colbert was not content to keep an eye on the state of finances. He had begun even by then to inquire into naval affairs and above all to participate, by order of the king, in committees "to take care of commerce." To Fouquet again came the honor of projects and decisions, but Colbert was present at meetings, such as the one on April 10, 1661.[3] And Fouquet's personal holdings were chiefly maritime and commercial ones. Finances, the sea, trade: Colbert was surrounding, determining, and unmasking the superintendant's universe.

According to what Colbert wrote two years later, the king had made up his mind to take the administration of financial matters away from Fouquet on May 4, 1661. Why then was his arrest put off until September? The collection of taxes and the harvest were not complete. It seemed wiser to wait to overthrow a man from whom one still wanted to obtain large and pressing sums. It was certain that Louis would be reluctant to take a step of which his mother would be sure to disapprove strongly. Anne of Austria did not seem convinced by Colbert's attacks: She still supported the superintendant. Finally, the king may have been hesitant to arrest a minister who had rendered him so many services in his foreign policy.

Fouquet's status still seemed elevated, and Louis XIV still showed him signs of favor. Colbert had to see to it that the king did not change his mind. Fouquet knew his enemy had not laid down his arms. The superintendant continued to seek Anne's support, smothering her with attention. He placed his spies everywhere—at court, around the queen, and in Colbert's own household. The plan of Saint-Mandé was being followed methodically. Neuchèze's faithfulness should guarantee that the Atlantic fleet would be Fouquet's; what was left was to secretly appropriate the Mediterranean galleys. The commander of the galleys was then

[3]Jean de Boislisle, *Mémoriaux du conseil de 1661*. In 1664 Colbert transformed that committee into the Council of Commerce.

the marquis de Richelieu. Fouquet had been in negotiations with him for some time, trying to persuade him to cede his office to the marquis de Créqui, son-in-law of Madame du Plessis-Bellière. At last, in July, Créqui bought the command with 200,000 livres given him by Fouquet. This gradual takeover of the king's navy was accompanied by the continuing work of heavy fortification at Belle-Ile.

It was clear that Colbert already had precise suspicions about Fouquet's hidden plans. As early as May he made inquiries into the condition of the navy, noted all irregularities, and contacted Duquesne and Neuchèze. On April 27 he had asked his cousin Colbert du Terron to obtain information about the strange activity at Belle-Ile, which were being noticed despite all the precautions Fouquet took to conceal the huge construction. Colbert received reports from his cousin that confirmed his intuitions. Fouquet forebade access to his island by unknowns. Terron's first care consisted in finding ways of sending spies into the superintendant's fortress. "A confident mason in a boat carrying dressed stone" could get into the island without arousing too much suspicion. Or else "three or four casks of wine in a double launch could be sent." The surest means, wrote Terron, "would be to house a man at Quiberon, the Breton port nearest Belle-Ile, who, disguised as a sailor or peasant, could often go over to Belle-Ile." It appeared that several times a great deal of powder and ammunition had been hauled from Bordeaux to Belle-Ile. It was also necessary to inform themselves about the cannons. Terron suggested that his cousin adopt a code to use in corresponding on that subject.

A few days later, they learned from a merchant that on Fouquet's island "things were being done in a magnificent style:" 1500 laborers were at work there. On June 10, Terron received a complete report, with a fully detailed map of the island. He hastened to share it with his cousin. The spy "will wait until his return to tell how he managed the intricate matter of entering (those are the terms of his narrative), and by what intrigue he came to learn of what is happening on the island." Fouquet was maintaining a garrison of 200 men. "There are 400 cannon in the fort, to wit 100 cast iron and 300 wrought iron, a quantity of bombs and explosives in the magazine, five cast-iron mortars, weapons and munitions for 6000 men. . . . Provisions include 300 casks of wine whose contents are replaced as they are used, and a proportional amount of wheat. The greater part of the weapons and ammunition came from Holland. The local people stand guard on the island and in the town."

The spy's map of the island, drawn in pencil, shows very exactly not only what had been completed but the work under way: "blacksmith's shop," terraces, esplanades, ditches, "future location of the basin," levees, town, church. The fortifications were well along. Terron's man noted that "they work day and night when possible. The workers are forbidden to leave the island, and no ship is allowed to take them aboard for any reason."

Later, Louis XIV would enumerate in his memoirs the actual offenses of which Fouquet stood accused: "Building forts, decorating his palaces, forming cabals, and putting his friends into important posts bought at my expense, in hope of making himself the sovereign arbiter of the state." Would Fouquet's financial doings have been enough to bring on his terrible disgrace? Was the king as convinced as Colbert of the need for a major financial reform? Perhaps. What does seem certain—and the memoranda of council meetings in the early part of his personal reign prove it—is that Louis XIV early possessed a very lofty conception of the majesty of his position and of the sacred legitimacy of royal and absolute power. It is easy to believe that Colbert showed Terron's reports to the king, and that Louis XIV felt a profound indignation at them. Weapons for 6,000 men, vessels, 400 cannon: That, neither the king nor the state could tolerate.

Now the time had come to win over Anne of Austria, the superintendant's most important ally. Colbert had the idea of employing the aged duchesse de Chevreuse to that end. She had been a source of great irritation at the time of the Fronde, but despite her evidently divided loyalties, she had retained her influence with the Queen Mother. The duchesse bet on Colbert and (in addition to marrying her grandson to Colbert's eldest daughter) agreed to take on the sensitive mission. In early July, Mme de Chevreuse received the court at her chateau of Dampierre. There, the Queen Mother, surrounded by Fouquet's enemies, finally promised not to oppose the disgrace of the superintendant.

Spying increased in both camps. Anne of Austria's confessor seems to have played both sides. Fouquet learned very quickly of the conversations at Dampierre, and made the mistake of expressing his displeasure to the Queen Mother. On July 21, an agent wrote to Fouquet that the confessor "complained that, when seeking to clarify things with the Queen Mother, you quoted her almost word for word, and when you told her that she had been among your enemies at Dampierre and had heard things said against you, upon her denial that she had been spoken to in that way, you told her to go ask her father confessor; and the next day the Queen said she could not fathom how you knew such things, and that you had spies everywhere."[4] Soon Fouquet received a message that one of his friends, Mme d'Huxelles, had written partly in invisible ink: "This is no exaggeration. . . . The Queen has forbidden her confessor to have any dealings with you, and said you were spending a million to corrupt her people."

The danger of disgrace had never seemed so great. According to Choisy, Fouquet went to Fontainebleau to meet the king, confessed all his errors, admitted to his excessive expenditures, and promised to reform. Louis XIV, who had already made up his mind, reassured him with that "wise dissimulation" that Colbert

[4]Quoted in Georges Mongrédien, *L'affaire Foucquet.*

admired. The superintendant had admitted his financial indiscretions, but had been careful to say nothing of his plots to take control of the naval forces and to build strongholds. Colbert did not fail to continue to inform Louis XIV.

On July 24, Terron added a postscript to a report sent to his cousin: "Since I finished my letter, M. Duquesne has arrived; we are to talk everything over once he has seen Commandant Neuchèze."[5] Clearly Colbert already suspected some sort of connivance between Fouquet and top naval officials. Terron's letter of July 28 denounced the secret trade the superintendant wanted to carry on in the Antilles. Two naval officers in Fouquet's pay had revealed that

> Their employer's intent was to become sole master of Martinique and to have up to fifteen vessels to support the inhabitants of that island and carry on all its commerce, to the exclusion of all other persons. And so that each element would be useful to the other, Belle-Ile must be the warehouse for all commerce, in such fashion that all food intended for Martinique would be kept there, such as wine, brandy, vinegar, vegetables, and flour, all of which could very easily serve as provisions for the citadel of Belle-Ile itself, for which supplies would need to be replenished continuously. All munitions needed to equip his ships will also be stored there, since the same ones are needed for the defense of a fort. And as for the upkeep of the ships, it is thought the proceeds from that [Caribbean] trade will provide for it and in time will even show a profit. . . . I think you will find this plan for trade . . . between Belle-Ile and Martinique well thought out. It is a fine pretext and an excellent cover for having both a war fleet and a store of munitions in abundance. And thus the master of Belle-Ile and of ten or twelve ships assuredly becomes a great lord.

Colbert had by no means abandoned the intention to have Fouquet judged by a special court. Yet as attorney general, Fouquet could be judged only in parlement and by his peers. On Colbert's advice, therefore, Louis XIV explained to the superintendant that he wanted to reduce parlement to its judicial role and that the plurality of Fouquet's functions constituted an obstacle to that reform. Perhaps the king may even have mentioned to Fouquet the coveted post of chancellor?

On August 2, Mme d'Huxelles begged her friend not to sell the office of attorney general, and reported to him Anne of Austria's anger when she heard of the secret purchase of the Mediterranean galleys command. "He'll see, he'll see," cried the Queen Mother, "how much good it's done him; he'll see what the king thinks of all that money he gave Créqui from his pocket." The plan of Saint-Mandé was still hidden behind the mirror, but Louis XIV had by then enough information to guess what its outline was.

[5]Quoted in Auguste Jal, *Abraham Duquesne et la marine de son temps.*

Despite the warnings of his friends, Fouquet—hoping to regain the king's confidence—sold his office for the sum of 1,400,000 livres and gave a million of that sum to the king. But from that point on, he made one blunder after another. It was the period when Louis XIV fell in love with Louise de La Vallière. Out of respect for his mother, the king wanted to hide his adulterous affairs.[6] Fouquet divined the king's feelings and (a terrible mistake) tried to buy off Louise to make her an ally. The politically innocent Louise, deeply shocked, told everything to the king, whose fury can be imagined.

Why, knowing of the king's growing distrust of his subject, would Fouquet want to display his grandeur by giving one of the most magnificent fetes Europe would ever see? He was too intelligent to show himself naive on that point. Was it a provocation, or was he mesmerized by the tragic, romantic dream of unattainable power?

The "triumph" of Vaux was set for August 17. Six thousand invitations were distributed throughout all Europe. The evening before, Fouquet and Colbert countersigned a free-colonization charter. By the afternoon of the seventeenth, thousands of carriages were blocking the Paris-Melun road. The king reached Vaux in his carriage drawn by six white horses about six in the evening. The unheard-of luxury of water made to do man's bidding among the gardens, the emblem of the sun centered in the sky, in the shape of a squirrel, in Le Brun's remarkable painting; the threatening snakes,[7] symbolic, dizzying, challenging, triumphantly joyous: all cut to the quick the greatest king of Christendom.

One must deny any truth to the legend that claims the king decided to arrest Fouquet because of it. Louis XIV, in Colbert's very words, had planned only to remove "the administration of finances" from Fouquet on May 4. It is more than likely that the reports from Colbert's agents, particularly those of Terron, dating from May and June, were what led the king to plan Fouquet's arrest under an accusation of plotting against the state. The decision to carry out that arrest during a trip to Brittany had already been made in July. In fact, on August 2 Mme d'Huxelles wrote to Fouquet: "I have been promised that I will learn things that are of the utmost importance to you . . . concerning the trip to Brittany, certain highly secret decisions of the king's, and measures taken against you."[8] All the events, the reports, the intrigues that followed after July may have exacerbated the fury of the king, but did not in any way bring about the already determined fall of the superintendant.

[6]We should recall that Maria Theresa was the niece of Anne of Austria.

[7]The snake appears on the Colbert coat of arms.

[8]Quoted in Mongrédien, *L'affaire Foucquet*.

The Fall of Fouquet

On August 25, Louis called a meeting of the High Council. The king proposed abolition of cash drafts, which Fouquet was using to cover his secret expenditures. Chancellor Séguier, who attended the meeting that day, gave the proposal strong support. Thunderstruck, Fouquet cried out in spite of himself, "So I am nothing now?" Le Tellier gave Brienne a nudge. Fouquet saw his error and said it would be necessary to find other ways of concealing the secret expenditures of the state.[9]

At the end of August, the king announced to his mother the superintendant's imminent arrest. Though she could not hide her sorrow, Anne submitted.

THE COUP D'ÉTAT

The court was to visit Nantes, where the king would attend a session of the Breton Estates. It was there, in his own fief, that the superintendant was to be arrested.

A study of Colbert's personal papers concerning the affair shows that the future minister of the king was simultaneously planning Fouquet's arrest and the actual seizure of power by the king in the domain of public finances. Georges Mongrédien has written correctly that the birth of absolute monarchy began after the fall of Fouquet. Colbert was aware that he was putting into effect a new political regime. The breadth of his plan, the attention to detail, the many erasures in his rough drafts, all show how high the stakes were. The abolition of the office of superintendant and the administration of finances by the king himself were to be proclaimed: That meant taxpayers' money was no longer to be lent to the king as an individual, but proceeds from taxes were to be paid to him as chief of state. It was a strong attack on many private interests. It was also a giant step on the road from feudal monarchy to national monarchy.

In his plan for Fouquet's arrest, Colbert specified the tiniest detail: "Prompt and immediate action," he wrote. Everything was arranged. The business had to be carried out with the utmost speed. Mme Fouquet was to be exiled, as was "la dame du P.B.," which proves that Colbert was informed of Mme du Plessis-Bellière's involvement. The superintendant's aides Bruant and Pellisson were to be arrested. Couriers were to be dispatched to the Queen Mother and the chancellor to "inform them that the plan had been executed." It was necessary to have a squad of *maîtres des requêtes* ready who would seal Fouquet's various houses and châteaux, and dismiss his workers. Belle-Ile was to be handed over to the king: "We expect that, several days ahead of time, under pretext of an outing upon the

[9]The anecdote was passed on by the younger Brienne to Abbé Choisy.

] 65 [

water, orders will be given to have ships disposed accordingly." Two royal regiments would be ready to land on Belle-Ile. After the island was delivered into the hands of royal officers, two *maîtres des requêtes* would conduct an investigation on the spot.

The arrest itself must be put into the hands of an absolutely trustworthy man. The faithful d'Artagnan, officer of the king's musketeers, was chosen. Colbert specified that: "On the day selected, on pretense of going hunting, orders must be given to have the musketeers mounted and the carriages ready." The whole sequence of the arrest was indicated in Colbert's plan: how the king could speak with d'Artagnan without arousing Fouquet's suspicion; when and where the superintendant was to be arrested; which valet and which doctor would attend the prisoner—without forgetting the dispatching of clothing and linens.

On a large sheet, Colbert drew up a list of things to be done immediately after the arrest:

As soon as the first matter [i.e., Fouquet's arrest] is completed and orders given for the entire plan to proceed, the king must proclaim the total abolition of the office, its title, and all its duties: because His Majesty's will is to reserve the entire and absolute authority for distribution of finances to himself; because he has resolved to establish near his person a council of limited numbers, which he will call the royal council of finances, in which His Majesty will determine said distribution, after which said council will carry out all the other functions of the department.

The principal passage, in Colbert's hand, bears many erasures and corrections. Colbert knew he had just summed up the essence of a revolution, of which—he could not forget—he would be the primary beneficiary after the king. Fouquet's arrest would abruptly deprive the state of the vast credit the superintendant undeniably possessed. The money could run out overnight. A large sum had therefore to be secured to serve as a treasury reserve until the financial system could be very rapidly reorganized and the tax farmers forced to make restitution for their shameless profits. Like Mazarin before him, Colbert paid a call on the comptroller general, Herwarth, "to draw two million livres from him, explaining that the *king wished him to send them to Fontainebleau* [underlined in the original] so that His Majesty will have them there upon his arrival." Colbert did not like Herwarth and had no desire to see the comptroller general join the future council of finance in which he himself intended to take the leading role. Therefore, the names of those who would compose the royal council were not to be announced, in order to keep Herwarth's hopes up until he had provided the two million.

The efficiency of a coup d'état derives principally from the promptness of its execution and the resulting effect of surprise. All the intendants and *maîtres des requêtes* throughout the country were to be simultaneously mobilized in order to put the reforms into practice. "Orders for the troops to be marched into the provinces and established throughout by the end of October" should be executed "expeditiously." All the enfranchisements given to towns were to be revoked; the *maîtres des requêtes* were to see to that. The tax farmers were to hand their accounts and supporting documents over to "Mister Colbert, intendant of finances." The removal of treasurers, the reduction of the tax farms, the auditing of the accounts of the treasury: An avalanche of precise plans was indicated by a quick stroke of Colbert's pen.

For years he had been reflecting on the reform of public finances. His plan was clear and confidently formulated. He wished with all his soul to strengthen the political power of the king—that is to say, that of the state; for him, the terms still meant the same thing. Two immediate measures would ensure the king's authority over public finances. In the first place, "it would be well to publish a decree forbidding payment of any draft without express order of the king signed by his own hand." In the second place, the king must demand secrecy.

Directly following this set of measures to be taken immediately after Fouquet's arrest, and on the same sheet, Colbert drew up a draft of the speech Louis XIV was to deliver at the initial meeting of the finance council. Therefore, the speech had already been written even before the superintendant was taken into custody. The first paragraph pardoned Mazarin for not having been able to remedy the disorder of the finances because of his immense preoccupation first with the war and then with the peace negotiations: a respectful lie!

Next the king was to explain how Fouquet had "confessed his thievery" and, despite his promises, had continued his mismanagement. In the margin, Colbert scribbled these words: "Monsieur le Cardinal-Superintendant—Building at Vaux and Belle-Ile—office of commander of the galleys." We may suppose that the king had asked him to mention the other charges that should be added to the offenses in the area of finances, in order to better justify so severe a decision. Louis XIV would demand secrecy, firmness, and sincerity of his councilors. Colbert then had the king say:

Where the handling of my finances is concerned, I am pleased to tell you that, having studied them quite thoroughly over the last six months, I have resolved to change completely the way in which they have been managed up to now, and to replace with order the disorder and confusion with which they have been administered. To that end, I have determined to defer for three or four years the payment of all notes drawn against anticipated revenues for 1662, and to use the surplus to meet the expenses incurred by my state.

The court departed for Brittany in late August. Colbert carried the plan for Fouquet's arrest among his papers. Only Le Tellier was taken into his confidence. On the twenty-seventh, Colbert and his former patron left by carriage, followed by Fouquet (who was suffering from a high fever), Mme Fouquet, and Hugues de Lionne. At Angers, boats were waiting. The barges of the two rivals seemed to be racing each other. An aide of Brienne's said one of the two would be wrecked at Nantes. Louis made the trip on horseback and settled into the old château of the dukes of Brittany.

Upon his arrival, the king sent for news of Fouquet, who was staying in the hôtel de Rougé with relatives of Mme du Plessis-Bellière's. Louis went to only one meeting of the Estates. Fouquet managed to arrange an outright gift of three million for the king. The king was losing patience; the days seemed long to him. D'Artagnan was ill: They had to wait another day or two. Le Tellier and Colbert were drafting the last details of the arrest. The written orders for the musketeers were transcribed by copyists that the two accomplices kept under lock and key.

On Sunday, September 4, 1661, Louis XIV summoned d'Artagnan. The officer thought the king wanted to look over his company's rolls with him. When he learned the truth, he could scarcely hide his astonishment. The king gave him his written orders: "M. d'Artagnan shall take care not to lose sight of him from the instant of his arrest, and not to allow him to put a hand in his pocket, lest he be able to remove any papers." Then the king asked him to go to Le Tellier, who would give him all the details. D'Artagnan was then fifty years old. In his entire career, he had never felt so moved. Once at Le Tellier's lodging, the musketeer felt unwell and asked for a glass of wine to restore himself. Out in the street, Fouquet's friends observed with suspicion the movements of the troops. Fouquet reassured them: "Colbert is lost; tomorrow will be the finest day of my life." That evening, Colbert came to visit the superintendant, who was still ailing, and extracted 88,000 livres out of him for the navy.

Louis XIV applied Colbert's plan to the letter. He announced that there would be a hunt the next day, preceded by a morning council meeting. On Monday, September 5, the principal ministers went to meet him at about six in the morning. Outside, the grey-clad musketeers were on horseback. The meeting over, Louis kept Fouquet a little longer than Le Tellier and Lionne. The super-intendant came out persuaded he "stood first in the king's esteem." Those were his last moments of liberty. D'Artagnan and his musketeers caught up with him and placed him under arrest.

Less than an hour later, Louis called his ministers together again in the presence of Condé, Turenne, and other important individuals. According to Brienne's testimony, Lionne was "pale and drawn like a man half dead." The king quickly reassured him. Coislin, who was present, left this account: "His Majesty told us that we should be surprised by what he had just done, which he had been constrained to do by very pressing reasons that he would make known in his own time; meanwhile, he wanted us to know that he had formed the plan more than four months ago, on the basis of information he had received concerning the superintendant's conduct, which was completely contrary to his duty."[10]

All the measures to be taken immediately after Fouquet's arrest had been carefully planned. Nothing remained but to apply them swiftly. On the same day, as the *maîtres des requêtes* went to seal all of Fouquet's properties, Colbert presented Louis with a model for two letters the king ought to send, the first to Herwarth, the second (never published) to the Queen Mother. Louis XIV paid no attention to the latter. Furthermore, it is amusing to compare the letter the king actually sent to Anne of Austria with the one drafted by Colbert. The tone of the king's letter is much more intimate and warm. Clearly, Louis wanted to establish an affectionate complicity between his mother and himself. Details abound. The young king appeared greatly excited by his far-reaching brilliant exploit, while Colbert exhibited the cold determination of great organizers.

"Moreover," wrote Louis to his mother, "I have already begun to taste the pleasures to be found in working on finances myself, having, in the little attention I have given it, noted important matters that I could hardly make out at all, but no one should doubt that I will continue."[11] Colbert was a good teacher and had doubtless made his own financial competence clear. As Le Tellier and Mazarin had before him, the king trusted Colbert completely.

Herwarth received the following letter, signed by the king and inspired by Colbert:

Nantes, September 5, 1661

The late cardinal having assured me during the last days of his life that I would always find assistance in the amount of two or three million livres from your funds, whenever the good of my service required me to make any change in the administration of my finances, now that for various reasons I have been forced to have the superintendant arrested, I am happy to write these lines to tell you that you shall do me the pleasure of preparing for me, either through your own resources or those of your friends, the largest sum you can, so that I can use it if I need to. I await your reply.

The reply came in the form of two million livres. In a hastily written report, Colbert counted up all the amounts he had been able to raise in order to cope

[10]Quoted in Mongrédien, *L'affaire Foucquet.*

[11]"Letter from King Louis XIV to the Queen Mother," found in the study of the late M. Rose, king's secretary, Clermont, 1862.

with the superintendant's abrupt departure. The total, seven million livres, included the million Fouquet had given the king from the sale of his office of attorney general, and a mysterious "million from C. . . ." Could that have been Colbert himself? Was he rich enough by then to be able to offer the king such a sum from his own money?

Fouquet's power had been financial and maritime in nature. It was, then, imperative that the king's signature legitimize a statute concerning the new financial administration. Furthermore, it was necessary to appropriate promptly Fouquet's maritime organization and to impose the king's authority on the principal naval leaders.

FINANCES

Over the weeks that followed Fouquet's arrest, Colbert summarily sketched out the urgent decisions to be made. The style was hurried and abrupt. It was necessary to act quickly: "To the king—power and function—Read the regulations. Orders to be given for provisions . . . Set the king's days," etc. The intimacy shared in the work between the two men was already great enough for Colbert to dare to show this kind of document to the king. In response to "Set the king's days," Louis XIV wrote in his own hand "Tuesday, Thursday, and Saturday."

Colbert himself conceived and prepared the regulation establishing the royal council of finance. The composition of the document was extremely arduous. The first draft includes many corrections; the first page was crossed out in its entirety.[12] The second draft was also heavily worked over. A clerk wrote out a synthesis of the two versions, under Colbert's direction. The regulation, in final form, was signed by the king at Fontainebleau on September 15. It officialy abolished the office of superintendant; thenceforth, His Majesty would "reserve to himself alone the right of signature on all orders of payment concerning expenditures whether on account or in cash, including both secret outlays, rebates, interest payments, and others of whatever nature." But further on, Colbert wrote a paragraph that placed the actual power in his own hands: "The intendant of finances, who will have the honor of appointment to said royal council, will have the treasury account as part of his department, and consequently he will keep accounts of all revenue and expenditures, to be shown to no other person except on His Majesty's express order." The keeping of the accounts would thus be taken away from Herwarth, who would, nevertheless, keep the honorary title of comptroller general for several more years.

[12]The definitive version of the statute may be found in François André Isambert's *Recueil général des anciennes lois françaises depuis l'an 420 jusqu'à la revolution de 1789* (Paris, 1822–33) 18:9 and also appears in Pierre Clément, *Lettres, instructions, et mémoires de Colbert,* vol. 2, pt. 2, p. 749. Colbert's draft variants have never been published.

THE NAVY

The appropriation of Fouquet's naval bases was accomplished without difficulty. On the evening of September 5, five companies of infantry set off for Belle-Ile, where they met with no resistance. The governor of Concarneau received orders to surrender his command. Before long, Créqui was to give up the command of galleys. The viceroy of the Americas found himself forced to resign.

On the other hand, the submission of Neuchèze and Duquesne seemed much harder to obtain. Neuchèze was at Brouage with ten ships when he learned of Fouquet's arrest. He was gravely worried. Should he flee or weigh anchor for the Levant, as ordered? He waited more than a month, hesitated, was afraid. Very cleverly, Colbert did not want to intensify the uneasiness that had taken hold of the high-ranking naval personnel (Duquesne called it "squabbling"). Those men would be needed for the reorganization of the royal navy. Neuchèze received a note from Colbert, who tried to reassure him about his situation: "I don't think it so desperate that you could not still patch it up."[13] Neuchèze made an initial confession to Colbert du Terron, who encouraged him to speak to the king. Louis received his complete confession. That ingenuous declaration, according to Colbert, is what saved him.

Dusquesne was an old countryman of Fouquet's and, some felt, his vassal. He was a man of a stubborn and difficult nature, but also a remarkable seaman. Despite the king's formal orders, he had not sailed from Brest, had not taken Fouquet's ships into his division, and had not seized the cannon at Belle-Ile, even after several months. Called before the general staff of the fleet, Duquesne submitted and was pardoned.

At the same time that Colbert was taking firm control of the navy and finances in the name of the king, searches were being carried out in Fouquet's various residences. On September 19, Colbert suddenly arrived at Saint-Mandé in order to encourage the search committee in its efforts as it turned things over and tapped on the walls and woodwork. Colbert was still there the following day and discovered the famous plan of Saint-Mandé hidden behind the mirror. He had capital proof of Fouquet's guilt. Without delay, he took the precious document off to the king at Fontainebleau.

The obstacles to the installation of an absolute monarchy and to Colbert's own rise seemed to have been overcome at that moment. Colbert's power was linked to the glory of the king and to that of the state. On December 21, Nicolas Colbert died, after having witnessed his son's triumph.

---

[13]Charles de La Roncière, *La vrai crime du Surintendant Fouquet.*

PART II

KING & STATE
[1661-72]

CHAPTER 6

The Minister, the King, and France

COLBERT TOOK FOUQUET'S PLACE in the High Council with the rank of minister of state. For more than twenty years, he would work with the king on the affairs of France. Did they have the same view concerning the state, the same political sensibility?

TWO PERSONALITIES

The king seems to have been created to embody the doctrine of an absolute monarchy. The exuberant vitality inherited from his grandfather Henri IV and the refined and, at first, slightly cold politeness he got from his mother gave him an air of health and majesty that was impressive and intimidating. By nature a lover of things rural, a handsome man and a lover of love, the chase, and the world, Louis was capable of closing himself up in his study for hours. Slow, meticulous, methodical, he never decided a question without having examined it at length.

"I shall see," was his customary reply to those who questioned or entreated him. He compensated for the weakness that can result from an insecure nature by the use of authoritarian formulae, by the secrecy with which he surrounded himself, and by a certain royal casualness that was disarming. The Fronde had taught him to trust no one. Colbert was one of the few men of whom he was absolutely sure.

Mazarin's recommendations had undoubtedly influenced the king. Colbert was a familiar figure: That was also important. Louis had been accustomed to his presence since childhood. Amid the tempest of treasons, Colbert was the messenger of faithfulness. At the beginning of his personal reign, Louis was twenty-three and Colbert forty-two. That nineteen-year difference in their ages allowed the minister to advise the king with a sort of respectful authority.

His deep black eyes, his pale complexion, his severe countenance, his glacial manners—everything about the minister suggested a somber severity that terrified those who approached him but that reassured the king. Each man had his place: Louis XIV that of king, Colbert that of minister—for one, the luxurious radiance of a monarch of divine essence; for the other, the conscientious rigor of a minister in the service of the state. Colbert's incredible capacity for work pleased a king who indisputably respected work. Colbert's methods suited Louis's personality rather well. Both enjoyed detail, as Mazarin had not: "Details for everything," the king demanded of his minister. Colbert's natural inclination toward order and formality in his paperwork was attractive to a king who needed clear and thorough information.

Louis XIV and Colbert shared the taste of the age for grandeur. Grandeur of the king, of the nation, of the state? For the two men, the nation could not exist without the unity inherent in the monarchy. France was then a patchwork of provinces and of disparate populations; the concept of a native country was still vague. The real link that joined Frenchmen together continued to be their common submission to a king invested with a sacred authority. It was at this point that the unifying role of the state intervened in its turn, which gradually, and without the knowledge of the two men, encroached upon the authority of the king. But these nuances pertain more to the realm of instinct or political sensibility than to that of political thought.

To be sure, Colbert seems to have been ardently devoted to the king's personal glory. But it was significant that he constantly wanted to situate the glory of that reign within a historical continuum that was already that of France. In 1663, he began to write his *Weekly Journal of Events Forming the Basis of the Royal History,* intended for future generations. Overwhelmed by his daily business, Colbert was soon forced to discontinue the journal, which has contributed no small amount to posterity's image of that young king, so deeply occupied with affairs of state despite his taste for amusements. In his famous *Memoirs on the Financial Affairs of France, of Historical Application,* Colbert described Fouquet's fall and the beginning of Louis's personal reign. The style sometimes evokes that of a legendary epic: "He was a young prince, twenty-three years of age, in strong and vigorous health, and consequently full of the fire and zeal that that age inspires." If he was engrossed in the France that was to come, the minister did not, for all that, forget her past. References to previous reigns frequently support his arguments: He seems to have preferred that of Louis XI.

In 1665 he wrote a *Report to the King Concerning the Education of the Dauphin,* which proves beyond any doubt that it was he who prepared the materials for the famous *Instructions to the Dauphin.* The first part dealt with "The State of European Affairs at the Time the King First Began to Govern." The second part was devoted to financial matters and conveyed in broad outline Colbert's political convictions, including the reform of the judicial system and the abolition of the sale of offices.

Colbert often used the term *grand design.* He never abandoned the great political projects he had earlier proposed to Mazarin. And these projects concerned the glory of the state (in the modern sense of the word) as much as they did the personal glory of the king. Monetary, industrial, maritime, and colonial power would bring glory and wealth to the whole nation, to the French state that could affirm thereafter its own existence without requiring support from the monarchy. Colbert had not yet foreseen that. Can the same be said of the king?

Louis XIV was undoubtedly impressed by the precise and clear conviction of the minister, who knew the art of presenting logical, ordered plans that had long been in preparation. The king—cautious and without great technical proficiency—seemed a bit ruffled by his minister's headstrong passion. He seems to have been convinced; the glory of France was not an empty word to him. But as we will see later, the strength of a centralized state that obeyed its own laws and could evade the arbitrary power of an absolute monarch would arouse Louis XIV's suspicions. Colbert worked obstinately to unify France by law. Louis sought to charm her into submission.

Instinctively, the king accepted the immutability of the three feudal orders. There were those who waged war, those who prayed, and those who labored. Colbert, who came from a social class of great diversity and high mobility (as his own family's history shows), wanted to shake the feudal structure by fighting with all his strength for a unified state, which would be the sole dispenser of justice.

According to Bossuet, kings derive their powers from God: And according to the feudal order, the king, like the military aristocracy surrounding him, justified his dominion through warfare. A Catholic king and a leader in warfare: That was how Louis XIV liked to see himself. The shades of meaning or the differences of opinion that occasionally brought the two men into conflict on religious and military matters reveal the beginnings of a serious misunderstanding.

Both Colbert and Louis attacked the political power of the clergy, which they felt could not be allowed to rival the king's. They had not forgotten the role some members of the church (such as Cardinal de Retz, former archbishop of Paris) had played during the Fronde. The king, however, saw religion as also a factor for national unity—indeed, as a sort of political banner. The century before, Queen Elizabeth of England had flaunted her Protestantism in a political struggle with Catholic Spain. Louis XIV, who showed no signs of mysticism in his younger years, professed a Catholicism that allowed him to declare himself the eldest son of the Church and first among Christian kings.

Colbert was never convinced of that point of view. For the minister, the power of the king depended on the material power of his state. On the one hand, the tax of the Catholic clergy was competing with the tax levied by the state. On the other, the clergy kept the records of baptisms, marriages, and deaths, and played a substantial role in university affairs. Consequently, the Church was an administrative power of the greatest importance, which annoyed the champion of a strong central government.

Finally, while the monks (whom the minister thought too numerous) produced nothing and gave France no children, the Protestant community seemed to provide a vital energy indispensable to the national economy. In the early years, Colbert was able to persuade the king to great religious tolerance. Much later, he would watch in consternation the persecutions ordered against the Protestants. Still, no one dared to revoke the Edict of Nantes while Colbert lived.

The money Louis devoted to his personal military prestige and to the luxury of his household distressed his minister. In 1666, Colbert wrote to the king in a frank style that he alone, perhaps, could take the liberty of using:

My duties in Your Majesty's service are far and away the most difficult of all; of necessity, I must take on the most difficult matters whatever their nature. . . . I tell Your Majesty that, speaking as an individual, I am given unspeakable pain by a bill of one thousand écus for a single meal. . . . You have so mixed your amusements together with the land war that it is very difficult to separate them. . . . If only Your Majesty were fully informed of all the disorders these perpetual troop movements cause in the provinces and how distasteful they are to the people.

The most significant passage in the letter concerns "the increase in numbers and splendor" of the troops of the king's household to the detriment (according to Colbert) of the nation's armies. The minister continued:

The prodigious difference now existing between these troops of the king's household and those of the armies will weigh on the hearts of the officers and soldiers of the latter, and ruin them, for as soon as a good officer or a good soldier appears among the troops of the regular army, he will make every effort to join those of your household. . . .

This excessive distinction of your household in all things diminishes the zeal of all your other subjects; great kings have always embraced their last and most distant subject as they did the nearest, with only some difference in the distribution of favors alone. Our great kings, François I, Henri IV, never made such distinctions; the latter was often guarded by the old army regiments.

It has often been written that Colbert's policy required peace and was totally opposed to the expenses of war. That is not quite correct. We shall see later on that the minister's economic policy led inevitably to war. And Colbert was the first to wish for a state equipped with an army as powerful on land as on sea. What he deplored was the sumptuous consecration of the king's own person that impoverished the state and distanced the monarch from his subjects. His courageous remonstrances had no effect.

Nonetheless, the king listened to him on many other matters. Colbert's numerous responsibilities bear witness to the king's great confidence in his minister. It would be difficult to present any one aspect of Colbert's policies without first mentioning the whole of his governmental activities. To do so would be to risk committing a serious psychological error. Colbert was much more a pragmatist than a theoretician. His true obsession was the greatness of France. Which systems he thought contributed more effectively than others to that greatness, which of his judgments were mistaken—these are entirely different questions. What he proposed to the king was an all-inclusive policy for France. We must first recall his ambitions for the nation before judging any particular aspect of his policy.

THE EXERCISE OF GOVERNMENT

Colbert attended the High Council together with the two other ministers of state: Michel Le Tellier, minister of war, and Hugues de Lionne, minister of foreign affairs. Finally, he could break the conspiracy of silence surrounding Richelieu and refer to his idol's grand designs. The king came to find his pious fidelity amusing and received with pleasantries the way in which Colbert presented an important matter to the council: "Here is Colbert, who will tell us, 'Sire, the great Cardinal Richelieu, etc.' "

Upon the creation of the council of finance after the fall of Fouquet, Colbert took over the bookkeeping from Herwarth and became responsible for financial matters. But the offices of the comptrollers general belonged still to Herwarth and Bretueil, both of whom were, on the whole, above reproach. Only after Herwarth sold his office in 1665 could Colbert be named comptroller general of finances.

In 1664 Colbert was given the post of superintendant of buildings, which the department of cultural affairs conferred on him in some sense. In 1668 he became secretary of state for the king's household. In 1669 he was named naval secretary, after having been involved in naval matters for some time. Thanks to the frequent encroachments of overlapping administrative boundaries during the ancien régime, and thanks also to the complaisance of the elderly Chancellor Séguier and then to that of the even more elderly Chancellor Aligre, Colbert slowly took control of the department of justice, which tempted him especially.

If we were to compare his duties with those of present-day French ministers, it could be said that Colbert was at one and the same time minister of finances and economic affairs, minister of industry and commerce, minister of the interior, secret keeper of the seal, minister of cultural affairs, and minister of the navy and of overseas affairs.

In the early days, the young king asserted his authority all the more by entrusting a large part of his actual power to a man who was himself quite authoritarian. He maintained distance by a certain casualness of tone. Louis sent this letter to his minister in 1661:

> As I believe there is nothing pressing today, I will not do any work. Bring the papers we were to discuss this evening to tomorrow's council of finance, so I can finish up what needs to be done before Mass.
> The Queen doesn't want the ruby box; she has nothing that fits it.
> If anything urgent comes up, let me know.
>
> LOUIS

Colbert left half the sheet blank when he wrote, and the king, like Mazarin, returned his letters after having written answers in his own hand. Colbert had improved his writing considerably, which allowed him to write to the king without using copyists.

Louis constantly assured his minister of his confidence in him and his satisfaction: "As you shall judge appropriate. . . . It is up to you to judge what is best. . . . I am pleased to hear my finances discussed as you do. . . . I am leaving it up to you." But Colbert was given to understand that the king remained absolute master. Louis's tone showed itself peremptory, superior, at times. But it is also true that he used that tone to utter the famous line, "I order you to do as you wish."

The minister was most careful to keep the king up to date on everything. Louis nearly always agreed with his suggestions, but insisted on giving his approval in all matters without exception before any action was taken. On the other hand, Colbert obtained from the king letters of confidence guaranteeing him unequivocal powers in the administration. In 1662, Louis sent a circular to the treasurers of France, ordering them to give "complete adherence" to everything the minister "required of them" in the name of the king. No decision or commission was to be carried out without Colbert's approval.

The system of the tax farmers and superintendants had accustomed the monarchs to request funds without concerning themselves with the state of the treasury. The accepted formula seemed to be: "It's up to you to straighten it out." Louis often showed a tendency to adopt it in his dealings with Colbert. Yet the latter was the true creator of modern public accountancy. The great innovation of his administration consisted in the requirement that three sets of books be kept—for receipts, expenditures, and cash on hand—accompanied by the regular preparation of a statement of expenses expected ("statement of estimate") and actually made ("statement of truth"). In other words, it was a matter of imposing the idea of a national budget—so natural today, so little a part of the customs of his time.

Colbert strove to find effective means of acclimating the king to this new concept of public finance. In addition to his respectful and incessant admonitions to the king, he regularly submitted small notebooks, illuminated with colored letters and initials of gold, in which a famous calligrapher had copied out the annual table of naval matériel and personnel, as well as a statement of the year's finances. Louis, who carried these notebooks with him, could know at any moment the state of his navy and of his finances.

Two departments were outside Colbert's control: foreign affairs and war. As finance minister, he involved himself indirectly with the first by raising the subsidies Louis sent to the courts of his foreign allies. He also wrote the reports that were used in the drafting of commercial agreements. But foreign policy was conducted by the king, with Lionne's collaboration. And war still remained the domain of Le Tellier and his son Louvois. That fact drove Colbert to despair, and he overwhelmed the king with genuinely passionate outbursts on the subject.

THE LE TELLIER CLAN

Louis had not forgotten the esteem in which his mother and Mazarin had held Le Tellier. The king even called him Monsieur Le Tellier, as he never did Colbert or Lionne. Flexible, patient, the war minister seemed quite different from his eldest son, François Le Tellier, marquis de Louvois. Brutal, authoritarian, quick-tempered, Louvois was a year younger than Louis XIV. Father and son shared remarkable organizational talents. By 1662, Louvois had joined the council, his father having arranged for him to inherit his office. We may easily imagine the ambitions Le Tellier nourished for his son's career. The immense powers of his former aide irritated the war minister a great deal. The rivalry between the Le Telliers and Colbert broke out very quickly.

Louvois soon noticed Louis's taste for pageantry and military display. He was not unaware of Colbert's reservations on that subject. To "embarrass" his rival, he advised the king to organize a magnificent jousting tournament in Paris.[1] Louis liked the idea but was afraid to oppose Colbert. Unexpectedly, the minister made no objection, asking only that the king keep the matter secret for a week, during which he would arrange to have the Paris octroi* temporarily turned over to the royal treasury. The tournament promised to be splendid and dazzling. Hundreds of visitors flocked to Paris from everywhere. A few weeks before the date set for the show, Colbert explained to the king that the preparations for the event would not be completed in time and that it would be advisable to postpone it for about two weeks. The short delay obliged the visitors to stay in Paris. Consumption therefore increased sharply in the city, whose octroi happened to be temporarily assigned to the king's account. The celebration netted the treasury more than a million livres.

Colbert sometimes allowed a glimpse of a passionate temperament that contrasted with his cold manner. His patriotic lyricism, a forerunner of revolutionary romanticism, bore witness to his national and political passions. His despair at not wielding exclusive influence over Louis reveals (beside his own ambitions) the emotional character of his relationship with the king. Warfare was not his province, but he could not keep from deluging the king with advice on the appearance of the troops, the movement of the armies, and the equipment of the soldiers. Let us recall briefly the 1666 memorandum in which Colbert complained of the needless expenses for the splendor of the parades and of the king's household troops. Why all that ostentatious luxury when foreign policy urgently required money? Louis insisted on befriending Poland in order to detach that country from Austrian influence. He had promised the king of Poland five or six thousand men to help him put down internal revolts.[2] The Hapsburg menace worried Colbert

[1]Mémoires of the duc de Luynes, vol. 2, Luynes family archives.

[2]The project was abandoned because of transportation problems. In any case, the unrest in Poland ended that July.

*The octroi was a municipal customs, a tax on commodities brought into a town or city.

also. It seemed vital to him for France to conduct an effective policy against the emperor. He heatedly remarked: "When millions in gold for Poland are involved, I would sell all my possessions, pledge my wife and children, and go on foot for the rest of my life if necessary to provide them." And further on, still fuming, he added: "But, Sire, with respect to the mustering of troops and their order of march, I would not have thought an affair of such consequence would be entrusted to a young man of twenty-four,[3] with no experience in such matters, very temperamental, and who thinks his job authorizes him to ruin the kingdom, and who even wants to ruin it because I want to save it."

Two years later, Louvois was named secretary of war. The court observed with the greatest interest the rivalry, which provided malicious gossip: "Monsieur Colbert is still perfectly well. . . . Monsieur Colbert is no longer so well." On October 23, 1668, the king gave Colbert an obvious sign of favor. The minister was sick. For several years he had suffered from terrible attacks of gout. Gui Patin noted that "The king today paid M. Colbert a brilliant visit. He had all his guards with drawn swords. They say Colbert has gout and a touch of dysentery: It's because his mind is overworked." The whole court was talking about it. According to the Venetian ambassador, the king told his minister, "Colbert, unhappiness is what makes people sick. Be cheerful and you'll get well."

In 1671, the office of chancellor of the royal ordinances fell vacant. Colbert coveted that office, but it was Louvois who obtained it. The marquis de Saint-Maurice, ambassador of Savoy, reported: "M. de Louvois has been visited and congratulated for his new office by every member of the court, except M. Colbert; they are not getting along at all, and it is thought that the father and son have tried to get Colbert into the king's bad graces." Louvois seemed to establish his predominance. In council, in the king's presence, Colbert gave free rein to his fury. On April 24, Louis sent him the following letter:

I was able to control myself the day before yesterday well enough to hide from you the pain I felt at hearing a man I have showered with kindnesses, as I have you, speak to me as you did then.

I am very well disposed toward you, as is apparent from what I have done for you, and I am still well disposed at present; and I believe I can prove it very clearly by saying that I restrained myself a moment for your sake, and that I did not wish to say aloud to you the things I am now writing, lest I lead you to displease me further.

The recollection of the services you have rendered me and my friendship are the cause of this attitude; take advantage of it, and do not risk angering

[3]In 1666, Louvois was actually twenty-seven.

me again, for once I have heard your arguments and those of your colleagues and I have judged all your claims, I never want to hear of it again.

Consider whether the navy wouldn't suit you; whether that wouldn't strike your fancy; or whether you would like something else; speak freely. But once my decision has been handed down, I don't want a word of reply.

I am telling you what I think, so that you will be working on a sound basis and take no fruitless measures.

We may suppose that Colbert begged his pardon with great humility and sadness, for on April 26 the king wrote to him thus:

Do not think my affection toward you is diminished while your services continue; that cannot be, but they must be rendered according to my wishes, and you must believe that what I do is for the best. The preference you fear I give others should not distress you. I wish only to avoid injustice and to work for the good of my office. I shall do so once you are all behind me. In the meantime, please believe that I have not changed at all where you are concerned, and that my feelings are what you might desire.

The king was master. He said so in terms that are still impressive. The majesty of his person remains fascinating through the ages. The regulated pomp of a submissive court supported his personal charisma very effectively. The king sensed that better than Colbert did. Still, like all his contemporaries, the minister was completely aware how important the court could be in gaining greater intimacy with the king and in better securing his family's position.

CHAPTER 7

The Court

THE MARQUIS DE SAINT-MAURICE, ambassador of the duke of Savoy, sent his master very precise and highly colored reports of life at Louis's court. He shows us Louis during the Flanders campaign, tanned, thin, always with the army, always elegant, his moustache twisted up and carefully waxed. He would spend "more than an hour and a half getting dressed, while sitting down; it is true that he isn't bored, since everyone talks with him and tells him witty and comic stories." The court also consisted of comrades in arms who fought, showed off, and enjoyed intrigues of their own, grouped around a king who understood their manners because they were his as well. The court had been domesticated, cut off from political power, but it seems to have been a sort of natural and necessary element in Louis XIV's life.

Colbert knew that well. Despite the respectful distance on which Louis insisted, the minister had to capture the king's imagination if he were to apply his policies freely. Participating in court life and in royal intrigues was practically obligatory.

THE KING'S MISTRESSES

Since childhood, Louis XIV had been accustomed to see the domestic affairs of his royal entourage entrusted to Colbert. Mazarin's agent had handled the education of the cardinal's nephews, had been an obliging messenger for the king and Marie Mancini, and had overseen all the details of the monarch's marriage. Naturally enough, Louis turned to his minister when it was a question of delivering to the person "whom I mentioned at the time of my parting" the letters "with nothing on the outside . . . you get my meaning."

Louise de La Vallière, the person in question, was pregnant about 1663. As long as the Queen Mother remained alive, Louis was relatively discreet about his liaisons and his bastards. Colbert was assigned to make arrangements for the birth and to provide for the child's needs. The king kept his minister up to date on the sufferings of "you-know-who." Louise gave birth to a boy. Colbert described the circumstances of the clandestine birth:

As far as the child's maintenance is concerned, in accordance with the secrecy ordered by the king, I gave orders to Beauchamp and his wife, long-time servants of my family . . . to whom I stated, in secret, that one of my brothers had gotten a well-born girl pregnant, and that for honor's sake I was obliged to take care of the child and to entrust its keeping to them, which they accepted joyfully.

In 1665 a second son was born to Louise and her royal lover. A beggar was found on the porch of a church to serve as the baby's godfather. Both children died in infancy.

On January 20, 1666, Anne of Austria died, and the king felt free to make his liaison public. In October, Louise gave birth to a daughter, Marie-Anne, and the next year she had a son, Louis. The two children were legitimized under the titles of Mlle de Blois and the comte de Vermandois. They were entrusted to Colbert and his wife, who raised them alongside their own children.

Colbert was most careful to inform Louis XIV of the state of his offsprings' health. On May 5, 1670, he wrote to the king:

Mlle de Blois has had the smallpox that is going around. My wife sent for Brayer, who took care of her; thanks be to God, she is now nearly over it.

M. le comte de Vermandois has a bad cold, which rather upset him. Your Majesty may be sure that my wife is giving him all the care she should.

And in the same letter, under the date of the sixth, in the morning, he added: "Mlle de Blois feels quite well, and will be purged tomorrow morning. The prince is no longer upset, and his cold is much diminished."

In 1667, the king fell in love with Mme de Montespan. To avoid the scandal of a new liaison, he kept up appearances by making Louise occupy an apartment adjoining Mme de Montespan's, with rooms that opened on each other and shared the same front door. In 1671, Louise fled to the convent of Chaillot. The king demanded her return. Neither Lauzun nor the maréchal de Belle-fonds could manage to convince the young woman to leave the convent. Then, as Mme de Sévigné informs us, "the king wept bitterly, and sent M. Colbert to Chaillot to beg her urgently to come to Versailles so that he could speak to her again. M. Colbert brought her there. The king spoke with her an hour, weeping bitterly, and Mme de Montespan came to her with open arms and tears in her eyes. All of this is entirely incomprehensible." Three years later, Louise retired permanently to the Carmelite community of the Faubourg-Saint-Jacques.

In 1670, Louis gave his new favorite the taxes inposed on the butchers of Paris—at the expense of the treasury. Colbert had the courage to protest, pointing out to the king that never had any of his forebears dared make such gifts. Mme de Montespan kept the privilege, nonetheless, but the king seemed a bit embarrassed. The king's favorite was furious with Colbert. According to Saint-Maurice, the old duchesse de Chevreuse, with the minister's approval, tried to put the duchesse de Mazarin in Montespan's place.

Colbert could see that the king's attachment to his mistress was unusually strong. He decided it was better to make her his ally. So he prevailed upon Philippe Mancini, duc de Nevers, Mazarin's nephew, to marry Mlle de Thianges, Montespan's niece. The king's favorite was enchanted, and seemed on the best of terms with the minister. A month later, when Louis wanted to give Louvois the office of chancelor of the royal ordinances, Mme de Montespan went so far as to go down on her knees in tears before the king to plead for Colbert. Louvois received the appointment, but the alliance of Mme de Montespan and Colbert—as we shall see—was never to be broken.

THE ROYAL FAMILY

During his absences, Louis XIV seemed in some way to entrust Colbert with the task of looking after his family. The minister kept the king informed about their health, read the mail to the Queen Mother as in Mazarin's time, or busied himself with domestic details. Thus, in 1662, Colbert asked his brother, who was intendant of Alsace, to send him mechanical soldiers from Nuremberg to give to the dauphin. The next year, he wrote the king: "Milord Dauphin was a little indisposed yesterday, because of his teeth; last night he slept very well, so that today he was as cheerful as ever." The king replied in the margin: "If the least thing happens to my son, send to me at once so that, being assured that he is well, in the absence of further news, I shall be at peace. I trust you, having no doubt that you will do as I command."

Several years later, Señora Molina, the queen's first chambermaid, asked the minister to inquire about a room in the château of Chambord with a fireplace, "where Her Majesty's bouillon may be comfortably prepared."

It was again Colbert who was the mediator between the king and his brother, Philippe d'Orleans, called simply *Monsieur*. In 1670 Louis, exasperated by his brother's relations with the chevalier de Lorraine, had the latter arrested and sent to the Château d'If. Outraged by the seizure of his favorite, Monsieur withdrew to Villers-Cotterêts and refused to return to court, despite the king's commands. Colbert was sent to bring him back.

On that occasion, Philippe wrote Colbert a very long letter. "Monsieur Colbert," he lamented, "as for some time I have thought of you as a friend, and since you are the only one among those who have the honor of being near the king who has shown me any signs of friendship in the dreadful calamity that has befallen me, I believe. . . ," etc. There follow interminable complaints about the unhappy fate of the chevalier and the innocence of his cherished favorite. "After that," the prince concluded, "I have nothing to add, except to assure you that I will be, M. Colbert, your most excellent friend for life." On his second trip to Villers-Cotterêts, the minister succeeded in bringing Monsieur back. The chevalier was set free two years later.

The king's cousins called on Colbert as well. La Grande Mademoiselle[1] had refused to marry the king of Portugal. Louis did not conceal his displeasure, and she suffered a partial disgrace. The princess wrote to Colbert several times: Her overtures were always rebuffed, she complained, whereas her stepmother, Gaston's second wife, was showered with favors.

Later, madly in love with Lauzun, she sought the help of Colbert and Mme de Montespan in convincing the king to consent to their marriage. Mme de Montespan kept her friend Lauzun informed of the progress of their suit: "M. Colbert is promising miracles after seeing the reports he has been given." When La Grande Mademoiselle had Louis's permission to marry Lauzun,[2] Condé and his sister, Anne de Longueville, vented all their anger. Mme de Longueville added: "If Mademoiselle wants to get on by marrying the king's favorite, she would do even better to give herself to Colbert's son."[3]

Mademoiselle, in turn, was furious that anyone had dared mention such a misalliance.

This disdain for Colbert's family in no way prevented Mme de Longueville from petitioning the minister with great friendliness: "I am sending the bearer to beg you to put an end to this business, which at present is entirely in your hands; I hope you will act as justly as your past treatment of our interests would lead us to expect you to. . . . I have no doubt that you will act as we would wish, hoping for the justice that you have always led us to hope His Majesty would do us, to which end I hope your good offices will contribute not a little."[4] The great Frondeurs had certainly changed their tune!

---

[1]The daughter of Louis XIII's brother, Gaston d'Orlean, and Louis XIV's first cousin.

[2]It was withdrawn again in 1671, to Mademoiselle's despair.

[3]Quoted in Philippe Erlanger, *Madame de Longueville*.

[4]Sold at Versailles under the auspices of J. P. Chapelle, P. Perrin, and D. Fromantin, March 8, 1977.

The Court

THE ELEVATION OF THE COLBERTS

In that race for favors, the minister never forgot his own interests and those of his family. Mme Colbert helped him with a discreet and tasteful efficiency. According to Mme de Sévigné, the minister's spouse was "extremely civil and has excellent manners." The Savoyard ambassador noted that "Mme Colbert presently rules the Queen [Maria Theresa] although all the princesses of the house of Lorraine are paying her court assiduously, Madame de Guise at their head."

The king greatly valued her advice with regard to the upbringing of his children by Louise de La Vallière. She knew how to remind the sovereign of the immense effort her husband devoted to his service, considering his poor health. When the minister had a painful attack of gout, the king enjoined him to get some rest, in terms that are worth quoting:

Mme Colbert tells me your health is not very good, and that your diligence in returning to work may do you harm.

I am writing this note to order you to do nothing that might make you incapable, upon your arrival, of serving me in all the important matters I entrust to you.

In short, I require your good health; I wish you to maintain it, and for you to believe that my confidence in you and my friendship for you lead me to speak as I do.

Colbert did not fail to profit from the usefulness of his services and the king's good opinion. In addition to his enormous salary, the minister obtained honorary distinctions that made his family de facto courtiers. In 1667 the king arranged the marriage of Colbert's eldest daughter, Marie-Thérèse, to the duc de Chevreuse and simultaneously affianced his second daughter, Henriette, to the comte de Saint-Aignan, future duc de Beauvilliers. On January 1, Louis announced the marriage to the duc de Chaulnes[5] in terms highly flattering to Colbert. "Dear cousin, I have arranged the marriage of Chevreuse with the eldest daughter of Colbert, and as I am thus linking the chief and sole male heir of your house to the daughter of a man who serves me in my most important affairs with the zeal and success Colbert has shown, I very much wished to tell you of the alliance myself, being sure that you will share in the satisfaction shown by both families."[6]

[5]The duc de Chaulnes was the son of one of the brothers of the high constable of Luynes. The duc de Chevreuse (Marie-Therese Colbert's future husband) was the son of the duc de Luynes (who was himself the only child of the high constable of Luynes), who had been the first husband of the elderly duchesse de Chevreuse.

[6]Pierre Clément, *Lettres, instructions, et mémoires de Colbert,* vol. 7.

87 { 87 {

We may well imagine what this social promotion meant to the merchants of Rheims. Colbert hurried to announce the news to the aldermen of his native city:

> The king, a prince who rewards beyond their hopes the fidelity of those honored to serve him, after all the favors with which he has already covered me, has chosen to arrange marriages for my first two daughters, to wit, the elder with M. de Chevreuse, only son of M. le duc de Luynes, and the second, who is now only ten, with the comte de Saint-Aignan, who has the right of succession to the post of First Gentleman of the King's Chamber. And as though it were not enough to have procured me two such great and important alliances, His Majesty did them the office of a father, giving each of them 200,000 livres, the greater part of their dowries.

On February 2, the wedding of Marie-Thérèse and the duc de Chevreuse was celebrated in the minister's house. A supper-concert, a play, a dance: the brilliant company was dazzled by the reception. One guest reported to Olivier d'Ormesson that "M. Colbert danced quite well, and that it was his greatest passion." The evening of the wedding, he "danced two courantes in private, and very well indeed."

The following year, Louis elevated the barony of Siegnelay to the status of a marquisate. Colbert, like Le Tellier, did not dare to take a title. It was therefore his eldest son who was known as the marquis de Seignelay, just as Le Tellier's eldest son was titled the marquis de Louvois. On August 31, Seignelay defended his thesis in philosophy. In those days a thesis defense was a social event. All the courtiers hastened eagerly to applaud the young man to such an extent that the king found his court nearly deserted and, according to d'Ormesson, showed "great jealousy."

In 1671 Colbert's second oldest daughter married Saint-Aignan. The king and queen signed the marriage contract, as they had done for the eldest daughter and would do for all Colbert's children.

The minister was much courted, but there were also many who hated him. His nepotism violently angered everyone hungry for positions and offices. "He wants everything for himself, his relatives, and his son," noted Saint-Maurice.[7] One of Colbert's brothers was successively bishop of Luçon and of Auxerre. Another, the comte de Maulevrier, was lieutenant general of the king's armies. His favorite brother, Colbert de Croissy, was appointed ambassador to London. His uncle Pussort became councilor of state and played a predominant role in the world of

---

[7]Seignelay's career was primarily naval, and it will be treated in a later chapter devoted to maritime affairs.

justice. His first cousin, Colbert du Terron, was councilor of state and naval intendant at Rochefort. Four of his sisters were abbesses and convent prioresses.

But these honors did not prevent Colbert's living a relatively simple life. To the great astonishment of certain diplomats, he went about unescorted. In a memorandum intended for his son, he wrote: "Consider well and reflect often upon what your birth would have made of you if God had not blessed my labors, and if these labors had not been extreme." Seignelay's entire upbringing was oriented to the administration of public affairs. The glory of the Colberts came essentially from political power not accessible to the courtiers. The courtiers were aware of this and feared the king's minister more than the king's favorite.

THE NORTH

"The North" was Mme de Sévigné's nickname for Colbert. Gui Patin called him *Vir marmoreus,* "The man of marble." The ambassador of Brandenburg recalled him in these terms: "He was large and advantageously formed. . . . His manners, though correct and composed, did not fail, upon reflection or after doing business with him, to leave the impression of a hard and haughty nature." The ambassador of Savoy, less disagreeable, wrote: "For my part, in spite of his severe disposition and bearing, I find him very obliging, quick to grant reasonable requests, a man of his word, and prompt."

Colbert held the purse strings, and his influence with the king was undeniable. His office was invaded by petitioners. The Venetian ambassador recalled that "On days when he gave audience, the other ministers' offices were like deserts." His cold manner was very useful for intimidating courtiers and discouraging requests. During one famous audience, Mme Cornuel said to him in her high-pitched voice, "My lord, at least give me a sign that you hear me!"

The king knew not to appear stingy. Pensions, dowries, and gifts rained down on submissive courtiers. The domestication of the nobility was very expensive for the treasury. Louis's expenditures for the court belong to the realm of caprice. Here again, the king accepted with difficulty Colbert's notion of public finance. How could a budget clearly set out in advance be reconciled with the fancies of an arbitrary monarch?

Colbert tried to watch the distribution of pensions closely. As Mme de Sévigné put it: "We must now solicit things that were formerly no trouble. A fine age indeed." With what apprehension the marquise went to confront "the waiting ice," when Colbert granted her an audience. With what care, she had prepared a whole speech designed to obtain a pension for her son-in-law. Mme de Sévigné reported to her daughter afterward: "I will not tire myself if I quote his reply: 'Madam, I shall see to it.' And he walked me to the door, and that was it."

The entire court had seen the merciless severity the minister had shown in preparing the trial of Fouquet and in punishing the crimes of certain landed nobles in their provincial fiefs. When a courtier approached Colbert, was it not also the world of privilege that was colliding with the state as dispenser of justice?

CHAPTER 8

The State as Dispenser
of Justice

"**D**ISORDER REIGNED EVERYWHERE." Thus the king expressed himself in his *Mémoires for the Year 1661*. These few words sum up the incredible tangle of jurisdictions, the disparity of laws and customs, the widespread disobedience to the central government, the tyranny of clans and localities. Nothing was more complicated than the heavy administrative machinery of the ancien régime; nothing more unjust than the many abuses practiced by a swarm of financial officers so anxious to reimburse themselves for their offices at the expense of the taxpayers and the royal treasury.

Le Grand Siècle had not left the Middle Ages—the waning, decadent Middle Ages, with a distinct resurgence of feudalism, lacking the spiritual drive of the cathedral builders. An intense need for unification, order, and simplicity went hand in hand with a very fashionable nostalgia for ancient Rome. Visits to Roman ruins were very much in vogue. The unhealthiness of the cities, the narrow, dirty streets, the ever-present danger of fire, called for town planning that was more functional, better ordered, and inspired by ancient designs. For Colbert's contemporaries, Rome evoked a certain idea of modernism. The minister had researchers find for him the great principles of Roman law. He had a sort of sentimental conception of Augustan Rome—powerful, deriving its strength from its unity and the clarity of its administration.

How then were abuses to be punished; how were that righteous order and that simplifying unity to be imposed? Only the personal authority of the king could overcome an infinite number of barriers and obstacles.

Louis was highly conscious of the importance of his role in all the areas dealing with justice. There were several reasons why this was so. According to Capetian tradition, judicial power legitimized the majesty of the royal office. The Estates of Normandy had begged God and Louis XIII, "his lieutenant on Earth," to have pity on their suffering. The king, God's delegate, consecrated by the Church, was the natural protector of the people and the supreme judge.

Besides, Louis XIV had observed that the organization of justice that existed at the beginning of his reign constituted a restraint to monarchical absolutism. The *parlementaires,* so jealous of their independence, were, above all, judges. By selling financial and judicial offices in ever-increasing numbers, the kings of France (as Pierre Goubert put it) lost in authority what they gained in money.

At the beginning of his personal rule, even before Fouquet's fall, Louis wanted to reduce the authority of the sovereign courts and of the corps of officials. Troublesome magistrates were exiled; remonstrances were refused; the use of royal commissioners in the provinces was encouraged.

Colbert would never have thought of calling into question the king's sacred authority in all matters of justice. With all his soul, he worked to increase the sovereign's political power, But in his reforming dreams, Colbert was bolder than Louis XIV. The minister favored unity and leveling even more than the king. A single, nationwide code of law seemed to him the best guarantee of equitable justice and the best defense against the caprices of private interests.

He proposed "that grand design" to the king in a 1665 speech before the council of justice, of which, naturally, the minister was a member. Could that council be satisfied to correct the inadequacies in the administration of justice that various reports had pointed out here and there? Colbert suggested to His Majesty: ". . . some grander design, such as restricting the whole kingdom to the same law, the same measures, and the same weights, which would certainly be a design worthy of Your Majesty's grandeur, worthy of Your spirit and Your times, and which would bestow on you unfathomable blessings and glory (although only the honor of its execution would be yours, since the design was first fashioned by Louis XI, beyond question the most competent of all our kings)."

Louis, more cautious than his minister, preferred to follow a more cautious, less brutal, and less hasty policy of unification than the one Colbert wanted. Colbert recommended "great zeal, great diligence, and great firmness" to the king. Although less passionate, Louis still remained deeply interested in the unification of the judiciary, and he stood behind Colbert's actions. The latter would have to use all his energy and willpower—which were very great—to attack that immense task that was so dear to him. The "thousand tyrants" (to use his phrase), who annoyed with impunity, were prepared to fiercely defend their privileges.

THE THOUSAND TYRANTS

A trip through the provinces under Louis XIV continuously contradicts the traditional picture of absolute monarchy. Just as royal taxes were but one tax among others, so royal law remained one law among others. The unification of the kingdom was scarcely begun. Each province, each commune, continued to dispense justice according to its own customs. Suppose the king wanted to impose a decision in a matter of law? A flood of overlapping jurisdictions was employed to drag out the affair. Bailliages, seneschalships, lower courts, supreme courts, docketing, deferring, pronouncing, publishing—to be executed, such a decision had to pass through the hands of a process-server who summoned each interested party individually. And what is one to say about the multiplicity of specialized courts that sat only at certain times of the year? Delay, complication, and inequality characterized the enormous judicial machine of the ancien régime, whose continuation was assured by the countless magistrates who owned their seats as personal property.

The weakness of royal control and the poor quality of much of the judicial personnel led to staggering abuses. The gentlemen of the robe, the "robins," devoured the ruined country squires whose estates they wished to buy. They provoked a decision of bankruptcy through the expenses incurred from an onerous trial, and they mobilized all the barons and retainers of the judiciary for their profit. Laws, customs, usages, royal justice, and seigneurial justice were completely intermingled. Whom should one ask for justice? Loyseau remarked that "a peasant in Poitou entering a plea for his cow or his sheep would rather give them up altogether than go through five or six different jurisdictions." Village justices more often followed the customary law of the neighboring jurisdiction, where their overlords happened to be located, than the laws of the locality. Village judges—ignorant and venal men, half peasant and half magistrate—frequented markets and fairs, readily accepting bribes. They were often seen in taverns drinking with persons whose cases were pending. On a higher level, it was not uncommon to see *parlementaires* render decisions as connections and clientele dictated. Quarrels and personal grudges were violent. In general, the judiciary endeavored to recover the costs of their offices by any means.

Seigneurial justice existed alongside royal justice. Every gentleman thought himself to be sole proprietor of judicial rights in his village, and if his village was only a hamlet, why then he was the sovereign judge of its three men and two women. One often comes across nobles who exhibited a good-natured paternalism and were relatively generous, as was Mme de Sévigné. But there were also numerous seigneurs, veritable criminals and leaders of brigands, who terrorized their regions with impunity. The baron de Sénégas was convicted (among other crimes) of two or three murders, of imprisonments, and of having locked an enemy in a damp wardrobe. M. du Palais tortured bailiffs who tried to serve him with papers. Other gentlemen were, in effect, highway robbers, holding travelers and peasants for ransom or kidnapping rich marriageable girls.

In addition to the tithe he paid the clergy, the taxpayer was subject to two direct taxes, one owed the seigneur and one set by the royal finance officers. The fiscal system of the ancien régime was extraordinarily unfair in its structure as well as in its application.

The peasants paid nearly all the direct taxes. Saint-Aulaire made the point well: "If we take into account the scarcity of capital and the state of agriculture; if we consider that the *taille** was paid solely by the commoners who owned less than a third of the land and who had to pay, besides the tithe, the feudal dues and the local assessments as well; if we consider that this tax had grown even more oppressive because of the arbitrariness of the assessment, then we are terrified by the burden borne by the people at that time."

Certain seigneurs, such as the terrible baron de Sénégas, demanded irregular payments in specie and in kind. In Auvergne, the vicomte de Canillac collected a *taille* for Monsieur, one for Madame, and one for all their children, above and beyond the royal tax.

The collection of the royal taxes also created an occasion for abuse. Let us recall very briefly some characteristics of the organization of royal taxation. Since Richelieu's time, the kingdom had been divided into thirty-two *généralitiés*. Twelve of those belonged to the *pays d'état*, which had retained the right to propose the amount of their taxes to the king. The twenty others were located in *pays d'élection*, where royal appointees set the taxes as they pleased. In each *généralité*, chief collectors gathered in the revenue from each region, paid off local debts, and transferred the surplus to the *trésorier de l'épargne*, the central treasurer. The *trésor de l'épargne* (central treasury) was a financial institution created by Francis I to serve as a central depository for both ordinary revenues (those deriving from the king's lands) and the special revenues of the state (direct and indirect taxes).

The king's idea was to break the monopoly of the old financial aristocracy; but, in turn, the treasurers and chief collectors came to form an independent group and often acted in concert to the detriment of the state. It was not rare to see the chief collectors advance money to the *trésorier de l'épargne* in return for a rebate of one-tenth of the revenues, which cut down the total amount collected.

The financial officials responsible for setting rates of taxation readily over-charged certain poor parishes unable to pay bribes, to the advantage of those rich enough to buy off these strange civil servants. Or else local toughs, the *coqs de village*, won a decrease by threatening the collectors.

Indirect taxes on salt, wine, and the like (*fermes, gabelle, aides*), tied to the price of consumer goods, affected the entire population in a superficially more equitable fashion. But their collection also led to abuses. The tax farmers demanded interest in order to be able to pay in advance. The populace hated the *partisans*, government creditors often confused with the finance officials, who pried into

*The *taille* was the main tax, a direct tax supposedly levied in proportion to income.

private lives, made inquiries, acted as informers, or practiced blackmail. In Mazarin's time, Colbert was already indignant at these many abuses. To combat them, he relied on the usual instruments of royal power, the *maîtres des requêtes*.

THE MAÎTRES DES REQUÊTES

Theirs was an ancient body.[1] They were the true successors of Charlemagne's *missi dominici,* and the kings endowed them with extraordinary powers and sent them to tour the provinces on horseback. They set out, then, with powers superior to those of the parlements. They inspected local administration, heard subjects' complaints, and could in specific circumstances pronounce even the death sentence without appeal or recourse. Considered to be members of the judiciary, who had fixed tenure, they had access to all the parlements. Most of them, moreover, were of the *parlementaire* class. Besides the circuits on horseback, their duties were numerous in both the administrative and the judicial spheres. Like the members of the Council of State, the *maîtres des requêtes* were at the same time civil servants and officeholders. The cost of buying their offices was considerable. The famous La Reynie, later head of the Parisian police, paid 300,000 livres for his position in 1661. To obtain the office, one had to be over thirty-three, although occasionally dispensations were granted: Fouquet had become a *maître des requêtes* at twenty-five. These magistrates were highly conscious of representing the state as dispenser of justice, and in general they were more than faithful to Colbert. They were almost the only ones to have understood him at all times, perhaps the only ones who sometimes felt affection for him.

The intendants, chosen from among the *maîtres des requêtes*, were put in charge of one or more *généralités*. During the Fronde, they lived permanently in their *généralités* and supervised the police, judiciary, and finances there, to the fury of the parlements and the holders of royal offices. The revolt of the parlement had forced Mazarin to abolish the intendants. The cardinal got around that obstacle by reestablishing the circuits on horseback by the *maîtres des requêtes*. Once the Fronde had been put down, the intendants reappeared with the title of "departmental commissioners for the execution of the king's orders."[2]

In the first years of his personal reign, Louis XIV limited their role, or at least the outward signs of their power, to avoid reawakening the rebellious impulses

[1]The title itself dates back to the reign of Philip V. These magistrates were originally assigned to receive the petitions (or *requêtes*) addressed to the king in his palace (*hôtel*): Hence their full title, *maîtres des requêtes de l'hotel.*

[2]The *départments,* the territories in which they exercised their financial power, were in part the forerunners of the geographic departments into which France is divided today.

of the Fronde. The king strictly forbade their encroaching upon the duties of the officeholders, whom they were expected simply to oversee. Little by little they were again domiciled throughout the kingdom, each in charge of a single *généralité*, with their old and glorious title of *intendants de police, justice, et finances*. As such, they were responsible to both the chancellor and the comptroller general. As long as Séguier and Aligre were at the head of the justice department, Colbert was entirely in charge of that administrative staff, so useful to the implementation of his policies.

Under Louis XIV, there were twenty-five intendants: twenty-one in the *pays d'élection* and four in the *pays d'état*. The number is incredibly small in comparison with that of the officeholders. On several occasions Colbert had expressed his desire to see the state governed by a very small number of civil servants. He wrote that where financial matters were concerned: "It is certain that the easier they are to understand, and the smaller the number of persons controlling them, the nearer they will approach perfection." An important civil service threatened to escape central government control and to weigh down the administrative machinery, already so unwieldy and complex.

On the other hand, the minister attached the greatest importance to the quality and competence of that staff, which was very carefully selected, trained, and supervised. In 1661 he had a list of the eighty *maîtres des requêtes* drawn up, and beside each name he wrote his appraisal: "A good man, but not worth his province"; "The king knows him"; "mediocre"; "He has always been considered one of the best," etc.

Before entrusting them with the job of intendant, Colbert initiated the young *maîtres des requêtes* in the exercise of their office, by giving them special missions all over the country, "so that they may visit the interior of the realm from end to end in seven or eight years' time, and thus become capable of greater things."

The administrative functions of the intendants became, in time, as varied as they were broad. Sanitation in cities, police investigations, judicial powers, maintenance of roads, financial matters: All had an important place in the enormous correspondence between Colbert and the intendants. The minister overwhelmed them with recommendations, occasionally with reprimands, or with threats that he always put off until later. As privileged civil servants, the minister provided them with a sort of tacit support and a kind of complicity.

In 1664 Colbert charged the *maîtres des requêtes* and the intendants with conducting a general survey throughout the kingdom to learn the state of the Church, the nobility, the judicial system, and the finances. An inventory of abuses would assist in the preparation of a set of reforms. One need only read the results of an investigation concerning Poitou that Colbert de Croissy sent his brother to realize that a veritable police file covering the whole country was being set up.

The primary responsibility of the intendants was still that of ensuring an equal distribution of the *taille*. Abuses, secret agreements, and corruption were so widespread that the task of the king's envoys sometimes seemed superhuman. The misfortunes that befell Claude Pellot, intendant of Guyenne, who was related to Colbert by marriage and was also his personal friend, allow us to make that judgment. One day, two of his bailiffs insisted on imposing the *taille* on persons under the protection of M. d'Orbussan, counselor in the Parlement of Toulouse. Orbussan was furious, and he contrived a way to get revenge. Supported by false witnesses, he lent all his influence to a slanderous warrant for rape. The bailiffs were prosecuted before the Parlement of Toulouse and were convicted, but not for long. Pellot investigated the matter himself and convinced Colbert to have the case removed to the jurisdiction of the *maîtres des requêtes*. That same tribunal gave Orbussan a decree of adjournment.

That was in 1665; by then, the king felt strong enough to lessen the judicial power of the "sovereign" courts, which were henceforth merely "superior" courts.

Royal control over the parlements was also exercised through their First Presidents, appointed by the king and often chosen from among the *maîtres des requêtes*. Claude Pellot became First President of the Parlement of Normandy in 1670. He continued to send the minister specific information on the region, its leading citizens, and its *parlementaires*.

Judgments rendered at that time by the Parlement of Normandy against witches or accused witches were still cruel. In July 1670, the Parlement of Rouen sentenced a man and two women to be hanged, then burned, for the crime of witchcraft. Pellot was indignant at the lightheartedness and cruelty of his colleagues. The women had been found guilty on the simple deposition of some boys of fifteen or sixteen who claimed to have seen them at a witches' sabbath. There was no one to accuse them of poisonings, witchcraft, or casting spells. As for the man, he was said to cause sickness in persons he disliked.

Pellot wrote to Colbert in haste:

We are to judge another witch tomorrow; besides that, another twenty-one or twenty-two from one gang, and eight or ten from another, are supposed to come in a day or two from the same place as these, between Coutances and Carentan. . . . They say that in that part of the country they daily discover persons to accuse of witchcraft, and we are afraid that the more there are found guilty, the more there will be discovered. Therefore, if His Majesty were to find it appropriate to give a few orders concerning this matter, they would come at a good time, for the three sentenced today are not to be executed for three or four days, in order to await those who are still to be convicted and take them all together.

And President Pellot added:

I consider it most dangerous, my Lord, to sentence people to death on the deposition of four or five wretches who often have no idea what they are talking about. . . . The matter is important enough, I think, for His Majesty to draw up some sort of regulation concerning it, and for the judges to know what proofs are required to convict such people. For while some treat the evidence as a joke, there are others who do not and who burn them, and it is shameful to see human lives toyed with in this way.

Pellot and Colbert saved the accused by obtaining a decree from the Grand Council overturning the verdict of the *parlementaires,* despite their spirited protests. In 1694, after Colbert's death, other such sentences were pronounced. The intendant Foucault was able to save some of those condemned, but others perished at the stake.

Colbert gradually took over supervision of the personnel normally within the jurisdiction of the chancellery. Ormesson noted, not without some irritation, "For ten years Mr. Colbert has been carrying out the principal duty of the chancellor, handing out employments to the *maîtres des requêtes,* proposing on his own the appropriate persons to fill vacant posts, giving them to his relatives, etc."

But the installation of a loyal staff was not enough to punish or to reduce the most obvious abuses. During the first years of the king's personal reign, a series of immediate measures were undertaken that threatened numerous interests and stirred up long-lasting hatred against Colbert.

IMMEDIATE MEASURES

A chamber of justice set up in 1661 for the purpose of striking a blow at the tax farmers, and more generally at all those creditors who had abused the state, would cause the financial structure to tremble for almost eight years.[3] The major defendant was Nicolas Fouquet, brilliant symbol of an entire world. From Angers, the ex-superintendant had been taken to Amboise, to Vincennes, then to Moret—where Colbert, agreeing with d'Artagnan, "had considered it very advisable that bars be placed in the windows"[4]—and finally to the Bastille at the time of his trial. Pellot and other *maîtres des requêtes* had seized and sealed the papers of Fouquet and his secretary, Pellisson. All those papers were delivered to Louis XIV.

The king had briefly considered handing Fouquet over at once to a special commission that would have initiated proceedings against him without delay. That project was not carried out. Instead, it was thought better to prepare carefully

[3]It set out to investigate every case of financial misconduct since 1635.

[4]Letter from d'Artagnan, *Catalogue Charavay,* no. 751.

the establishment of a chamber of justice. Fouquet had to wait three years before being brought to trial before a tribunal composed partly of *maîtres des requêtes* and counselors of state and partly of members of various parlements. The king first appointed Lamoignon, First President of the Parlement of Paris, to preside over the chamber of justice. Concerned about legal forms, Lamoignon insisted as early as 1662 that the defendant should be shown the evidence gathered by the prosecution and should be provided with counsel.

The trial dragged on so long that Louis personally asked Lamoignon to withdraw. The chancellor himself, Pierre Séguier, took his place. Fouquet and Séguier had long been enemies, although for rather droll reasons: While Fouquet had remained loyal to the king during the Fronde, Séguier had sided with the princes. The defendant did not fail to point that out during his trial, to the chancellor's great embarrassment. Something of an opportunist, Séguier liked to follow the man of the moment—in this case, Colbert. Mme de Sévigné, who lamented the misfortunes of her friend Fouquet, wrote to Pomponne: "Puis [Séguier] is always afraid of displeasing Petit [Colbert]. He begged his pardon the other day because Fouquet had gone on too long, saying he had not been able to interrupt him."

Despite the seriousness of the plan of Saint-Mandé and the initial steps taken to carry it out, the judges paid much more attention to Fouquet's misappropriation of public funds. Strangely enough, succeeding generations would react in the same way. Fouquet's arguments in defense of his handling of finances were skillful, intelligent, and not entirely without effect on the judges, even though Colbert had secretly picked them himself. First, the ex-superintendant explained that his methods had been prescribed by Mazarin, who had himself unhesitatingly intermingled the state treasury and his private fortune, with Colbert's help. The cardinal's unbelievable greed had forced Fouquet to come up with enormous sums on short notice. In the second place, great financial reforms could not be carried out in time of war. Extraordinary and unforeseen expenditures implied a lack of order. Finally—and here we come to the heart of the political and economic differences between Fouquet and Colbert—the ex-superintendant defended a public-financing policy that differed radically from that of his enemy.

A few days before Fouquet's fall, the question had been raised of whether to refer the usurpers of public revenues to a special chamber of justice. The numerous objections had made it clear that such an exercise of authority would destroy the state's financial credibility, put an end to commerce, and drive foreign money out of the kingdom. Besides that, the financiers had been ready to offer twenty million to avoid prosecution.

Fouquet persisted in thinking that it was necessary to encourage capital—or more precisely, speculation—by pleasing the financiers. As he put it in his *Défenses*: "cease speaking of taxes on financiers, show them favor, and instead of contesting their legitimate interests and profits, give them gratuities and indemnities as a sign of good faith, when their support has been important. The principal secret, in a word, is to give them incentives, that being the only reason why anyone would be willing to run some risks."

In 1661 Colbert put forth the principle that the state should refuse to resort to any form of borrowing and public financing; the state should instead derive its entire resources solely from tax revenues and revenues from the royal domains. For the minister, state creditors were public enemies who speculated shamefully upon the distress of the treasury. While Fouquet's trial was taking place, Colbert fiercely hounded everyone bearing the slightest resemblance to a king's creditor.

The thunderbolts of Louis and his minister fell upon the tax farmers, who were the leading profiteers. Olivier d'Ormesson, who, it is true, had never liked Colbert, wrote:

Financiers were vigorously investigated, and that investigation passed from fathers to their children, from the children to any relatives who had an inheritance, and then to sons-in-law, and also had an impact on buildings and land that had been the dowries of the financiers' daughters, so that sons-in-law paid the taxes of their fathers-in-law, without exception for the gentlemen of the robe, as established in the first indictments, and also without exception for the ancient military nobility. Garrisons were put in the homes of chief justices because they were married to tax farmers' daughters.

These inquisitorial suspicions spared no social class. In 1662 the duc de Guise asked "the favor of being treated differently from the tax farmers, since instead of getting rich through the king's business, I have always spent everything I had."[5]

Next, Colbert went after the *rentiers*.* During periods of unrest, many of them had acquired *rentes* issued by the government, assigned to the city of Paris or to other administrations. Bought cheaply, these *rentes* came to produce exorbitant interest.

Colbert acted without restraint. He simply canceled a million's worth of *rentes* secured by direct taxes, 600,000 livres worth secured by the salt tax, and all of those secured by the revenue of the city of Paris or other administrative bodies from 1656 to 1661. Others were redeemed at purchase price, after a

---

[5]Letter from the duc de Guise to Colbert, *Catalogue Charavay*, no. 754.

*"The *rentes* were a system of concealed borrowing at interest under which fixed annual or quarterly payments were sold for cash. The crown's own credit was generally so bad that many *rentes* were nominally assigned on the municipality of Paris, the clergy, and other third parties" (Robin Briggs, *Early Modern France, 1560–1715* [New York: Oxford, 1977], p. 230).

deduction had been made for any interest the government had already paid above the legal rate. These draconian measures, which at times seemed to be actual expropriation, involved a multitude of interests and affected both large and small holders. President Lamoignon felt personally injured, and put up a vain resistance to the policy. Mme de Sévigné claimed she was in the shadow of the poorhouse.

The numerous *rentiers* detested Colbert. A pro-Fouquet cabal began to take shape. The intendant Foucault[6] loyally warned the minister: "Threats are everywhere; Monsieur d'Artagnan tells me that you, My Lord, should take greater precautions than ever."

In December 1664, the verdict was about to be delivered in Fouquet's case. Turenne made the terrible quip: "I think that Colbert greatly hopes he will be hanged, and that Le Tellier greatly fears he will not be." The verdict was made public on December 20: Out of twenty-two judges, thirteen had voted for banishment and nine for the death sentence. His handpicked court had given Colbert a slap in the face. His own judicial brutality; the moderation shown by d'Ormesson, the prosecutor; a touch of pity for that man, once so much courted, whose hair had turned white after his arrest—all of these may have contributed to the judges' clemency. The next day, Louis commuted the sentence of banishment for life to one of life imprisonment. Fouquet was taken to the fort of Pignerol, where he died in 1680, after a particularly harsh confinement.

The chamber of justice was still in effect in 1669, terrorizing some and keeping others in a state of continual anxiety to such an extent that the government eventually had to become somewhat more flexible. The decisions of the chamber of justice obtained a total of 110 million livres for the state.

Persons who falsely claimed noble status to avoid taxes were sought out and prosecuted. Real nobles guilty of threatening or harassing the populace or the tax collectors were brought before special assizes that made a strong impression on the entire kingdom. Colbert had already thought of holding *grands jours* (those most powerful of inquests) as in Mazarin's time. Extraordinary tribunals were called for by the general populace and even by certain *parlementaires* who seemed overwhelmed by the powerlessness of the local courts in the face of the many extortions.

In 1665 the *grands jours* of Auvergne began at Clermont. The Auvergne nobility lived in terror. Death sentences were passed, judicial rights suspended, fines levied, woodlands razed, and fortresses demolished. Many seigneurs fled to the mountains. There were 340 sentencings in absentia; those who had escaped royal justice were burned in effigy before curious onlookers.

[6]Nicolas Foucault (1643–1721) was intendant at Montauban, at Poitou, and at Normandy. He showed great fervor in the struggle with the Protestants after the Edict of Nantes was revoked.

The following year, the *grands jours* of Languedoc were held, and again there were executions and judgments in absentia.

The psychological effect of these *grand jours* was considerable. Royal justice was affirmed impressively. Colbert convinced Louis to reduce the number and extent of officeholders. Thousands of new and meaningless offices had been created and put up for sale since 1630. Payment of the wages was costing the treasury over eight million yearly. And the frantic rush to purchase official posts was diverting capital from commerce and industry. Despite outcries, entreaties, and offers of bribes, Colbert abolished a large number of offices, which he bought back at rock-bottom prices (see the Edict of 1665, renewed in 1669 and 1671). The remaining officeholders would be more and more subject to the intendants.

With the establishment of the chamber of justice, the minister was able to watch the treasury and the honesty of the treasurers closely. In a hitherto unpublished report, he wrote: "There can be no doubt that the results of the chamber of justice will depend entirely upon the information we get from the treasury, that is to say, from the books kept by the treasurers. . . . Having seals placed on their offices and those of their bookkeepers would be a brilliant move." Especially, he added, because they will not fail to remove their books to a safe place. "It is much more appropriate to force them to produce their books by royal proclamation."

The "discounts" offered to tax collectors, which had reached the scandalous rate of 25 percent, were cut back sharply to 4 percent. In 1664 Colbert abolished the title of *trésorier de l'épargne* and took over the duties himself. The *trésor de l'épargne* became "the royal treasury" in 1666.

What were the financial results of all these efforts? First, a large decrease in fixed budget outlays, which in ten years dropped from fifty-two million a year to twenty-four. Second, a gradual rebalancing of the budget. Let us recall that when Mazarin died in March of 1661, the anticipated revenue for 1661 and 1662 and a part of that for 1663 had already been spent. Third, the *taille*, which had been a shameful burden on the peasantry, especially in the *pays d'élection,* was reduced spectacularly. The *taille,* which had risen to fifty-three million in 1657, dropped from forty-one million in 1662 to thirty-eight million in 1679 (and was no more than thirty-five million in 1680).[7]

On the other hand, indirect taxes, which all consumers paid, went up remarkably. The revenues from the tax farms rose from thirty-seven million to sixty million. The king was thus obliged to idemnify the supervisors of the tax farms—the notion of substituting state control for the tax-farming system being

---

[7]In the *pays d'état,* on the other hand, the distribution of taxation had been fairer to begin with, being usually based on accurate surveys; and there the *taille* increased.

too new for that time. They were released from the requirement that they retain agents, who consumed part of their profits. The abrupt increase in indirect taxes, notably the salt tax, caused riots, or what were then called *emotions.* The repression by the state was sometimes quite harsh.

The minister also went to work to alter the state of the public debt. Over six years, Fouquet had borrowed about 171 million at an apparent interest rate of 5.5 or 5.75 percent, but at an actual rate of 15 to 18 percent. Colbert reduced the legal rate of interest from one in eighteen, or 5.5 percent, to one in twenty, or 5 percent, in order to place France on an equal footing with her commercial rivals in borrowing and trading money.

Elsewhere, the minister struggled tirelessly to obtain reductions in the debts too often contracted by elected municipal officials. This gave the intendants an opportunity to intervene in municipal affairs.

Despite its clear and evident successes, this policy of systematic opposition to public debt was to be severely criticized more than once. Does that mean Fouquet might be exonerated? The superintendant seems to have been closer to a state of mind foreshadowing a sort of private and imaginative capitalism. Colbert believed in the strictness of a state that was ideally just and beneficent. The fact is that both approaches were wide of the mark, given the somewhat unstable character of a transitional age.

Existing structures were not adaptable. Behavioral patterns whose roots were deep had become obsolete. Fouquet was mistaken. Leaving aside the question of his personal dishonesty, no policy, however imaginative and intelligent, can be effective in the face of generalized corruption and institutionalized financial disorder. And Colbert was wrong to hope that a policy of moralizing financial affairs could work economic miracles when the basis of taxation remained iniquitous, and when the king could demand any sum of money at any time. The state still could not dispense with public financing without first having carried out a very wide-ranging national reform. It is undeniable that Colbert made efforts in that direction. But once again he was too early.

THE GREAT REFORMS

With the Fouquet affair at an end, the king and Colbert turned their attention to implementing a general reform of the judicial system. There is no doubt the minister gave impetus to the project. Nevertheless, he cleverly credited the king with having the idea. It is true that Louis, who was very interested in that issue, insisted on examining every aspect himself. In 1665 the first preparatory conferences took place, held before the king and called "councils of justice." Every minister attended, as did the terrible Pussort, Colbert's uncle.

Colbert wanted to proceed swiftly. He was of the opinion that the plan prepared by the council should not be communicated to anyone, but should be promulgated at once by registering it in a *lit de justice*. But Louis wanted to proceed in a more deliberate manner and ordered that the council be enlarged. The undated letter he sent Colbert shows clearly his prudent approach:

Versailles, Thursday

It would be a good idea for you to see the Chancellor [Séguier] tomorrow, and for you to tell him that I wish him to ask the opinion of the royal representatives in parlement on what is to be done to reform the judicial system, and also of those belonging to the other deliberative bodies in Paris. Ask him if he thinks it appropriate to send for advice from the First Presidents in the provinces[8] and from the king's representatives in all the parlements if you think that advisable.

Press him to agree; otherwise speak lightly of it.

Louis

Besides that, the king told Lamoignon that the preparation of such plans without the involvement of the latter disturbed him: "Go see Colbert, and discuss the matter together." The minister was surprised but had to go along.

The new conferences began early in 1667. They took place in Séguier's rooms, and as the king wished, they involved five counselors of state, including Pussort, three *maîtres des requêtes*, First President Lamoignon, several presidents of various parlements, and representatives of the king. The minutes of these meetings bear witness to the continual ideological conflict between Lamoignon and Pussort.

Lamoignon, whose career owed a great deal to Fouquet, was honest, traditional, and very respectful of the prerogatives of the magistracy, and he seemed systematically opposed to Colbert's initiatives. Saint-Simon left this portrait of Pussort: "A tall, dry man, lacking in social graces, hard to approach, a bundle of thorns, knowing neither amusement nor any other diversion; but withal, great integrity, much capacity, great knowledge, extremely hardworking."

Despite Lamoignon's moderate suggestions, it was the inflexible and reforming spirit of Pussort—and of Colbert through him—that usually carried the day. In April 1667, the "civil ordinance concerning the reform of justice," or Code Louis, became law. It was the first real attempt at the unification and codification of the rules of judicial procedure. Colbert hoped that eventually such procedures would be free of costs. Three years later the ordinance covering criminal law was

[8]We should remember that, unlike the other *parlementaires,* the First Presidents were approved by the king.

published. Here, we may find it regrettable that Lamoignon was unable to impose his views, which were much more humane and respectful of civil rights than those of Pussort.

As long as Colbert lived, an overall, coordinated effort toward codification was carried on relentlessly.[9] The parlements accepted with great acrimony the reforms desired by the king. The attitude of the Parlement of Rouen seemed close to rebellion. In general, the members were furious to learn of the suppression of the *droit de remontrance,* their right to impose legislation. The jurisprudence of the Parlement of Paris was the best impetus for the unification process. Very slowly, the practice of the capital spread everywhere. Little by little, a "French law" emerged from the mass of varied and entangled traditional laws.

Ultimately, didn't the monarchy contribute to setting in motion forces that would soon be able to do it harm? A powerful administrative body was taking the machinery of government into its own hands and threatened somewhat to evade royal authority. In contrast to the divine rights of kings, the rights of man began imperceptibly to emerge. Above all, men were progressing toward a coherent and unified administration of justice. The codes then being drawn up—ambitious, unchangeable, logical—offered an alternative to all that was arbitrary. A new order had made its appearance.

[9]Statutes for waters and forest, for commerce, for the navy, for slavery, to be discussed more fully below.

CHAPTER 9

Paris and Versailles

COLBERT WANTED THE KING to identify himself with the new order by settling in Paris, the center of the state. But Louis XIV, the living incarnation of France, wanted the nation and the world to bow down before Versailles, the temple of royal majesty. Was it only the memory of the Fronde that made the king keep his distance from Paris? Here and there, one can glimpse the curious ambiguity of the role he played. He tamed the aristocracy, but the nobles were also considered and treated as Olympian demigods. He promised a powerful administration, yet he mistrusted it. He promised a powerful administration, yet he mistrusted it. He proclaimed Paris "the royal and capital city of the kingdom, center of government," or "the common fatherland of all our subjects," and yet he showed no further interest in the city and did not like to remain there. The choice of Versailles was a serious matter. The men involved in the political, economic, scientific, and artistic life of the nation lived in Paris or went there. Versailles was a dead city when the king was gone. An entire class—active, ambitious, hungry for government posts—bitterly resented the scorn heaped on them by an almost magical court, from which they were excluded. The center of the state would never be the center of the monarchy. The effects of that separation for the future of the regime were incalculable. Colbert would foresee the danger, and would submit to the king's passion for his "temple" with dismay.

As part of his official duties, Colbert was involved in the administration of Paris as well as in the building of Versailles. Indeed, the management of the municipality of Paris lay partly with the comptroller general and partly with the secretary of state for the king's household; Colbert held both offices. On January 1, 1664, Louis offered him a royal New Year's gift: the office of superintendent of buildings, with an income of at least 40,000 livres a year. Thus, Colbert would carry on the construction at Versailles begun under his predecessor, Antoine de Ratabon, and would attend to the royal buildings, in Paris as elsewhere.

KING AND STATE

PARIS

Paris then had between 400,000 and 500,000 inhabitants. For the time, that was enormous. It was probably the most important city in Europe. It still retained its medieval appearance, with its countless bell towers, its ancient houses, and its narrow, very dirty, ill-paved, and unsafe streets. By day, pedestrians had to thread their way among carriages, horses, or pigs and chickens. "Watch out for the water!" was the only warning given when a Parisian dumped his ordure out the window. Itinerant vendors and artisans added to the great vitality of the street that had so diverted Henri IV, and that his grandson shunned. By night, any of a number of ruffians assaulted passersby with complete impunity. An almost nonexistent police force and streets lit poorly if at all made crimes and thefts easier to commit.

In 1667, La Reynie became the first "lieutenant general of police" for Paris, the word *police* having also the meaning of "civil administration." He undertook to clean up the city, to pave the streets, and to install several thousand lanterns that burned from dusk past midnight during the winter months. That innovation dazzled all Europe.

A police force was organized and outfitted with prestigious uniforms. The pursuit of thieves and other criminals was intensified. La Reynie sometimes softened the harshness of the directives given by the king and by Colbert. On the other hand, Louis was often very indulgent toward certain courtiers, or toward the troops of the king's household, who were guilty of frequent extortions.[1] In 1672 the king, in agreement with Colbert, forbade new building beyond the recently constituted suburbs, because "it is very difficult to maintain law and order handily throughout all the parts of so large a body." Despite some progress, the lieutenant's initiatives were not sufficient to greatly improve the sanitation or safety of Paris.

Colbert was especially involved in urban renewal. He widened the streets (at the property owners' expense), built new fountains, planned canals, ordered plantings in the Tuileries and along the Champs-Elysées, and built new bridges. By 1669 the pathway along the Seine had been replaced by an ashlar embankment, called Le Cours, an elegant meeting place for ladies and gentlemen. The Parisians also enjoyed walks in the gardens of the Tuileries, which Le Nôtre had laid out. Women were often molested there, however. Colbert considered closing them to the public, until Perrault successfully intervened on the promenaders' behalf. The minister's desire for modernization was mingled with a dislike for the Gothic style. Paris still contained a large number of wooden houses dating from the

---

[1]Jacques Wilhelm, *La Vie quotidienne des Parisiens au temps du Roi-Soleil.*

Middle Ages. Fires were frequent and spread fast: The scarcity of water meant disaster under those conditions. All the narrow old alleyways had become extraordinarily unsanitary.

The cleanup of Paris was to serve as an example for other cities. The provincial intendants often wished to imitate the work done in the capital. But Colbert's grand design for Paris was to build monuments to the glory of the reign. To his son Seignelay he wrote: "As Paris is the capital of the realm and the seat of its kings, it is not to be doubted that she gives her impetus to the rest of the kingdom, that all internal affairs begin with her." The courtiers who thronged to Versailles nearly all maintained their dwellings in the city. Mme de Sévigné said: "We have a thousand errands in Paris." The artists who worked for the king lived there. The scientific world met in the city, where all the major administrative bodies of the state were located. Buildings worthy of the scientific and artistic glory of the age were erected under Colbert's supervision. The Gobelin tapestry works were renovated, the botanical gardens were reorganized, and Claude Perrault was put in charge of designing the observatory. It is to Colbert that Paris owes the Saint-Martin Gate and the Saint-Denis Gate as well.

The minister thought that the Louvre should remain the king's principal residence. He dreamed of making it the most beautiful palace in the world through renovations and by linking it with the Tuileries. The east facade, which faced Paris, was considered to be the main entrance. Colbert devoted himself wholeheartedly to its completion. Le Vau, François Mansart, and Italy's Pietro da Cortona submitted plans. Finally, the decision was made to invite the famous Bernini, Italy's foremost artist, to submit his designs for the facade and for the courtyard that would later be known as the Square Court. Bernini responded without delay and sent his sketches. Colbert thanked him, flattered him, admired his sketches, but asked for a second plan. For two years the architect and the minister carried on a strange comedy. Colbert simultaneously praised Bernini for his genius and overwhelmed him with suggestions. Bernini, he said, was paying too little heed to security requirements for a palace that was to be "the principal seat of kings in the largest and most populous city in the world, subject to various revolutions." The whole structure of the edifice should "inspire respect in the minds of the people." Besides, the plans submitted seemed ill-suited to the French climate. Bernini lost his temper. What was expected of him? Colbert and the king decided at that point that it would be better to clear up the matter in person.

In 1665 Bernini left his countrymen, who feared he might not return. France received him with exceptional honors. The architect made new proposals, and the minister new critiques. Colbert studied the smallest details of Bernini's designs; went over them one by one; plied the architect with a multitude of incredibly precise questions on the cornices, the balustrades, the shape of the staircases, how the arcades were to be closed off, the moats, the thicknesses of the walls, the placement of windows, etc. The plan was at last adopted, and on October 17, 1665, the cornerstone was laid. But Colbert was still not satisfied. He continued to inspect, and find many new faults. Bernini, furious, pointed out that the Pope and the Romans were summoning him home. Colbert took him at his word and was much relieved when he left.

The truth was that Colbert had always preferred the designs proposed by Claude Perrault, brother of the storyteller Charles Perrault and chief agent to the superintendant of buildings. The minister obtained the king's approval, and in 1666, the construction of the magnificent colonnade was begun, as well as work on the Square Court.

Were the Perrault brothers solely responsible for the new plans? Boileau would later stir up a spirited controversy on the subject. Some said Perrault had only carried out Le Vau's designs as modified by his son-in-law François d'Orbay. Others recalled that Le Brun had been involved. Were the designs the work of an individual or of a team? Fraud or wrongdoing? The mystery remains. In any case, the colonnade exhibits an admirable French Classical style, free of Italian Baroque influence.

In the winter of 1666 Louis left the Louvre to the workmen and moved into the Tuileries. Colbert did not know at the time that the king would never again return to "the most superb palace in the world." Louis XIV was passionately in love with Versailles. Although the correspondence between the king and his minister is full of references to Versailles, not a single letter shows any real interest in the Parisian buildings. He barely took the trouble to inspect them rapidly. In 1670 he wrote Colbert this note:

Sunday evening

I will leave Tuesday at nine, and will be at the Triumphal Arch at eleven at the latest.[2] I shall go from there to the Observatory, and then dine at my brother's. After the baptism, which will be early, I will go to the Louvre, and from there, proceed to the Tuileries, whence I will leave to return here. I'm letting you know my plans early so that you can take appropriate measures.[3]

Colbert had the great disappointment of never seeing the colonnade completed. Work on it was suspended in 1676. The splendor of Versailles was increasing, to the detriment of Paris and other châteaus, such as Fontainebleau or Chambord, which Colbert would have liked to restore.

[2]Not, of course, the modern Arch of Triumph, but the one under construction at the end of the Faubourg Saint-Antoine, which was never completed.

[3]Not included in Clément's *Lettres*.

VERSAILLES

In the first years of his personal reign, Louis had asked Le Vau to renovate Louis XIII's château at Versailles. In 1663 the architect began the first orangery and the menagerie, while Le Nôtre laid out the flower beds. When Colbert became superintendant of buildings, he did not suspect that the king had meant for Fouquet's team to build the world's most glorious palace at Versailles.

Soon the minister was having to erect temporary structures intended for the series of marvelous entertainments at Versailles. In 1664 Molière performed *Tartuffe* during the festivities for the "Pleasures of the Enchanted Island." A contemporary account tells us that "Monsieur Colbert spent his time on these divertissements despite his important occupations." The minister, who at the same time was working with all his might to wipe out the enormous debt left behind by Fouquet, obeyed the king's wishes with dismay. By September 28, 1665, he could stand it no longer and admonished the young monarch:

> Your Majesty is returning to Versailles. I beg you to permit me to say a word or two concerning the palace, whereof I think often, and that I hope it will please you to attribute to my devotion.
>
> That house has more to do with Your Majesty's pleasure and entertainment than with your glory. . . . Nonetheless, if Your Majesty should wish to seek evidence within Versailles of the more than 500,000 ecus that have been spent on that palace these last two years, you would hardly be able to find any. . . . While spending such great sums on that building, you have neglected the Louvre, which is certainly the most superb palace in the world, and the most worthy of Your Majesty's grandeur. . . . Oh, what a pity, that the greatest and most virtuous of kings, whose true virtue is of the kind that makes the greatest princes, should be judged by the standard of Versailles.

The minister's bitterness seems to have had some effect on the king. Whereas in 1664–65 Versailles cost 1,617,000 livres, in 1666–67 it cost only 741,000 livres, or less than half as much. Louis ordered the construction of the Grand Canal, and in 1668 the first Versailles was completed. Charles Perrault wrote: "The château was scarcely finished and Monsieur Colbert had barely had time to enjoy seeing a completed royal palace, to which he would only have to go two or three times a year to have necessary repairs made there, when the king decided to augment it with several buildings in order to be able to live there comfortably with his council during a stay of several days." The work on the second Versailles was directed by Le Vau and, after his death in 1670, by François d'Orbay, who carried out his father-in-law's plans. Colbert had to resign himself. He went to Versailles, sometimes daily, to inspect the work. The king insisted on being kept informed of the slightest details. When Colbert wrote: "I beg Your Majesty to let me know if these reports seem either too long or too short, so that I may follow your will in this matter as in all others," Louis wrote in the margin, "Long ones, full detail."

By 1670 the costs of Versailles rose to two million livres. The king was enthusiastic, impassioned, impatient. "Speed up work on the Trianon, for it must attain perfection before my arrival," he wrote Colbert.[4] Precise and peremptory orders arrived from the king. Colbert obeyed, giving faithful accounts of the construction. All the work is progressing in such a way that, I hope, will give Your Majesty satisfaction." The king replied, "I am satisfied with what you write me concerning Versailles. See to it there is no letdown, and continue to remind the workers of my return."

In June 1670, the quarryworkers were forbidden to leave their posts to help bring in the harvest, "which would have delayed His Majesty's buildings and prevented the completion of what he had ordered done in the present year." During certain periods, between 20,000 and 30,000 men were employed at the building sites. There were scores of fatal accidents; the widows of those killed were given pensions by the king. Sometimes Louis was overcome with pity for a particular individual. In April 1672, he wrote Colbert: "I forgot to tell you yesterday that something has to be given to poor Brontin, who was working on the pumps, and if he can't be hired, give him the means to retire, for he is in a pitiful state; you decide what he ought to have."[5] Let us recall that 46 million livres were spent on the work at Versailles during Louis's reign; ten million for the Louvre and the Tuileries and four million for the rest of the buildings in Paris, including the Invalides, built at Louvois's urging.[6] But the beauty of the buildings were not enough to proclaim France's artistic and intellectual supremacy. Both king and minister were aware, each in his own way, of the need for a genuine cultural policy, a policy that would be seen as one of the most brilliant in French history.

[4]Unpublished letter of May 19, 1670.

[5]A note not published by Clément; the king added it at the bottom of the letter that appears as no. 51 in vol. 6 of Pierre Clément's *Lettres, instructions, et memoires de Colbert.*

[6]Robert Mandrou, *Louis XIV en son temps,* p. 169.

CHAPTER 10

The Arts and History

COLBERT BUSIED HIMSELF with a "fine-arts policy" from the first years of the personal reign of Louis XIV, well before he was officially named superintendant of buildings. For him, the arts had an essential political function, that of glorifying the king in the eyes of his contemporaries and of future generations. In a complementary fashion, the image of a monarch who was patron of the arts and sciences ought to testify to the primacy of seventeenth-century France among the great stages of Western civilization. It was an immense ambition; but the king's taste was exceptional: "The Age of Louis XIV" is not an idle phrase. In his *Memoirs of Historical Application,* Colbert wrote, "it is good to note all that the king has done this year [1663] so that science and the liberal arts might flourish within his kingdom." All the great men, "bewitched" by the high royal patronage of the king, wrote, painted, and bore witness to that glorious reign. Art writes history. Artistic glory had to serve the glory of the king.

Consequently, Fouquet's dazzling patronage, and the sun symbol of Vaux, seemed like an insult to royal majesty. Fouquet was arrested in September 1661; in 1662, at the festival of the Carrousel, Louis chose the sun as his own emblem. The fallen superintendant's whole artistic staff entered into the service of the monarch. Le Vau began the early work at Versailles, where Le Nôtre designed the formal gardens. La Quintinie ruled over the royal kitchen garden. Le Brun was named first painter to the king, and he brought Colbert the Maincy workshops, formerly under Fouquet's patronage, which were quickly transformed into the Gobelin tapestry works. Châtelain wrote: "The tapestries begun by Fouquet were finished for the king, with the fleur de lis taking the place of the squirrel." All the "engineers" of water, all the contractors that the superintendant had employed, went to work at Versailles. With bitter admiration, the king and Colbert went through an inventory of Fouquet's marvelous collections: furnishings, books, rare plants, and statues. A state councillor sent in his report to the minister:

Found, in the gardens of Saint-Mandé, 200 large orange trees, several statues, and many plants whose names were unknown to me, but which I was nonetheless

able to inventory with the help of two German gardeners, one of whom had
been summoned from the royal garden for that purpose. . . . In the library,
7,000 volumes in folio, 8,000 in octavo, and more than 12,000 in quarto . . .
in one room of the library, a chest full of medals, including 122 gold ones
. . . in one room, 1,900 volumes, including 760 folios.[1]

Among the rare books were Talmuds and Korans. The king would acquire a large
part of Fouquet's collections, including furniture, books, orange trees, and statues,
even unfinished ones such as Puget's *Hercule gaulois*. The authors who had sung
the praises of the superintendant forgot their unfortunate benefactor and, under
Colbert's auspices, glorified the rising star of the monarchy. Only La Fontaine
still wished to remember. Themes from his *Fables* decorated certain chairs at
Versailles, but Colbert kept the doors of the Académie française closed to him.
In order to present himself before that illustrious body, the pleasant writer had
to wait for Colbert's death—whereupon he took over his seat.

Among Fouquet's papers there was an essay of Saint-Evremond's attacking
the Treaty of the Pyrenees. That brilliant and witty author, finding himself
threatened with the Bastille by Colbert, went into exile in England. Despite a
royal pardon granted by the king, he refused to return.[2]

Four men, three of whom had belonged to the superintendant's entourage,
were to collaborate closely in the cultural policy carried out by Colbert.

Le Brun directed in dictatorial fashion weavers of tapestries, cabinetmakers,
painters, and sculptors. He had a talent for grand historical decoration and for
allegorical scenes.

To help him with the writers, Colbert called on the elderly Chapelain, author
of *La Pucelle,* an epic poem that succeeding generations lost no time in forgetting.
It may be difficult to understand how Chapelain could become a veritable literary
oracle in Colbert's view, but Voltaire would later account satisfactorily for the
minister's choice: "Chapelain knew an immense body of literature, and, although
it may seem surprising, he had taste and was one of the most enlightened of
critics."

When Colbert was looking for a secretary to help him run the department
of fine arts, Chapelain recommended Charles Perrault, a civil servant concerned
with finance under Fouquet and the future author of *Fairy Tales*. Before winning
Colbert's approval, Perrault had to write a prose piece on the recent acquisition
of Dunkirk. It was a great success, and Charles was made clerk, then first clerk,
and then comptroller general of buildings (a position created especially for him).

[1]Quoted by Adolphe Chéruel in *Histoire de Nicolas Fouquet.*

[2]George Mongrédien, "La vie de société au[x] XVIIe et XVIIIe" (Paris, 1950).

He was Colbert's right-hand man where cultural affairs were concerned. It was a curious combination. A figure between "fabrication and myth,"[3] an ingratiating and wily political animal, Perrault enjoyed the full confidence of a brusque and realistic minister. He served Colbert loyally and faithfully for nearly twenty years.

Finally, Claude Perrault, the brother of Charles, became the minister's favorite architect and, in a way, his delegate within the scientific world.

TO THE KING'S GLORY

On February 3, 1663, Charles Perrault, Chapelain, Bourzéis, and Abbé Cassagne were puzzled to find themselves called to a meeting at Colbert's residence. The minister had called them together after having requested secrecy concerning what he was going to reveal to them. At that meeting, Colbert told them that they were to join with him in making up a small council to examine everything relating to architecture, "the life of the mind, and erudition." In fact, the king would define the precise responsibilities of that "little academy" (later the "Académie des inscriptions et belles-lettres") when he told its members: "I am entrusting to you the one thing in the world that is most precious, which is my glory." Twice a week, on Tuesdays and Fridays, the little academy met formally at Colbert's residence. Carefully, it designed or selected the emblems and legends that were to decorate tapestries and medals. The series of emblems that would go with the tapestries ordered by the king for his apartments at Versailles would be depicted, on Colbert's order, in a superb manuscript collection.[4] Later, Colbert would have the emblems published, accompanied by a prose commentary and a poem written by different members of the academy.

The council was greatly interested in the job of selecting designs and mottoes for the medals. The king was overjoyed to see the medal with the emblem of the sun and the motto *Nec pluribus impar*.

In 1663 the king was recovering from an illness. A chorus of praise was hastily organized to celebrate his convalescence. Before long, a veritable royal propaganda service was set up by Colbert and his collaborators. Charles Perrault recalled in his *Mémoires* that "When there was no commissioned work to be carried out, the academy labored to revise and correct works, either in prose or in verse, that had been written in praise of the king, to put them in shape to be printed at the press in the Louvre." Chapelain busied himself with finding "several trumpeters of the king's virtues." Colbert then suggested drawing up a list of French and foreign authors to whom the king would grant stipends in return for their

[3]Marc Soriano, *Le Dossier Perrault*.

[4]The miniaturist Jean Bailly would be responsible for the painting.

writings on the glory of his reign. Louis approved the enterprise and a list containing eighty-eight names. Mézeray, the official historiographer; Godefroy, who acquired books for the royal library (and for Colbert); and Chapelain received enormous grants of 3,000 to 4,000 livres a year. True, they were considered to be highly placed civil servants, and these amounts represented salaries as well as subsidies. Corneille received 2,000 livres. Initially, Perrault was granted 1,500, Molière, 1,000; and Racine (who was still quite young), 600. Chapelain had been perceptive enough to notice the latter: "In a few days," he wrote Colbert, "I shall have in hand an ode in French by a young man named Racine, which he has brought to me and is now polishing under my guidance." Understandably, La Fontaine's name is not on the list, because of his indestructible loyalty to Fouquet. At first, Boileau received 1,200 livres, but that grant was soon withdrawn— which is easily understood when we realize that the young writer had poked fun at Chapelain, whom he called "Pucelain" in his *Satires.* He later wrote a poem called "Chapelain decoiffé" ("Chapelain Hatless"). Such insolence seemed astounding. Several years later, after Chapelain's death, Boileau would share with Racine the title of king's historian and would receive 2,000 livres a year.

Colbert also summoned foreign authors. Often, they responded eagerly to the promises of the king of France. Thus it was that Carlo Dati of Florence proclaimed his acknowledgement to Chapelain, who had obtained his grant for him. But his words, "mixed with conceits and figures," irritated Chapelain: "Sir, it is in praise of heroes that one must spread the great sails of eloquence."[5] Dati followed Chapelain's specific recommendations, and he did not forget to write three letters of thanks: one to the king, another to Colbert, and a third to M. Besque, treasurer of buildings.

To Vossius, historian of the United Provinces in Windsor, Colbert wrote "Though the king is not your sovereign, he wishes to be your benefactor." Similar letters were sent to Antwerp, to Stockholm, to Strasbourg. Frenzied panegyrics began to be heard throughout Europe. Foreign princes grew disturbed and angry. The pope ordered Allatius to refuse the money sent him; the emperor made a higher bid by doubling the grant made to Boeklerus.

In France, the king's generosity created fierce jealousies. The trial of Fouquet and the prosecution of the tax contractors encouraged the secret circulation of virulent pamphlets against Colbert or the king's policy. Boileau's brother Gilles detested the minister and attacked him spiritedly. Colbert arranged to have "antipamphlets" written. In the Tuileries gardens, the pamphleteers gathered, exchanged information, and were on the lookout for indiscreet gossip that they would publish in their clandestine writings. La Reynie's policemen kept an eye on them and

[5]*Catalogue Charavay,* no. 750, September 1973.

sometimes succeed in arresting some imprudent ones, who soon found themselves in the Bastille.

Printing had not been an open trade since 1618, when it was decided to grant only one master's license per year. In 1663 Colbert ordered the printers of Paris to gather in the upper rue Saint-Jacques, so that he could keep a closer eye on them. The order was circumvented by the printers located in the city. In late 1666 the minister intensified the activity of the police, and he proposed a radical measure, the sharp reduction in the number of licensed printers, excluding "those who were not citizens of good character or were incompetent." From ninety-six, the number of licensed printers fell to an incredibly low thirty-six. But the proposal was very difficult to enforce. Colbert tried to obtain a complete list of the provincial presses; distances and customs often stood in his way. And before long, the large number of clandestine works coming from Holland became a serious problem for the royal government.

It seems that the minister was much more successful when he exerted himself to enrich France's artistic patrimony.[6]

THE ROYAL COLLECTIONS

Mazarin and Fouquet had been true connoisseurs, more "inquiring" than Colbert. He liked to surround himself with works of art, but, less sure of himself, he readily consulted experts, hesitating to spend large sums on rare paintings and furnishings. Nonetheless, in one area his great competence is indisputable: that of books. Colbert, a remarkable bibliophile in his own right, was already dreaming in Mazarin's time of the reorganization of the royal library, the *Librairie.* At his request, the cardinal had named his brother, Nicolas Colbert, custodian of the *Librairie,* and when Nicolas became bishop of Luçon in 1661, Colbert succeeded him. Two years later, he passed that office on to the learned Carcavi.

At that time the *Librairie* was consigned to a humble building in the rue de la Harpe and contained only 16,746 printed or manuscript volumes. Colbert would quadruple that number over the next twenty years, through legacies and purchases and also by means of the *dépôt legal* (a law requiring new works to be deposited into the royal collection for purposes of copyright), which still exists today. One of the minister's first concerns was finding a location worthy of the king's library. In 1666 he grandly installed the *Librairie* in two houses next to his own private residence in the rue Vivienne.

[6]One cannot recommend too highly the remarkable catalogue of the exhibition *Collections of Louis XIV,* which was held at the Orangerie in 1977.

The collection of the comte de Béthune (1,923 volumes of manuscript documents and letters) soon joined the Brienne collection of manuscripts, which the library had bought in 1662, thanks to Colbert. The minister sent agents and scholars throughout the kingdom, to try to acquire—or, failing that, to copy—records, archives, all manuscripts "of use to history." The resulting collections still represent a very important part of the wealth of the manuscript department at the Bibliothèque nationale today.

Colbert was especially interested in the purchase of books and manuscripts from the Orient. His activities in that regard would enrich the library in an exceptional way. The major acquisitions began in 1667. In that year, Fouquet's marvelous Oriental collection (including an illuminated Koran and splendid Persian manuscripts) went to the rue Vivienne. In the same year, the minister bought on the king's behalf the remarkable collection of the senior *maître des requêtes*, Gilbert Gaulmin: 246 Arabic, 214 Turkish or Persian, and 127 Hebrew manuscripts.

The following year, a fruitful exchange for the king was arranged between the *Librairie* and the Collège des Quarte-Nations, which had inherited Mazarin's collection. Thus, the royal library received several hundred priceless Oriental treasures, including a famous Hebrew Bible and the magnificent Coptic Gospels in the Mesopotamian style. At Colbert's request, experts and scholars began a systematic search for rare manuscripts in the countries of the Near East. The best known was the German Vansleb, who combed Egypt, Turkey, and even Ethiopia. Ambassadors and consuls were also involved in these efforts.

Hundreds, even thousands, of masterpieces, Hebrew, Syriac (including 650 volumes brought back by Vansleb), Persian, Turkish, Greek, Coptic, found a place in the king's library—and, not incidentally, in Colbert's own, "the Colbertine,"[7] admired and celebrated throughout Europe. Upon their arrival in France, the precious volumes were carefully sifted by the minister's librarian, Etienne Baluze. Some needed to be bound. Colbert had the finest morocco leather bought in the Levant.

It was Colbert who decided to create the cabinet of medals and to make it an annex of the royal library. Thanks to his efforts, the king's collection was enlarged with many rare pieces, sometimes bought at high prices in Europe as well as in the Orient. Located first in the Louvre, that royal collection would later be moved to the rue Vivienne.

In 1667, during an illness that confined him to his room, the king looked through two volumes from the great collection of engravings belonging to Abbé

[7]The Colbertine would be purchased by Louis XV and serves as a remarkable foundation for today's Bibliothèque nationale.

Marolles. The abbé wanted to sell the complete collection of 120,000 engravings. Upon the favorable recommendation of the "little academy," Louis bought it at a ridiculously low price, thanks to the abbé's unworldly nature. The cabinet of prints was born. Colbert made it part of the royal library so that it could be available to artists and the public. Like the library, it was enriched by gifts, purchases, and the *dépôt legal*.

Engravings seemed to both king and minister an excellent way to make a wide audience aware of the successes and grandeurs of the reign. Engravings showing battles, captured cities, festivals, and scientific discoveries were made under the direction of Van der Meulen, Israel Silvestre, and others. In 1670 it occurred to Colbert to have these prints bound into volumes. The collection was called the *Cabinet du Roi*. On February 22 of that year, he described the project:

> The size of everything we engrave in the future must be reduced, whether the subject be animals subjected to dissection and anatomical study, plants ditto [*sic*], antique medals from the *Cabinet du Roi*, mottoes and medals for the king, busts and statues of His Majesty, paintings, carrousels, tapestries, royal residences, and, in general, everything else of the same sort. We must, I say, reduce them all to a format such that they can be made up into volumes of equal size so that at the end of each year we can make up volumes of everything that has been done in all sorts of endeavors.[8]

All these engravings and plates were part of the cabinet of prints at the rue Vivienne. Later, under the Empire, the 956 plates of the *Cabinet du Roi* were taken to the Louvre and became the original nucleus for the present-day Chalcographie nationale.[9]

Colbert noted the great artistic wealth amassed by the tax farmers with a great deal of irritation: "buildings, furnishings, silver work, and other ornaments were only for financiers, for which they pay enormous sums." The king ought to have the finest collection of furnishings, paintings, and objects d'art in the kingdom. To achieve that goal, Colbert pursued a dual policy: On the one hand, he was always on the lookout for any chance to make a purchase, in France or elsewhere; on the other, he organized and encouraged royal factories and workshops under the strict and privileged supervision of the state.

Two months after Fouquet's arrest, Colbert had already resumed contact with Mazarin's Italian agents. He begged Abbé Strozzi in Florence to buy cabinets and tables "luxurious enough and well enough made to serve a prince as great as our king." The quality of the materials should be almost perfect: The abbé should

[8]*Catalogue Charavay,* no. 750, September 1973.

[9]These plates are still being used for printing and engraving.

send nothing at all rather than sending anything "common or mediocre." At one point, Strozzi was warned that the lapis lazuli he had sent was not blue enough and had too many white veins. Colbert was the first to think of importing Tuscan alabaster. The king, who liked rare stones, seemed quite pleased. Travelers and diplomats were transformed into procurers of objects and paintings. The high prices often alarmed the minister. True, it seemed difficult to be superintendant of buildings and chief financial officer at the same time. Despite his caution when making purchases, however, Colbert increased the royal collections spectacularly. In 1661 Louis had fewer than 200 paintings; at Colbert's death he had 2,500. Many of the paintings of the Italian masters that adorn the galleries of today's Louvre were acquired by Colbert. Rare fabrics, statues, and vases came to Paris, where he examined, inspected, and assessed their quality conscientiously.

One of his best counselors where paintings and drawings were concerned was the rich Jabach, a German banker who had taken French citizenship and who owned a fabulous collection himself. From time to time he agreed to cede one of his masterpieces to the king—for example, Titian's *Woman at Her Toilette* and Leonardo's *Saint John the Baptist.* Whenever a collection of drawings was offered to Colbert, Jabach was summoned to his residence to authenticate each one. In late 1670, Jabach experienced extreme financial difficulties. Colbert saw the long-awaited opportunity to get his hands on the banker's treasures. Negotiations were conducted ruthlessly by Perrault and the minister. On March 11, 1671, Jabach transferred 101 paintings and 5,542 drawings of the highest quality to the king for the very low price of 220,000 livres. That exceptional group went to the Louvre and represented by far the most important purchase Colbert made for the king.

In 1664, to satisfy the king's weighty commands, the minister reorganized the old tapestry works known as the Gobelin and the Savonnerie, and made them royal factories. Le Brun was named director of the Gobelin, where not only tapestries but also furniture, cabinets, locks, and silver objects were made. The sculptors Caffieri, Coysevox, and Tuby, cabinetmakers, draftsmen, printers, and many others worked under Lebrun's authoritarian direction. The Gobelin employed up to 700 skilled craftsmen who worked only for the king. The weavers were Flemish for the most part, and the marble cutters, Italian. If they wished, they could live on the premises. The Savonnerie produced its wonderful rugs, which are well known. As both factories were under direct state control, they were not subject to guild regulations.

Little by little, Colbert improved the workshops at the Louvre that had been organized by Henri IV. The old palace became a veritable city of art. Tapestry workers, goldsmiths, painters, chasers of medals, and engravers worked there and lived on the ground floor with their families. The great cabinetmaker Boulle had an apartment decorated with valuable art works, two workshops where he employed twenty-six workers, and storage spaces. Colbert also set up the royal printshop (later to be the national printing office) in the Louvre. The minister repaired and enlarged that state institution, which did not intend to compete in any way with private printers; it even lent them the matrices of its Greek and oriental characters. Political, scientific, and historical works were printed there at government expense.

Outside the royal factories and workshops, so carefully organized and firmly administered, French artists carried out important royal commissions. Colbert's impetus in this regard is beyond doubt. For example, in 1660 Gaston d'Orléans bequeathed to his nephew the king his marvelous collection of paintings on vellum. We should remember that this was the supple, white, and very fine parchment that was particularly favored by painters whose subject was natural history. Over the years, Nicolas Robert had painted flowers and animals for Louis's uncle. Colbert found the collection infinitely attractive and wished to have the work continued. He commissioned Robert to create around eighty vellum paintings per year for the king. The models (plants and birds) came from the royal botanical garden and the menagerie at Versailles. Colbert's admiration for these paintings may have been tinged with envy; he had the delicate paintings copied for his own library by three students of Robert.[10]

The minister saw drawing as something more than ornamental: The artist should bear witness to an entire civilization. This may be the most vast expression of Colbert's policies. Under his influence, astronomical discoveries, industrial machinery, buildings, battles, and royal festivals were drawn by the greatest artists of the time so that posterity might remember the age of Louis XIV.

THE AGE OF LOUIS XIV

The king looked at, admired, and enjoyed his collections. Without Colbert, would he have given them such scope and universality? Nothing could be less certain. Mazarin had given his agent precise orders concerning the purchase of works of art, and Colbert learned and executed. After Mazarin's death, his initiative in artistic matters was immense.

On the other hand, Louis protected writers such as Racine and Molière with remarkable discernment. He had a sort of instinctive talent for spectacle, decor, and ornamentation. He personally reviewed all architectural designs (especially those for Versailles); he worked directly with Le Nôtre on plans for the gardens and on the choice of flowers (to such an extent that Le Nôtre once spontaneously

[10]Colbert's copies were sold in 1728 to Prince Eugene of Savoy and are now in the National Library of Vienna.

embraced Louis in front of the astonished courtiers); and he devised fascinating entertainments for the court. Colbert's role in this regard was purely administrative.

The minister liked to surround himself with writers during his rare periods of leisure. For their part, the authors flattered him and wrote admiring odes in his honor when the occasion presented itself. Admittedly, their motives were not always unselfish. Fouquet and the tax farmers had proven generous toward them. The chamber of justice, by attacking so many private fortunes, had undeniably played a part in drying up a source of favors for men of letters. The allowances and gratuities proposed by the king and his minister had come at an appropriate time.

By 1663 Molière was already famous, and it should be emphasized that to a great extent his reputation was the king's doing. Colbert summoned him and his troupe to his residence for a performance of *The School for Wives*, for which the minister paid Molière 220 livres. When the *cabale des dévots** had Molière's *Tartuffe* temporarily banned from production (between 1667 and 1669), Colbert, as well as the king, spoke on Molière's behalf in opposition to Lamoignon. In 1669 Molière wanted Mignard, who had always taken a back seat to the irascible and all-powerful Le Brun, to complete the fresco in the Val-de-Grace. The comedian pleaded for his friend in an ode intended for the minister, but to no avail.

> *Persevere, O great Colbert, to desire in France*
> *To establish in the arts o'er which you rule, excellence.*
> *You owe the universe these hands, worn and skillful,*
> *Knowing hands of which the age is ne'er prodigal.*
> *It is your ministry to go out and find them*
> *To employ them in tasks that only you determine.*
> *And to choose for assignment each one's proper task;*
> *For your own greater glory you must not delay;*
> *It is known that great men, Colbert, make bad courtiers.*

Some say Colbert was the model for the character Harpagon in Molière's *Miser*. Others claim that the minister—wishing to make fun of an insufferable Turkish envoy—had asked Molière to create the Mamomouchi interlude in *The Would-Be Gentleman*. There is no evidence either way. The relationship between the two seems, in fact, to have been sufficiently good and sufficiently neutral.

Racine, on the other hand, would always show a real liking for Colbert. His play *Bérénice* would be dedicated to him and *Brittanicus* to the duc de Chevreuse,

---

*The *cabal des dévots* were a group of Catholics with a reputation for great piety. They often promoted religious and nonreligious causes of interest to them.

the minister's son-in-law. In his dedication to Colbert, Racine wrote: "My lord, in the midst of so many important tasks to which your devotion to our prince and to the common welfare continually bind you, you do not disdain to lower yourself betimes to our level, to ask us how we have employed our leisure."

Everything was done in the name of the king, and the king, moreover, assumed responsibility for all that took place. But perhaps Louis imagined a patronage that was more personal and more individualized than the sort of patronage envisaged by Colbert. The minister thought all the artistic and intellectual undertakings of the reign should be orchestrated in a methodical, grand, and official fashion by the academy concerned. That was Colbert's style: The patron or the instigator was no longer the king alone, but the state acting in the king's name.

The Académie française had been founded by Richelieu in 1635. *Le grand cardinal* had ordered it to "purify the language and to determine correct usage." We should remember that at that time all higher education was carried out in Latin under the direction of the church. Marc Soriano has correctly emphasized the political implications of the task entrusted to the academicians. The political and administrative unification of France would be greatly facilitated by the use of a single, clear, and rationalized national language throughout the kingdom. The centralizers of Revolutionary times would share that attitude. The writing of a dictionary and a grammar thus became almost a political act. Colbert became impatient. Work on the dictionary was taking too long.[11] The minister devised a system of tokens intended "to inspire the academicians to be more assiduous in their attendance at the meetings."

Until 1672 the Académie française met at the home of its protector, Chancellor Séguier. Colbert was admitted to the académie on April 21, 1667. The duc de Saint-Aignan called for him at his house and accompanied him to Séguier's. The *Gazette de France* wrote that "after having been admitted with the usual ceremonies," the minister "made a speech in praise of the king, with such grace and success that all the learned company was filled with admiration."

There are several anecdotes concerning Colbert's presence in the académie. Hearing himself addressed as "Monseigneur," Colbert insisted that in the future he be called simply "Monsieur," since he came as a colleague. It seems to have been from that day that the custom originated of addressing new members as Monsieur no matter what their titles or position. And why is a membership in the académie known as a *fauteuil,* or an "armchair"? Because the minister, wanting

[11]The dictionary would not be published until 1694, eleven years after Colbert's death.

to sit down, saw in the midst of many chairs an armchair in which an elderly man was seated. Out of concern for equality, Colbert had thirty-nine other armchairs installed.

In fact, Colbert, overwhelmed with work, attended few meetings. How was he to keep an eye on the illustrious company? Charles Perrault could do so, but he was not an academician. With the greatest casualness, Colbert ordered him to become a member. "The king is very fond of that society, and as my concerns prevent me from attending as often as I would like, I would be very happy to be kept informed, through your agency, of all that happens there. Ask for the first vacant seat."[12] The académie, its back up, did not immediately accept this compulsory candidacy. But Perrault was nonetheless elected in 1671, and his suggestions were accepted docilely by the members, who were not deceived concerning his true mission.

In 1672, Séguier died. Louis became the académie's patron and Colbert its vice-patron. Where would its meetings now be held? Colbert wrote to the king: "There is only the Louvre or Your Majesty's library. The Louvre is more dignified and more troublesome; the library would be less dignified until it is attached to the Louvre, and more comfortable." The king replied, "The académie should meet at the Louvre; that seems more appropriate, though a little uncomfortable."

It was in Mazarin's day, in 1648, that the Royal Academy of Painting and Sculpture was founded in opposition to the claims of the guild of "masters of the arts of painting." The latter had wanted, in effect, to ban those who were not members of their group. Many painters and sculptors, especially those working for the king, begged the cardinal to create an academy that would distinguish them from "those daubers, marble masons, and marble polishers." In 1656, letters patent granted the royal academy a monopoly on the teaching of drawing. The guild painters resisted. Each group wanted to apply the law "each in his own favor." Le Brun was named director for life, the curriculum of the academicians was fixed, the monopoly on teaching was solidly confirmed, and the lesson plan was drawn up by Colbert himself. In 1664 the parlement registered the letters patent despite the outcry from the guild painters forced to comply. The academy was installed in the Louvre, and before long almost every painter of talent was admitted. We should, however, mention the independent stance of Puget in Marseilles, who remained faithful to the baroque style. And Mignard had a long wait until Le Brun died and he could become an academician and King's First Painter.

Instruction in the academy was principally in life drawing; the students also learned geometry, perspective, and anatomy. Historical painting was the most

[12]Soriano, *Le Dossier Perrault.*

] 124 [

highly esteemed. Le Brun organized lectures in which the composition of heroic themes, religious and ancient stories, and mythology were studied. All official art is despotic. But on the other hand, the statutes of the academy were broad enough to allow all sorts of talents to participate. No painters were censured. Three women miniaturists, Madeleine and Geneviève de Boullongne and Sophie Chéron, were members.

Colbert sometimes lost his temper: The students were left to themselves; the models lacked discipline. He did not hesitate, when necessary, to intervene in the discussions of the academicians. The rule was simple: It was necessary to return to the worship of antiquity and to nature. Hence it seemed logical to extend the academy's schooling to Italian soil. The French Academy in Rome was founded in 1666. Twelve scholarship students were received there every year. Subject to mercilessly strict rules of conduct, the students were expected to copy ancient sculptures and Renaissance paintings. The best student each year was given a prize on Saint Louis's day. Bernini was supposed to advise the young Frenchmen; he did so rarely. The director was to assert his authority; the first, Errard, had none to show. Colbert plied him with recommendations, exhorted him to severity, waxed indignant at the poor behavior of some students, who went out at night, got into fights, and so on.

The results from that academy were often very disappointing. Nonetheless, after having proved themselves, the students were assured of finding work, upon their return to Paris, in the royal workshops or building sites. In the artistic realm as in commerce and industry, Colbert stood for full employment as a political commitment. It was rare at that time for an artist of even the slightest talent or skill not to receive employment from the state. The most qualified, as we have seen, might even be housed at government expense.

In 1671 the minister created an academy devoted especially to architecture. That group completed or extended the council for buildings. Its most useful role was its involvement in the preservation of "ancient churches and buildings." The creation of the Academy of Music was the work of the king. Louis XIV had a great passion for music and the dance. He recognized very early the great talent of the young Italian Lully. Colbert would have preferred to give the responsibility for musical affairs to Perrin, who already held the privilege of establishing "academies of opera," but he had to accede to the king's will. Lully bought Perrin's privilege from him and in 1672 founded the Academy of Music in Paris by order of the king.

Louis wanted to take personal charge of everything having to do with entertainment. On the other hand, he gave over to Colbert the control of an area that interested and even fascinated the minister: that of the sciences.

THE STUDY OF THE UNIVERSE

"From the point of view of mental representation, the modern world begins in the seventeenth century," Bertrand Russell has written.[13] People became aware of the immensity of the universe, as well as of the variety of religious beliefs. It is significant that men of science in Colbert's time were involved generally in all those disciplines that seek to disclose the mysteries of creation: philosophy, mathematics, astronomy, and physics. The church did not allow philosophical doubt, and even less the concept of a universe whose center was not the earth. Remember that Galileo was forced to renounce his theories in 1633 to avoid the stake. That scientist died in 1642, when Colbert was already twenty-three.

Still very close to the Middle Ages and Thomist postulates, the age of Louis XIV at the same time heralded the eighteenth century. The disparity of these influences can be seen in the contentions with royal policy: Science was encouraged, and a watchful eye was kept on philosophy.

The king shared the age's interest in rare animals and plants. The menagerie at Versailles welcomed exotic animals. Colbert carefully advised Charles Perrault to be careful of the "live crocodile" that had come in from Guinea and had his agents search the islands of America for the green shrubs or the extraordinary flowers that his master loved so much. There is no doubt that the king supported Colbert in scientific policy.

But let the scientists beware of departing from the views of orthodox religion! When Descartes's remains were brought from Stockholm, Louis forebade all funeral eulogies, just as he would ban the teaching of Cartesian philosophy in the university.

Did Colbert have a broader outlook? The truth is that theological quarrels were of absolutely no interest to him. To all appearances, the man was a believer, but without a trace of mysticism. In his view, the church mattered only to the extent that it aided or hindered the state. He wished to replace with state control the church's monopoly on higher education. The churchmen's way of teaching seemed to him incompatible with modern discoveries and poorly prepared the students for public service. But it was hard to weaken so powerful and well established a fortress.

At first Colbert dreamed of a general academy somewhat like the modern-day Institut de France, which would be divided into four sections: literature, history, philosophy, and mathematics. He was able to carry out his plan only in part. In 1666 he founded the Academy of Sciences, which met at first in his own library, then later in that of the king, on rue Vivienne. He gave this new organization the task of studying mathematics, astronomy, botany, anatomy, and

---

[13]Quoted by Maurice Ashley in *Le Grand Siècle*.

chemistry. These sciences were separated from all other disciplines; and the academy promised not to discuss theology or politics, and especially not astrology or the philosopher's stone. The academy would have twenty-one members, including foreigners—to whom Colbert offered lucrative sums as inducements to come to France.

Among the French members, Claude Perrault, an excellent organizer (to the minister's delight), proposed a plan for the study of plant physics and especially of comparative anatomy, his personal passion. Mariotte was to produce a remarkable study of the changes in a gas according to the pressures to which it is subjected.

Three famous foreigners joined French scientists: the Dane Roemer; the Dutchman Huyghens; and the Italian Cassini. Huyghens had been the first to discover a satellite of Saturn and to use the pendulum in clocks, according to the theories of Galileo. Colbert invited him to live in France, where the enormous benefits he received convinced him to stay: In addition to a stipend of 6,000 livres, the scholar was given lodgings at the Louvre. Cassini was highly regarded in Bologna, where he had recomputed the longitude of the church of San Petrone. This great astronomer had discovered the orbitational periods of Jupiter and Mars. Colbert negotiated at length with the city of Bologna, which agreed to part with Cassini for several years. But the exorbitant salary Colbert granted him (9,000 livres!) was so attractive that Cassini ultimately requested French citizenship.

Nothing was too good or too expensive if it would help the scientists in their research. Colbert procured laboratories and advanced instruments. An astronomical observatory was a prime requirement. Where should it be built? It was originally to have been placed on Montmartre, because of the height, but the smoke of Paris hindered observations to the south. It was finally located at the far end of the Faubourg Saint-Jacques, where, besides the good visibility, the abandoned quarries could be used for experiments in mathematics and physics. Colbert entrusted the plans to Claude Perrault. Work was begun in 1667 and was finished in 1672. Cassini had moved in by 1671. When necessary, scientific expeditions as far as Guyana were arranged to verify the accuracy of that scientist's calculations. All of these scientific endeavors were written up in the excellent *Journal des savants,* which was being published again under Colbert's protection after having experienced some disagreements with Rome and the Jesuits when it first appeared.[14]

Very interested in the early developments in machinery, which had the potential to transform industry, Colbert established a Conservatory of Machines, Arts, and Trades under the direction of the engineer Antoine Niquet and attached

[14]Rather literary in its outlook when it first appeared in 1665, the *Journal des savants* had spoken well of a Gallican work. Publication had been suspended, then it reappeared thanks to Colbert.

to the Academy of Sciences. Engravings depicting the conservatory's new machines in detail were used by Diderot in his *Encyclopedia* a century later.

Remarkable work was being done in France in this area: We should briefly mention that of La Hire and Varignon on applied mechanics, that of Azout and Picard on measures and levelings, and that of Mariotte on pneumatics and hydraulics.

In 1673 it was Colbert also who asked Huyghens to take on as a student a protégé of his, the famous Denis Papin. The young man would invent a steam engine that could power a boat, and he carried out joint experiments with his Dutch master on the coefficient of expansion of gunpowder, which led to the 1691 discovery of the "fire machine."

In 1671 Colbert took over the administration of the botanical garden himself. Founded by Louis XII, the garden was simultaneously a school of botany and of medicine. Its superintendant had full latitude in the choice of lecturers and gardeners. This had led to abuses, and Colbert therefore decided to reorganize the garden under his personal supervision. It was later reported that during a visit Colbert noticed that an area intended for botanical cultivation had been planted instead as a private vineyard for the administrators. In a wild rage, he ordered the immediate destruction of the vines and took a pick axe in hand to start the uprooting himself. The English botanist Salisbury witnessed the scene, and this vigorous action so impressed him that he named one of the plants in his catalogue the Colbertia.

Colbert's productivity in what we would call "cultural affairs" was as remarkable as it was astonishing. Nonetheless, his actions leave us with a somewhat disconcerting sense of contradiction. Isn't this contradiction inherent in the age? Colbert seems to have been simultaneously a pessimist and an optimist. As Maurice Ashley has written, classical art is pessimistic. The canons of beauty were fixed once and for all. Could not imagination, then, displace perfection? The conception of a world rooted in a dogmatic and necessary hierarchy paralyzed any idea of progress. And yet Colbert believed as wholeheartedly in scientific progress as in the progress of justice and the steady improvement of the material condition for the greatest number. His passionate willfulness was also a form of optimism.

This duality of feeling recurs exactly in his economic activity. He believed in technological progress, and in the industrial techniques conceived by the scientists. Yet his economic theories were marked by a fundamental pessimism that led inevitably to economic warfare.

PART III

THE ECONOMIC WAR [1661–72]

CHAPTER 11

Mercantilism and War

WE ALL KNOW THAT RICHELIEU had dreamed of a grand economic design for France. But the endless struggle against the power of the Hapsburgs and the detestable financial system prevented him from creating "an affluent state." During a twelve-year period of relative peace and financial reorganization (1661–72), Colbert would attempt to apply the broad outlines of Richelieu's famous testament.

There is no worse misnomer than "Colbertism," if by that term we mean to designate an economic theory. Colbert's economic ideas were those of his age, and essentially those of Europe. This type of economic ideology, which was imposed with the force of dogma upon the contemporaries of the minister, would be called "the mercantile system," or "mercantilism," by the physiocrats of the following century. Eighteenth-century economists considered their predecessors to have ascribed too important a role to commerce. The mercantilist ideal, originating in England in the mid-sixteenth century, held that the state should be a seller rather than a buyer. Thus, one increased the stock of precious metals, the most obvious index at that time of a nation's power. Let us remember the incredible anarchy of the times. How could the foreign commercial debts be paid except through the use of an international currency, i.e., gold? If a gold drain provoked an increase in foreign exchange rates, however, one might be unable to obtain credit or indispensable goods.

On the other hand, the balance of payments would, of course, remain favorable as long as raw materials were imported (though as little as possible) and manufactured goods exported in return. Thus, industry came to be seen as inseparable from commerce, especially since (as Henri Hauser has explained) it was through commerce that the initial capital was amassed that would then be used in manufacturing.

Sixteenth-century England was the first to use "Colbertism," without Colbert. To encourage the creation of industries and to increase the supply of metallic currency, foreign manufactured goods had to be taxed or their entry prohibited, while national products were allowed free export. In complementary fashion, foreign raw materials were allowed free entry, and the export of the nation's raw materials was forbidden. In short, this was an economic protectionism that seems quite commonplace to us today.

Industry had a further advantage: that of suppressing the "idleness" of the people. All European governments shared Colbert's concern for full employment. As early as the sixteenth century, one discerns an inclination toward centralized planning that could, if necessary, lead to the nationalization of industries in order to ensure employment for the citizenry and to guarantee national independence. We must not forget that the advent of mercantilism was contemporaneous with the birth of the concept of nationalism. Mercantilism thus became a patriotic act, or even a system of power.

A state affirms its power "against" other national powers. This aggressive competition, a necessary implication of mercantilist theory, was to grow notoriously worse during the sixteenth century.

The great influx of American metals during the sixteenth century had given considerable impetus to domestic commerce. People were buying, selling, and producing more. After about 1620, however, the rate of production of precious metals decreased, or at best remained stationary, whereas economic needs had greatly increased. Undeniably, seventeenth-century Europe suffered a veritable monetary famine. In certain countries (especially England and France) the government completed mercantilist protectionism with what is called "bullionism"—a doctrine that consisted of preventing the export of precious metals—especially since a shortage of metallic currency could lead to a decline in prices that was unfavorable for trade.

Such monetary restriction encouraged the economic pessimism that characterized the period, a pessimism that was directly rooted in the religious and philosophical thought of the century. As Henri Hauser has so rightly put it, "There is no such thing as economic history, only economic aspects of human history." The influence of Thomism remained quite strong and reinforced a sort of instinctive and tenacious belief that money could not be productive. The notion of an economic stability that excluded all possibility of expansion came into being quite naturally. Consequently, if there was only a fixed stock of precious metals available in Europe, only a determinate quantity of a particular raw material on the market, and only very limited possibilities for increasing the volume of trade, then it was to each nation's advantage to obtain for itself a greater quantity of metallic currency at the expense of other nations, a monopoly in some raw material, or exclusive rights to some market. In other words, every action, every economic deed of that period, should be considered in the context of economic warfare.

Nevertheless, the considerable expansion of commercial activity and the recent great geographic discoveries should have obviously contradicted such a static and submissive concept of the economic universe; but attitudes ignore facts, whatever the age.

It is true that if we consider twentieth-century trade and that practiced in mercantilist times, we observe enormous differences in volume and mass. A German economist has equated the total volume of commerce for one German port over several years at the beginning of the sixteenth century with the cargo of a single transatlantic freighter today. The dangers of the sea, the main commercial route, were immense. They were risked only for rare commodities, which helps to explain the importance of a monopoly.

Colbert's contemporaries could scarcely conceive of the possibility of extending trade outlets indefinitely. For centuries, production had been determined by the existing market, even though much later everything would be overproduced in order to create new demands for disposing of an ever-increasing stock of products. Because the market governed production rather than the other way around, a somewhat naive notion became accepted, that the more a nation produced, the less the other nations could hope to produce: A market's capacity for absorption was filled by the nation that produced the greatest amount.

Another manifestation of this economic pessimism was a belief in the advantages of regulation, which only served to prolong the medieval tradition.[1] Nature is evil; man is irrevocably marked by original sin. The need for a benevolent tutelary authority seemed obvious. The strict discipline imposed in the workplace by guild regulations shocked almost no one.

Mercantilism presupposes a full diplomatic context for state planning. Full-scale economic war could only lead logically to military warfare. The three great rival economic powers in Colbert's time were France, England, and Holland. All three understood the link between political power and commercial success. Nonetheless, all three differed in the exact relationships they established between the state and commerce.

MERCANTILISM FRENCH STYLE

Following the lead of Elizabethan England, France under Henri IV adopted the mercantilist doctrine. For some time the French commercial class in its formal grievances had been calling for the imposition of economic protectionism. It was a Protestant businessman, Barthélemy de Laffemas, an autodidact with a practical turn of mind, who convinced the king to protect the French economy and employment through the creation of industries and the reorganization of guild regulations. Named comptroller general of commerce in 1600, Laffemas practiced mercantilism in a manner both pragmatic and exaggerated. His mania for surveys, his ferocious xenophobia, his anger at the free-exchange liberalism of the city of Lyons, his ambitious industrial policy—all were to influence Colbert considerably.

At the time Richelieu began to govern France, Europe was feeling the first effects of a restricted money supply. It appeared urgent that a vigorous export policy be undertaken to bring in metallic currency. A protectionist, but less autarkic and aggressive than either Laffemas or Colbert, le grand cardinal, a man with a superior and lucid mind, foresaw the possibilities for the expansion of future commerce over a wide range. Colonial maritime enterprises were actively encouraged.

It was generally acknowledged that only luxury items or goods of superior quality, made to well-established standards, could be readily exported. Inspection of manufactured goods was carried out with formidable rigor by officials of a central administration strengthened by Richelieu. The Code Michaud (1629) specified the permissible dimensions for all silk, wool, or cotton, a measure intended

[1]Eli Heckscher has written in *Mercantilism* that Colbert applied medieval economic principles on a large scale.

to preserve the Spanish market. Manufacturers guilty of repeated violations were threatened with fines or confiscation of their goods. Inspectors checked the cloth produced in each city, even in each borough.

The tyranny of the inspectors sometimes caused serious riots. In 1640 the craftsmen of Poitiers revolted with cries of "Long live the King and public freedom!"

The production of luxury goods was taken over by the state. Laffemas encouraged the production of Gobelin tapestries, crystalware, and silk goods; Richelieu protected the Savonnerie and the Venetian mirrors manufactured in Paris and Picardy.

From the beginning, mercantilism in France was employed at the government's initiative rather than that of a social class. The whole nation—not just a merchant oligarchy—was expected to profit from a policy desired and run by the government. That was also how Colbert saw things. His concept of mercantilism was the narrowest, the toughest, the most bellicose—and also the most pessimistic. He held as an absolute principle the idea that economic expansion was impossible. To give only one example, he thought that only a fixed and specific number of vessels could carry on the worldwide sea trade. Consequently, an increase in France's merchant fleet would develop at the expense of those other nations.

In general, any national economic progress had to impede the economic power of other countries. One would think it was cause and effect. The theory of a single monetary pie for all of Europe that Colbert propounded to the king was tantamount to a declaration of war. Colbert explained to the king that it was a matter of "increasing the money in public circulation by attracting it from the countries whence it comes; keeping it within the kingdom and preventing it from leaving; and giving people means to make a profit from it." After this bullionist credo, the minister added:

In these three points consist the greatness and power of the state and the magnificence of the king owing to the expenditures that large revenues permit, and this magnificence is all the greater because it simultaneously abases all the neighboring states; since there is only a fixed quantity of money in circulation throughout Europe, augmented from time to time by what comes in from the West Indies, it is certain and demonstrable that if there are only 150 million livres in public circulation in France, one cannot manage to increase that amount by 20, 30, or 50 millions without simultaneously taking the same amount away from neighboring states—a fact that caused the double elevation that has increased so appreciably for several years: on the one hand, increasing the power and the greatness of Your Majesty and, on the other, reducing that of Your enemies and of those who envy You.[2]

[2]Memorandum to the king concerning finances, about 1670.

It was not the first time Colbert had tried to convince the king that economic power should be sought as eagerly as territorial power. Economic warfare was equivalent to military warfare. It is not certain that Louis believed him entirely. Nonetheless, Colbert agreed with the king and even with Louvois on one essential point: A country's power is measured by the number of its troops and its logistical strength. Stalin's famous question, How many divisions?" seems a distant echo of the preoccupation of Louis and all of his ministers, without exception.

An abundance of metallic currency was above all a means to a political end, the grandeur of the state: "An abundance of money alone makes the difference between grandeur and power." A significant increase in the money supply could only be had "by trade alone, and all that depends on it." But there should be no mistake about the ultimate goal of all this economic activity: "Commerce is the wellspring of finance, and finance is the sinew of war."[3]

Colbert did not disagree with Louvois for wanting to create a very strong army. He regretted that his younger colleague too quickly diverted large sums for the needs of war that were also indispensable for setting up industries where practically none existed, for improving a deplorable network of roads and water-ways, or for creating a real merchant navy. The dispute was primarily over the order of priorities.

Colbert carried all the consequences of mercantilist doctrine to the extreme. Only in this regard may we speak of "Colbertism." Protectionism became more and more intransigent. The regulations on goods for export were draconian; but the absolute necessity for a favorable balance of trade obliged them to satisfy the tastes of foreign consumers.

As in the days of Laffemas and Richelieu, the state took direct control of an economy whose production, in the final analysis, served the state itself. Never had an economic system been applied with such energy and rigor throughout an entire kingdom. Nowhere else but in France had mercantilism been so clearly a factor in national unification. No other government in Europe had sustained so great and continuus an effort to subsidize and promote the national economy. Undoubtedly, Richelieu had foreseen a more flexible and a broader economic universe than that foreseen by Colbert. But no one in France before Colbert had truly understood the obvious and necessary relationship between financial order and the possibilities for economic investments.

Another peculiarity of French mercantilism, then, was that the system was desired and put into practice by one man alone, or nearly alone. The odious institution of the *paulette* (the yearly fee paid by an official to assure for his descendants the office he had purchased) had diverted the French bourgeoisie from

---

[3]Colbert to his cousin Colbert du Terron.

capitalistic ventures. The honors of a safe and comfortable government post were preferred to the risks of commerce or industry.

Colbert tried unceasingly to win over the French, and above all Louis XIV. As was his custom, the minister proposed a precise and detailed plan to the king at great length. Its tone was very sure, very affirmative, one might almost say professorial. The sovereign had to be swayed, for his backing was indispensable for giving a major impetus to the economic movement. That also seems to have been peculiar to France. The royal charisma was needed to encourage the initiatives and efforts toward an economic grand design that was rather poorly understood by most of the people. The king's will must be made known everywhere. Only rarely did an order from Colbert or one of his subordinates not begin with the words "His Majesty wishes that," or "The king has ordered me to tell you that." How different the relationship was between the king of England and the merchant and industrial class in his country.

The Merchants of England

Indisputably, the inventors of mercantilism were English statesmen such as Burghley, Lord Treasurer to Queen Elizabeth. Economic protectionism, industrial policy, increased employment: All the major tenets of "Colbertism" had already been very clearly expressed in England nearly a century earlier. But the application of these common theories was quite different on each side of the Channel. The feudal hierarchy in Britain had never been as rigid and compartmentalized as that on the Continent. Commercial activity did not lead to a loss of status for the English nobility. The king and the government had difficulty controlling a merchant and industrial class that encompassed a wider social range and was much more independent than that of France.

Queen Elizabeth I had as her successor the son of her enemy, the Catholic Mary Stuart, Queen of Scots. James I and then his son, Charles I, were Anglicans but were very impressed by the great Catholic monarchies on the Continent. They tried by their authority to introduce in England the principles of kingship by divine right, dominating all the powers of the state and protecting art and literature by means of its prestige.

Charles I, husband of Henrietta of France, who was the sister of Louis XIII, refused to persecute Catholics and governed as an absolute monarch, without convening Parliament. Furthermore, he extended his political authority to the economic life of the kingdom. Only a small number of courtiers were granted charters for large trading companies or industrial monopolies. Like Richelieu and Colbert, the Stuarts strengthened the regulations governing the manufacture of products to be exported. A vast majority of the merchant and industrial class proclaimed that "liberty is the soul of commerce," and sanctioned the insurrection led by Oliver Cromwell and his army of Puritans. Charles I was executed in 1649, while Mazarin was governing France.

We should not forget that the advent of Cromwell owed a great deal to the hostility felt throughout commercial circles toward French-style mercantilism. Cromwell broke up what was left of an administrative system copied from the central administrations of Continental nations, and initiated internal economic freedom, while pursuing a very protectionist foreign policy.

After Cromwell's death in 1658, friends and foes of the Republic finally came to terms and brought the Stuarts back to the English throne. The reign of Charles II could not resemble that of his father, Charles I. The new Parliament jealously defended all the Republican laws concerning commerce and industry. The king looked enviously upon the powers of his first cousin, the king of France, and felt somewhat hostage to the merchants and the manufacturers.

Contrary to what we saw in France, it was the "businessmen" in England who breathed life into the national economic movement. It was they who influenced the government's economic policies, while in France it was up to the state to propose capitalist alternatives to an entire class mesmerized by the civil service. Was nostalgia for the great administration of ancient Rome still very strong in France? Probably it was, whereas in England, Roman structures had blurred where they had not disappeared altogether.

There is no point in trying to find a public servant even remotely like a French intendant in Charles's kingdom; he did not exist. If the king of England had wanted to impose controls such as Colbert's on manufactured goods, he could not have done so. No administrative power could fetter the free initiative of an active and enterprising commercial milieu. The mercantilist dogma that imposed rules for the manufacture of products for export was adhered to less and less. Luxury items were not the only possible exports. Larger markets opened up to English industry.

But this liberty, unknown in France, should not make us forget the common concern, or even the common obsession, of the two countries: the incredible economic successes of little Holland. For the English shared the French view that the insolent prosperity of another country could only jeopardize their own prosperity.

THE DUTCH OBSESSION

In 1665 Colbert gave a greatly exaggerated overestimate of the size of the Dutch fleet. He claimed it included 15,000 to 16,000 vessels, or 75 percent of the entire European fleet. In reality, it had at most 8,000 or 9,000 ships. Was it the haunting presence of the Dutch in the great ports of Europe, and even of the world, that created this illusion of great numbers? Holland had replaced the sacrosanct notion of the commercial balance with the idea of working for commissions. They had become the great carriers over the seas. Enormous stocks of raw materials and tons of manufactured goods were transported from one country to another in their flat-bottomed, round-sterned ships. As Daniel Defoe put it, "They buy to sell again, and the major part of their vast commerce consists of taking on supplies in every part of the world in order to supply the whole world in turn."

According to Colbert, Amsterdam seemed to be "the warehouse of the world's goods." Merchandise from everywhere was sometimes stored there for several months, then sold when the best prices were available. Masters of the market, masters of prices, in some areas the Dutch nearly became masters of production or of local industries.

That economic domination had already distressed Richelieu: for Colbert it was a veritable nightmare. The "lethargy" of his countrymen in the face of this special sort of invasion infuriated him. The lower Loire region gives an especially clear example of the Dutch presence in a foreign country. Let us visit Bordeaux, for example, during Colbert's time. The wine merchants' quarter had become a Dutch district. There was even a chapel where the sermons were in Flemish. In the taverns of this wine-producing region, beer was being drunk. From time to time the local bourgeoisie accused these active foreigners of controlling the trade of their city, but the majority would never have dreamed of replacing them. Hungry for honors, offices, and ennobling estates, the Bordeaux merchants carried on a quiet, discreet, and risk-free trade. And major maritime commerce in those days was extremely dangerous. La Fontaine describes it clearly in one of his fables:

> *One ship, its cargo badly stowed, sank in the first wind.*
> *Another ship, found wanting in the needed weapons,*
> *Was taken by pirates as a prize.*
> *A third reached its mooring safely,*
> *But failed to sell its merchandise.*[4]

The great merchant was thought to be like an adventurer, in the worst sense of the word. A peace-loving merchant might risk a little money on some great "adventure," but not too much. And all these activities did not seem very honorable to him. In a great exporting city, he would be content to work on commission for a foreign correspondent, usually Dutch. If he happened to speculate in wines,

---

[4]La Fontaine, *Fables,* bk. 7, no. 19, cited in Charles Higounet, comp., *Histoire de Bordeaux,* vol. 4, *Bordeaux de 1453 à 1715.*

he took care to do it under an assumed name. Tax farming in the great tradition, tolls, income from the archbishopric, and his own lands held greater interest for him. Sometimes his commercial nonchalance could cost him the ownership of his vineyards, which he valued so highly. At the beginning of the century, the Dutch had formed veritable syndicates that monopolized wine trade. They dealt directly with the producer, and in case of nonpayment, they seized his vineyard. Local industry could benefit from their spirit of enterprise: In Bordeaux, for example, they set up a sugar refinery.

Who were these Dutchmen? How had "a handful of people reduced to a corner of the world where there was nothing but water and fields," as Richelieu put it, managed to attain such affluence? What might the observations of a Frenchman be upon visiting their country? Let us imagine a fictitious trip taken by the son of a Bordeaux merchant to the Republic of the Netherlands. Suppose that the father of our traveler, like so many other merchants in Bordeaux, Nantes, La Rochelle, or Bayonne, has a contact in Holland, a rich merchant who invites the young man to stay in his home in Amsterdam.

Before leaving, our traveler might read up on the political organization and the geographical situation of his host's country. At that time it was already common to use the word *Holland* to refer to all the United Provinces, of which there were seven.[5] It is true that Holland, the province, was the most powerful and the richest of the seven. As a subject of an almost sacred monarch, our citizen of Bordeaux would be eager to visit a "popular republic" whose reputation for intellectual freedom and comfortable living in egalitarian simplicity had caught the imagination of many Frenchmen.

At the beginning of the sixteenth century, the Spanish Netherlands separated into two groups of provinces. The Catholic provinces in the south—which were also collectively called Brabant and which corresponded roughly to present-day Belgium—still remained under Spanish control. The United Provinces in the north, corresponding to today's Netherlands, would carry on a bitter struggle for independence under the guidance of the house of Orange-Nassau, which had become a sort of national symbol. Spain ultimately recognized the independence of the United Provinces, or the Republic of the Netherlands, in 1648.

Each province had its chief of state, the Stadtholder, and a prime minister, the "Pensionary." The federal government included the Grand Pensionary and the Stadtholder General, who in practice were always the Pensionary and the Stadtholder of the province of Holland. All of the internal politics of the republic is summarized in the struggle between these two personages, who represented each

---

[5]Holland, Zeeland, Utrecht, Gelderland, Overijssel, Frisia, and Groningen. Spain had also relinquished to the Dutch the Generality, a strip of land south of the Meuse, and the enclave of Maastricht.

of the very different social groups. Behind the Stadtholder, that is, the head of the house of Orange, was the Calvinist church with its fanatical ministers, and also a proletariat of consequence. Patriotic and nationalist, the partisans of the house of Orange remained loyal to a policy of independence vis-à-vis Spain or any other possible invader. Louis XIV and Colbert underestimated their latent strength. For although he was titular military commander, the Stadtholder no longer governed the Republic. The house of Orange had been supplanted by the Grand Pensionary's party, which included the liberal "third force" between the Catholics and the strict Calvinists, representing the powerful class of merchant magistrates. The Stadtholder had lost his judiciary and fiscal powers.

Our traveler might nearly forget the existence of the prince of Orange, confined to his French-style court. For him (as for the king and Colbert) the true head of state and maker of foreign policy was Jan De Witt, Grand Pensionary from 1653 onward. The originality of the policy of the great merchants with De Witt at their head consisted in separating economic war from military war. Unlike what happened in France, prosperity was an end in itself and not a means to greater military strength. Political and military peace was a necessary condition for the particular kind of economic war the Republic was waging.

When our young traveler visits Holland (around 1665) the United Provinces are at peace with France. The Republic is considered a traditional ally against the Spanish enemy, in spite of Colbert's exasperation. Our Frenchman's first impression upon entering Dutch territory is bewilderment at its geography. The sea, the wastelands, the marshes, the rivers seem to isolate the country from the rest of Europe. While the soil of France seems capable of furnishing all necessary products, that of the Netherlands must be conquered over and over again by the inhabitants. An economic autarky such as Colbert envisaged would not be possible in Holland.

Agricultural techniques are much more advanced, although the traveler may not notice it immediately. At first glance, farming seems as archaic as in France. On the other hand, he is astounded by the number of towns he passes through over a short distance. The country is essentially urban. The inhabitants of the town represent two-thirds of the population, an enormous proportion compared to essentially rural France. The appearance of the cities is often neat and clean. The commercial areas are full of life, but without the deafening uproar heard in French streets. The state does not attempt to control economic activity in the cities as the French government does, but the power of the guilds over the various crafts is often tyrannical. Respect for guild regulations has remained a common European feature.

While walking from one store or workshop to another, our traveler observes with astonishment the amount of metallic currency in circulation. Good coin is so hard to come by in France! Even in Paris, a merchant or a craftsman often had difficulty in obtaining payment. Nearly all work is done on credit, because of the monetary famine of the times. Intrigued, the Frenchman promises himself he will get an explanation of all this from his host.

Next he arrives in that famous Amsterdam, economic capital of Europe and Colbert's obsession. Rising out of a world of marshes and fog, the city—admirable, spacious, airy—is lined with red-brown, black, or pink houses on piles along its semicircular and concentric grand canals. Street life is intense and disciplined, always within hearing of the city's countless bells. The Frenchman observes the numerous warehouses along the canals.

The home of his hosts is fairly large, comfortable, clean, but without ostentation. On the wall are hung paintings that show scenes of family and city life in all their truthfulness, all their simplicity. In the main room there is a portrait of the master of the house, painted by a certain Rembrandt, who is struggling against poverty. Here a painter is one tradesman among others. Patronage is an unknown concept. A rich patrician pays for his order, and that is all. Art does not contribute in any way to illustrating the grandeur of the state or divine power.

Our traveler, accustomed to the diversity of dress among the French, who are always careful to reveal their social stature or acquired privilege through their clothes, notes with some surprise the sad, somber, black or violet clothing of his hosts. He is aware of their great fortune, and notes the near absence of servants. The mistress of the house does her own shopping. This simplicity of life extends to the important personages of the state. Mrs. Ruyter, wife of the celebrated hero of the Dutch navy, does her own shopping too, and Jan De Wit, the Grand Pensionary, himself goes about on foot.

Meals are taken in near-silence. The food is not especially refined. Our traveler dreams of the lively feasts of the Bordeaux region. He has further occasion to speak[6] with his hosts in their little private garden, which almost all the Amsterdam burghers possess, over a cup of tea, coffee, or chocolate, all commodities brought in by the ships of the great colonial companies.

The Dutch ask the young Frenchman his plans for the future. It is their turn to be surprised by the limited interest he shows in his father's export business. The young man's great preoccupations seem to be the office of treasurer that his father wants to buy for him soon and the beautiful estate that his family is preparing near Bordeaux.

The son of the household, about the same age as the guest, also speaks to him about his future. He evokes with enthusiasm the ships that adventure to the

[6]It showed good breeding among Dutch patrician families to know how to speak French.

four corners of the globe in search of rare goods; he describes the fantastic commercial activity that animates the quays of his city. What is his ambition? It is to become a rich merchant like his father. For him, trade is a sort of epic. He is even learning the languages of far-off lands. Holland possesses the greatest center in the world for the study of Oriental languages.

How will he invest his profits? Just as his parents did, in his townhouse. The properties of the landed aristocracy, few in number, hold no interest for him. A few paintings, some Delft porcelain, and polished cooper cookware will adorn his only investment in real estate: a fine urban residence where he can lead a simple, virtuous, and closed family life.

All this talk gives the young Frenchman a glimpse of a new idea: Success confirms virtue. Of course he is not aware to what extent this idea prefigures an "American dream" that France will understand with difficulty.

The Dutch read an enormous amount. Greater intellectual freedom and lax censorship have made this corner of Europe a publisher's paradise. Our traveler finds numerous botanical works and popularizations of science in his host's library. The Dutch know how to combine their love of the concrete and of science with their commercial genius. Thanks to the advanced techniques of their processing industries (such as certain ways of dying cloth), they dominate major markets. Our Dutch family also owns a work of Jan De Witt[7] entitled *Holland's Best Interests*. The Grand Pensionary declares, in the forms of maxims, his faith in a happy capitalism successfully represented by his own class and his hatred for the House of Orange and the Calvinist church.

The coming war between France and the Republic of the United Provinces is also an ideological confrontation. According to De Witt, the dynastic spirit was, by its very nature, violent and irrational. It led inevitably to the centralization of the state, which suppressed free trade, without which no economic, prosperity can exist. Furthermore, it leads to war and then to bankruptcy.

The tyrannical rigor of the Calvinist church disturbed the Grand Pensioner equally. A republic, land of asylum, religious tolerance, and the death of the state: The Frenchman thinks a long time after finishing Jan De Witt's book.

The tolerant Republic did not spare the Catholic Church, however. The Jesuits were banned from the entire province of Holland. Our young visitor from Bordeaux finds no Catholic church in the city. A private home is pointed out to him, specially remodeled, where he will be able to attend Mass on Sunday. He knows that Catholics, although in the majority, are blocked from taking any important positions. Louis XIV was greatly irritated by this antimonarchical, anti-Catholic merchant oligarchy. Colbert would use that irritation—political in nature—

[7] Actually written by a certain De la Court, the work was published in 1662.

to influence the king to crush a nation that so insolently mocked French economic power.

Our traveler might then wish to observe more closely "the world's greatest warehouse" and Europe's leading financial marketplace. The extraordinary activity on the quays and docks of Amsterdam astonishes every visitor. Among the peculiar mobile cranes, Baltic cereals, English wool, wine from Aquitaine and the Rhine, iron and wood from Scandinavia, spices from the Indies, sugar from Brazil or the Antilles, and countless other goods from everywhere are loaded or unloaded before the ships depart for destinations all over the globe. Around August the Indies fleet returns: twenty enormous ships with fabulous cargoes. In April nearly two hundred vessels raise anchor for the Baltic.

Because of its geographical situation, the Netherlands found itself not far from the major river routes, at the center of the great sea-lane that linked northeastern and southwestern Europe. Trade with Holland had taken the place of the Champagne trade that had so enriched the Colbert family. Remarkable shipbuilders, the Dutch designed ships for each sea and for each particular trade. The approach to the coasts was terribly dangerous. The sea was at once both violent and shallow. The merchants' spirit of enterprise did not allow itself to be intimidated by the wrecked ships broken up by the waves. All foreign visitors noted the appetite for work and the extreme frugality of the Dutch. All the world's goods passed through their hands, and they consumed almost none of them. Even the best products of Holland were meant for exportation.

Their sailors were the most sober and hard working in Europe. The captains were often of modest origins. The sailors were paid incredibly low salaries, one-third lower than those of French sailors, for much harder work. Dutch boats had a crew of eight, while twelve or sixteen manned similar French ships.

Everything was designed for the best possible return on the lowest possible investment. The famous "flutes" (from the Dutch *fluit*), flat-bottomed ships with round sterns and narrow decks, were inexpensive to build but could hold vast amounts of merchandise. Transportation costs were by far the lowest in Europe. Thus the Hollanders became indispensable go-betweens in European trade.

In order to deal with the tremendous risks of the sea, Dutch shippers had organized a remarkable system of maritime insurance. Insurance companies multiplied in Amsterdam, to such a degree that they could lower their rates to ten percent and even eight percent of insured value. By comparison, the mean French rate was about 25 percent in the same era.

Dutch trade invaded the world. Whereas in France Colbert was fighting desperately (as we shall see) to create colonial companies, the Dutch merchants spontaneously formed associations to conquer the trade of the West and East

Indies. To the great anger of Louis XIV's minister, part of French colonial production wound up in the warehouses of Amsterdam.

The great Dutch merchants, notably from Amsterdam, utilized with formidable efficiency the weapon of information in the service of commerce. No European country possessed a regular postal service so perfected. Nowhere were there so many gazettes, nor were any as well informed of economic events worldwide. Dutch businessmen were always the first to know of shifting prices in distant markets, as well as of shipwrecks and natural calamities. Because they were also largely responsible for transporting raw materials and manufactured goods, speculation became easy. The Dutch could dictate prices in foreign ports, which hampered local trade considerably.

Let us take as an example the tradesmen of France's interior provinces, who sent their local products to the ports for export. At what price will they sell them? At that fixed by the Dutch organized and installed in the port city: that is to say, at a low price. After having turned a small profit, the French returned to their provinces with imported goods. And those goods had been brought in most often through the agency of the Dutch, who had held them the requisite amount of time in their warehouses and sold them, of course, at the highest price. When French merchants wanted, in their turn, to resell those goods in the interior of the kingdom, they were hampered by their high purchase price.

Colbert's xenophobic mercantilism was not only a consequence of a theoretical concept of world economy. France actually was fighting an economic war, led with extraordinary commercial intelligence by the Dutch.

The Dutch also had the genius to connect commercial and financial power in a manner never before seen in Europe. Colbert rightly said that only trade, "the source of finance," could bring a country metallic currency. But Dutch methods were different. After having seen the foremost port of Europe, our traveler visits the leading financial market in the West, the famous Stock Exchange of Amsterdam, what Pierre Goubert called "the Wall Street of the Seventeenth Century," a sort of permanent commercial fair where world commerce is discussed. The building is classic, elegant. Some thirty columns support covered galleries, where the great merchants meet. Regular visitors know they will find the East India merchants by one column, and those of the Levant or the Baltic by another. Here a ship is chartered that, a few steps farther on, will be insured. In the courtyard, the talk is of real-estate values, of long-term deals, of speculations in universal trade. All the world's goods, or nearly all, were given their price there.

Businessmen quickly understood that this immense commercial monument could not exist without a healthy and stable currency accepted in all countries.

Here, as elsewhere, monetary anarchy reigned that, in our day, seems almost improbable. Perhaps less preoccupied than Colbert by that diversity of metallic currency, the Dutch had decided as early as 1609 to protect resolutely a single currency, backed by a great bank on the Italian model. The florin of the Bank of Amsterdam (not the florin in public circulation) soon became the most secure of Western currencies.

The foremost secret of that success consisted in the bank's always keeping on hand at least enough silver to cover all deposits. And as Henri Hauser has explained, Holland, unlike other mercantilist states, had the audacity (enormous at the time) to make no effort to protect the metallic currency in its possession through prohibiting the exit of precious metals.[8] Resolutely antibullionist, the United Provinces allowed the exportation of currency, and even of ingots from 1647 onward. A merchant knew he could withdraw at any moment what he had deposited in the Bank of Amsterdam, without having to borrow. That certainty attracted masses of capital. Depositors accepted the low interest that the bank offered them, in exchange for absolute liquidity. In this way, the bank accumulated considerable holdings in metal without charging large fees. That is the explanation for the abundance of metallic currency in circulation in the United Provinces.

This financial strength served the businessmen, who in their turn augmented the capital of a bank capable of giving them long-term credit at reasonable rates and of guaranteeing stable rates of exchange. The deposits of capital, which were attracted like a magnet, were not the only cause of Dutch success. Like any private citizen of the Republic, the bourgeois government of the United Provinces knew how to proportion its expenditures to its revenues. Fear of deficit and easy access to credit went hand in hand. The government borrowed at very low rates because it was never insolvent. Moreover, the Dutch law punished any insolvent debtor with prison.

The balanced management of Dutch government depended on the considerable advance of the United Provinces in their political and social structures. It is essential to understand that fact in order to understand the unprecedented obstacles that Colbert had to face to establish French economic power. The government of the Republic could maintain its budget through a healthy tax income. The United Provinces were two centuries ahead of France here. Excise taxes were extremely high; moreover, everyone paid taxes, which presupposes an absence of feudal privileges that visiting Frenchmen always found startling. The properties of the Catholic Church and of certain nobles had been sequestered or purchased by the government, then sold or rented to farmers. There was no difference in the legal

[8]Henri Hauser, *La prépondérance espagnole, 1539–1660*, p. 441

status of burghers and of peasants, who owed no feudal dues except certain money payments. Government credit existed in the United Provinces because the public credit system was organized, generalized, and logical.

This was exactly the opposite of the situation in France, where there was no organized public credit. Colbert was highly aware of this. Whatever faults we may find with him, he had the merit and the courage to introduce concepts of order and justice in the area of public finance. Only financial regularity and security could sustain long-term economic planning. The minister tried to increase indirect taxation and to terrify a veritable "mafia" of businessmen who speculated without scruples on the state's financial infantilism. He obtained results: The growth in royal income shows it. But how could he balance the budget only through taxation in a country where so many inhabitants had the privilege of exemption? How could fresh cash be obtained from the taxpayers when they were mostly peasants who could not pay in valid currency?

Nevertheless, money circulated in the privileged layers of society. Mme de Sévigné borrowed and lent constantly. Credit was widespread, but without any control. What was needed was a central bank on the Dutch model. Yet attempts to set one up were always failures. No financier, no great merchant, wanted to risk his fortune in the bank of a state where an absolute monarch reigned who could take out huge loans at any time on the basis of policies he alone decided without appeal.

The financial habits of the monarchy confirmed their fears. The king borrowed but never reimbursed: It was, as we have seen, the taxpayers who reimbursed the tax farmers for what the king borrowed. A government bank could only inspire mistrust and skepticism. In order to direct capital into national industry and the export trade, there was only the immense energy of a minister who was not always understood, and whose strength of will was a source of irritation.

All was not idyllic in the Netherlands—much was needed. The efficient and unbending capitalism largely profited the bourgeois class—a very large class, it is true—but it also engendered widespread poverty, as a visit to the edge of any city could demonstrate. There, miserable agglomerations of slums contrasted sadly with the neat comfort of bourgeois neighborhoods. There, in the slums, William of Orange raised with ease the troops to overthrow the government of merchants and repulse the French invader. For war was on the way, and the United Provinces were poorly prepared to meet the threat. They had a sizable navy, but the merchants tended to use it to convoy their trading vessels, and the army was clearly too small. England, and then France, wanted to profit by this military weakness to strike down, by force of arms, this little country that made such a mockery of their economic systems.

THE ECONOMIC WAR

FROM ECONOMIC WARFARE TO MILITARY WARFARE

Already in Richelieu's time, the French traders were complaining of the Dutch takeover of their Atlantic ports. A neighborhood in Nantes was called "Little Holland." There were even reports of Dutch sailors who stole French merchandise while disguised as Turks.

The cardinal's first priority was the fight against encirclement by the Hapsburgs. The United Provinces hoped to free themselves from Spanish domination forever. The Franco-Dutch alliance against the enemy seemed obligatory. This principle had a profound effect on French foreign policy until Holland, exasperated by Colbert's bellicose protectionism, considered a commercial alliance with Spain against France.

It is necessary to be aware of the image of Spain in public opinion in the seventeenth century. The shadow of Charles V was still there. The gold of Europe came from the mines of Spanish America. The power of Spain traumatized minds throughout the century, even though reality did not justify that famous "Spanish obsession" of which historians speak. As long as the war lasted, Mazarin followed the same policy as that of Richelieu with regard to the United Provinces. The Dutch were very precious allies; one submitted in silence to their economic hegemony.

England did not have the same imperatives, and its important merchant class refused to submit to the veritable Dutch dictatorship in matters of trade. Until 1650, the balance of trade was almost entirely in favor of the Netherlands: For every loaded ship that left Britain for Holland, there were ten Dutch ships that unloaded their goods on English docks. Cromwell obtained the Navigation Act from Parliament in 1651: It provided that goods coming from Asia, Africa, or the Americas would be imported in English ships, while those coming from Europe might sail under the flag of the producing country. (Colbert would try to introduce somewhat similar measures twenty years later.) This act of economic warfare provoked the first armed war between England and the Netherlands (1652–54). The Republic of the Netherlands had to yield. Its navy was large, but it had to do convoy duty for the merchant marine of the Dutch patricians while fighting against England's navy. The Amsterdam Stock Exchange foundered. Despite the return of peace, anti-Dutch propaganda remained lively under Charles II.

In France, in the year warfare with Spain ceased (1659), Fouquet felt less obligated to deal gently with the powerful Dutch merchants. He adopted the moderately protectionist measure of charging a customs tax of fifty sous per ton for vessels entering French ports.

Mercantilism and War

Colbert's policy consisted of practicing progressive protectionism—growing gradually stricter as French industry and the merchant marine, battered by years of war and civil strife, took shape again. It was necessary at first to permit freedom of trade in order to awaken economic activity and to assemble the capital required for large-scale industrial and maritime ventures. Only when France would be capable of exporting her manufactured goods in her own ships, could she attack Dutch trade sharply. In 1662 Colbert even suppressed in part the fifty-sou tax; but in 1663 he reestablished it entirely. The chamber of justice had forced numerous contractors to make restitution. It was time to rebuild industry. It was the year of the famous memorandum in which Colbert—loyal to the mercantilist theories—explained to Louis XIV that the economic strength of England and Holland was the principal cause of France's weakness. His terms implied a strategy for combat.

The next year, 1664, he established the first, very detailed customs tariffs; thus, for example, "skinned sheep will require payment of five sous per dozen, live sheep fifteen sous apiece." But the rates were still moderate. It was a matter of protecting a nascent industry without impeding a European trade that French manufacturers were not yet able to dominate.

On August 3, the king called the first council on trade. Colbert sent him an important memorandum in which, after a long historical study,[9] he demonstrated to the king the extent to which the power of his state depended on its economic strength.

The masters of the economy could become the masters of the affairs of state. Was Louis XIV convinced? It is doubtful. The letter he sent to his ambassador in London in 1666 proves that either the king had not understood, or he did not truly believe in his minister's theories. Louis XIV actually wrote: "If only the English would content themselves with being the greatest merchants of Europe, and would leave me as my share whatever I could win in a just war, nothing would be easier than for us to reach an agreement." The "just war" was the one he was preparing against Spain: The conquest of Flanders would be his compensation for the dowry of Queen Maria Theresa, which had never been paid. Besides, he hoped in this way to consolidate France's northern borders. Louis XIV thought of war in the traditional terms of political strategy and territorial conquest.

At the same time, the English exhibited a completely contrary approach. From 1665 onward, they were engaged in a second war against the Netherlands. The motives of that war were completely economic. England and the Netherlands

---

[9]Colbert often showed a true historical education. All action should, for him, refer to history.

were fighting over the Guinean slave trade and American spices. The two maritime powers inflicted spectacular naval defeats on one another. France now found herself in a very uncomfortable situation. Holland was more than ever a commercial foe, but she was also an indispensable ally at the moment when French troops were preparing to enter the Spanish Netherlands. Jan De Witt complained bitterly to the king that he was receiving no aid in his war against England. Louis was greatly annoyed. He wanted to humor Holland, but had no desire to back a republic he disliked against his cousin Charles II, whose friendship he hoped to keep. France nonetheless dispatched 6,000 soldiers toward the Dutch enclave of Maestricht and officially declared war on England.

Natural disasters came to Louis's rescue, so to speak. A gigantic fire and a terrible outbreak of plague ravaged London. The efforts of the English government were turned from combat. In June 1667, the Dutch fleet under Ruyter appeared on the Thames. A panicked England was eager to come to terms with Holland at Breda, while Louis XIV was commencing what was called "The War of Devolution," by invading Flanders.

In the year 1667 the Dutch felt doubly the victims of French aggression: French troops were drawing dangerously close to their territory, and Colbert was increasing customs rates considerably. Jan De Witt hoped for a military alliance with France, but he demonstrated at length to the French ambassador, Pomponne, "how much the preservation of friendship was often incompatible with being neighbors," especially when the neighbor was as powerful as the king of France. The ambassador did his best to dispel these unjustified suspicions.

On his side, Colbert considered that France's domestic and foreign situation now allowed for a true declaration of economic war. The king was getting out of the quagmire into which the Anglo-Dutch war had drawn him; and French industry was recovering. The customs tariffs of 1667 were what Robert Mandrou has called a combat tariff. Rates were often prohibitive and showed a considerable difference from those of 1664. Here are some comparisons:

	1664 rates	1667 rates
Silk stockings, per dozen	3 livres 10 sous	8 livres
English flannel, per piece	6 livres	12 livres
Wool caps, per hundredweight	8 livres	20 livres
Tapestries from Antwerp and Brussels, per hundredweight	120 livres	200 livres
Dutch and English cloth, per 25 ells	50 livres	100 livres

It was time to protect French industry and above all to force the French to manufacture at home instead of importing what others manufactured. The English had not done otherwise. Cromwell could not admit that England conducted itself as an underdeveloped nation by exporting unprocessed wool and having it returned processed by the Dutch factories. Similarly, Colbert could not bear to see the sugar from French colonies refined by the Dutch. In 1664 "foreign refined sugar" was charged 15 livres a hundredweight at entry; in 1667 it was charged more than twice that much.

Colbert would explain these new tariffs well to his cousin Colbert du Terron: "When I drew up the tariffs, we had two problems in this area, which were considerable: one, that all the merchandise from our islands was going to Holland; and the other, that we had no refined sugar except from Holland, England, and Portugal."

The Dutch retaliated with taxes on wine and spirits. Colbert laughed at that. Germany wanted French wines that passed through Holland. The Dutch would be forced to import them. Actually, these measures did harm French trade. Besides, the merchant marine of Louis XIV was in no shape to compete with that of the United Provinces. Colonial trade suffered. An active black market undercut the minister's plans; he even thought of making Antwerp a rival to Amsterdam.

The idea of a war against the hated Republic began to attract the king. Holland had made a serious political error. In May of 1668, Holland joined forces with England and Sweden (by the Treaty of the Hague) to hasten peace negotiations between France and Spain. Thanks to the alliance, the Treaty of Aix-la-Chapelle failed to give Louis XIV the borders he had hoped for. It was easy for the king to break the alliance by giving subsidies to England and Sweden. But he still had a grudge against the Dutch.

In November 1670, Colbert granted the Dutch ambassador an audience, which the comte de Saint-Maurice describes. The minister "asked him why the Estates General[10] was arming; he replied: So that they will not fear France. Monsieur Colbert answered that the king was not their enemy; the ambassador told him that nonetheless his superiors had reason to think so, since His Majesty was ruining his own subjects in order to hurt the Dutch, and that the proof was to be found in Guyenne and in Brittany, where the people were going begging because the taxes on wine and grain that they once sold in Holland were preventing such sales, while in Holland they had Prussian and Silesian grain and German wine, which in truth was slightly dearer than in France, but that there was no shortage for all that."

[10]The Estates General was a dependency of the Dutch government.

Furious at these claims, Colbert issued an order forbidding the loading of spirits on Dutch ships (January 1671). In turn, the Dutch entered into a trade alliance with Spain against France. Louis XIV was in a towering rage against the merchants who, he later wrote, "were enticing my kingly cousins to join offensive alliances against me." Troops were raised. The Dutch became frightened. But the king, Colbert, and Louvois, for once in agreement, wanted war, with the help of England. One of Colbert's unpublished reports shows that he had been working prudently, and with a touch of skepticism, for just such an alliance over the past two years. England remained a commercial rival all the same. On July 8, 1672, the minister revealed his true intentions: "If the king were to subjugate all the United Provinces of the Netherlands, their trade would become His Majesty's trade; there would be nothing left to wish for."

The invasion of Holland began. This war was to be a turning point in the reign of Louis XIV and in Colbert's political life. All the great economic activity of his early ministry (1661–72) would be hostage to the Franco-Dutch conflict.

CHAPTER 12

"Colbertism" and the French

COLBERT'S JUDGES HAVE EXAGGERATED the gap between the minister's passion for the grandeur of the state and his scorn for individual happiness. Certainly, taxation is more fruitful the richer "the people" are. The accounts of his intentions are suspect. Colbert had also hoped to create "abundance for all" and not "luxury for the few." He would tell the king, after the tragic war against Holland, how painful the sight of poverty was to him.

He asked all Frenchmen for an immense effort, in the context of a national perspective. Everyone should benefit from the economic recovery, but the state most of all. There was only one way to ensure that recovery: France must win the battle of exports. It was necessary to direct the economy with that goal in mind and, if need be, to force the French to follow the itinerary that led to abundance, as it was conceived by the minister.

There is no doubt that Colbert belonged to that race of men who wanted to make others happy in spite of themselves. An army of *maîtres des requêtes* and intendants fought tenaciously to shape economic forces to the minister's grand design. Couldn't seventeenth-century Frenchmen make economic progress on their own, without the heavy guiding hand of the administration? Here we find again the mission of the state as dispenser of justice. The weight of privilege, the complication of customs, the endless hindrances caused, not by the state, but by localities and private groups: Was not that weight as hard to bear as the strong and heavy hand of the minister? Let us observe the various economic areas of the Sun King's disparate, divided, complicated France.

THE WORLD OF MARKETS AND FAIRS

Today we can scarcely imagine how isolated a given region, county, or village was in Colbert's day. Means of communication were haphazard. Postal service was very limited and disorganized. The best meeting places were still, as in the Middle Ages, the trade fairs that were held in the same towns at fixed times. Savary[1] counted 194 fairs in the Parisian region and 301 more in the provinces. A few large cities, such as Paris, Lyons, Rouen, Bordeaux, and Orléans, had become market places of national and even international importance. But most markets and fairs were provincial or regional. A fair was a considerable event in regional life. It was a chance to get in touch with others at last. Here people bartered; there a wholesaler bargained with a retailer. Colbert's inspectors took advantage of this concentration of merchandise to open bales and check the quality of the fabrics. Further on, a tradesman called in debts. Everywhere, measurement, calculation, and accounting went on. The variety of weights and measures from one province, or even one town, to another is staggering to us. Savary gave novice traders a warning: "If a Paris merchant goes to buy in a trading center where the yardstick is longer or shorter than in Paris, he must allow for it . . . or he may be cheated." If it is necessary to measure "liquids such as wine, oil, honey, and the like, one must be aware that in Paris liquids are measured in *muids*; in Champagne, in *queues*; in Tours, in *poinsons*; in Anjou, in *pipes*; and in Bordeaux, in *tonneaux*. Of course, a buyer had to verify that the quality corresponded to the amount he wanted. It was impossible under those conditions to negotiate over any distance. One had to go and render accounts in person.

Colbert tried to persuade the king that the best "grand design" of his reign would be a unification of weights and measures, similar to the reform of justice. But the force of habit was too strong, and the state was still too weak to impose such a reform.

To this variety in weights and measures was added the complexity of a monetary system that, moreover, was not peculiar to France. Metallic currency was used for payments, but one reckoned in livres tournois, an artificial standard used to establish values for metallic currency in circulation.[2] In other words, all accounts, all transactions, all contracts were established in *monnaie de compte,* or account money—which was the livre tournois (itself divided into sous and denires). But all payments were settled in gold, silver, or copper. The king alone had the power to fix in account money the value of real money in circulation.

For Colbert, a strong and stable currency was not only a symptom of economic health but also a matter of national prestige. Near the end of his life, he would write again: "Nothing better indicates the dignity and grandeur of states than uniformity in their currencies; and once that grandeur and that dignity decline, the first indication is a decline in the currency and fluctuations in value from

[1]Author of *The Perfect Merchant,* a work written under the inspiration of Colbert.

[2]By "weakening" the metallic amount of the unit of account, the government provoked inflation (and a de facto devaluation), while the "reinforcement" of that amount led to deflation (and to a revaluation).

province to province."[3] The principal silver coin—the crown, or ecu—was valued at three livres tournois from 1641 onward. That rate held until 1689, six years after Colbert's death. Thus, the minister was successful in maintaining monetary stability: The foreign rates of exchange for French currency scarcely varied during the period.

But the situation became complicated where gold and copper were involved. How could the relative values of the three metals (gold, silver, and copper) be adjusted, when each state increased the value of one metal in proportion to the others according to its own needs? The imbroglio often seemed hopelessly entangled. Great international merchants calculated the amounts of metal they wanted to receive, not at the rates established for France, but according to a more-or-less international standard. One understands the drama for a nation represented by the lack of precious metal. If strict mercantilism seems obsolete to us, perhaps it was not so in the time of Colbert.[4]

French minting technology had improved greatly. Nevertheless, counterfeiters still got rich: Certain foreign coins (especially the pistole from Spain) were in common use in France, and copies were difficult to control. Colbert was merciless regarding the counterfeiters whom the police unmasked.

AGRICULTURE

Who doesn't know La Bruyere's famous passage describing the peasantry? "We see throughout the countryside certain wild animals both male and female, blackened, livid, and burned by the sun, attached to the earth, which they dig and turn with invincible stubbornness." Not all agricultural workers lived in misery, but numerous statements by the intendants and by Colbert himself confirm the famous text repeatedly.

Peasants were frequently owners of a small parcel of land insufficient to nourish them.[5] In most of the richer provinces they lived under the system of sharecropping and thus had to pay the landowners (usually in kind) almost a third of their harvests. Farming methods were archaic. Animals were few in number and small in size. There was never enough manure to enrich the land. Harrows still had wooden teeth. Noxious plants intermingled with the wheat: They had

---

[3]From a 1681 letter of Colbert's to the intendant of Provence, cited by Clément. We should note that the letters of the minister concerning currency were very rare.

[4]Colbert had great illusions—and the people around him fed them—about the chances that new mines would be discovered. But searches were unsuccessful.

[5]It is admitted that the peasants possessed a fifth of the land, as did the bourgeoisie. The rest was divided between the king, the nobility, and the clergy.

to be weeded by hand when the spring came. Crop rotation was a must. In some places half the land was fallow at a given time. Yields were poor and plantings uneven, depending on the region and the year.[6] Furthermore, it was difficult to practice crop specialization. Poor transportation meant each region had to be self-sufficient and produce every sort of crop in small quantities. Provincial autarky and limited importation caused vast differences in prices. Who profited from these differences? It was never the farmer, who—always in need of money—sold his harvest as quickly as possible to an astute speculator.

We should not, then, be surprised that poor technology, reinforced by scandalous speculation and enormous taxes, often led to horrible famines. Black buckwheat was the peasant's chief food, flour being too expensive. When the harvest was bad, prices became prohibitive and famine spread quickly. If the harvest was good, prices dropped, and speculators ruined the farmer.

There were frequent famines under Louis XIV, many extreme, as in 1662. The king and Colbert took emergency measures. They hurriedly imported wheat from foreign countries, especially from Danzig, to be sold or given away on the very steps of the Louvre. They attempted to act on a national scale by requisitioning wheat in the provinces despite the resistance of local magnates. The roads and rivers were obstructed in many places by local tollgates and internal customs. It took all of Louis's power to arrange free passage for wheat. The sufferings of the country people that year of 1662 were dreadful to behold. Whole families perished. The parish priests of Blois stated that, "Said parishioners have been living these three months on cabbage stalks and roots that they steal from gardens and eat in the open like animals."[7]

The famine of 1662 would haunt Colbert until his death. In the following years rural France continued to suffer. In 1663 the intendant of Dauphiné wrote to the minister: "I am assured that in a few places where snows and the cold winter have killed the wheat, the peasants had nutshells and acorns ground with black wheat and a bit of oats or rye to make their bread." And in 1665 it was the intendant Robertot's turn to write: "In the province of Berry and the ones around, all the inhabitants, but especially those who till the soil, are worse off than the slaves of Turkey or the peasants of Poland."

Colbert's policies with respect to wheat unfortunately often had disastrous consequences. In the time of Henry IV, Sully, following the lead of the ministers of Elizabeth I of England, favored the export of and even a great trade in grain.

---

[6]According to Jean Meuvret, the mean yield was nine to ten hectoliters per hectare, roughly ten and one-half bushels per acre. Some lands were larger, but most were smaller.

[7]Georges Mongrédien, *La vie quotidienne sous Louis XIV.*

The cultivation of wheat should be a profitable business, which would encourage large and medium landowners to produce more. Colbert settled for limiting grape-growing, then practiced quite widely in France, as being nonessential. He was so afraid of famine that he forbade the export of wheat and he imported cereals, which he put on the market at low prices in hopes of lowering the price. He was following the theories of Laffemas, who had disagreed with Sully. While trying to guarantee that France would be fed, Colbert hoped above all to keep wages down, thus lowering industrial expenses and contributing to the export effort. Like Laffemas, he was aware that salary levels were tied to the price of food, i.e., of bread. Besides, the army had to be fed cheaply and easily in winter.

Yet he constantly feared famine, and he seemed to worry about the peasants' plight. In 1662 he tried to protect them from unpaid levies by forbidding the seizure of animals and farm implements for back taxes. His orders were not always followed. In 1667 he had Louis take measures to prevent the usurping of communal goods by the great landowners. Three years later he wrote to the intendant of Tours: "During your inspections, try to see if the peasants are any better off, how they are dressed and furnished, and if they enjoy feast days more than before, these four points being the only way we have of knowing if they have attained a better state than the one they were in during the war and the first years of peacetime."

He worried about harvests ceaselessly. According to the results of his inquests, he authorized or forbade buying and selling of grain. His policy was erratic. He allowed grain to circulate for a short time, then he would lose his nerve and not allow any grain out of a region where a shortage seemed likely. The uncertainty of these governmental orders, coupled with the risk of suspension of trade and the freezing of prices, discouraged production. Marginal land was abandoned, and production fell off greatly.

Rural France was situated in large part outside the system of monetary circulation. The peasant usually paid in kind; hence no new money passed through his hands. By neglecting agricultural production in favor of industry for reasons of metallic currency, Colbert made an immense mistake. Involuntarily, he contributed to the continued danger of famine. And by lowering the profits from the large and moderate agricultural properties, he cut down on private investments in industry, for, as is well known, many of the bourgeois, whom the minister was asking to invest money in manufacturing and trading companies, would do so only in proportion to the profit margin on their crops.

His livestock policy was more successful. Besides forbidding seizure, he tried to introduce foreign strains, cattle and also sheep for the wool industries. He hesitated to import English sheep for rather picturesque reasons. He wrote his brother Croissy on September 14, 1670: "As I have fully examined what might cause the difference in our wools, I found no other except that English sheep spend the night outdoors in the fields, because there are no wolves, and we cannot do the same."

Plants for industrial use interested him especially. Like Sully, he encouraged the growing of mulberry trees and silkworms. He favored the planting of woad and madder, of tobacco in Languedoc and Guyenne, and especially of hemp, which the navy had need of for its sails and ropes, in the west of France.

Following mercantilist tradition, he tried to avoid the purchase of foreign horses, which would mean a drain of currency. Need we recall the vast importance of horses in that time, not only for the needs of war, but for those of daily life as well? As early as 1662, Colbert worried about that matter. He created an administration to deal with their breeding, and when needed, he distributed specially bred stallions[8] to private breeders. The results were noticeable; horse breeding improved considerably in Normandy, Poitou, and Berry.

ROADS AND WATERWAYS

Up a steep, sandy road, unpleasant in the heat,
While on all sides without escape, down the sun beat,
Six strong horses pulled a coach.
Alongside the coach, women, monks, and old men walked
But, even so, the team sweating and blowing, had
balked.[9]

Except for a scanty network of royal roads—which converged, even then, on Paris and lacked transverse connections—transportation remained deplorable in Colbert's time. The rare highways were paved only in the neighborhood of large cities. Once autumn came, carts could be mired to the axle. Maintenance was the responsibility of property owners along the road, who could neglect the roads as they pleased. Plowmen encroached upon the roadway by one or two plow-widths. An impassable road was also a good excuse not to go to the tax-collecting station. Garbage was even dumped in the roads.

On the rivers and streams, bridges were extremely rare. Thus, on the Garonne, there was no bridge before Toulouse.[10] Frequently, fishnets, fish holding ponds, or watermills blocked the rivers. Most travelers went by water, complaining

[8]Vauban was later to criticize his lack of interest in mares.

[9]La Fontaine, *Le Coche et la Mouche.*

[10]Yves-Marie Bercé, *La vie quotidienne dans l'Aquitaine au XVIIe siècle.*

of the insolence of the boatmen, who made them wait and set them down too soon.

Everywhere, tollgates and internal customs brought the flow of travelers and goods to a halt and (as Vauban put it) made Frenchmen foreigners to each other. From Orléans to Les Ponts-de-Cé on the Loire, there were twenty-odd tolls to be paid. Some were granted by the king as privileges, the beneficiary paying a tax in return. But there were also many illegal tolls levied. Individuals, under pretext of having made improvements blocked the roads and rivers and demanded fees for the transport of merchandise. In the age of Louis XIV, the concept of liberty was rarely separable from that of privilege. Once the state tried to establish a sketchy collective discipline that, in the last analysis, would benefit the greatest number, it was looked upon as the enemy of liberty—that is to say, of established privilege. Colbert paid no attention and endeavored, with a handful of civil servants, to put into effect a sort of nationalization of roads and rivers, as well as a reduction in the scandalous customs barriers. A good communications network was essential to extend the king's authority, to facilitate troop movements and to free economic exchanges. The slowness of travel hindered the disposal of perishable goods. For example, it took four days to go from Paris to Lille, ten or eleven days from Paris to Lyons. To export a product from a factory in Touraine or Anjou to Spain, four customs duties had to be paid internally, not to mention countless minor tolls. Under these conditions, transportation costs could reach 50 percent and even 100 percent of the net cost of products at the factory.

To the tolls on roads were sometimes added privileges of cities, which seemed senseless. The minister was exasperated by the "alleged privileges" of the city of Bordeaux: The "wheat privilege" allowed the city council to halt grain convoys from the interior in order to procure food for the city when needed! And because of the "wine privilege" of Bordeaux, the products of the highlands could not be disposed of freely, since Bordeaux was the outlet for a vast region.[11] Can Colbert be reproached for attempting to undertake elementary and sensible modernization that submitted certain economic sectors to administrative authority? One forgets that in the minister's day economic freedom often meant permission to obstruct and even to do damage.

Delays caused by the inextricable complexity of relationships between the provinces and the administration of Paris (delays of which we still complain) existed before Colbert. Yves Bercé describes the endless formalities required under

---

[11]During the famine of 1662, the city councillors of Bordeaux tried to withhold three-quarters of the wheat bought in Guyenne. The king was opposed to this and wrote to the governor: "It is a matter of the health of my people; I want to be obeyed without another reply or delay."

Mazarin to get repairs made on a bridge near Bordeaux.[12] The first complaints arrived in 1643, and the bridge was repaired in 1660.

When Colbert came to power, the treasurers of France were still responsible for inspecting the roads, bridges, ports, and thoroughfares of the kingdom. The first care of the minister was to strip them of these administrative and technical duties, which he gave to the intendants. The intendants had to make inquiries, to order work to be done, to regularly inspect its quality, and to guard against cost overruns. As usual, Colbert bombarded them with recommendations. He even contacted the engineers directly. He sent Leveau this order: "In all these things be sure to note every defect and have it repaired by François, who is at the site, and will not stir, by my orders, until the construction is entirely complete." To Charmois, he wrote: "It is necessary that this work and all other of the same kind be done so solidly that it may last, if possible, to eternity." The intendants did their best to suppress illegal tolls. Vincent Hotman, intendant of Guyenne and a relative of Colbert's by marriage, succeeded in opening the Garonne to free trade from the highlands, despite the opposition of city council and the local parlement. Another ally of Colbert's, the intendant d'Aguesseau, put into order the navigable part of the Lot. Not all the intendants showed such zeal. In 1669 Colbert assigned them assistants called "commissioners of bridges and highways."[13] Many of the property owners had encroached on the public road to their profit. The roads had to be actually expropriated in order to enlarge them again.

The minister was very concerned with the upkeep of roads designated as being "for the king's passage alone." Sometimes they had to be hastily graded or paved before the sovereign's arrival. Such practices were common all over Europe. Under those circumstances, Colbert used the detested system of statutory forced labor, the *corvée*. We should be aware that the minister little liked resorting to such means. Let those who abused the practice beware. In the following century, Orry, the comptroller general, would not share these scruples, a fact which did honor to Colbert; the system of forced labor would be extended, and France would finally have its first real highway system.

Colbert regulated the proper width for roads, prosecuted those who set up barriers or used the roads for their own profit, and raised the budget considerably for the department of bridges and highways, from 22,000 livres in 1662 to 623,000 in 1671. Foreigners noticed the improvements, but the personnel of high quality whom Colbert placed throughout France were too few in number to wipe out such an accumulation of abuses and routines from the country.

[12]Bercé, *La vie quotidienne dans l'Aquitaine*, pp. 48–49.

[13]The administrative department known by the title "Ponts-et-Chaussées" was not created until 1761.

The minister wrote that nothing "is more useful and advantageous to the populace than river navigation." Natural obstacles to navigation were frequent. He gave a patent to the inventors of a machine for cleaning and dredging navigable streams. Always impressed by Dutch technological advances, he sent an engineer, Lafeuille, to the Republic of the Netherlands to examine hydraulic works, canals, locks, bridges, jetties, mills, and machines. He had some failures and some successes. Flooding of the Loire was reduced thanks to the construction of levees. Always concerned for the technical competence of his civil servants, Colbert replaced the intendants of dikes and levees with engineers.

A set of canals was expected to supplement the river network. Colbert's ambition is revealed by his numerous plans: to link the Mediterranean, the Atlantic Ocean, and the North Sea. Wars would destroy that dream. The most spectacular creation remains the construction of the canal Deux-Mers, or the canal of Languedoc, which joins the Mediterranean to the ocean by way of the Garonne. That link allowed merchants to avoid Gibraltar. And, in case of famine, the exchange of wheat between Guyenne and Languedoc would be easy. National unity circulates by means of transportation routes.

The operation of the canal was made a fief, and was granted to its builder, Riquet, who farmed the salt tax in Languedoc. He was impartial, audacious, and carried away by the difficult task, even to the point of paying unforeseen expenses out of his own pocket when necessary. The canal was not completed until 1681, but it seems to have had the effect of bringing down the cost of land transportation. The merchants of Gaillac, who hadn't succeeded in selling their wines in Bordeaux would sell them in Languedoc by way of the canal.

Colbert kept constantly abreast of the progress of its construction. He wrote Riquet on January 31, 1670: "Do not fail to report to me on your progress every fifteen days, regularly." And on February 28, he added: "I recommend to you that your works be built in such a way as to last eternally." Despite Riguet's successes and the quality of his work, Colbert began to reproach him gently for not punctually producing his payments from his salt-tax farming. As the years passed, terrible rages replaced light reproaches.

WATERS AND FORESTS

One of the minister's prime concerns was to avoid dependence upon foreign countries for raw materials. The future sometimes showed how right he was. Wood from the forests of Provence was more expensive than that from Holland, and inferior in quality to the Norwegian. It was, nevertheless, the wood from Provence that the minister preferred to make masts for ships.

The picture of Colbert protecting forests intended for naval use has become legendary in our time. It is easy to forget that wood was then an essential material for economic life. The primary material for construction, raw material for many manufactured objects, wood was almost the only fuel. Tileworks, ironworks, forges, glassworks, all were built near forests. The forests were an important part of the king's fortune. Louis XIV called them, "a noble and precious part of our domains." Yet their administration, before Colbert, was deplorable. For several generations a flood of indulgences and privileges had little by little allowed forests to be handed over to nearby landowners and to the officials theoretically responsible for protecting them. By insisting on rights of "passage," "grazing," "heating," or "wood for construction and repair," the townships pillaged the royal forests. Louis wrote in his *Memoirs*: "They would burn certain living timber on purpose so as to have an excuse to claim the rest as having been burned accidentally." Corruption was rife among civil servants. They cut trees for personal gain, or for that of their friends, without government permission. Or they sold wood for profit without letters patent. Certain nobles usurped communal property and abused hunting rights.

Colbert took up the forestry problem on October 15, 1661, only a month after Fouquet's fall. The king's vast forests had to turn a profit as quickly as possible to balance the budget inherited from Fouquet, which had accumulated a large deficit. In that period the administration of forests was attached to the finance department. A group of *maîtres des requêtes* and commissioners was sent throughout the kingdom to take an inventory of royal forests and private ones as well, and to note all infractions and prevarications. The minister kept in constant touch with his emissaries by sending each one instructions. No one was to be spared. In a general circular to the commissioners, Colbert recommended: "If you find that gentlemen have committed infractions, you should no more spare them than if they were officers or merchants."[14] The king was lenient in a few cases, but punishments were inflicted with a terrible harshness.

At the same time he was carrying out this policy of justice, the minister was working on the famous text of the ordinance for waters and forests, which was registered as law by royal authority in August of 1669. As its preamble explains, "It is insufficient to have reestablished order and discipline if we do not consolidate it by good and wise regulations, so that its fruits may be passed down to posterity."[15] Its stipulations considerably strengthened the power of public interest over private interest and that of the central government over local authorities. A special independent court was established by the king and the minister:

[14]July 9, 1663, Pierre Clément, *Lettres, instructions, et mémoires de Colbert,* vol. 4.

[15]The ordinance for waters and forests remained in effect until 1876.

"The judges appointed for the department of waters and forests shall alone examine both civil and criminal cases pertaining to this area." All other royal judges and even the parlements were forbidden to intervene. The ordinance prescribed "the demolition of huts built on stilts by tramps and the useless members of society."

Elsewhere, there was new legislation on woods, hunting, and fishing, involving private lands as well as the royal forests. Religious and other private proprietors kept a part of their woods uncut for the state, according to the regulations fixed by the ordinance. For the first time, the government planned the cutting of timber to suit its needs and with a view to conservation. Everyone was required to make known where any road ran through the woods. But where hunting and fishing were concerned, the new ordinance did not remove any distinctions between classes. Hunting and fishing remained the privilege of ecclesiastical and lay lords. Feudalism was jostled, but it still seemed unthinkable that it could be destroyed.

The progress concerning the rent of the forests was quick and spectacular. By the end of the year 1663, net revenue from the royal forests reached the figure of 320,705 livres, which was six times the revenue for 1662!

THE INDUSTRIAL WORLD

Historians always refer to the "dictatorship of labor" that Colbert imposed. It was essential to increase considerably the volume of merchandise exported and to conquer the international market by the quality of goods. In other words, the rhythm of French labor had to be accelerated, according to the minister, and manufacturing had to be regulated to ensure the quality that would render merchandise competitive.

Production volume, of course, depended on the number of workers. An advocate of high birthrates, Colbert encouraged marriage before the age of twenty and lowered taxes progressively on large families (Edict on Marriages, November 1666).

The minister was exasperated by the proliferation of church personnel and monks who paid no taxes and produced nothing.[16] The remarks on church personnel that the *maîtres des requêtes* and members of the Council of State made to Colbert already prefigure revolutionary claims. In 1665 one of them wrote: "One can say, and it is true, that they now possess more than a third of the kingdom's income. . . . [They attract to themselves] all the wealth while depriving the public, who at this moment is cut off from a third of its revenues and will soon be by half, in

---

[16] A survey around 1660 roughly indicated that 266,000 of 18,000,000 Frenchmen were ecclesiastics, and of these, 181,000 were monks and nuns.

order to feed all those lazy and unproductive, not to say useless, souls. . . . The state must get some advantage from their wealth, for it is the case that that wealth in inalienable because it is public." In 1666 Colbert drafted an edict forbidding the foundation of convents without letters patent from the king. He also tried to raise the age of ordination to twenty-five for men and twenty for women, but the Church forced him to abandon this project.

Like Laffemas, Colbert considered that the civil wars brought with them industrial anarchy, and thus also the numerous shoddy products that had injured the reputation of French products on the market. France found itself invaded with foreign merchandise—German scythes, English wool, Dutch cloth—which hindered the sale of French goods in their home country. Unemployment led to emigration of workers and a frightening increase in poverty.

Besides, as Fernand Braudel has written: "Between the fifteenth and the eighteenth centuries, the world was still nothing but a vast peasantry, where 80 to 95 percent of all men lived off the land alone. The rhythm, the quality, the insufficiency of harvests, ruled all material life."[17] We have noted the uncertain character of agricultural production. And the kingdom was in the throes of a "little ice age," catastrophic for the countryside. The innumerable poor were unable to find work in the cities, which repulsed them ferociously. Many then became peddlers (water-carriers, hawkers). A great mass of peasants became supplementary manpower for agriculture and for industry. Day laborers, journeymen helped with the grape-gathering and with the mowing and worked also in some fashion in factories and shops. If the peasants always needed money, the craftsmen also needed grain and did not hesitate to work in the field.

The world of the laborer and the manufacturer seems very small, dispersed, and family-centered. The spirit of the Middle Ages still influenced all of economic life. The mania for rules had not been invented by Colbert: Rules had been customary for many centuries, since the time when corporate rules were demanded by guilds who banded together in wardenships. Generally, professional groups had gone to the suzerain (seigneur, city, or king) with a request to be granted the privilege of being formed into wardenships, with precise rules and their own police to enforce respect. Today, that attitude seems very hard to understand. But regulation then seemed absolutely necessary to many, not only for the consumer's sake but also to protect the craft itself from competition. One's clientele was a vested interest, to be conserved by offering it products that had been made according to established norms. There was, once again, no belief in economic expansion. The world was immutable like that of the stars. The number of crafts and the men who practiced them could not increase nor could the number of

[17]Fernand Braudel, *Civilisation matérielle et capitalisme.*

consumers. The rules consecrated the privilege given to a certain manufacturer, a certain guild, to make a specific product in a specific fashion. Rules also implied privilege and monopoly.

Master craftsmen expected their rules to guarantee them a means of honestly earning their living according to their class, neither above it or below it. They fought with all their strength against the first great industrial concentrations (much as small companies still do in France) and sought to limit the number of fellow workmen allowed.

Colbert remained equally skeptical about the possibilities of economic expansion, though on a worldwide scale. He judged that France was not getting her proper share of the European pie. The two bywords of his industrial policy were national expansion and commercial quality.

Merchants were often in disagreement with manufacturers. To get around guild rules, they engaged numerous small workshops around the countryside, or gave families raw materials to be processed at home. They produced cloth of lesser quality than that made by the masters, but it was lighter, cheaper, and easier to sell within France.

In order that French industry produce quality goods able to be exported, the minister tried to subject that dispersed mass of more or less independent workers to guild rules of the wardenships. Some merchants wished for that solution. Thus, in 1670 the merchants of Orléans, who trafficked in "silk, wool, cotton threads, or wool blends," asked the king earnestly to grant them regulations. "Being neither guild nor community," they were powerless to put an end to the abuses "committed in the manufacture and preparation of said merchandise." They obtained satisfaction and were at last able to elect wardens and jurors who could prosecute those guilty of fraud. But when Colbert in 1666 gave legal notice of the order requiring all free craftsmen to join guilds, he could not make everyone obey him. Supervision was too difficult to carry out.

For the minister, the wardenships of the guilds had the advantage of imposing regulations on what was manufactured. It was also immensely inconvenient: By limiting the number of manufacturers and workmen, it opposed all expansion and, above all, full employment, a major concern of Colbert's. While simultaneously freezing the evolution of the guilds, the minister would, as Henri Hauser writes, "introduce an element of disorder" by creating factories. The proliferation of privileges finally reached the point where they nearly canceled each other out. Factories, of course, also submitted to the rules, which, being dependent on the king, could be adapted easily to technological inventions. And above all, they could employ large numbers of workers, unlike the guilds.

[18]Henri Hauser, *Les débuts de capitalisme.*

As ever, Colbert began by ordering investigations. Each region was written up: Its resources, it work force, and the characteristics, tastes, and aptitudes of the population were all noted. In 1664 the Council of Trade met for the first time. It was made up of royal civil servants and of delegates from eighteen industrial cities. Colbert also worked closely with a group of collaborators responsible for introducing or developing various industries. Thus the Dalliez brothers supervised the creation of foundries.

Camuset was to set up knitting mills in Burgundy. How would he obtain the assent of the populace? Colbert did not hesitate to use somewhat coercive methods. On October 27, 1671, he had the king sign the following letter: "To the Mayors and Aldermen of Autun and Arnay-le-duc: Dear and Beloved Friends, having sent M. Camuset to establish a factory to make knit stockings, we wished to tell you that you should give him at the same time all the assistance in your power to carry out the said establishment, and to that end you shall require men and women as well as children over the age of eight who are unemployed to work in the said factory."[19] Camuset was expected to send Colbert information during his lengthy trips, whose stages the minister had fixed himself.

Mme de la Petitière was charged with developing the lace and embroidery industry. With much zeal and energy, she organized a sort of public school in Auxerre where women were taught how to make French lace. Colbert saw to it that she was granted a free residence and a pension of 600 livres.

A few factories were royal property. They produced furnishings for the royal household (such as the Gobelin or the Savonnerie) and military equipment (the Saint-Etienne weapons factory).

The minister ordered his agents, "Actively exhort any individual who desires to open an establishment to succeed in it, and if he needs the king's protection, you may promise him that he will not lack for it."

In most cases the new factories had partial state support, and some older ones in difficulty were subsidized. These "royal factories" were permitted to bear "the king's arms," to mark their products with a crown and three fleurs-de-lis, and sometimes—as a supreme honor—to have porters in royal livery at their doors.

The greatest difficulty consisted in finding capital. To encourage the bourgeois to invest in industry, Colbert stopped the sale of public offices while discouraging purchase of Paris bonds, the *rentes de l'Hôtel de Ville*. Over a few years, he seemed to be getting some results. But private enterprise remained very timid. Colbert would later be criticized for his subsidies, but one may wonder whether the bourgeoisie, so attached to honorific offices and to real estate holdings, would

[19]Quoted in Franc Bacquié, "Un siècle de l'histoire de l'industrie."

ever have supported industrialization alone, without those subsidies and the king's charisma.

Colbert was the first to be irritated by this lethargy. The subsidies were only "crutches" to support a factory's first steps. The system was dangerous: If the state went through a financial emergency, the whole industrial apparatus could collapse (which happened in part after Colbert died). But factory owners liked being subsidized and managed to obtain further loans from the government. Thus the textile industry in Languedoc, artificially created to stem the flow of money to the Mideast, could barely stay alive. Like hungry chicks, its constituents endlessly begged the government for money. The minister was furious. In a letter to the intendant Bessons (October 2, 1671), he expounded the problems inherent in his own system: "The merchants never apply themselves to surmount by their own efforts the difficulties they encounter in their business, as long as they hope to find easier paths at the king's order. It is impossible for these establishments not to have to face changing conditions from time to time, and if their backers lack the industry to find other outlets when one is lost, no authority and no aid can make up the lack."[20]

To ensure outlets for production, Colbert often granted monopolies for new processes (a little like our patents) or for a given product. The French Lace Company, founded in 1665, was given a monopoly for nine years on lace imitated from the Venetian. The Dutchman Van Robais had exclusive rights to the weaving of fine cloth within a ten-mile radius of Abbeville. Here again the minister was being more pragmatic than it might appear. Monopolies served to introduce new industries. Thus the making of silk stockings was first entrusted to privileged factories and then, in 1672, was organized by Colbert himself into "a community and masters."

The majority of factories were in fact made up of several workshops, more or less grouped, working under a single management. A few were more like our factories, employing up to one thousand workers. The most famous example is the factory of the Dutchman Van Robais, who received from Colbert in 1665 a loan of 80,000 livres and a grant of 20,000 to found in Abbeville an important factory for fine cloth in the Dutch style. He brought along, or hired locally, more than 1,600 workers. The king granted him and all of his workers permission to "continue to profess the alleged Reformed religion."

It was absolutely necessary to prevent the French from buying luxury goods outside of France. Foreign manufacturers and especially skilled workers who could

---

[20]Don't we seem to be hearing a contemporary French government official speaking to the Conseil National du Patronat Français?

teach the French their techniques were brought in, sometimes at great expense. The Dutch, troublesome rivals, were especially sought after: They were also rope-makers, carpenters, and shipbuilders. German miners and metallurgists were also brought in. Despite the opposition of Venetian authorities, mirrormakers from Murano moved into France. In 1665 the French government officially forbade all foreign technicians to leave the kingdom. Three Venetian workers holding valid Venetian passports to return to Murano were arrested in Lyons and thrown into jail. Shortly afterward, several silk workers trying to leave and find work in Spain were also imprisoned, and Colbert recommended that they be fed "sparingly."

Contrary to what goes on today, France in Colbert's time sent a considerable labor force to Spain. The minister saw nothing wrong with this: The Spaniards had gold, and upon his return each émigré brought back "some amount of money that adds up when you take them all together." But skilled French laborers ran a great risk if they tried to work outside France: From 1669 onward, they were forbidden to "settle in foreign countries on pain of confiscation of body and property."

Colbert wanted to impose on the entire industrial world—merchants, man-ufacturers, workers—a merciless and strict discipline. It was illegal to produce cloth without strictly respecting the rules for the width and length allowed, the specified dyeing procedures, and the required thickness. The minister thought "the highest degree of perfection" could not be obtained without a sort of police terrorism. The cruel edict[21] he sent the kingdom's mayors and aldermen is still amazing. It stated that:

> Cloth manufactured in France if found defective and not in conformity with the rules shall be exposed on a post of nine feet in height, with a signboard giving the name and surname of the merchant or worker found responsible, and after having been thus exposed for forty-eight hours, the merchandise shall be slashed, torn, burnt, or confiscated, according to ordinance; in the case of a second offence, the merchant or worker shall be reprimanded before the full assembly of the guild, besides the exhibition of their products; and finally, in case of a third offense, they should themselves be placed and attached to said pillory for two hours, along with specimens of the goods confiscated from them.

The aldermen refused to apply this law fully, but occasionally (in Tours, for example) defective goods could be seen hung from posts.

In 1669 Colbert organized the industrial inspection service. As usual, he sought staff of high quality to gather information, investigate, and see to it that the rules were applied. The merchants were often irritated by this inquisitorial

[21]Edict of February 17, 1671, in Clément, *Lettres,* vol. 2.

surveillance, and craftsmen complained of having to copy foreign products and of being forced to abandon personal invention and local tradition.

The most notorious example was that of the lace industry in Auxerre, where Mme de la Petitière was in charge. The city traditionally manufactured a local lace. But Colbert wanted to impose the style of Venice on it, which he called "French lace" (and which was also called "Colbert lace" by others). It was high-relief needlework with designs inspired by Renaissance scrolls, and decorated with garlands and flowers. The women workers wanted to make traditional lace. The aldermen were indignant at these draconian rules. Colbert persisted. To better verify that the work was being done properly, it was forbidden, on pain of corporal punishment or fines, that any work be done outside the factories. It was also forbidden to make lace "after any design other than those furnished by the contractor." A black market in traditional lace arose. The new style clung to life for a time, but died with Colbert.

There can be no doubt that the quality of French industry had been in a decline before Colbert's time and that the minister had clearly improved the reputation of French products abroad. But why that excess, that rigidity in his commercial ideas, when a city like Lyons—with its countless free artisans who furnished her great merchants such quantities of cloth and silk—seems to have run counter to his theories?

Understandably, the minister hoped to stamp out the French habit of untrustworthiness and the lack of seriousness with which foreigners found such fault. The preparation of an ordinance concerning trade was not enough.[22] It was necessary to employ means of popularization and publicity. Colbert had the happy idea of asking for the collaboration of Jacques Savary, an old friend of Fouquet's. Savary dictated *The Perfect Merchant,* a sort of practical commentary on the ordinance. He got results: The book was a great success in France and elsewhere. The minister showed, as we have already noticed, a great competence in the use of publicity.

Colbert's attitude toward the working class seems, in a sense, more modern than that of some of his contemporaries, but it still had the severity colored by paternalism current in his time. Unemployment and extreme poverty increased in terrifying fashion. There had been civil wars, which had devastated the country. There had also been, as Henri Hauser has written, "the gradual expulsion of the worker from guild governance," begun three centuries earlier. All guild regulations favored the sons of masters over the *compagnons,* or journeymen. Hence the *compagnonnages*—more or less clandestine groups that celebrated rites the Church had condemned, and that tried to create a secret monopoly on jobs. The "antipathy" between capital and labor had already been born in the fourteenth century.

[22]The ordinance would not be published until 1673.

In response to the scourge of poverty, numerous charities sprang up, some-times admirable, but they were of no interest to the minister. For him, the only effective and durable remedy was maximum production, not only for export pur-poses but to ensure full employment. The incredible energy he devoted to creating a "dictatorship of labor" was worth, in his eyes, all the charities in the world. Whatever the critics say, he never accepted the inevitability of poverty, and he hoped deeply for "abundance for all,"[23] though it might not come about for a very long time.

His humanitarian reasons were joined to moral ones. Work must be found for men and unmarried women of all ages in order to "protect them from oppor-tunities to do ill, which are inseparable from idleness." Colbert genuinely hated idleness, to such a degree that he could scarcely conceive of leisure for himself or anyone else.

Working conditions were extremely hard from today's point of view. The working day, for a journeyman, varied between twelve and sixteen hours, "without respite, except to take proper and necessary refreshment." He reached the workshop at six in the morning and never left before nine at night. Fortunately, there were many holidays—about 110 days a year counting Sundays. In 1666 Louis XIV asked the archbishop of Paris to abolish about twenty holidays to speed royal building.

Colbert, following Dutch practice, wanted to reduce definitively the number of holidays, which halted the rhythm of production. An edict of 1669 suppressed seventeen. The reasons invoked are rather surprising: "Most workers are uncouth men who give over to debauchery and disorder these days intended for piety and good works."

The factoryworker's life as Colbert conceived it was a great deal like life in a barracks. Even when he did not live in the factory, the worker had to respect moral rules. In the mints, the minister fixed the length of the working day at fourteen hours in winter, and sixteen hours in summer. In general, workers of all factories were not allowed to take any work outside the shops, where their pro-duction was closely overseen. The women who made lace in Aurillac staged a revolt and provoked riots; the intendant could calm them only by authorizing work at home. Let us note, in addition, the enormous importance of women—particularly concentrated in the textile industry—in the minister's economic plans.

Colbert foresaw the dangers for the worker inherent in an excessive concen-tration of capital—and thus of workers—in a given factory. His remarks are worth citing. Increasing the number of factories would oblige "the master to give perhaps something more to the workers," so that "the masters of a single factory may not

[23]Preamble to the edict on the foundation of the East India Company, 1664.

make themselves masters of their workers, to whom they would perhaps give only what it pleased them to."[24]

Around 1669 the minister took stock of his industrial efforts; the industry producing luxury goods was successful. The mirror factory, which copied the Murano techniques, soon manufactured "glass more perfect than that of Venice."[25]

France was dotted with factories.[26] All foreigners noted this economic revolution. The Venetian ambassador wrote enviously: "French merchandise is in demand on all coasts, which forces [people] to send their currency to France, to the obvious detriment of other markets and to the satisfaction of Colbert, who seeks only to despoil other nations so as to enrich France."

As far as can be known, Louis XIV supported his minister's economic policy. Colbert begged him over and over to give open backing to the immense undertaking. On May 12, 1670, he wrote to the king: "I don't know if Your Majesty will find it apropos, in your reply to the speeches of the magistrates of the captured cities, to speak to them of their trade, and of their factories, and of all the kindnesses you have shown them, and wish to show further in every situation, and to tell them to apply to me where this subject is concerned."

"I shall speak to them accordingly, in the sense you say," the king replied, and he took the trouble to confirm again a few days later: "I have done as you wished concerning the merchants, and I have spoken of commerce, to those who made speeches, in the manner I thought best, ordering them to send you reports on commercial matters."

On May 16, Colbert again asked for the king's cooperation:

The two largest and most important factories that Your Majesty has established are those in Abbeville, for textiles, and in Beauvais, for tapestries; both have their grandeur and are worthy of the kindness Your Majesty has for your people. I know it is difficult, and even impossible, for you to visit them; if, nevertheless, by visiting these cities, or, as you are passing by, if you could go inside them, it would be very advantageous. . . . These signs of Your Majesty's kindness and of your concern with all things will give new life and energy to all of these factories, which, without that, are languishing and could even perish.

In other words, nothing can live without the light of the royal star. Louis replied: "I will go to the factories at Abbeville and Beauvais, and will speak as I think

[24]Quoted in Hauser, *Les débuts du capitalisme,* p. 29.

[25]In 1692, the various glass factories in Paris, Tourlaville, and Cherbourg joined to create the Saint-Gobain Company.

[26]The long list has been established region by region by Professor Renaudet.

best, and as you have set forth. I strongly exhorted the people at Oudenarde to work, and they gave me a report that we shall examine together upon my return." The king never toured any factories except his own (such as the Gobelin). It was not that he disregarded economic problems, but for him, the affairs of state and the greatness of France lay elsewhere.

CHAPTER 13

The Sea

Whoever is master of the seas has great power on land—RICHELIEU

THANKS TO THE GREAT NAVIGATORS of the two preceding centuries, Europe began for the first time to conceive of the planet in its geographic reality. Fleets and ships, wrote Fernand Braudel, were the glory of Europe: "The maritime unity of the world was at the service of the white man." European superiority in navigation on the high seas seemed obvious. National ambition had to attain an even vaster field of play. It was not enough to be the leading power in Europe; it was necessary to become the leading power in the world. The considerable progress of international maritime trade, the numerous colonies, confirmed the essential role of seapower.

Several European nations—Spain, England, Holland—had understood that quickly. France's backwardness in maritime matters contrasted with her strength on the Continent. French lethargy and apathy with respect to naval matters have given rise to many explanations, all of which contain a grain of truth. Thanks to her geographical position, France had long been the only possible center for land trade in western Europe. The Long Vestu company had brilliantly utilized these great commercial routes that drew merchants away from the major sea-lanes. And as a general matter the French seemed indifferent to the sea. Land ownership and public office interested them much more. Probably it was above all the endless civil and foreign wars that made all the efforts of the state to establish real maritime and colonial power fail.

With discernment and inspiration, Richelieu sketched a naval policy that Colbert would take up almost religiously. Holland's success had mesmerized the cardinal. He was furious at the idea that French merchants were obliged to use Dutch ships. He ordered the construction of merchantmen as well as warships; he created commercial associations in imitation of the Dutch companies, pursued the colonization of Canada, and attempted to regulate the naval hierarchy. But nearly all his work disappeared or was jeopardized. Strife within France, the war against the Hapsburgs, and the continuing insecurity of central government prevented him from applying his broad policies effectively. Insurrectionary feudal powers during the time of Richelieu and Mazarin had understood the strategic importance of naval forces. Only with difficulty did Richelieu manage to abolish the independent admiralities in order to impose the idea—so natural in our day— of a central admirality dependent on the government. The sea was thought to be virtually a private business. Fouquet, better placed than anyone to know the cardinal's intent in this matter, had nonetheless felt, as we have seen, the temptation of rebellion on the seas.[1] Ever faithful to "le grand cardinal," Colbert attacked the superintendant as much for his maritime intrigues as for his financial embezzlement.

In fact, Colbert was involved in maritime affairs as early as 1661. At that time, the naval bureaus were under the jurisdiction of the office for foreign affairs, directed by Hugues de Lionne. There was also a "Grand-Master of Navigation," a sort of commandant who theoretically commanded the naval forces. The title then belonged to César de Vendôme, illegitimate son of Henry IV and Gabrielle d'Estrées, a blundering and incompetent former Frondeur. Lionne was overwhelmed by foreign policy, and Vendôme let things slide.

It was with the simple title of "member of the Council of the Grand-Master of Navigation," and with the consent of Lionne, that Colbert began to take the future of the navy in hand. That situation brought on numerous conflicts with the officials in foreign affairs, until Colbert formally became head of the navy department on March 7, 1669. He often seemed greatly saddened by the king's lack of interest in naval affairs. To Louis XIV, sea warfare was incompatible with royal majesty. He even said this, in his *Memoirs:* "In my own interest, I held that since the welfare of the state does not permit a king to expose himself to the caprices of the sea, I would be forced to entrust the fate of my armed forces to my lieutenants, without ever being able to act in person. . . . Warfare on land is a more advantageous business than naval war, in which the most valiant almost never have occasion to distinguish themselves from the weakest." The king inspected no dockyard, not even a single ship, before 1681. How different from the king of England, who so frequently reviewed his naval forces, and, in Louis's absence, those of France, just before waging war on Holland!

"His Majesty shows great disgust with naval affairs," Colbert noted bitterly. The monarch was losing patience. Despite the sums dedicated to seapower, brilliant feats of arms were not forthcoming from the navy. The problem was that everything had to be created from scratch. France's backwardness with respect to the rest of Europe was considerable. It was in that connection that Colbert tried to arouse the pride of the king, who, despite his lack of enthusiasm, gave genuine support

[1]Let us recall that Fouquet's father had been one of Richelieu's principal counselors in maritime affairs.

to Colbert's gigantic undertaking. The monarch also wished to organize punitive expeditions against the Barbary pirates, who terrorized the seas, especially the Mediterranean. He agreed finally that a major expansion of maritime trade was necessary. Colbert always showed great psychological talent when it came to convincing his master—Mazarin as well as Louis XIV—to adopt his own views. When the minister attempted with his utmost power to protect the many Protestants who served or worked in the navy, he did not hesitate to stir Louis's indignation by explaining that major sea trade was shamefully in the hands of "heretical nations."[2]

He had to awaken the monarch's interest, and that of his court, in things having to do with the sea. Never lacking means for gaining publicity, the minister created "Little Venice," an authentic naval museum, in the grand canal of Versailles, where a complete miniature fleet amused the courtiers. To the doge's gift of two gilded gondolas were added, among others, two yachts built in England, several Neapolitan feluccas, some Dunkirk launches, and a light galley after the style of Le Havre, armed with thirty-two minuscule cannons. It was a charming scene, but the king still did not visit his naval forces at anchor in the ports Colbert had created or renovated. On the other hand, Colbert noted that the sovereign was "extremely touchy about salutes and points of honor." French ships were forbidden to give flag salutes. Things reached such a point that the English and the French avoided one another on the high seas, even while they were allies. Merchantmen proudly hoisted a blue flag bearing a white cross emblazoned with fleurs-de-lis. And on naval tokens where an eagle glides above the waves, can be read Louis XIV's famous motto: "All yield, or fly before me."

THE CREATION OF A NAVY

This was Colbert's least questionable achievement. Let us recall briefly that the minister had inherited eighteen warships in 1661 and left 276 in 1683. During that period, moreover, the merchant marine was linked to the war fleet: the acute danger of pirates forced merchant ships to travel in convoy with a heavily armed warship. After the fall of Fouquet, France could claim, besides the eighteen warships, only four transports, eight fireships, and the hulls of six galleys, nearly all in poor repair. The naval yards were nonexistent or totally disorganized. The best seamen sometimes spent years on shore. The naval budget was laughable.

Colbert began by assigning three million livres to naval affairs for the year 1662. At first, he relied on other countries in building up important naval forces. He was short of time: He had to punish the Barbary pirates—which was done at

[2]First meeting of the Council of Trade, August 3, 1664.

Gigeri, not far from Algiers, in 1664. Above all, the threat of imminent naval warfare with England, at the time of the War of Devolution (1667–68), somewhat flustered the king and his minister. Vessels were hastily procured from the Dutch, raw materials from Norway and Sweden. Copper for the casting of cannon was imported in great quantity. Yet that could only be a temporary policy, for it was too much the opposite of mercantilist notions and too dangerous strategically. Obviously one's navy should not depend on foreigners. Colbert made that clear to one of his agents:

> I have written you several times that you must not buy, if you can help it, any goods for the navy that come from foreign countries, especially when we might be able to find them within the kingdom. Yet I have learned that you bought eight to two hundred hundredweight of pitch in the North. You may judge for yourself that this is not the way to boost Digne or Vidaubau, nor to oblige individuals to improve their production, if we give preference to what the Dutch supply. I myself am convinced that they make it just as well in Provence as in the North and that we should use that rather than the other. I think that in this matter you will agree to follow the king's will, which, in a word, is to dispense with foreigners wherever the navy is concerned.[3]

Colbert set an example himself by growing hemp for cordage on his estate at Seignelay.

As soon as he had taken in hand all the personnel Fouquet had bribed, he worked to set up a true maritime infrastructure and to reorganize the naval hierarchy.

PORTS AND CANALS

The poor state and disorganization of the dockyards before Colbert were pitiful. Let us listen to the testimony of the intendant d'Usson de Bonrepaus concerning the dockyard at Toulon:

> There was at that time no dockyard there, but only a few small enclosed warehouses, with workshops that were not at all enclosed, so that individuals went in to carry off surreptitiously whatever they needed to equip privateers. Monsieur Colbert, in order to remedy this disadvantage, had all the different warehouses consolidated in the same place by a walled enclosure, which was called a park. There was only one gate, guarded by the Swiss, and these Swiss detained those who carried anything away. Once this first arrangement had

[3]Letter to M. d'Ingreville, March 29, 1670 (Pierre Clément, *Lettres, instructions, et mémoires de Colbert,* vol. 3).

been made, he undertook to build larger and more commodious dockyards, worthy of the king's magnificence.[4]

As for the yards at Brest, the duke of Beaufort, son of César de Vendôme, described them as "trash." But before long, under the direction of the chevalier de Clerville, Colbert's chief engineer, there appeared large drydocks, long wharves with three-story warehouses, forges, and a powder magazine, not to mention vast sheds to hold sails, longboats, and ropes.

All the coasts that bordered the realm had several large ports, either modernized or built from the ground up, with dockyards under rigorous police control, in which at last the minister could easily impose uniform weights and measures.

Richelieu had wanted to establish three naval bases in the north and west of France: Le Havre, Brest, and Brouage. Only Brest seemed successful. Le Havre was navigable only at high tide. Colbert gave Duquesne the job of improving the access to the port. Dunkirk, which Louis XIV had bought back from England in 1663, was later to replace Le Havre, thanks to Vauban's efforts. Brouage had silted up irremediably. To replace it, the minister, with the aid of his cousin Terron, created the entirely new port of Rochefort. The chosen location was where the Charente River emptied into the only large roadstead in the region, formed by the islands of Ré, d'Oléron, and d'Aix. Rochefort quickly became a large town of 20,000 inhabitants, many of them Protestants. François Le Vau (brother of the builder of Vaux-le-Vicomte and Versailles) was responsible for the completion of its facilities.

In 1671 the minister traveled to Rochefort to prepare for the visit of the king. He wished to show the king the stores of hemp and tar, the hemp-spinning mills, and the ropeyards. The sovereign was to see the fabrication of a huge anchor and the masting of a ship. Colbert even described for his cousin how the vessels were to be arranged for best effect: "In the center, the one that is to be the flagship, then the largest, and so forth, so that whatever direction he comes from, he will see the smallest first, then the largest, on up to the flagship." But Louis XIV never came.

The port of La Rochelle, heavily damaged in the civil wars, was repaired; it was later to be the scene of intense activity. Along the dangerous shores of the provinces of Aunis and Saintonge, the minister installed continuously burning beacons, fueled with logs and pitch, visible within a radius of thirty-eight kilometers, four times the usual range of contemporary beacons.

In the southern part of the kingdom, the three major ports were Sète, Marseilles, and Toulon. Sète was, like Rochefort, a creation of the government. Clerville opened up the harbor; a medallion commemorated the event in 1666.

---

[4]Quoted in Charles de La Roncière, *Histoire de la marine française.*

Toulon had once been an important port, but it had deteriorated to the point that a large ship could enter only with difficulty. Colbert reestablished its importance by recommending to Clerville: "This is not a reign for small things; it is not possible for you to imagine anything too great." Marseilles, too close to Toulon to be itself a great naval base, should be (according to the thinking of the minister) the center of sea trade with the Levant. Arnould, intendant of galleys, doubled the area of the old city. Puget—who was faithful to the baroque style, preferring to stay in Marseille and keep his independence rather than submit to the rules of the Academy of Paris—was nonetheless entrusted with the "alignment" of the buildings. He proved himself to be as great an urban planner as he was a brilliant sculptor.

Every effort was made to improve shipbuilding. Specialized observers were sent to study Dutch and English techniques. At Rochefort, Terron engaged fifty-four shipwrights (forty of whom were hired on an annual basis) to work with Flemish and English wrights. Colbert offered large salaries to attract skilled foreign workers who could train French laborers. Spectacular progress was made in the speed with which vessels were built. In a sort of race among the ports, Rochefort succeeded in erecting a frigate in thirty hours, Brest in twenty-two, and Marseilles in seven.[5] By 1670 the royal fleet included nearly one hundred ships of the line, not to mention frigates, corvettes, galliots armed with bombs, and so on. It should, however, be noted that despite the establishment of foundries, French naval artillery remained inferior to that of the English navy, whose guns were more accurate and had greater range.

The outfitters of the merchant marine were offered construction bonuses. In order to compel the citizens of Bordeaux to "commit themselves to seafaring," Colbert combined threats and promises. Access to the bourgeoisie, to the guild-wardenship, or to consular posts were subordinated to the outfitting of a ship! Thus it was that in 1671 the "Charter Company of Merchants of Bordeaux" was created. The company's first ship, *La Ville de Bordeaux,* was a magnificent vessel with three decks and three masts, which from 1672 on was outfitted for whaling in Greenland.

NAVAL STAFF

Colbert, like Richelieu, dreamed of having a permanent and competent naval staff. The minister made that fact public with a concise statement: "The king grants naval commissions only for merit and not upon recommendation. There is

[5]Ibid.

only one way to rise in the service: time and feats of arms."[6] The "scarcity of competent people" in the navy made him unhappy. The weight of feudal hierarchy was still too heavy for the office* of Grand-Master of Navigation to be abolished. This often exasperated Colbert: "Ambition gives men pretentions in an age when merit is less important than favor."[7] The Grand-Master, César, duc de Vendôme, was as inconsistent as he was incompetent. His son, the duc de Beaufort, went so far as to write to the minister, "Use all your credit and your skill to prevent Vendôme from going to sea. After all, he goes in the service of the king."

Yet Vendôme saw to it that his son inherited the office. Beaufort's temperament was fretful and insufferable. The people of Paris nicknamed him "king of the markets"† during the Fronde. He was one of the best pistol shots in the kingdom, but he stupidly declined to accept a single lesson on nautical matters. His "rashness" was upsetting to Colbert, who tried to bring him under the control of the navy's intendants and officers. Beaufort paid no attention and gave the most contradictory orders at will. Whereupon the minister asked the king for help. The king sent the "king of the markets" a memorable reprimand. All Beaufort's defects were harshly recalled: "I am happy to have spoken at length of these details, to show that nothing can be hidden from me."[8]

Beaufort died in the course of a campaign against the Barbary pirates in 1669. Colbert had named as Admiral of France and Grand Captain of the Seas a two-year-old boy, the comte de Vermandois, the son of Louise de La Vallière and raised by the minister. The marquis of Saint-Maurice expressed the common opinion: "a coup of Colbert's, to make him master of the navy." The coup was so obvious that Beaufort had to be replaced by a more effective person. Jean d' Estrées, a good army officer but a bad naval officer, was named vice-admiral of the fleet of Ponant. A bungler, he was asked by Colbert to "change his style." The duc de Vivonne, brother of Mme de Montespan, became general of galleys in the Mediterranean. That was fair enough: It meant each of the king's mistresses had a close relative (son and brother) among the highest-ranking naval officials.

The truly great figure in the naval hierarchy was Abraham Duquesne, already fifty-one years old in 1661. The sea was his domain. Son of a Protestant merchant captain, on occasion a pirate, Duquesne went to sea aboard his father's ship as a child. At seventeen he distinguished himself by capturing a Dutch ship. He always

[6]Clément, *Lettres,* vol. 3.

[7]Cf. La Roncière, *Histoire de la marine française,* p. 345.

[8]October 20, 1666.

*The office was a hereditary one.

†Beaufort's vocabulary was that of a market vendor's: coarse.

remained loyal to the king and Richelieu even during the siege of La Rochelle against his coreligionists. Disgusted by the deterioration of the navy, he enlisted in the service of Sweden, but returned to France at Mazarin's request and was named squadron leader in 1647. Duquesne was a very handsome man, robust, blond, and blue-eyed. He was married to Gabrielle de Bernières, who did not hesitate to abjure the Catholic religion to wed him. Despite a smiling exterior, his character was as cantankerous as Colbert's. Their correspondence was a droll mixture of respectful wrath on the part of Duquesne—always angry at everything and in particular at the slowness of his promotions—and patient and tactful authority on the part of Colbert, who held the officer's competence in high esteem. Duquesne had to wait until 1667 to become lieutenant general of naval forces.

The ships were undermanned. Colbert tried several remedies in succession. First, the townships of the seacoast were asked to furnish a number of men proportional to their population. But instead of sailors, the minister received money. At first this expedient was accepted, so much the more since vessels were still few. After a few years, a regular system of recruitment became urgent. The French fleet had grown, and, above all, it had to be able to defend itself in case of war with England and later with Holland.

The hateful press-gang system was common during that period. Colbert preferred to replace it with a system of "classes," which would ensure a fairer and more regular recruitment. He had a general roster of sailors drawn up—first those in Poitou, Aunis, and Saintonge, and finally, in all of France. Then he divided these men into three, four, or five "classes" depending on their locality. Each man would owe the state a month's service every three, four, or five years. Those were, in brief, the principles of the famous "maritime registration," which did not outlive its creator, at least in that form. The system worked well in some places (in Brittany for example), and poorly in others. Local parlements, aldermen, and merchants often conspired to help evaders. These novelties inspired no confidence among the sailors, and they were not mistaken: The exigencies of war forced the minister to prolong the terms of service beyond their promised lengths. Still, the "classes" were a step in the direction of fairness. But the minister's contemporaries were too imbued with feudal concepts to understand that. Sailors often preferred to take their chances with the press-gangs, rather than accept a common discipline, which seems fairer to us.

In 1669 there were 60,000 men on the maritime rolls, or 12,000 to 15,000 per class. When not in service, sailors were free to enroll in the merchant marine. The minister insisted on rapid publication of the rolls, so that the merchants would not be hampered in their own recruiting. The same year he forbade all officers and seamen "to take regular service in other countries, on pain of the galleys in perpetuity." Those then abroad were called upon to return to France within six months "upon their lives."

New rules fixed the relationship among ranks. The captain was called *maître* and his first officer *contremaître*. One also found in the crews a ship's carpenter, a pilot, sailors, and cabin boys, called *garcons*. While many seamen were Protestant, the surgeon-barber was always Catholic, that profession being denied to Protestants. French sailors were better paid and better fed than the Dutch sailors, which, of course, increased transport costs. An eyewitness recounted that the Frenchmen required four meals a day, including "wine, bread, wheat biscuits, fresh and salted meat, codfish, herring, eggs, butter, peas, beans; and when they ate fish, which is only on fast-days, it had to be well-seasoned."

The minister's cruelty in filling the Mediterranean galleys is disquieting. Everyone knows the terrible conditions of the galley slaves. Only criminals, convicts, or slaves were used to drive the galleys. The number of galley slaves was very insufficient. Colbert procured them through iniquitous means when he needed them. In 1662, a revolt against taxes broke out in the Bourbonnais region: Four hundred peasants were sent to the galleys, followed by dealers in contraband salt arrested in Poitou, Auvergne, and the Limousin. The minister even asked the presidents of the various parlements to sentence "the greatest number possible" to the galleys, by commuting death sentences to forced labor. Some judges held back; others turned out galley slaves eagerly.

To the intendant of Toulon, who had just bought three Turkish slaves, Colbert wrote: "There is nothing as important, for strengthening our galleys, than having Turks mixed there; we must at once seek means to raid Barbary and get slaves." The minister belonged to an age when cruelty and charity mingled with a startling casualness. He didn't hesitate to recommend to the intendant of Toulon: "Take care to protect your convicts, see that they are given good bread and beans . . . be charitable to those that are sick." But he wrote to the intendant of galleys, Arnould, on March 29, 1669: "A large number of people here who have experience with galleys say that your convicts cannot be any good, because you give the slaves too much liberty and feed them too well, since nothing is worse for a slave than grease and obesity. You should take this under consideration."

Need we add that Colbert insisted on strict discipline for all naval personnel? Intendants and commissioners oversaw officers, sailors, and even the directors of naval yards, who did not hesitate to employ the workers from the dockyards in their own households.

Colbert wanted the navy to carry out naval operations alone, without support from the army on land. Understandably, he didn't want to introduce any confusion between the Department of the Navy and the Department of War, where Le Tellier ruled. To have infantry troops aboard his warships, he created two regiments, the Royal Marine and the Vermandois, one for the Ponant and one for the Levant. Le Tellier and Louvois immediately complained to the king that Colbert was commissioning officers without their knowledge, claiming he was "undermining their offices." To Colbert's great displeasure, Louis agreed with them. Thenceforth, the officers of the two regiments served aboard ship with such distaste that they had to be relieved in 1671.

Nautical science had made little progress since the preceding century. Longitudes could not be calculated, and a precise chronometer did not exist. Errors were frequent. Colbert asked three of the departments he had created—The Academy of Sciences, the Observatory, and the Hydrographic Service—to collaborate on furnishing maps, instructions, and exact details. In every port, hydrographers taught and described new knowledge. Schools multiplied. The minister wanted to attract "quality people." The problem of calculating longitude obsessed him, and he spared no expense to solve it. The Dutchman Huyghens whom, we have seen, Colbert had attracted to France, came close to the solution with his pendulum clocks. A multitude of maps were made available to sailors.

It is remarkable that such a vast undertaking would be carried out by such a limited number of civil servants. Colbert was aided by a secretary general[9] and only seven or eight clerks. All of the naval administration was eventually centralized.[10] The minister drafted everything himself, observed the smallest details, and, in short, wore himself out for the sake of what he called "the most beautiful part of my administration," which he had decided to pass on to his eldest son, Jean-Baptiste, marquis de Seignelay.

THE MARQUIS DE SEIGNELAY

Seignelay was intelligent and very gifted, but overconfident because of his facility. He liked luxury and the better things in life. His father gave him a memorandum in which he wrote: "Think well and reflect often on what your birth would have been if God had not blessed my work, and if that work had not been extreme."

His father held him to a strict schedule: "You have asked me, son, whether it is better to work at night or morning; I reply to you that one must work morning and night." The minister had a specific plan: to make his son his principal

[9]Louis Matharel, then Le Foin, starting in 1670.

[10]Let us note, however, the particular situation of Brittany, which succeeded in keeping the autonomy of its admiralty until the eighteenth century.

aide in maritime affairs. In 1670 Seignelay was sent to his cousin Colbert du Terron at Rochefort. Colbert asked his cousin to introduce his son to seafaring, to give him a taste for work, and to oversee his conduct and his waistline as well. Seignelay was inundated with injunctions, being told to avoid "falling into any of the mishaps of excessive gaming, love affairs, or other faults that can disgrace a man for life."

Later Colbert himself took over his son's training. The letters[11] he sent to his son reveal the passionate energy he devoted to naval affairs. Nothing escaped him: not the comings and goings of warships, nor the orders given officers, nor the amounts of cast-iron or copper to be sent to the warehouses, nor the details of the construction of a port. Seignelay became a representative for his father, observing, transcribing, carrying out, or rapidly transmitting the orders his father had drafted in an abrupt and peremptory style. In his turn, Seignelay sent his father reports in which he recapitulated the impressive list of his activities. The minister occasionally allowed some signs of his satisfaction to be seen: "Nothing could be better done, my dear son, than this report; do not slacken, soon you will be as competent as I wish."[12]

Colbert's surveillance was incessant, almost obsessive. Seignelay was expected to keep in mind the contents of all his father's recent letters: "Observe, if you please," he wrote to his father, "that I do not read excerpts of letters, but read them all attentively so as to keep in mind what has gone before, which always has some relationship with what is being done now."[13] "Good" replied Colbert, "you must always take care to read five or six of my earlier letters before answering any letter." To complete his training, the young man was sent to Italy, the Netherlands, and England to study the layout of ports, the dockyards, and the duties of officers.

The French ambassador to England was then Colbert du Croissy, the minister's brother. The minister wrote him: "While my son is with you, I beg you to see to it that there are always four or five of the principal officers of the English navy eating lunch or dinner with him, so that he can converse with them, and hear what they have to say about their profession or what they have seen." Louis XIV backed Seignelay's career with his full authority, which shows the immense favor Colbert enjoyed at the time. The sovereign sent his minister the following letter: "I am writing to tell your brother to thank the king for his good treatment of your son. You can tell him he may accept the gift offered him. I am

[11]Unpublished in part.

[12]Unpublished reply to a memorandum of October 23, 1671.

[13]Unpublished note of Seignelay with a reply by Colbert, October 25, [1671?].

pleased that he has done even more for his education in England than he did in Holland."[14]

Finally, in 1672, Seignelay was allowed to sign naval dispatches, after his father examined them. The young man was expected to discuss naval matters, often with the king. His father was pleased, but mortally worried. Over and over he sent Seignelay little scraps of paper with hastily scribbled instructions.[15] The minister still became angry at times: "Your reports are not handsome enough; what I mean is, you are galloping through them." He still arranged his son's schedule:

> I think my son should polish off today all the work I have given him, and that tomorrow he should work all day, from the moment he gets up, on copying into a notebook the full list of vessels, their ports, their ages, the lists of squadrons that are at sea this year and those that are to go to sea next year, the lists of officers, and the number of pieces of artillery both cast-iron and iron in all the yards; it will be much to his advantage to have these lists in a notebook the day after tomorrow when the king is at work.
>
> Tomorrow evening and the next morning, he should prepare what is needed for the council meeting.[16]

Seignelay was to become a remarkable collaborator for Colbert. The work of the two men would be as closely associated with the navy as the work of Le Tellier and his son, Louvois, was associated with the army. The creation of a true navy could not have been carried out—in France, in any case—except by an efficient and powerful central administration, which had never found a better justification. On the other hand, we can ask if the weight of that administration did not do a disservice to maritime trade.

MARITIME TRADE AND COLONIES

Maritime trade implied, for the contemporaries of the minister, the possession of colonies. Possession did not necessarily mean forced colonization, but it meant at least establishing settlements where raw materials could be obtained without middlemen, and where manufactured goods from the mother country could be sold. The notion of free trade still seemed suspect. A monopoly on some

[14]Not published by Clément.

[15]Seignelay kept these bits of paper and handed them down to his descendants in the family papers.

[16]Unpublished note.

product or in some region was reassuring to merchants and nations alike. Mercantilism sprang up quickly after the great maritime discoveries. The share of trade that a nation controlled throughout the globe should only profit that nation, to the detriment of other nations. Spain, Portugal, England, and the Netherlands had taken a considerable lead over a France absorbed by wars and turned inward upon the continent.

The France of Henry IV had had practically no navy or merchant marine. Despite Sully's advice, the king wanted to pursue the colonization of Canada, begun by Jacques Cartier under Francis I: A depot had been established on the Saint Lawrence estuary, on the future site of the city of Quebec. Richelieu would channel maritime trade and colonial enterprises to the Americas. He wished to lay the groundwork for major trade with the Orient, but political problems and the navy's weakness prevented it: Colbert would take up again the idea of colonizing Madagascar.

Richelieu sent colonists and missionaries to Canada, where they soon founded the city of Montreal. Following the example of England and Holland, the government gave charters to great trading companies. While, in England, the hope of being able to practice freely one's religion in the new world encouraged emigration, in France, the charters included a clause that almost always excluded Protestants. Mazarin, engrossed by the disastrous political situation in France, could not carry on his predecessor's grand design for trade. Besides, did he really consider it? For him, sea trade was, above all, a means of speculating on his own account. As early as 1652,[17] Colbert wanted, nevertheless, to persuade him to revive—for his own profit, but also for the profit of the kingdom—the companies of which Richelieu had dreamed.

Fouquet, dissembling and secretive, as was his custom, carried on trade with the Antilles and the East Indies exclusively for his own profit. Too preoccupied with the superintendant's trial and with restructuring finances, Colbert contented himself, during the first years, with commissioning studies that would lead to a broad commercial and colonial policy. It is more than probable that he looked through the papers "le grand cardinal" had left on the subject. By 1662, he was asking his brother Nicolas, bishop of Luçon, to convey "the king's intent" to the inhabitants of the entire coast: Individuals should no longer be afraid to get involved in trade with foreign countries, or to build new ships, for they could be sure of the king's support. It was vitally important to pull merchants and shipbuilders out of their desolating "lethargy," for already nearly all major international trade was by sea.

[17]See the letter from Colbert to Mazarin of October 13, 1652, in Clément, *Lettres*, vol. 1.

THE ECONOMIC WAR

At the first meeting of the Council of Trade (August 3, 1664), the minister noted bitterly that the French merchant marine had been reduced to "200 seaworthy ships." That was not much when one knew that the Dutch and English merchant ships were counted by the thousands. "The king's power on land is superior to all others in Europe; on sea it is inferior. It is necessary to make it equal throughout."

Like Richelieu, Colbert was rankled to see the trade between the French Antilles and France monopolized by the Dutch. The near-monopoly Holland had in the North Sea was a veritable nightmare. He offered ship-outfitters and merchants bonuses; like subsidies were given to industrialists.

The risks of seafaring forced shipowners to band together, most often to carry on a rather minor trade. Colbert wanted more: He wanted to create large companies, following the example of England and Holland, in which all the capitalist forces in the kingdom would participate. Later, commentators would willingly place the French charter companies, desired and sustained by the state, in opposition to the English and Dutch companies created by private capitalists. The distinction is poorly made. The foreign companies were also charter companies, owing to the privileges granted by the king of England or the government of the Netherlands. But in England as in the Netherlands, the merchant class was much more intermixed with the government's personnel: The feeling of a strong separation between the castes according to function—a feeling common in France— was much less evident in England and Holland. The French mistrusted all intervention in economic matters. They were constantly suspicious of an underhanded preparation of a new tax.

The great contradiction, with which all the economic work of Colbert clashed fundamentally, consisted in wanting to impose civil peace by strengthening the monarchical authority while, at the same time, imposing a broad capitalist transformation despite the arbitrary nature of that regime. Whatever their reasons might be, the subjects of Louis XIV seem to have grown sluggish with a certain satisfaction in the medieval economic conditions, often very distant from capitalist conceptions as they are perceived today. Charles Seignobos explained clearly the capitalist innovation, so poorly understood or accepted in France, that the very nature of these companies implied: "Instead of being a local group of persons attached to a set of moral rules, without capital in common, the commercial companies became a national enterprise, impersonal, operating with a permanent common capital, with a view to unlimited gain, without any moral restrictions."[19]

Colbert had to struggle on all sides against the deep-seated individualism of the French, who were hostile for the most part to these large associations. The merchants of Bordeaux turned a deaf ear to the appeals of the minister. The

[18]At the time, the term *merchant* was also applied to shipowners.

[19]Charles Seignebos, *Essai d'une histoire comparée des peuples de l'Europe.*

intendant explained why to Colbert: "In this province one does not form societies. Everyone wants to handle his own business as an individual, and does not want anyone to know about it." The men of Marseilles were not in any hurry either, and Colbert showed his anger in a letter to one of his agents: "You tell me the English and the Dutch are doing ten to twelve millions' worth of trade in the Levant. They do it with large ships. The gentlemen from Marseilles stick to small crafts so that each of them can have his own, and thus one succeeds and not the other." There were, nevertheless, a few great merchants of enterprising character. Thus, the brothers Formont, from a Protestant family of Rouen, became close collaborators of Colbert's. Cosmopolitan merchants, bankers, and shipowners, they belonged somewhat to the race of the Colberts of the Long Vestu. They shared the same conception of an ambitious international trade, associated with a great financial movement.

Pierre, the eldest, was the head of one of Europe's leading banks. He had correspondents throughout Europe: Madrid, Rome, Venice, London, the Hague, Danzig, and Berlin. Furthermore, he owned, or had a share in, several merchant ships based in the principal ports of France. He traded with the Antilles, Guinea, or Morocco as easily as with Italy, England, Holland, or the powers of the north. For twenty years he was an intelligent and active supporter of Colbert's.

Alas, the Formonts, with a few others, were the exceptions. Foreign trade remained lazy and timid. The companies seemed suspect, they were seen to be potentially harmful. However, the government granted them extensive privileges. When the companies had colonial interests, they could even exert, in the territories that had been conceded to them, considerable political power. In sum, it was a matter of breaking up of royal power, the companies remaining, of course, submissive to the king by a feudal contract.

Privilege was, in those days, inseparable from monopoly. In that regard the companies made no innovation. No one could imagine mounting a large-scale commercial operation without a monopoly. Exclusive rights to a raw material could allow profitable increases in prices or political blackmail. The commercial supremacy of a foreign power in a region that produced such materials was a national humiliation. Thus, international trade was conceived in terms of economic war. The large companies were charged with conquering for France the trade of the world. To each, the minister reserved a part of the globe.

THE ORIENT

Founded in 1664 at the same time as the West Indies Company, the East Indies Company received from the king a monopoly on trade and navigation in the seas of the Orient and the Southern Hemisphere for a period of fifty years. When the Parlement of Paris ratified the two charters, its president tried to add a clause stating that in the countries conceded them, no religion could be practiced other than Catholicism, but Colbert managed to have it removed with much difficulty. On the other hand, he caused to be inserted in both charters a clause specifying that participating nobles would not lose their status. Shortly after, an edict even gave nobles permission to refer to their gentlemanly standing in the public record of maritime commerce, "provided they do no retail business."

To attract subscribers, the minister organized active propaganda, not only in France but also in Europe, even in Holland, to the fury of Jan De Witt and his friends. The academician Charpentier was asked to draw up the prospectus. Here again, the king was to be the prime mover, the supreme example. The initial capitalization for the company was set at fifteen million livres. Louis XIV signed up as first shareholder for the vast sum of three million livres. The royal family followed suit. The two queens and the dauphin each put in 60,000 livres; Condé, 38,000. Then came the court: 100,000 from Mazarin, 30,000 from Noailles, 10,000 from Luynes. Chancellor Séguier subscribed for 40,000; the comptroller general, Herwarth, contributed 60,000; and Colbert himself, 30,000. Judges and merchants of Paris, subsidized industrialists, and high-ranking civil servants all felt obliged to sign up. The shares sold in Paris, including the king's, furnished something over a third of the expected capital. There remained nine millions' worth to be gotten in the provinces. But their inhabitants had no desire to participate in what they saw as a dangerous adventure. The intendants sometimes showed a regrettable zeal in forcing members of parlements and officials to subscribe. The intendant of Auvergne even thought of using the "ministry of dragoons."

Colbert sent a circular to the treasurers of France to enjoin them to set a good example. Nothing could have been less spontaneous than these investments. Colbert was given a current list of subscriptions by généralité and by province. By each name he noted with his own hand, if the subscriber had showed himself to be rather generous, or if the subscriber was being too slow in announcing the amount of his pledge. In turn, Louis wrote the mayors and aldermen of the kingdom. Boissonnade describes the impromptu arrival of a royal messenger in the tranquil town of Poitiers:

On June 24, 1664, the city council, including the mayor and aldermen, was just about to conclude. The postal clerk came into the meeting room and handed over a large packet, which was immediately opened. We can imagine the stupefaction of these men, who had just been peacefully discussing local affairs, when faced with the statutes of the company, a circular from the society's twelve directors, and a letter from the king ordering them to immediately call a general assembly, to inform Colbert of "everything that happened," and, added the king, "to omit nothing in your power to notify everyone of the use and advantage for all those who subscribe . . . for such is Our pleasure." The inhabitants of each parish were ordered "to assemble at the sound of the bell." Neighborhoods and parishes chose delegates to examine the documents. The Poitevins remained skeptical and even hostile. Despite Colbert's urgent reminders, it seemed impossible to raise the money. The mayor claimed there were local financial problems. The municipal council, threatened with the suppression of privileges, finally sent 3,000 livres drawn from the city's "special funds," in September 1665. There was not one further subscriber before 1667.[20]

Poitiers was not an isolated case. The minister met the same resistance and the same inertia all over France. It is not surprising that by 1669 the king was saying, "The company is compromised in the public eye throughout my realm."

Still, ships went to sea, and trade missions were organized. Colbert hired several Dutch advisors. Taking up again the projects of Richelieu, he attempted the colonization of the island of Madagascar. The financial problems the company had to face to assure the flow of trade discouraged all colonial effort. Madagascar had to be temporarily abandoned. At least a precedent had been set for the future. Colbert also tried several times to avoid sending ships around southern Africa, by negotiating a passage through the Red Sea with the Egyptians—but, alas, without success.

It sometimes happened that the company's representatives were successful in the most distant lands. To establish commercial bases in India, Colbert named a Persian advisor, Marcara Avanchivz, who knew the area well. The minister wanted to set up a trading post in the territory of the king of Golconda, who received Marcara with pomp. No doubt on Colbert's recommendation, the Persian played upon Louis XIV's brilliant reputation for commercial ends. The French monarchy, he explained, was the oldest. The king of France was superior to all the princes of Europe both in military might and in personal qualities. He was not eager, like the Dutch and the English, to carry off the treasures of India, for he had riches enough in his own kingdom. He wished only for peace and good faith in matters of trade. The king of Golconda happily accepted a portrait of Louis XIV and granted the French better trading conditions than those offered their rivals, despite all the intrigues and bribes of the Dutch aimed at spoiling the negotiations. In December 1669, Marcara returned to Masulipatam, where he installed the first French commercial outpost in India, able to send spices directly to France, aboard French ships. But successes like these were unfortunately too rare. French indifference brought on the company's collapse in 1672.

[20]Prosper Boisonnade, *Colbert et la souscription aux actions de la Campagnie des Indes, spécialement en Poitou.*

The currency drain toward the Mideast obsessed Colbert. In 1665 he was planning to separate Mediterranean trade from that of the other oceans, and to entrust it to a special company. Marseilles, principal commercial port of the region, carried on a large part of the trade with the Levant. But, the people of Marseille had, according to Colbert's agents, the reputation of being disorderly, quarrelsome, and unenterprising. The intendant of galleys, Arnould, wrote spitefully to the minister: "Since they are sober and idle, great talkers and gossipers, they no longer care to do anything except stroll through the port, sword at their side, with pistols and daggers, which it would be good to correct." Colbert hoped to discipline their commercial habits by creating the Company of the Levant in 1670. It had no exclusive rights, but received bonuses and escort ships from the king. It was a success for two years.

The minister's relationship with the city of Marseilles often was tense. First, the Marseillais were ordered not to send any more spices to the East. Unlike the Atlantic ports, Marseilles did not have enough foreigners ("foreigners" included Frenchmen from other cities) in its port. To attract them, Colbert made Marseilles a free port in 1669. The institution seemed then a needed corrective to contemporary protectionism, but the people of Marseilles were furious. They had kept the prejudices of the Middle Ages and they did not want to grant to others their rights as bourgeoisie, of which they were so proud. The edict was maintained, despite rather liberal concessions: The new neighborhoods had to be filled, and commerce given new life.

The minister was determined to protect the Jews and Armenians of Marseilles despite the anger of the town. The Jewish community had been driven out a century before. In 1670 Lionne allowed three Jewish merchants to settle in Marseille. Two years later the chamber of commerce requested they be expelled. Colbert wrote to the intendant, Rouillée:

> You should not be surprised if the Marseillais have had so much to say about Jewish settlement there: The reason is that they do not care whether trade increases, but only that it pass through their hands and be done their way. Nothing is so valuable for trade in general as an increase in the numbers of those who engage in it, which means that what is not advantageous to individual inhabitants of Marseilles is very much to the advantage of the kingdom.

THE ATLANTIC

There may not have been enough "foreigners" in Marseilles, but there were too many in the Atlantic ports. The English and, above all, the Dutch carried on most of the trade with the North and the islands of the Americas. In La

Rochelle as in Bordeaux, the merchants accommodated themselves very easily. In order to force the French merchant marine to show more ambition, Colbert founded the West Indies Company, which was immediately given a monopoly on trade with the American colonies and the west coast of Africa from Cape Verde to the Cape of Good Hope. According to that "exclusive" right, all export and import trade in the region was reserved for French ships.

Colbert tried to encourage the company to get involved in the slave trade, to bring agricultural workers to America. But, too absorbed by the exploitation of the Antilles, the company almost completely abandoned that unhappy traffic.[21] The minister still was able to arrange two expeditions to Africa: The first, under Villaret de Bellefond, went to the coast of Guinea; the second, led by Lemaire, went up the Senegal River. Shortly afterward, Frenchmen living along the coast were able to take certain Dutch territories[22] that were to become the nucleus of the French empire in Africa.

Since 1635, some ten Caribbean islands, including Martinique and Guadeloupe,[23] had belonged to the French, mostly former shareholders in the companies Richelieu had created. Colbert began by liquidating those companies and abolishing the regime of hereditary overlordship. Thus, Guadeloupe was bought back from its owner in 1664. Undoubtedly, the evaluation of indemnities often proved very difficult. In 1665 the French moved into the western end of Santo Domingo. For a few years management of the colonies was entrusted to the company. The colonists were exasperated by the rule of the exclusive monopoly: On the one hand, they could sell only to the mother country, and only raw materials at that; on the other, they were expected to buy all finished goods from France. The French navy claimed the right to confiscate the cargo of any foreign ship found in the area.

For the minister, the interests of the colonists were totally subordinated to the interests of the state, whose monetary reserves had to be protected above all else. It was a common opinion in Europe at that time. The job of the Creoles was to furnish France the goods she did not produce—sugar, tobacco, cotton, cocoa, and coffee—and to serve as an outlet for her industries. The sugar problem poisoned the relationship between the colonies and the mother country. By the terms of the exclusive charter, the Creoles could export only raw sugar, and only to France. But they sold raw sugar very cheaply and they found themselves obliged

[21]The slave trade would be renewed by the merchants of Saint-Malo. Cf. L. Cordier, *Les compagnies à charte et la politique coloniale sous le ministère de Colbert.*

[22]The island of Gorée, Rufisque, Portudal, Joal, and Arguin [Senegalese towns].

[23]And Saint Christopher, Saint Martin, Saint Croix, Saint Lucia, Marie-Galante, Grenada, Tortuga.

to buy refined sugar on the French market at a high price. They were not allowed to refine their sugar themselves until much later.[24] They were also forbidden to sell such by-products as rum and molasses in France. In vain did they ask the minister to be allowed to export them to Canada or Boston. Paris's intransigence encouraged black-market trade with the English and the Dutch.

The French colonies in Canada were also included in the edict conceding the West Indies. But the company was quickly discouraged by the hostility of the colonists, who were determined not to be harrassed by its agents. Furthermore, it was engrossed in the Caribbean trade. After hesitating, Colbert gradually withdrew its Canadian privileges, in particular that of choosing the governor or intendant, which in fact the company had almost never exercised.

Directly administered by Paris, Canada was organized like a French province, with a governor, an intendant, and courts of justice similar to those of the mother country. The intendant, Jean Talon, was a fortunate choice: He had the intelligence to favor the interests of the colonists as much as those of France. For him, the preservation of a populated colony was at stake. The minister listened willingly to his advice, but enjoined him to stamp out even the slightest desire for political autonomy. Colbert, like Louis XIV, feared encroachment by the bishop and the Jesuits upon civil authority. This preoccupation reappears endlessly in his correspondence. In 1669 he wrote the governor, Courcelles: "Concerning the excessive authority that the bishop of Petrée and the Jesuits, or more precisely the latter in the former's name, are claiming, once the population of the country grows, royal authority will surely outweigh the ecclesiastical and take on the extent it should have in truth. In the meantime, you may still prevent cleverly, without signs of hostility between you or partiality on your side, the too great enterprises that they might carry out."

A few years later, he opposed governor Frontenac's plan to call a meeting of the Estates General in Quebec. Any organized local group was a threat to central power. And the governor received this curious confidence: "With time, and once the colony is stronger than now, we should gradually dispense with the trustee who now offers petitions in the name of all the inhabitants, it being best that each one speak for himself, and no one for all."[25]

In 1663 French Canada had some 2,300 inhabitants, settled primarily on the shores of the Great Lakes and Hudson's Bay. The minister's ambition was, not the conquest of a vast expanse of territory that the mother country risked being unable to control or keep, but the creation of a strong, well-populated colony solidly implanted in a safely administered region. It cannot be doubted

[24]In 1682.

[25]Clément, *Lettres*, vol. 3, pt. 2.

that the "populating" of Canada was Colbert's work, even if his methods for enforcing that populating may seem a bit surprising today. The minister disliked the solitary trappers, the *coureurs de bois* who hunted fur-bearing animals and lived after the Indian manner. They were beyond the administration's reach, and above all, according to Colbert, they prevented the settling of a large population.

One of the things that has brought the most obstacles to the populating of Canada has been that the inhabitants have put their homes where they pleased without taking the precaution of joining them one to the other and clearing adjoining tracts so as to help each other. Thus these dwellings, being isolated on all sides, are exposed to the ambushes of the Iroquois. For this reason, two years ago the king caused Council to order that there would be no more piecemeal clearing of lands, and that our dwellings would be made to conform to the pattern of other parishes and townships.[26]

Talon was required to grant land to the first colonists to cultivate while clearing adjacent tracts for new arrivals. The French were slow to emigrate. The minister, according to his custom, would force the issue. Several infantry companies coming from France or the West Indies were set ashore at Quebec to put down the Iroquois.[27] The Indians were defeated or driven off. Several companies were disbanded. The men were requested to settle in the colony. Did the soldiers know, when they embarked, that their disbanding had already been decided upon? Talon gave each of them land and a sum of money proportionate to his rank. Colbert hoped to prevent the officers from returning to France. They settled in the country for the most part, and gave their names to various Canadian villages (Sorel, Chambly, Saint-Ours, Contrecoeur, Varennes, Verchères, and so on).

It was necessary to furnish wives for these makeshift colonists. Colbert cleared out the poorhouses responsible for the education of abandoned children, and Louis even drew 40,000 livres from his personal treasury to aid in sending nubile girls to Canada. But men were still much more numerous than women. The prisons were also cleared. Prostitutes took the road to Quebec.[28] The mother superior of the Convent of the Incarnation of Quebec had her hands full with the guidance of these special newcomers.[29] First she pointed out, with reason, that the Canadians

[26]Instructions from Colbert to Talon, March 27, 1665, Clément, *Lettres*, vol. 2, pt. 2.

[27]The most important regiment was that of Carignan.

[28]Cf. Cordier, *Les compagnies à charte.*

[29]At that time, the mother country wanted to furnish wives to the buccaneers and freebooters of the Antilles. Fifty prostitutes were sent to the island of Tortuga. The number was inadequate, so the new wives were put up for auction.

only wanted "village girls who would work as hard as the men; experience shows that those who were not bred to it were not right for here, being in a state of poverty they could not surmount." But Colbert wanted the disbanded soldiers to marry quickly. He sent whoever showed up, with virtually no selection. A certain M. Bourdon brought over 150 girls in 1669. The mother superior said the poor man experienced a difficult voyage: "They gave him no respite during the long trip, for, as they were of all conditions, some were quite rude and hard to handle. There were others of better birth, who were better bred and gave him better satisfaction. . . . It is true that a lot of people are coming from France now, and that the country is becoming better populated; but besides the decent people, there are a lot of scoundrels of both sexes, causing much scandal."

Talon asked the minister to select "girls who have no natural deformity nor ugly appearance, but who are strong so that they are able to work in this country." Colbert wrote to the archbishop of Rouen asking him to encourage the priests in his diocese "to find in each parish one or two girls willing to volunteer to go to Canada." Thus, some 1,500 women were brought to the colony. It was a considerable number for the time. Marriages followed upon their arrival. One witness, the baron de Hontan, recounted jokingly: "When word came of the new merchandise, all those well disposed toward multiplication hastened off to market." Parents who had not married a son of twenty years or a daughter of sixteen had to pay a fine to the colony's poorhouses. On the other hand, they received an annuity of 300 livres if they had ten living children.

Colbert's policy toward friendly Iroquois was remarkably free from racism. He hoped the native population would form "a single people" with the colonists. The Indians should be converted, then drawn into the French community, "which can be done through marriage and the education of their children." He thought the Jesuits showed too strong a tendency to keep them separate from the French. The trappers eagerly sold alcohol to the Indians in exchange for cheap furs. The Church complained to the governor. Colbert was perplexed. He asked the exact number of "sins, murders, fires, and other excesses brought on by the use of spirits." If the number was small, it was necessary to consider that one courted "the risk of being deprived of their trade, and forcing the savages to take it to the English and the Dutch, who are heretics." The bishop would carry the day.

In Colbert's day, the English did not really fear French competition in the New World. Their relative passivity was rather well founded. Colbert did little to encourage distant explorations. Still we should mention here the appearance of an exceptional figure, that of Cavelier de La Salle, one of the greatest of French explorers, thanks to whom France would later possess a gigantic territory between the Great Lakes and the Gulf of Mexico.

Born in 1643, son of a wholesale merchant and nephew of a stockholder in one of Richelieu's companies, La Salle was a Jesuit novice and a teacher of mathematics and natural science. In 1667 he resigned from the novitiate and went to Canada. Talon was greatly interested in finding a route to the Pacific and China. Supported by the intendant, La Salle sailed Lake Ontario and reached the Ohio, alone, living from hunting and fishing. In the summer of 1670 Nicolas Perrot, the most famous of the trappers, came across La Salle hunting with a few Frenchmen and a dozen Iroquois. The explorer learned that the Ohio emptied into a much larger river and suspected that he could find a way to Mexico. He returned to Quebec in 1672 for money and official permission. As we shall see below, he was to go all the way to France and meet with Colbert before continuing his great discoveries.

We must not forget that Canada's function then was to serve the economic interests of the mother country. Colbert at least showed some flexibility. The colony was too important a population center for mercantilist theory to be applied in all its rigidity. The minister even encouraged the Canadians to set up their own factories. He would even rejoice over the fact that Canada furnished a part of the commodities needed by the Caribbean islands. On the other hand, he outlawed tobacco-growing in Canada because it suited the Antilles better and might detract from fishing or manufacturing. The colony had superb forests: "They are a treasure to be carefully preserved." Canada could "build some shops for the construction of royal ships." The conquest of maritime trade remained his major preoccupation.

THE NORTH

To Colbert's despair, Holland held a near monopoly on commercial transport in the Baltic Sea. It was especially in these regions that he hoped to destroy Dutch economic strength. By 1661 he had had the council order voyages by three ships that were to bring back wood from Göteborg, hemp from Riga, and cannons and munitions from Stockholm, in exchange for salt, spirits, and spices. Duquesne insisted that the North could furnish quality materials for boat-building. Soon Colbert was trying to establish direct economic relations with the Nordic powers. His agents, notably the Formont brothers, studied various marketplaces in Sweden, Norway, and Denmark as well as in Russia or Prussia.

In 1663 Colbert signed a commercial treaty with Denmark and negotiated another with Sweden. He already had in mind the creation of "a good company" to trade in the Baltic. Alarmed, the Dutch ambassador wrote to Jan De Witt: "There is no doubt that those people have in mind to take over trade in the north and to drive out those who are presently in possession. They will neglect no means to attain this goal."[30] And De Witt replied: "We have learned to our sorrow that in France they are working to usurp trade and navigation in the north, and hence to exclude all others." That correspondence is of prime importance, for it shows the beginnings of the fatal war of 1672 already existing in 1663.

After having formed the two Indies companies, the minister attempted to find subscribers for a North Sea Company. They were as rare as ever. Henri Hauser, who has so often shed such brilliant light on world economic history, saw the secret reason for the success of trading companies in Holland and their failure in France.

> To defeat the Dutch traders, Colbert had recourse to a method that seemed simple: to take from the Dutch their favorite weapon, the grouping of merchants into companies. But it is here that Colbert's basic error appears. The institution could not be transplanted. Since about 1601, there had been a sort of spontaneous flowering of companies in the United Provinces, encouraged by the country's economic and political conditions as a whole. The associations, or "chambers," of merchants in each port had federated themselves, just as the Provinces themselves had. The companies were the reverse side, the economic lining of the Dutch state.[31]

It is, in fact, more than probable that in France the unifying character of the state, counterbalanced by the individualism of the French, strongly impeded the minister's commercial policy.

Beyond that, the rudimentary character of the French banking system was a major obstacle to the establishment of large-scale trade. The minister was quite aware that in order to do business in the north, he had to be able to use Dutch bank drafts. At the most, there was only the bank of Hamburg for him to turn to.

In France, banking activities were often in the hands of Protestant businessmen. It was primarily the Huguenot bankers, led by the Formont brothers, who helped Colbert set up the North Sea Company. Most of the North Sea and Atlantic ports were solicited in vain. The people of Dunkirk shared too many common interests with the Dutch to want to compete: They were in the habit of buying half shares in Dutch trading ships. In Dieppe they preferred to safely continue their everyday business rather than to risk difficult competition. The people of Rouen reproached the companies with concentrating all commercial activity in the hands of directors who thus lost contact with their clients. And

[30]Boreel to de Witt, August 21, 1663, cited in Boissonnade, *Colbert*.

[31]Preface by Henri Hauser to the work of Boissonnade and Charliat in *Colbert et la compagnie de commerce du Nord*.

besides, children could no longer be sent to foreign countries "to learn business and foreign languages." As far as the Rouennais were concerned, individual trade was as profitable as the trade of associations. Besides, they concluded, "the French spirit does not tend to the forming of companies as do the English and the Dutch." Colbert's agents urged with reason that since trade to the north involved mostly heavy, bulky, low-cost materials, to make it profitable, it was necessary to deal directly with the owners of forests and mines, and then to transport the goods in specialized ships that only large companies could build. Why persist in acquiring only small quantities of wood and metals in foreign ports? Rouen did not allow itself to be persuaded.

Despite all the efforts of Claude Pellot, then intendant of Guyenne, the merchants of Bordeaux preferred coastal trade, to which they were accustomed, rather than to undertake direct trade with the north. Governmental promises and threats secured a few subscribers. The minister wrote to Pellot: "I am impatient to receive the sheets with the names of those who have pledged, and for what amount."

In La Rochelle, Colbert du Terron found a merchant, Henri Tresmitten, who tried to establish direct relations with Sweden. The city, a Protestant center, seemed more open to Colbert's schemes. It became the company's headquarters. Its location had many advantages: It was near salt marshes and vineyards; it belonged to the customs union of the Five Farms, created by Colbert. The export of salt and wine, as well as the import of products for sale, without having to pay multiple customs duties, was made easy. But if the merchants of La Rochelle were more conciliatory, they did not at all want to associate with their rivals in Bordeaux!

The company was founded at last, in June of 1669, with a capital of 600,000 livres. The king invested 200,000 in the first two years. The company lived mostly on government contracts. A Dutch shipwright and twelve journeymen directed French workers: All had the status of workers in royal factories. The company had some ten ships by 1670, plus escorts furnished by the navy. It succeeded well enough despite its problems. The Dutch began to panic. De Witt went to Danzig in the vain hope of negotiating better conditions than those obtained by the French. On his side, Colbert sent Pomponne to Sweden to try to detach that country from the Netherlands.

The minister wanted to merge the trade of the West Indies Company with that of the North Sea Company. American goods would then find a direct outlet without going through the Dutch. In response, the Dutch tried to replace French wines with Rhine wines in the markets of the north.

The Anglo-Dutch war, customs tariffs instituted by Colbert in 1667, and the commercial offensive led by France ended, all the same, by provoking an economic crisis in the United Provinces. Workers and sailors alike felt the sting of unemployment. Four-hundred silk looms shut down. In October 1670, Pomponne, then French ambassador to the Netherlands, wrote Colbert: "It is certain, monsieur, that trade is weakening every day, that one sees the cargoes of ships diminish, and that many [ships] are still in port. That is what causes the reasoning of most people in this country that a war where Europe would be divided would be more profitable to them than peace."

Grotius's sons asked Louis XIV to retract protectionist measures. The king refused. Colbert exhorted the directors of the company to "do more harm to the Dutch than they do to us."

A conflict had become inevitable. In April 1672, placards appeared in the ports, proclaiming that His Majesty had resolved to make war on the Netherlands. The war was to confirm the notion that victories are sometimes ambiguous things. It brought the Sun King, and hence his minister, a great deal of glory, but also deep bitterness.

PART IV

GLORY &

BITTERNESS

[1672–83]

CHAPTER 14

The Sun King's War

FORTIFIED BY AN ENGLISH ALLIANCE, by Swedish friendship, and by the Empire's neutrality, Louis XIV went crusading against the "cheese-sellers." The United Provinces were invaded, the unfortunate Jan De Witt savagely assassinated; but it was a most ambiguous victory. Louvois's magnificent army was forced to retreat before the fierce patriotism of the Dutch, who flooded their lands. The king of France had caused a formidable enemy to come to power: the twenty-two year old William of Orange. Frail, sickly, wily, and remarkably intelligent, William would use the same diplomatic weapon as Louis XIV: money. The Bank of Amsterdam was rich. The florins were adroitly distributed. William succeeded in recreating the old alliance of the Hapsburgs against France. Spain and the Empire joined forces with the Netherlands. The war had changed in nature and in direction. The economic war desired by Colbert to overthrow a commercial enemy was succeeded by a traditional war led by the House of France against the House of Hapsburg to defend or enlarge territory. But Colbert's war, the future would confirm, would be lost. The king's war, against the encirclement of the Hapsburgs, would be won. The treaty of Nijmegen, in 1678, would confirm both the commercial defeat and the territorial conquest.

For Louis XIV, his function as leader in time of war derived from the sacred nature of his person and, in a certain manner, his own legitimacy. His numerous victories seemed to increase his divine stature. Versailles more than ever became the temple of the sun. The axes of the palace and the park were laid out conforming to the motion of a star. Le Brun and Van der Meulen hastened to paint the glorious campaign of this new god of war by decorating the admirable "Ambassadors' Stairs,"[1] a masterpiece of trompe l'oeil. Work proceeded apace on the great apartments of the king and queen. The gods and goddesses of Olympus accompanied the sovereign. The salons were decorated with Diana, Mars, Mercury, Apollo, Venus. . . .

Magnificent blonde tresses, beautiful violet eyes under chestnut brows, a formidable tongue, a naughty wit: Mme de Montespan, a goddess fond of good living, was adored by the king.

The court joyfully followed the royal army. Between victories, the loveliest entertainments ever seen in the West were given at Versailles. A sort of magical beauty, willed and directed by Louis XIV, deified the king and his epic. Colbert himself was carried away: The adulatory praise he addressed to Louis for his feats of arms surprises us. Despite the growing influence of Louvois, the two men were then very close to one another. Their cooperation was exceptional. Ever the privileged man of confidence, Colbert watched over Mme de Montespan. He had to entertain her, to direct the building of her house at Clagny. The minister, so severe, and the mistress, so seductive, got along marvelously, to Louis's great satisfaction.

As superintendant of buildings, Colbert, of course, had final authority over the work at Versailles, and at the same time, the conduct of the war involved him in two principal capacities. Head of the Department of the Navy, he felt responsible for the management of the naval war. On land, the illogical administration of the time divided between him and Louvois the control over various fortresses: Louvois handled those in Artois, Roussillon, Dauphiné, and Flanders;

[1]The stairway would be destroyed in the eighteenth century. See the remarkable works of Alfred Marie—for whom Versailles has no secrets—for the entire history of the palace's construction, e.g., *Naissance de Versailles* (Paris: Editions Vincent Fréal et Cie in conjunction with the C.N.R.S., 1968).

Colbert had charge of those in Picardy (along the old border), Champagne, Burgundy, Languedoc, the three Lorraine bishoprics, and Alsace.

Finally, as comptroller of finances he had to see to the expenses of the war and Versailles. His devices for getting money—in reality the gradual abandonment of an entire economic policy—were baptized "emergency measures," to underscore their temporary character. The period of bitterness began with the war on Holland. Colbert managed, thanks to prodigious efforts, to furnish the sums the king wanted, but at the price of what concessions!

Louis was full of praise for the minister and his son. Seignelay became a sort of messenger between his father and the king, not only for naval matters but also for business in general. Louis's letter to Colbert dealt pell-mell and simultaneously with the war on land and sea, the progress of the construction at Versailles (with an incredible attention of detail), Mme de Montespan, never-ending gifts for foreign courts, finances, and Colbert's health. The king's remarks sometimes showed solid good sense, if a bit slow-witted, and an amiability bordering on humility with regard to the minister's competence. Yet the man seemed excessive in his megalomania. And his genius for theatrical presentation of the unreal was astounding. His was a curious personality, as ambiguous as his war.

Before following more precisely the action of Colbert in the unfolding of the conflict, we must describe the relationship between the minister and one of the most interesting figures of the century, the future Marshal Vauban. The scion of minor Morvan nobility, poor and orphaned at the age of ten, Sébastien Le Prestre de Vauban was raised by a parish priest in the countryside. In 1651, at eighteen, he managed to enroll in Condé's army. Warfare in those days implied the taking or the defending of forts. Roads were few, and all were studded with towns that were more or less fortified, which, in the hands of the enemy, could be used to block convoys loaded with cannons and supplies. Furthermore, captured cities could eventually be used as pawns in future peace negotiations. Vauban was involved in many sieges. Upset at the loss of so many of his subordinates, killed at his side, he tried to perfect the methods of attack. A student under the chevalier de Clerville, he became the great engineer of whom we know. Colbert was probably the first to point him out to Louis XIV. On April 20, 1663, the minister wrote to his brother the intendant of Alsace: "I would not fail to speak to the king of the competence and energy of M. Vauban."

Vauban was given a company in the Picardy regiment and worked on the fortification of Brisach, in Alsace. There, the new intendant, Colbert de Saint-Marc (a cousin of the minister's), foolishly implicated him in an embarrassing swindle. The good faith of the engineer was abused by an agent of Saint-Marc's, who made him sign forged accounts. The minister realized his cousin's blunder: By then (it was 1667), Vauban had entered Le Tellier's services. Colbert and

Louvois, for once in agreement, did everything to extricate Vauban from the responsibility. But the engineer never forgave the offense. He detested Colbert and was totally devoted to Louvois. Loyal to Colbert out of duty, he often directed the fortifications of fortresses. His resentment was so tenacious that in 1671 he tried to convince Louvois to take control of the fortification of the port of Dunkirk. Louvois did not dare attack his rival on his own ground. Vauban fortified the port, but it was under Colbert's direction.

When the war with the Netherlands began, Colbert was fifty-three; Vauban, thirty-nine. The minister vainly multiplied praises regarding the engineer. Vauban executed his work conscientiously and adopted a frigid politeness around the minister.

The administrative confusion in the maintenance of the fortifications uselessly fueled the rivalry between Le Tellier and Colbert. Louvois employed military engineers, while Colbert used civilian architects. The king often met with the first group and neglected the second. The services of Colbert suffered.

Let us note, finally, the contrast between Colbert's simplicity and Louvois's pretentiousness while on inspection tours. Colbert refused any ceremony; he formally forbade the firing of the cannons for his reception and advised Seignelay to follow his example. Louvois demanded, as soon as he could, an escort of dragoons to mark his entrance into towns. The military expenditures that Louvois called for were a major factor in the failure of Colbert's economic policies. But—we must not be deceived—both men agreed on one essential point: that Dutch power should be destroyed once and for all.

THE ATTACK ON HOLLAND

Louis XIV left Paris on March 27, 1672, at the head of an army of 120,000 men. His lieutenants were Condé, Turenne, Luxembourg, and Vauban. War was declared on April 6. Jan De Witt, foreseeing the imminent conflict, had hastily raised 20,000 men since the month of January. Until then, the Estates General of the Netherlands had budgeted money for trade rather than warfare. The young William of Orange was brought out of his retirement and made captain general, under the strict surveillance of the ruling bourgeoisie.

The campaign appeared easy. On April 28, the king wrote to Colbert: "I do not desire to be sent my sword; it is of no use to me in itself. If our excursion from Paris has its effect, you will not regret having stayed there;[2] you cannot do too much to reestablish the credit that may be strongly needed in a thousand circumstances."

[2]Passage not published by Clément; see vol. 2, note p. ccxxi.

The Paris *parlementaires* were extremely cooperative. On May 5, Colbert asked the king if he thought it proper to "give some gratuity" to "those who have served the best." Louis replied prudently: "You have my permission to do what you think serves me best concerning gratuities, only take care that that does not have consequences for the future." And he added: "You have no need to commend your son to me; you know what I told you in parting. I will keep my word, and take very good care of him. He won't do anything improper, but if he did, I wouldn't let him get by with it. Except for finances and any private matters, which you can write me about, the rest can be sent through him."[3]

Seignelay transmitted the king's very precise orders for furnishing Versailles and helped his father with naval affairs. The French war fleet organized by Colbert numbered about one hundred vessels. Its firepower was limited, and its crews were not trained. But the king of England, Charles II, added 130 English ships under the command of his brother, the duke of York. Their crews had a long experience of combat against the Dutch warships.

On May 13, Charles II reviewed the French fleet (which Louis XIV had never seen) off the Isle of Wight. Charles showed real competence in his judgments. The qualities and defects of the fleet—commanded, alas, by Jean d'Estrées—were quickly perceived. The ships of the line were well designed, but the absence of lighter ships, "speedy under sail," to drive off fireboats, was regrettable. French launches were ill-adapted to the North Sea. Colbert was eager to learn from the naval campaign. He advised d'Estrées to observe "all the English practices."

The advance of the armies of Louis XIV was spectacular. Four sieges were under way simultaneously. On June 12, William's troops were taken by surprise while crossing the Rhine. Despite the wounds suffered by Condé and Longueville's death, it was a clear-cut French victory. Condé advised the taking of Amsterdam, without any waste of time. Louis committed the greatest error of the war when he preferred to follow the prudent and traditional siege strategy. On June 20, the sluice gates were opened at Muyden, and Amsterdam became an island in the Zuyderzee. The French underestimated the importance of the waters as a means of defense, and no one more so than Mme de Sévigné, who wrote her daughter: "When I got back from town, I found peace had been made, according to a letter I was sent. It was easy enough to believe that all Holland is frightened and defeated; the king is happier than has ever been seen."[4]

Peace had not been made. The Dutch plenipotentiaries came before the king on June 29. They offered the land south of the Meuse, all the conquered cities,

[3]Passage from a text incompletely published in J. Champollion-Figeac, *Œuvres de Louis XIV*, vol. 5.

[4]Letter from Mme de Sévigné to Mme de Grignan, June 20, 1672.

and ten million. But at Louvois's instigation, Louis again committed a terrible error by proposing in turn some particularly humiliating conditions: more land, the reestablishment of Catholicism in the United Provinces, commercial submission, and even a sort of feudal homage represented by the yearly presentation of a gold medal. This was more than military or trade war. It was a divine-right monarchy punishing once and for all and in exemplary fashion a base merchant republic that had dared to mock it.

But the Dutch plenipotentiaries knew that Holland could no longer be attacked except by sea. Admiral Ruyter had just defeated the Anglo-French fleet at Solebay. The glorious capture of Utrecht by the French troops in early July did not impress the envoys from the Estates General. They left the king, refusing all conditions. The war went on for another six years. Already the beginnings of a coalition between the Emperor Leopold and the Elector of Brandenburg threatened France. And the alliance with England was shaky. The Parliament and the merchants of London were skeptical, even hostile. The war was essentially desired by Charles II, who, with his entourage, received vast subsidies from Louis XIV. Holland rose up in favor of William, who became Stadtholder of five provinces, and then, on July 8, of the entire Republic. The arrest of Cornelius and Jan De Witt was demanded. They were accused, one of treason, the other of embezzlement and adultery. A furious crowd broke down the prison gates, cut the throats of the two brothers, disemboweled them, and mutilated their bodies. William scarcely punished anyone. The end seemed at hand for an entire caste, even a whole universe. But the aristocratic William mistrusted the populace. Little by little the prince allied himself with the bourgeoisie and merchants who had hurt his pride by restricting him to private occupations.

While French troops sacked and pillaged the Republic of the Netherlands, Louis and his minister were overseeing the creation of Versailles with care. Mme de Montespan wanted to participate in the decoration of the park. She drew a plan for a grove, to be called "the Marsh," and Colbert was assigned to carry it out. On May 4, the minister wrote to the king: "The sandstone shelves for the pond in the Marsh are coming along; but it seems to me we should put up a retaining wall for the pond above, although Your Majesty has not allotted any funds for that, because it would surely collapse during the winter." There followed a multitude of details about the cement for the terrace of the chateau, the settings for valves, the volume of water running in the fountains: The king wanted to know everything.

The prior of the Grande-Chartreuse in Dauphiné was obliged, on receiving a request in Colbert's hand, to furnish spruce trees for the royal gardens. The intendant of Tours was asked to send swans. On November 25, Colbert told him: "If possible, require the sellers to deliver them alive to the canal of Versailles; if not, you must contract with someone to transport them, and take care to send along a man of intelligence, who can feed them and see to it that they don't die." Rare plants came from the islands. The grand apartments were fully furnished. The decor of royal Olympus was taking shape.

Still convinced he had conquered Holland, Louis came home to his palace. In December, he learned with stupefaction and some dismay that William of Orange was besieging Cambrai. The king returned to the campaign. His first goal: to protect Saint-Quentin. Colbert fell back on the forced-labor system to reinforce the defenses of the citadel. The war, more difficult than he had foreseen, demanded new "emergency" funds.

On New Year's Day, 1673, the king wrote prettily to Colbert:

I was agreeably surprised by the letter you wrote me informing me that my revenue is increasing. I'll admit I was not expecting it. But I can count on your industry and enthusiasm to accomplish anything. I assure you that you have helped me start the year off in gaiety. I hope it will be as good as last; if not, it won't be your fault, I'm sure. Tomorrow, give me a more detailed account of all things; in the meanwhile, please believe that as you have given me the first pleasure of the year, during its course I will show my satisfaction with your services and with you.

Nonetheless, a small budget deficit had appeared, and it grew over the course of the war.

By March the domestic situation in England portended the breakup of the alliance with France. Though himself a Protestant, Charles II showed open sympathy for Catholicism: "Besides its spiritual superiorities . . . I am convinced that it is the only way to reestablish the monarchy." Parliament was not misled; its response was the Test Bill, which required all civil servants to solemnly renounce the Catholic faith and its forms of worship. The duke of York, a recent convert, was obliged to relinquish the post of Grand Admiral.

Louis XIV wanted to maintain the alliance at all costs. On April 6, he wrote Colbert:

I have seen the plan for Saint-Quentin: There is a point I have not been able to settle without Vauban. I'm taking a copy with me and will send it back to the intendant of Arras after having heard the opinions of the said Vauban. He will no doubt let you know what I have ordered him to do about Corbie and Le Castelet.

Pomponne[5] tells me the English ambassador is not very happy with the gift I presented him. There is no way to change it, but since his wife is leaving for England, I think we should give her one, in the queen's name, capable of

---

[5]Pomponne had replaced Hugues de Lionne, who had died in 1671, as minister of foreign affairs.

pleasing her. Think about it, and carry out my intentions well, which are that it should be as those I am accustomed to making.

LOUIS[6]

Colbert proposed to make a present of "10,000 or 12,000 livres." Louis wondered "if the gift to the ambassador's wife would not be better if it were a bit more, say 15,000 or 16,000 livres."[7] On the 18th of May, the epilogue occurred: The cupidity of the envoys seems staggering. Colbert wrote to the king:

> Following Your Majesty's order to increase the English ambassador's gift, I tried to have the bracelet base that was given him returned, but he replied that he found it so beautiful that it would be difficult to take it away without giving him displeasure. I found it easier to withdraw the diamond box of the ambassador, and he was given another, which cost Your Majesty 18,000 livres and looks to be worth more than 30,000, so that including the bracelet base the gift cost Your Majesty 28,000 livres and will still be thought worth 40,000.

The minister never missed a chance to economize. Louis replied, "I am well pleased with what you did with respect to the box."

Colbert was extremely worried about the progress of the war at sea. He wrote the king:

> All of Your Majesty's vessels are now at sea. The Rochefort ships have been held up at Belle-Ile by contrary winds; those from Brest are awaiting them in the roadstand; and the ones at Le Havre are also out. Dispatches from England say the king is at Scherness in order to put his whole fleet out to sea. The situation means a great deal to the campaign, for the first fleets at sea will have a large advantage over the others.
>
> I am sending Pomponne a notification of the bill of exchange that I am sending Verjus to pay the German subsidies. I am working to raise the 300,000 livres that must be paid to the Elector of Brandenburg.
>
> Finances are operating as usual.[8]

To which the king replied, "You know I always approve your handling of finances, and am well pleased."

The king was also eager to preserve his alliance with Sweden. And the meeting between the French and English fleets, impeded by the wind, preoccupied

[6]Unpublished handwritten letter written by the king from Peronne.

[7]Unpublished memorandum from Colbert, with a response by the king on May 8, 1673.

[8]Not published by Clément.

him. On May 17, he sent his minister this fine letter (published here for the first time):

Send Desnos as soon as possible with the horses for the king of Sweden. Give him what he needs for his trip and to keep them fed, so that they can travel slowly and have time to rest. Get the harnesses ready at the same time, and give some care to the completion of the matter, which is not important, but which could be useful.

I've just had news from Dunkirk that the Dutch fleet was in the Strait of Calais. I have sent to captain d'Estrées. I admit I am worried and will be glad to know the fleets have met. But I think he will reach the English coast before anything can go wrong.

Condé and Turenne were waiting in vain for the allied fleets, while pillaging and burning Dutch villages. On May 26, the king wrote Colbert: "You must get off a letter to the archbishop of Paris asking him to say public prayers for the prosperity of my armies, the same as last year. You must also write to all the bishops in your department for the same thing."[9]

On June 7 Ruyter succeeded in defeating the Anglo-French front, which had attempted to block the Dutch coast. The French armies retreated from Holland, which was protected by flooding in the interior and warships on the coast. A new exploit of Louis XIV's army would mask the veritable failure of the Dutch campaign—a failure that, unconsciously, no one wanted to admit.

The king laid siege to Maastricht, the Dutch enclave in the Spanish Netherlands. By June 11 he could write Colbert, "I have told your son to send a painter, for I think there will be something beautiful to see. All goes very well."

The epic of the warrior-king made Colbert lyrical: "Financial matters do not merit interrupting the concentration Your Majesty gives to his great and glorious enterprise. God willing, you will soon complete it to your full satisfaction. But, sire, everyone is trembling here at the thought that Your Majesty exposes himself to battle. Respectful silence prevents me from speaking of that, and I beg Your Majesty's pardon if these few words have escaped my pen."

On June 30 the town was taken. The entire court cried out in admiration. Mme de Sévigné wrote to her cousin Bussy-Rabutin, "What do you think of the capture of Maastricht? All the glory belongs to the king alone." In fact, the siege was carried out with Vauban's counsel. Colbert joined in the general admiration. On July 4 he sent the king a letter that shows how he felt about the war at that point. Like the court, and like the other ministers, he thought, mistakenly, that the campaign was an immense success for France. He showered Louis with praises:

[9]Unpublished response of the king to the memorandum of May 18, cited above.

All of Your Majesty's campaigns have such a surprising and astonishing nature that seizes our minds and gives them only the freedom to admire, without the pleasure of being able to find any equivalent. First, in 1667, twelve or fifteen fortresses and the better part of three provinces. In twelve days, in the winter of 1668, an entire province. In 1672, three provinces and forty-five fortresses. But, sire, these great extraordinary exploits pale beside what Your Majesty has just done. To capture 6000 men in one of Europe's strongest places with only 20,000 infantry; to attack in only one place without even using your entire force, to give a greater challenge to Your Majesty's prowess; one must admit that such an extraordinary means of winning glory was never thought of except by Your Majesty. We have only to pray to God for Your Majesty's preservation. For the rest, your will shall be the measure of your power.

Louis XIV returned to France in stages. He and Colbert exchanged letters almost daily. All the administrative and judicial bodies of the kingdom hastened to show how willing they were to satisfy the glorious sovereign. On July 18, the king wrote to Colbert from Rethel: "Your decision concerning the proclamation you have sent the parlement is a good one. The way in which it was ratified pleases me greatly, and you may tell the First President and the attorney general that I am very satisfied with what they have done on this occasion."[10]

At the suggestion of the king of Sweden, there was a meeting of diplomats in Cologne, in order to seek a compromise. Peace proposals in those days were usually backed by gifts and subsidies. Louis called for more money, doubling the sum set by Colbert for the emergency war fund, starting in November and December. On July 19, Colbert wrote: "Your Majesty can reckon on 600,000 livres. If you need more, please let me know." The king replied: "It would be good to go up to twelve hundred thousand livres." And Colbert followed: "I will authorize payment of the 30,000 livres for gifts that Your Majesty has offered Prince William." The king wrote in the margin: "Good."[11]

Negotiations in Cologne were difficult. Louis offered William the same conditions proposed by the Dutch in 1672 and which France had so haughtily refused. Now it was the Stadtholder's turn to refuse the offers of Louis XIV and to slyly prepare to extend the war. Louis multiplied the subsidies; he feared Spain's intentions were hostile. On August 6, he wrote to Colbert from Nancy: "I told your son to inform you what ships it would be good to have at Dunkirk and the

[10]Unpublished reply to a memorandum of Colbert's of July 13, 1673.

[11]Unpublished memorandum from Colbert, July 19, 1673, with the reply of the king written at Thionville on July 23.

] 206 [

Biscay coast so that we can intercept vessels carrying letters to Spain, and throw them into the sea. You can see why I want to disturb those exchanges." And the king added, after having written his signature: "Since the presents I brought with me are getting numerous [*sic*] because of the great number of emissaries that have come to see me, I wish for you to send me six golden chains with medallions weighing from 600 livres to 1,000, I mean two at 600 livres, two at 800, and two at 1,000. Also send four boxes of portraits between 3,000 and 5,000 livres.

Little by little, William's florins, and the general hatred caused by the strength of the French armies, brought about a European coalition opposing Louis XIV. Every fortress had to face the eventuality of an attack. From Nancy, the king told his minister: "Send orders to Saint-Quentin and Le Castelet not to leave any approaches open. From the state I see the Spanish are in, I think it is a good idea for there to be no place for them to try anything."[12] On that same day, Ruyter succeeded in a second attack. The Dutch fleet opened a passage that allowed the merchant ships of the Dutch India Company to unload their merchandise on the docks of Amsterdam.

On August 22, Louis was on his way to Alsace "to rid myself of the trouble the caterpillars [the Germans] could cause me."[13] He was worried about the state of his fleet: "It would be troublesome to call in the fleets so early; what consoles me is that mine is still in shape to stay at sea for a while, so that any blame for such a retreat would fall on the English. But that would not prevent their being displeased to see our enemies be the last to leave the water, which I do not doubt they will be if our vessels retreat this early."

The king still did not know about Ruyter's action. He was not told of it until eight days later, after he had written to Colbert on August 31, "I am impatient for news from the fleet, for according to what I have heard, there has been a battle."[14] In other words, Colbert was unwilling to be the first to announce the fleet's reversal to him.

There can be no doubt that the king was satisfied on all points with his minister, who was, more than ever, the administrative equivalent of a one-man band. On August 29, he wrote this fine letter:

I am glad you have paid the 400,000 livres I asked for.

[12]Part of the unpublished reply of Louis XIV on August 20 to Colbert's memorandum dated August 17.

[13]The paragraph on the "caterpillars" of this handwritten letter of the king's, written in Nancy, has been published in volume 5 of Champollion-Figeac, *Œuvres de Louis XIV*.

[14]Unpublished handwritten letter from Brisach.

I am also glad that you have sent the orders to my ships and galleys with more precautions so that they will surely receive them. I think that very important.

I am pleased by what you have to say about places, for I think the orders you have given will shortly put me at ease in that area.

Everything you have to say in your letter about Versailles and Saint-Germain gives me pleasure. Get everything ready so that nothing will be lacking, especially the pumps, when I arrive. I think that will not be so soon, but we shall not fail to think ahead. Let me know by exactly how much the pump that carries the water to the upper reservoir raises the level.

I think you will not be unhappy to learn that Colmar and Sélestat have received my troops and that we will begin moving the cannons to Brisach and razing them tomorrow.[15]

On August 30, the duke of Lorraine, the Holy Roman Emperor, and Spain joined the Dutch. The treaties were signed in the Hague. William succeeded in changing the course of the war. France, which had abandoned the fight against Holland, now had to face encirclement by the Hapsburgs.

THE EUROPEAN WAR

Colbert was more necessary than ever. His health was often very bad.[16] He knew war expenditures would increase considerably and for a long time. Fortunately, the king's cooperation and friendship made him forget somewhat his pains and cares. On September 8, 1673, Louis wrote him this magnificent (and unpublished) letter from Nancy:

It is time to tell you that I think it would be good to have the twelve hundred thousand livres.[17] from December at the end of this month, and to remember that advances to the emergency war fund from other months should begin next month. I am telling you this early so that you can arrange things so that nothing I think necessary will be missing.

Trier has capitulated, and I am back from a trip that has made me very happy. The Spanish will not leave me idle for long. It is my pleasure to tell you my intentions now, for I may have several busy days ahead of me. I think it would be worthwhile to raze three fortified towns this winter; they can only

[15]Unpublished handwritten letter from Rebanville.

[16]Colbert suffered from terrible attacks of nephritic colic.

[17]This is the twelve hundred thousand livres mentioned above in the king's reply to the memorandum of July 19.

harm us and are of no possible use. I haven't made up my mind yet, so don't mention it, but since two of them are in your care, I am warning you, so that nothing will be done to them except what is absolutely necessary to keep the Spanish from taking them. First there is La Capelle, and then Le Castelet; the third is Marienbourg. All three are small and rather pitiful.

They tell me you have not been well, but that it is over. Nonetheless I am greatly pained, for I wish to see you in good health for many reasons, but the strongest comes from the friendship I have for you.[18]

The financial situation was beginning to worry the minister deeply, especially since the king still seemed unsympathetic to the notion of budgeting ahead of time. On September 19, he tried to warn the king: "Concerning finances, I tell Your Majesty, as I think it is my duty to, what difficulties there are, and what means should be applied in advance, if they are to be overcome. At the same time, I am continuing to work, employing what little industry I may have to any order Your Majesty may give me."[19] The king replied, "I hope things go well and we lack nothing that is needed." Then he insisted, "The 1,200,000 livres from December must be paid in full by October 10."

Amidst his armies, busy with a campaign that seemed as though it would be difficult, the king dreamed endlessly of his palace. He wrote down the least details for his minister to carry out:

Think above all of the pumps. If the new one can discharge 120 inches of water, that would be admirable. (September 29)

The doorway has to be opened between the small apartment where Mme de Montespan lives and the guard room of the great apartment, and it has to be readied for use.

The doorway from my small apartment to my large one also has to be opened, in the room where I sometimes go during the council meetings, when it is necessary, I mean the place where the commode is. (October 3)

The year 1674 began with England's defection. Charles II yielded to the growing hostility of public opinion, which reproached his growing submission to the king of France, his naval failures, and the harm that this vain and hopeless war was causing to trade. On February 19, he signed a separate peace with Holland. The French fleet was alone against the Dutch and Spanish vessels. The French

[18]That same month, Louis XIV ordered Colbert to quickly have the fortifications of Guise and Saint-Quentin repaired.

[19]Unpublished memorandum of Colbert's with the reply of the king written at Nancy.

subsidies would, despite everything, continue to rain on Charles II: It was absolutely necessary that he remain neutral—the lesser evil—rather than enter the war on the side of William of Orange.

On the Continent, the encirclement of France by an angry Europe was growing more defined. Denmark joined the emperor on May 1, and Brandenburg followed suit on July 1. One of the gravest consequences of this war for the future was a resurgence of the German nation, which resisted Louis's many gifts. The king's determination was great, and France was lucky to have, at that moment, exceptional generals. Louvois—an excellent organizer, but choleric and peremptory—irritated Condé and Turenne. Those two men had not supported the way in which the war had been conducted in 1673. Condé kept quiet, but Turenne sometimes spoke out. Mme de Sévigné made this comment to her daughter: "It is certain that M. de Turenne does not get along with M. de Louvois, but that is not apparent, and as long as he get along with M. Colbert, it will not be."

The expenses brought on by the extension of the war frightened Colbert. It is probably about this time that an episode reported by Charles Perrault in his *Mémoires* took place. The king demanded 60,000 livres personal expenses. Colbert, alarmed, began by saying he could not furnish that sum. Perrault goes on: "The king told him that he should give some thought to the matter, and that a man had come forward who would try to be equal to the task if Colbert was unwilling to be involved." We can imagine Colbert's despair. Should he have recourse to loans and bring back the practices of Fouquet? "That's your problem," the monarchy seemed to be saying, again. The coup d'état of 1661, the arrest of the superintendant—who, sick, lived as a recluse at Pignerol in horrible conditions—was it, thus, all for nothing? According to Perrault, Colbert avoided the king for "a rather long while," working at home, "shuffling all his papers." He thought of retiring. His family dissuaded him. Finally, he decided to send Perrault to the king at Versailles with a few plans for construction. The king called in his minister the next day, and things went back to "their normal course."

From this moment on, Colbert's life was marked by a mixture of glory and bitterness. He was sincerely enthusiastic about the glory of the king's war. The failure, more and more evident, of the economic war would make him die "in despair" according to contemporary reports.

The war rekindled the old demons of the Fronde and its rebellious factions. Corrupted by William's money, the chevalier de Rohan conspired against France by attempting to facilitate the entry of Dutch troops through Normandy. He was discovered and arrested. The chevalier was related to Colbert's son-in-law, the duc de Chevreuse.[20] Many thought the minister would protect him. To remove any

[20]The old duchesse de Chevreuse was born a Rohan.

pretext for talk, Colbert withdrew briefly to his château at Seignelay, from where he corresponded with La Reynie. Colbert, who still held the idea of the power of justice, approved the decision for an exemplary punishment. After a stay in the Bastille, where he brought five servants to wait on him, Rohan was beheaded, along with his accomplice, Renee d'O.

Colbert sought desperately to raise money through taxation rather than by borrowing, in order to save what he could of his financial reforms. To the tax on stamped paper (stamped "forms" were obligatory for all judicial and civil acts) were added royalties on tin, taxes on objects made from gold and silver, increases in taxes on salt and tobacco. Revolts burst out, especially in Guyenne. The king, with great common sense, proposed a compromise (May 18, 1674): "If one could make some compromise, that is to say, to diminish the imposition of the tax on paper by two-thirds, under some pretext that seemed natural, and to reestablish the forms at a lower price than before! I'm telling you what I think and what seems best, but, after all, I end as I have begun by entrusting to you all there is to do, being assured that you will do what is to my best advantage."[21] His advice was followed. Colbert abolished the tax on the manufacture of paper, but maintained the stamped forms.

Starting with the month of May, a few diplomatic successes and some great military victories would mark that year, so somberly begun. Turenne and Condé saved the northern and eastern borders. The old marshal briefly abandoned Alsace, then won it back in the course of a surprise campaign in the winter.

In the spring, the court followed the king into Franche-Comté. One by one its old citadels fell. The court was dazzled. In April the king wrote from his camp before Besançon: "This is not a small matter I have undertaken here but I hope that my energy and my concentration will bring me success."[22] In May, still outside Besançon, he wrote again: "Let me know the effect the orange trees make in Versailles in the place where they should be."

On May 25 Colbert learned of the capture of Besançon, apotheosis of "the most important conquest ever made." He wrote immediately to the intendant of Bordeaux, who was struggling with local sedition, "Judge for yourself whether, after these master-strokes, we need fear the ill will of a few scoundrels in Bordeaux." The next day, he sent the king words of praise: "In the very instant, sire, when we were trembling over the attack on the fortress of Besançon, we received the happy and pleasing news of its fall."

The sovereign was drunk with glory, in love with Versailles and Mme de Montespan. He ordered the minister to carry out the plans for the house of

[21]Pierre Clément, *Lettres, instructions, et mémoires de Colbert,* vol. 2.

[22]Not published by Clément.

Clagny,[23] destined for his mistress. Versailles must be made ready to receive the hero. M. de Montespan, who had never admitted his wife's adultery, came to Paris on business. The king was worried. Colbert had the bothersome husband followed, and all his activities were reported to the king.

Once back in Versailles, the king organized, in the summer, festivals whose description fascinates us still, to celebrate the conquest of Franche-Comté. They were more than a political means to subjugate a rebellious court or arrogant nations; they were the true celebration of a cult of pagan characteristics allied to war. The ritual function of the court could be glimpsed here. War was then considered an inevitable necessity, as omnipresent and capricious as fate itself. The nobles, still a military caste, and their chief, the king of France, were its celebrants.[24]

Glowing amphitheaters of greenery, bending under the weight of flowers, framed by orange trees, statues and fountains, a banquet in the marble courtyard around a gigantic flower-bedecked column, a magical ride on the canal, and fireworks created the marvelous setting. So that Quinault's opera *Alceste* could be clearly heard, vases of flowers were placed where they would catch the falling waters from the fountains and muffle their noise.[25] Lully directed his musicians in an octagonal salon of greenery built near the Trianon. The grotto of Thetis was the setting for a performance of Molière's *Imaginary Invalid* (without the participation of Molière, who had died the preceding year). Near the orangery, on a walk bordered by orange and pomegranate trees, among fountains with gilded Tritons and flower-covered grottoes, Racine gave his tragedy *Iphigénie*.

Thenceforth the pageantry of Versailles and the intoxication of war would slowly come to possess the mind of Louis XIV. The basic misunderstanding between Colbert and the king worsened with each year, despite their very close relationship. Perhaps without even realizing it, Louis XIV instinctively chose the feudal authority of a warrior chieftain and neglected that of a national state, which escaped him, but which, little by little, the bourgeoisie possessed. Buildings, feasts, and war held the center of the political stage, while financial problems increased dramatically.

In 1675, when Louis went campaigning again, Colbert kept busy entertaining Mme de Montespan, catering to her every whim. The king's beloved wrote to tell him that the minister asked her always "if she wanted something." The delighted Louis wrote to his preferred confidant: "She also tells me she went to

[23]The little château was constructed following the plans of Mansard on ground now crossed by the boulevard de la Reine in Versailles.

[24]The nationwide surveys of the aristocracy ordered by Colbert show that many of them had fallen in battle.

[25]Alfred Marie, *Naissance de Versailles*.

Sceaux[26] and had a pleasant evening; I advised her to go to Dampierre some day, and assured her that Mme de Chevreuse and Mme Colbert would be happy to receive her. I am sure you will do the same. I will be glad for her to have some amusements, and those are quite proper pastimes, quite what I have in mind. I am pleased to let you know so that you can make whatever arrangements you can that might distract her." Mme de Sévigné hastened to tell her daughter about her visit to Clagny: "We were at Clagny. What can I say? It's the palace of Armida. The building is growing before our eyes. The gardens are finished; you know Le Nôtre's style. He left a dark little woods that is very effective. There is a whole forest of orange trees in large boxes."

Between two campaigns, Louis returned to Versailles, where the number of entertainments kept growing. He wrote to Colbert from a camp "near the Asembre" on July 15: "I have decided to leave for France Wednesday. You will find out why when I get there. But I want you to make everything ready at Versailles, because I plan to go there directly. I think that I'll be there Sunday evening. I'm sending to Bontemps to have him set the furniture up. Tell Dumets to have whatever is needed brought in."

One day in July, sad news brought grief into the divertissements of the court. Turenne had been killed during the French victory over Imperial forces at Salzbach. Mme de Sévigné wrote her daughter about it: "You speak of the pleasures of Versailles, and just as we were off to Fontainebleau to plunge into revelry, M. de Turenne is slain, consternation reigns, the prince[27] is racing for Germany, and France is desolate."

Condé saved Alsace once more. Sweden, ally of the king, was beaten by Denmark and Brandenburg, while Vauban methodically besieged all the frontier fortresses. Once in a while Colbert's subordinates had complaints about Vauban, who, they claimed, gave more attention to the works under Louvois. Here the minister stood by his colleague and the engineer, and he forbade that sort of complaint: "The excuse you think to be a good one, that M. Vauban does not find anything well done but what is done under other auspices, has no weight with me, and I do not advise you ever to use it." The French took Liège, Dinant, and Limburg, but lost Trier. Colbert reinstituted or created taxes, instituted a monopoly on tobacco. He advised, in vain, to "avoid coercion as much as possible."

There were violent uprisings in Brittany. The king saw the threats to provincial autonomy grow. On July 3 he wrote Colbert: "I have seen what you have told your son and what you wrote me concerning the Estates of Brittany. I will do nothing about it until I have further news from you, but the moment does

[26]Property acquired by Colbert.

[27]Condé.

not seem to me good to have them meet at that hour. Let me know your opinion in this, and your reasons for it."[28] Despite the moderate counsel of the governor of Brittany, the duc de Chaulnes, Louis sent troops to punish the revolt. Part of the army took up winter quarters in the west of the kingdom. Pillagings and hangings by the hundreds terrorized Brittany and Guyenne for a long time.

At sea, Jean d'Estrées tried to justify his losses by accusing Duquesne of softness and insubordination. The old sailor wrote Colbert in a towering rage, asking for leave: "Please don't abandon me, my lord, in the mire into which an enemy's trickery has cast me." In 1674 the minister succeeded in conferring on d'Estrées a mere division, while Duquesne went to lead a squadron in the Mediterranean. Messina was in revolt against Spain: France hastened to send ships to her aid. Vivonne, Mme de Montespan's fat and good-natured brother who was commandant of galleys, was honest enough to admit his ignorance of naval matters. The irascible Duquesne was won over. At last he could lead as he saw fit.

On February 10, 1675, off Stromboli, near the Aeolian islands, he met forty-three Spanish vessels, while he had only nine. In full agreement with Vivonne, he split his ships into three groups and sank five Spanish ships. The other enemy ships fled in disorder. After having congratulated him warmly, the king and Colbert ordered him to prepare to meet a great Hispano-Dutch offensive.

It was essential to keep the English out of the war at all costs. Louis's payments even reached certain members of Parliament. On July 7, the king wrote from his camp at Reist:

> I have here three special ambassadors from England to whom I should give larger presents than I have. That is why you must send me suitable ones for those to whom I must give them, who are the dukes of Monmouth and Buckingham,[29] and the count of Arlington, who is in his master's complete confidence. Get them ready, and, since I doubt they will be here long enough, keep them until I tell you what to do with them. They must be very beautiful. Send a few more boxes of ordinary portraits, for I am afraid I'll run short, being overwhelmed by envoys from several princes.[30]

At the same time, Duquesne was getting the fleet ready at Toulon. His terrible disposition exasperated everyone. The intendant Arnould, pushed to the limit, stated to Colbert that he would rather go home than deal with him. The minister

[28]Unpublished passage of a letter incompletely published by Clément. (see 6:329n). The king ends thus: "You can rest assured of my friendship. I think this ends my letter agreeably for you" (unpublished).

[29]The king wrote "Bouguingam" for Buckingham.

[30]Unpublished handwritten letter.

ordered him to bear up under the officer's wrath, and to show respect for his great competence. On December 16, from the stern of his ship the *Saint-Esprit,* Duquesne looked out over his twenty ships and six fireboats, ready to give combat to the famous Ruyter, or "Reutre" as it was pronounced then.

1676 was to be a glorious year for the young French navy, with several victories near Sicily. Duquesne and Ruyter met for the first time at Alicuri on January 8. Strengthened by the arrival of twelve vessels under Almeiras, whom Vivonne had secretly warned, Duquesne's squadron forced Ruyter back toward Palermo. Three months later a very bitter engagement took place between the French and the Dutch, supported by the Spanish, at Agosta, opposite Mount Etna. The sea of Sicily seemed on fire. On April 22, Ruyter was seriously injured by a projectile from the *Lys.* He died seven days later. All Europe was moved by the news. Louis XIV ordered French ports to honor the body with artillery salutes if it came within sight.

Pressing for a final victory over the Hispano-Dutch fleet, Duquesne fought and won the battle of Palermo. The French losses were heavy, but the victory was immense. Louis, who was on campaign, wrote this very beautiful letter to Colbert: "I have not been able to write since I got the first news of the action carried out by my vessels and galleys at Palermo under Vivonne. I now have confirmation, and the army will express its joy this evening with several salvos of musketry and artillery. It is what we have wanted for a long time, you and I, and there is nothing left to wish for in that area. We must still work to improve what is already becoming superior to other nations. It is necessary that France prevail over the other nations on sea as she does on land."[31]

That naval victory brought a little joy to a minister more and more over-whelmed by financial difficulties. The king demanded ever more and more money, and he knew what words to use to be heard. On June 2, he gave these orders: "Pomponne will also be writing you about a bill of exchange that has to be sent in connection with the treaty that was signed with the bishop of Münster. You know how important it is. Do everything possible to have this carried out. It is enough that I desire it for you to find the means."[32] And the king added this fine text:

I need patience in the position I am in. I want to have that quality in war also, and make it clear that I can trouble my enemies by my mere presence, for I know they wish nothing so ardently as my departure for France.

[31]Handwritten letter "from a field headquarters June 22, 1676." Not published by Clément.

[32]Unpublished passage from a letter very incompletely published by Clément (*Lettres,* 6:332).

I am delighted that you are in perfect health, both for the sake of my needs and because of my friendship toward you.

The new generation of generals lacked Turenne's military genius, but the French still took Condé, Bouchain, and Aire-sur-la-Lys, while losing Philippsburg to the Imperial army.

The spring of 1677 was marked by a series of victories by the armies commanded by Louis XIV. On March 17, Valenciennes was taken. Then, Cambrai was besieged. On March 28, the king wrote Colbert enthusiastically: "We begin entrenchments at the city this evening; if our wishes are granted, it will soon be taken. The citadel will take longer. I'll admit it is a great pleasure to find myself at Cambrai. I am sending you a letter for my daughter [Mlle] de Blois."[33]

The city was taken April 5 and the citadel April 17. In the same month the French were victors at Mont Cassel and Saint-Omer. On the twenty-first, the king wrote from Béthune: "Have a payment order for 11,000 livres cash sent me, and see to it Fourbin and Lornelle are each paid 500 pistoles against that order, to be applied to upgrading my musketeer companies, which are pretty shabby. I don't want anyone to know that they are receiving money, for fear of the consequences; that is why you must see to it that they get the money without anyone knowing."[34]

The king personally took great care of the condition of the fortifications, as is shown by a letter he sent May 4 from Lille: "Your son has gone to see the fortresses on this border, which he had not seen, to see how the expenses spent on them this year could be reduced so it can be used at Calais, which is not in the condition I would wish it to be in, given its importance. We must work there with application and diligence."[35]

By November, the very serious threat of an Anglo-Dutch alliance loomed larger. The French victories at sea, and the progress of Louis's armies in the north, had frightened the English. Charles II began to yield to ever more virulent opposition. William of Orange married Princess Mary of England, niece of Charles II and daughter of the future James II. In January 1678, a treaty of alliance was signed, even as the diplomats were negotiating in Nijmegen.

On the continent, Louis appeared to be in a position of power. Spain was worn out; the Dutch merchants wanted to recover the ease of peacetime trade;

[33]Unpublished passage from a letter incompletely published by Clément (*Lettres*, 6:336).

[34]Unpublished handwritten letter from Bethune.

[35]Unpublished passage from a letter incompletely published in Champollion-Figeac, *Œuvres de Louis XIV*, and in Clément, *Lettres*, vol. 5.

and the Emperor feared the Turks. Paying no attention to the peace negotiations, Louis had further strengthened his position by taking Ghent and Ypres in March. But two letters the king wrote to Colbert at that moment show the king's real uneasiness at the danger of a naval offensive by Charles and William. Only such uneasiness can have justified the surprising concessions to Holland granted in the Treaty of Nijmegen. On March 4 and 5, Louis wrote the following letters:

From camp before Ghent, March 4 at 8 p.m.

I have just now received your letter of the second to which I reply from the field so that you lose no time in giving orders to the ships under Château-renault. Your son has proposed to me what he told you, and I have agreed, thinking several small vessels to be more useful than large ones. But now that I see what you propose, I agree, because I am sure you have studied it thoroughly. Give orders to the effect you think best. All I can say from here is things are going as one would wish.

From camp before Ghent, March 5, 1678

Barillon tells me that the money that was in England has been withdrawn and he is afraid of running out; it is important to avoid that. That is why, as soon as you have received this note, have Fromon write so that what Barillon asks for can be given him, or else withdraw a large sum, that is, 50,000 ecus, and give them to Barillon at once.[36]

The Treaty of Nijmegen, signed on August 10, 1678, legitimized French domination in the eyes of contemporaries, and also of many historians. Spain was the big loser of that war. She abandoned to France Franche-Comté, the rest of Artois, parts of Flanders and Hainaut, and the Cambrai region.[37] Twelve fortified cities, including Cambrai, Valenciennes, and Maubeuge, became French. Vauban, named commissioner general of fortifications the preceding year, undertook to protect the new borders with impregnable fortresses. The material fact of this frontier would also contribute to reinforcing the concept of nationhood.

William of Orange had won an exceptional diplomatic and commercial victory. The United Provinces lost no territory. Louis restored Maastricht to them. Furthermore, he returned to William his personal estates, confiscated during the war: the principality of Orange and Charolais. Finally, to Colbert's despair, the navigation and trade clauses reestablished equal commercial treatment. In other words, the tariff of 1667 was annulled, and the merchants of Amsterdam were

[36]Unpublished handwritten letters.

[37]Pierre Goubert, *Louis XIV et vingt millions de Français.*

free to trade under better conditions than before 1672. There is no point in deceiving ourselves. The war against the Hapsburgs had been won. The war against Holland had been lost, even though the terrible suffering endured by that country had inflicted a palpable blow to their economic power.

Yet the king tried to maintain the absurd fiction of a Dutch defeat. Le Brun and Van der Meulen decorated the Ambassadors' Stairs by painting all the episodes of the glorious martial epic in allegorical figures, tapestries in trompe l'oeil (the four victories of 1677 painted by Van der Meulen), and scenes framed by trophies. A humiliated Holland was represented, significantly, by a merchant bowled over among his bales of goods and his account books, or by an armed female figure whose shield, bearing the name Maastricht, was being ripped away. The Spanish lion was shown in retreat, the Imperial eagle tottering on Herculean columns that were ready to fall. Around the balconies painted in trompe l'oeil, thronged the whole world, come to admire the magnificence of the Sun King. Versailles had become the temple of monarchical glory. Louis had decided to settle there. Plans were settled upon for the Hall of Mirrors, which was to be one of the world's marvels. The glory of the king reflected on those principal ministers who had contributed to the victory. Colbert, flooded with honors and gifts, also experienced a personal glory.

CHAPTER 15

The Minister's Glory

COLBERT'S FORTUNE WAS IMMENSE. His holdings in real estate had grown considerably. Louis paid him an enormous salary, without counting valuable public offices given him for free, special gifts and for favors of all sorts. His various salaries added up to 55,000 livres a year, not counting his income as secretary of the navy. In 1677 and 1679, the king gave him gifts of 400,000 livres "in recognition of his services and in order to give him the means to continue them." Of course the family of the minister also received rather substantial royal gifts. These sums are all the more stupefying given the budget deficit at the same time.

It has been shown that Colbert received 6,000 livres every three years from the Estates of Burgundy, "by reason of the services he can render the province."[1] It is possible that other provinces wanted as well to attract the favor of the all-powerful minister in that manner.

Rarely has one seen a statesman accumulate so many duties. Colbert's capacity for work is unbelievable. Up at five in the morning, late to bed, the minister regularly worked fifteen hours a day, barely distracted by two short meals of bouillon and bread. His permanent nervousness probably contributed to the severity of his stomach pains. He rarely interrupted the severity of his diet. His wine cellar was rather poorly stocked; he had, however, a predilection for the white wines of the Rhine, which he had brought in, in great quantities. He often suffered from gout and, especially, from dreadful episodes of nephritic colic. Mme de Sævigné tells us his remedy: "I am accustomed to take, every morning, a glass or two of linseed water. With that remedy, I will never have nephritis; it is to this marvelous water that France owes the preservation of Colbert."[2] In 1673 he begged his brother Croissy, ambassador to England, to buy him a pair of glasses,

---

[1] Seignelay's lands were in Burgundy. A vote of the Estates of Burgundy in 1691 proved the existence of the bribe. "6,000 livres will be given to M. de Pantchartrin at the same time they are paid to M. Colbert and M. Le Peletier."

[2] Letter to Mme de Grignan, February 16, 1680.

"the best and the finest that are in England," for his sight was "beginning to fail considerably." And, was it reminiscent of Mazarin? That man so severe and so sombre liked Roman perfumes. He had oils, essences, orange water, and even perfumed gloves sent from Italy.

In the last years of his life he had an apartment in the superintendancy of Versailles, within the south wing of the palace. Most of the time he worked at home, especially in Paris or in Sceaux. One guesses that he could not devote much time to the numerous inhabitants of his house. Besides his seven unmarried children (his two older daughters, we recall, were married before the war with Holland), Colbert housed and raised the king's children by Louise de La Vallière, the comte de Vermandois and Mlle de Blois. That immense mark of confidence on the part of Louis XIV truly impressed courtiers and diplomats. Mme Colbert very ably assisted her husband. While retaining the esteem of Louise, she was also on intimate terms with Mme de Montespan and with the queen.

The rank to be assigned illegitimate children during official ceremonies posed several problems for the minister, which Louis tried to resolve while on campaign:

[Your son] has told me what was in the report concerning the comte de Vermandois. There is nothing more to say about that, for I have ordered that he be treated as the princes de Conti are. It is necessary only to avoid his being too conspicuous on occasions, such as the shirt and the towel; and it would even be well if he were not quite on the same level as the princes of the blood while in church. This should all be done naturally, and this order be kept between you and me, for when what I am saying cannot be avoided, then he must do as the princes de Conti do.[3]

In January 1674, Mme de Sévigné told her daughter of an evening at the Colbert residence: "Mlle de Blois danced: She is a prodigy of charm and grace. . . . The duchesse de La Vallière was there; she calls her daughter 'Mademoiselle,' and the princess calls her 'belle-maman.' M. de Vermandois was there too." A few months later, Louise retired to the Carmelite convent to prepare her vows. Before leaving the world for good, she received the court and her two children for an entire week. In early 1680, Louis XIV married Mlle de Blois to the prince de Conti. "They are in love just like in a book," wrote Mme de Sévigné. The little princess wept with joy when her father told her his decision. The marquise described the fiancé's condition: "He didn't know what he was saying or doing; he passed by everyone he found in his way to go and find Mlle de Blois. Mme Colbert did not want her to see him except at night. He forced the doors open,

[3]Letter of Louis XIV to Colbert, July 3, 1675.

threw himself at her feet, and kissed her hand; and she embraced him without affectation, and started to weep again."

THE CLAN

The rise of Colbert's three brothers continued.[4] Nicolas was bishop of Auxerre from 1671 onward. He died in 1676 while the minister was still alive. Charles, marquis de Croissy, was France's ambassador to England, minister plenipotentiary to the congress of Nijmegen in 1678, entrusted with negotiating the dauphin's marriage with the daughter of the Elector of Bavaria in 1679, and, ultimately, secretary of state for foreign affairs in November 1679, replacing the disgraced Pomponne.

This last advancement was a victory of the Colbert clan over the Le Telliers. Two years before, after the death of d'Aligre, Michel Le Tellier had become chancellor of France, and hence the kingdom's chief justice. It was a terrible blow to Colbert, who had, until then, officiously directed that department. The Le Telliers hoped to weaken the enormous power of their rival even further by appropriating the department of foreign rights. Pomponne's negligence had displeased the king. Louvois plotted to obtain his disgrace. Pomponne was dismissed but—very careful to maintain the balance within his council—Louis gave the position to Croissy. Mme de Sévigné had this commentary: "A certain man had been striking great blows for a year, hoping to gather everything together; but one man beats the bushes, and the others catch the birds." The "upper" council thenceforth would seat two Le Telliers and two Colberts.

Edouard-François Colbert, comte de Maulévrier, continued in his military career. In 1676 he became lieutenant-general of the king's armies. Charles and Edouard-François married rich heiresses from the milieu of high finance.[5]

Colbert had five sisters; four—whom their parents had intended for the religious life in childhood—were now abbesses and prioresses. The son of the one married sister, Nicolas Desmarets, entered the service of his uncle in 1667. He was *maître des requêtes* in 1674 and intendant of finances in 1677.

Colbert had ten children, of whom one, born in 1658, died in infancy. There remained six sons and three daughters. Jeanne-Marie-Thérèse and Henriette, the two elder daughters, were married, as we have seen, to the duc de Chevreuse

[4]The minister was nine years older than Nicolas, ten years older than Charles, and fourteen years older than Edward-François.

[5]Françoise Bérault, whose dowry was 176,000 livres, and Marie-Madeleine de Bautru, whose dowry was 600,000 livres.

and the comte de Saint-Aignan. Colbert obtained a lieutenancy in the light-horse guards for his son-in-law Chevreuse. Saint-Aignan became duc de Beauvilliers after the death of his father in 1679. A third daughter, Marie-Anne, married the duc de Mortemart, nephew of Mme de Montespan, in 1679. That was another victory over Louvois, who had desired the match for his own daughter. Colbert's new son-in-law was impoverished. The couple received a million livres from the king!

Though the sons of the higher aristocracy often married commoners' daughters with ease, the daughters accepted a "misalliance" with more difficulty. In 1671 Seignelay was twenty. His father hoped to marry him to Marie-Marguerite d'Alègre. It would be a wealthy match. But the marquis d'Alègre wanted to marry his daughter into the Vendôme family. Mme de Montespan, the minister's faithful ally, intervened. Louis curtly notified the Alègre family of his preference for Seignelay, speaking through Mme de Montespan's father, the marquis de Mortemart. The marrige took place in 1675. Three years later the young woman died in childbirth. Mme de Sévigné wrote to her cousin Bussy-Rabutin on March 18, 1678: "But let us talk of Mme de Seignelay, who died day-before-yesterday morning giving birth to a boy. Fortune dealt a very rash blow there, daring to anger M. Colbert. He and his whole family are inconsolable. It's a great subject to reflect upon. That great heiress, so sought-after, and taken at last with such a to-do, is dead at eighteen." Louis wrote to Colbert from his camp before Ypres on the same day:

I learned with sorrow of the loss you have had. You know well enough the affection I have for you to believe that I felt it profoundly. I wish I could lighten your grief somehow, but I know that is difficult. I've allowed your son to leave as you wished, and I have ordered Saint-Aignan to accompany him. Firmly believe that I am greatly involved in what happens to you, and that no one can have greater friendship than I do for you.

I am touched by your joy at the taking of Ghent; it is important for the present and for the future.

Sixteen months later Seignelay made an even more brilliant match than the first: Mlle de Matignon, whose grandmother was of the house of Orléans-Longueville, and the daughter of a Bourbon. La Grande Mademoiselle made this rather acid comment: "Thus they have the honor of being as closely related to the king as Monsieur le Prince, Marie de Bourbon being a cousin of my grandfather the king. That gives Monsieur de Seignelay great airs, who, naturally is rather vain anyway."[6]

[6]Pierre Adolphe Chéruel, *Mémoires sur la vie publique et privée de Fouquet*, 4:516.

Colbert's second son, Jacques-Nicolas, born in 1654, was destined for the Church. When still quite young, he was already at the head of the famous abbey of Bec, which brought him an income of 60,000 livres. The sum was considerable, especially since the abbot did not even live there. In 1678, at twenty-four, he was elected to the Académie Française. Racine received him by detailing good-naturedly all of the family's accomplishments. Two years later the abbot became coadjutor of Rouen, at the king's will and with the Pope's blessing. On the day of his consecration (August 4, 1680), the affluence of the prelates in the church of the Sorbonne was notable. On that occasion he received a letter from the Pope, full of praise for the Colbert family. The minister used without scruples his good relations with the court of Rome to obtain relief for his relatives from taxes levied by the Church upon titular heads of abbeys and bishoprics. He left many requests and letters of thanks written to the Pope or to influential cardinals.[7]

The Le Telliers worked with the same intensity to place their relatives on the highest levels of the French Church. Bossuet, who found these abuses shocking, delivered an angry Easter sermon before the king and both ministers in 1681 at Versailles: "Let [your children] learn to work for the Church before they govern it."

Antoine-Martin Colbert, born in 1659, had a brilliant military career. He became bailiff and *grand croisé* of the Order of Malta, commander of the Order's galleys, commandant of Boncourt, colonel of the Champagne regiment, and brigadier of the royal armies. On March 23, 1677, Louis wrote from Cambrai to his minister: "You have thanked me for the flag-colonelcy in my regiment; it's a trifle, but he'll learn his trade there better than elsewhere."[8]

Jules-Armand Colbert, marquis d'Ormoy and de Blainville, was born in 1663. When he was nine, his father secured for him the post of Superintendant of Buildings. Louis, born in 1669, was baptized at Versailles in 1674, having the dauphin as his godfather and the queen as his godmother. His father meant for him to enter the church. He was only twelve when he received the bull for the abbey of Bonport. But the young Louis, who had no religious vocation, altered his father's plans and embraced a military career, after having been guard of the cabinet of books, manuscripts, and medals of the king's library. He became comte de Linières and captain general of the Burgundy militia.[9]

[7]See Pierre Clément, *Lettres, instructions, et mémoires de Colbert*, vol. 7.

[8]Unpublished passage from a letter incompletely published by Clément in *Lettres*, 5:379 and 6:336.

[9]He married Marie-Louise de Bouchet, daughter of the marquis de Souches.

THE LIBRARY

Colbert assiduously pursued the development of his exceptional library, which he housed in his Paris residence. In 1672 he sent this circular to the intendants:

> The pleasure of developing my library being nearly the only one I take . . . , I know from experience that sometimes old manuscripts that might be of value are found in abbeys and monasteries, where they lie neglected in the dust of the archives. You will be doing me a singular favor here if, in the course of the visits you make in your *généralité*, you could inquire without ostentation whether any are to be found, and if so, bargain for them or acquire them on the best terms available. You can easily judge that this sort of inquiry is more a matter of cleverness and of the respect the monks will have for you than of large expenditures and high prices. I beg you to take a little trouble and to show me some signs of your friendship in this matter.[10]

The intendants took a lot of trouble. Certain monks demonstrated the ignorance, or the compliance, that Colbert wished, while others, more aware of the true value of their treasures, refused to give away their manuscripts or to sell them for ridiculously low prices.

Once the young Louis Colbert had become abbot of Bonport (in 1681), the minister hastened to strip the abbey of eighty-seven of its most valuable manuscripts in exchange for worthless books. Ambassadors and consuls became purveyors. In 1682 he ordered M. de Barillon, then ambassador to London, to buy the books from the library of "the late Mr. Smith," of which he had the catalogue: "I believe you will be willing to help out in a literary matter that involve only my pleasure and has nothing to do with the king's business." He waited impatiently for the acquisitions, especially the *Treatise on the Trinity* by Michael Servetus, a rare book for which Calvin had had its author burned.

The protection and the keeping of Colbert's library was entrusted to Etienne Baluze, a famous scholar of the times. Colbert insisted on perfect order. In 1672 he noticed that certain volumes had disappeared. Baluze, very upset, wrote him: "My lord, you will find in this packet the list you do me the honor of ordering me to send you. I have attached the list I made in 1669 of the books then missing from your library, including several withdrawn by the marquis, who said he needed them."[11]

[10]Clément, *Lettres,* 7:618.

[11]Unpublished letter of July 26, 1672.

Furious, Colbert went to his son's home to recover his books. But there were many others missing. Friends and relatives, Charles de Croissy for example, had borrowed them without telling him. Thenceforth, Baluze sent a quarterly report of borrowed books.

The admirable library included, by the time of Colbert's death, more than 18,000 printed volumes, abut 8,000 Oriental, Greek, or Latin manuscripts (including the Bible of Charles the Bald), more than 1,600 "modern" manuscripts, 524 volumes of documents relative to the kingdom and to foreign affairs, 622 royal diplomas, and 722 original charters.

THE ESTATES

Colbert followed the French tradition according to which the solidity of a family depended on real estate. His properties were considerable. Besides his Paris residence, which he considerably enlarged, the minister owned land in several provinces. In Burgundy, the marquisate of Seignelay and the lands of Ormoy belonged to him. In Berry, he had acquired the marquisate of Châteauneuf-sur-Cher and the barony of Linières; in Maine, the lands of Percoux and Chanceaux; in Normandy those of Hérouville and Blainville. To that list we must add the domain of Saint-Julien-sur-Sarthe, several houses in Bourges (including Jacques Coeur's, which he sold to the city). Finally, near Paris, he bought the estate of Sceaux, as well as the lands of Châtillon and of Plessis-Piquet. His three principal residences were Paris, Seignelay, and Sceaux.

The Colbert house in Paris was formed from various properties that the minister had bought and added to the house Mazarin had bequeathed him in the rue Neuve-des-Petits-Champs on the corner of the rue Vivienne. The rue Vivienne separated the Colbert house and the Mazarin house (now part of the buildings housing the National Library). His most important acquisition had been that of the richly ornamented and decorated Bautru house in 1665. In 1672 he bought the residence of Claude Girardin, who was standing in for Bruant, Fouquet's former chief aide, who had fled to Liège. The chamber of justice had confiscated it, and sold it to the minister. Colbert added large areas of surrounding land.

His residence had magnificent tapestries (including two Gobelins) and rugs (one of them made at the Savonnerie). There were many paintings, mostly by French and Italian artists. The canvases of Le Brun, Mignard, Claude Lorrain, Veronese, Caracci, and Holbein could be seen.

For his study, Colbert had chosen many religious paintings by Carracci, Le Brun, and Raphael, among others. The minister, because of a rigorous schedule, had placed two clocks in his study, one with a Thuret bell, the other made of ebony with tortoiseshell ornaments, which sounded all the quarter hours. When he worked, Colbert used a desk and a writing table. The great desk was made of blackened pearwood, with floral and animal motifs inlaid. There were several drawers, with locks, on both sides. The top was covered with worn black cloth. The ebony writing table had an inkwell, a sandbox for blotting, a latch, and a bell.

Colbert had a predilection for black, which contrasted with the colors of the court, and was very different from Fouquet's tastes. Two of the three carriages he owned in Paris were black inside and out. The first had ten windowpanes, the second only two. The third was lined with crimson velvet with a floral design. In his stables there were eleven geldings for his carriages, all black, and two saddle-horses, one black and one light bay.

The inventory drawn up at Colbert's death shows thirty-six orange trees in his Paris orangery, with eight pomegranate trees, one male myrtle, fifty-three oleanders, forty-four viburnums (four in boxes and forty in pots), and seventy-five boxes and twenty-six pots of Spanish jasmine plants.

On August 19, 1677, Mme de Sévigné wrote her dear daughter from Aux-erres: "Here we are, my dear, and it's pretty hot. We saw the château of Seignelay on the way: We gave it our blessing, and we are persuaded that it will prosper." The château was indeed prosperous, and so was the village. The minister had installed two royal factories there, one for serge in the London style and the other for knitting and knee stockings. There were as many as 700 workers, for whom new homes were erected. A public market was built, as well as a public oven that could bake 2,000 pounds of bread at a time, a winepress, a salt warehouse, and a hostelry for travelers, "At the Sign of the Serpent."* The village grew into a town of 2,000, in which Colbert installed a doctor. About 1670 he brought in breeding studs for the horses of the marquisate.

During his visits, he occasionally observed wolf hunts. In 1672 he wrote his manager: "You must endeavor to drive out wolves, foxes, and other vermin, so that there are none on my lands, if that is possible. To the administrator of the manor of Châteauneuf-sur-Cher (acquired in 1679 for 165,000 livres), he wrote: "Endeavor, above all, to increase the amount of game, and let me know the quantity throughout my lands." He was constantly involved in the upgrading of roads, in hopes of reawakening travel and trade.

So that he could work in peace near Paris and not far from Versailles, Colbert bought the château of Sceaux in 1670. The building dated from the time of Henri IV. The minister undertook its demolition at once and entrusted Claude Perrault with the construction of a very beautiful building based on an original plan: five pavilions with mansard roofs linked by large pilasters. The chapel was at the end of the left wing, in a pavilion that was square on the outside and round on the

*A reference to Colbert's insignia.

inside. There Le Brun painted the story of John the Baptist on cameos set off with gold. On both sides of the court of honor, two long wings were added at an angle. One was furnished as an orangery. La Quintinie kept watch over 280 orange trees, 6 pomegranates, 8 myrtles, 150 jasmines, 125 laurels, 2 aloes, and even a passion-flower plant.

Following successive enlargements, the property had 700 acres within walls. On each side of the gate to the château stood two admirable groupings sculpted by Coysevox, symbolizing the virtues chosen by Colbert: Purity was represented by a unicorn transfixing a chimera, while a bulldog holding a wolf by its throat represented faithfulness. The park was beautifully laid out by Le Nôtre, who had many full-grown trees planted there, as had been done at Versailles. There were many statues, including Puget's famous *Hercule gaulois.* One could walk through the "Chestnut Room," or lose oneself in a maze full of fountains, or marvel at the "great Cascade," one of the finest decorative waterworks of the period, with waters flowing from urns held by two river gods that Coysevox had sculpted. One of the curiosities of the place was the Temple of Aurora, with an enchanting ceiling painted by Le Brun.[12]

The minister loved this residence more than the others. Many of his reports to the king are dated from Sceaux. His study was truly a museum of marble busts, dedicated to the glory of antiquity. Among others there were twenty-four busts, made of veined or white marble, of Roman emperors, empresses, and senators, placed on two plaster bases, which were also sculpted, one with a dog's head and the other with a unicorn's. On the walls there were twelve white marble medallions of emperors, in oval frames of gilded wood with silken tassels. There was also a bust of Homer, a group of wrestlers cut from white marble, and two sphinxes of red marble.

The château surely was emblazoned with Colbert's arms, which were gold with a blue serpent in the pale, with two lionesses for support, and, as a crest, a serpent bearing an olive branch with the motto, *Perite et recte* ("skillfully and rightly").

The minister and his wife enjoyed entertaining at their new property. Just as in Paris, they sometimes had orchestras, dancers, and singers. But in general, life at Sceaux was quiet and ordered. One day Colbert took Boileau and Racine to his home. He was alone with the two writers and enjoying their conversation greatly when he was informed that the bishop of ——— was asking to see him. "Let him be shown everything, except me," replied the minister.

In October 1677, he invited the members of the Académie française to Sceaux, informing them the day before by means of a note left at their homes. The entire company, including the archbishop of Paris, François de Harlay, came

[12]The Temple of Aurora is the only edifice that remains of Colbert's properties.

eagerly. The *Mercure galant* reported that "a thousand pleasant things were said at dinner,[13] whose only reason for ending was to allow the gentlemen greater freedom to show that wit that is found unalloyed in them." Going into an adjoining room, the academy engaged in friendly conversation. But Colbert had not forgotten the essential function of the academicians: What had been written to the glory of the king? The abbé Furetière responded with a reading of three works in verse that he had just composed on his majesty's latest exploits: "The Capture of Valenciennes," "The Siege of Cambrai," and "The Battle of Cassel."

After the reading, everyone went into the Temple of Aurora. It was there that Quinault recited his "Poem of Sceaux," 600 lines in praise of the minister and his residence. Charles Perrault spoke last. Still according to the *Mercure galant*— "He recited only a few stanzas, but they drew everyone's attention. The frequent applause they received was incontestable proof of their beauty." Upon leaving the Temple of Aurora, the academicians visited the living areas, and ultimately they were invited to walk in the gardens.

Louis XIV and his entourage were also guests at Sceaux. Mme de Montespan liked to visit Mme Colbert there. The king's brother came in 1673. The minister wrote to the king: "Today I received the honor that Monsieur was so kind to show me in coming to visit me. My son will report to Your Majesty on what His Royal Highness asked for." "Your son told me what you told him about my brother's entertainment," replied the king.[14] What Monsieur probably wanted was an appropriation to pay for a large entertainment. He did not hesitate to go to the all-powerful minister to ask for it.

In June 1675, the queen and her daughter-in-law visited Sceaux, and soon after were joined by the dauphin.

In July 1677, Colbert received the king. A festival was given in his honor. The festival of Vaux was still a recent memory. The court and the public rejoiced at the opportunity to compare the two receptions, and they awaited possible faux pas with curiosity. There had to be just enough pomp to honor royal majesty adequately and enough simplicity to remind everyone of the servant's modesty. The minister overcame all the difficulties with exceptional ability.

On the morning of the feast, he assembled the region's inhabitants and announced that he was going to pay a half-year's tax for them. In the evening, the same populace was invited to dance on the promenade, and when the king left, he was sure to be loudly acclaimed by people enraptured at having been so fortunately relieved from taxes.

Order, tranquillity, charm, and good taste characterized the day. The king noticed nothing on his way to Sceaux. All was tranquil there. The roads leading

[13]That is to say, luncheon.

[14]Unpublished memorandum of August 17, 1673, with a reply from the king.

to Vaux-le-Vicomte, however, had been jammed with carriages from all over Europe. At the gateway, the purity of the unicorn and the fidelity of the dog seemed to chase away the demons of embezzlement and Frondeur subversion. Their Majesties wished to inspect the living areas first. Everyone noticed the "marvelous cleanliness," a rare thing at the time.

Colbert next took the visitors to the gardens to hear the prologue of the opera *Hermione*. The walk was continued among the rare plants in the garden. Voices on one side and instruments on the other surprised them agreeably. At supper, the king and queen invited Mlle de Blois, Mme de Montespan, Mme Colbert, and her three daughters to their table.[15] Colbert served the king, while Seignelay served the dauphin. The minister's sons-in-law did the honors at two tables where, among others, "M. le duc," son of the great Condé, sat with the prince de Conti and the little duc de Vermandois. The supper was followed by a magnificent display of fireworks. To the great surprise of the guests, the surrounding villages lit up the whole horizon by firing countless skyrockets.

The king and his company then went to the orangery to enjoy Racine's *Phèdre*. Night had fallen. Upon leaving the orangery, the king came upon the entire population of the area, dancing and cheering under trees marvelously lit. The sovereign, enchanted, told his minister that he had never been so pleasantly entertained. The *Mercure galant* made this comment concerning Colbert's fete: "We may say that it was sumptuous without ostentation, and abundant in all things, without anything superfluous." It was a striking victory over Fouquet's ghost.

The reception bore a clear message: The glory of the minister was only a simple reflection of the glory of the king. Colbert never refused the private advantages of his political situation. But he remained above all, and to the depths of his being, a public man in the service of the state. His policies were in danger, however. Fortune and honors could not wipe out his bitterness.

[15]In other words, Queen Maria-Theresa had to accept at her table her husband's illegitimate daughter as well as his mistress.

CHAPTER 16

Bitterness

AFTER THE WAR WIDENED, Colbert's colleagues had to put up with his increasing peevishness. Charles Perrault, his top aide in the department of buildings, would later remember: "We noticed that until that time, whenever Monsieur Colbert went into his study, he could be seen starting work happily, rubbing his hands in joy, but that from then on, he hardly ever sat down to work, except with a downcast air, and even with a sigh. Monsieur Colbert, who had been easy to get along with, became difficult and troublesome."

His immense ambitions for the nation were costly. But the expenses of the war and the king's lavishness seriously compromised the program built up with such passionate energy and in such solitude. Let us remember once more: Colbert was and remained until his death a single-minded man. His political plans never changed, despite the difficulties that arose in the many agencies he headed, and despite the serious concessions he had to make in regard to his financial doctrines.

THE FINANCIAL PROGRAM COMPROMISED

In 1672, the budget deficit exceeded eight million livres; in 1676 it reached twenty-four million. The minister, faithful to his financial principles, hoped to cover the deficit through taxation before having recourse to borrowing. The direct tax, the *taille,* affected for the most part the mass of peasants overwhelmed by poverty and the terrible climatic conditions. The financial injustice of the ancien régime was fundamentally opposed to the effective application of the minister's doctrine. To be truly worth collecting, taxes—it was obvious—should be paid by all. Too many entrenched privileges prevented radical reform. A little more equity could, nevertheless, ameliorate financial conditions. Until the end of his life, Colbert tried to establish throughout Europe the system of the *taille réelle,** which

*The *taille* was levied in two forms. The *taille personelle* was supposed to be scaled to the individual's ability to pay. The *taille réelle* was a land tax. The *taille réelle* was only used in Languedoc, Artois, Hainault, Flanders, Provence, and parts of Guienne.

was already well-established in the *pays d'états*. The best way to succeed was to draw up a survey for each province. But local resistance was so strong and, to the minister's despair, the administrative machinery so cumbersome and complicated, that a general application for the *taille réelle* was almost abandoned. In 1682, Colbert admitted his helplessness to the intendant of Languedoc: "We, Monsieur Pussort and I, have again looked closely at the ordinance project for the *tailles réelles,* but I admit that we have found so many problems that it is very difficult to reconcile orderliness and rules worthy of a legislator with the customs of Languedoc."[1]

The auction of tax farms (that is, the sale of the right to collect indirect taxes) continued to obtain high prices. The treasury was refloated, but like their predecessors under Mazarin, the tax farmers reimbursed themselves inflexibly at the taxpayers expense. Colbert's statements on the subject did not change anything. Furthermore, the proliferation of indirect taxes for "special affairs" provoked violent revolts. The minister tried to simplify the collection of this infinity of taxes, realizing that it exposed the public to all sorts of harassment from the tax farmers, sub-tax-farmers, agents, and subagents. He banned physical searches for contraband tobacco. (The tobacco tax had been farmed out by the government in 1674). But again, the lack of civil servants under his direct orders, the difficulties of communications, and established customs hindered basic reforms.

Colbert quickly realized he was going to have to fall back on loans. The practice was, in his eyes, detestable and dangerous. Would he deliver the monarchy to the ancient blackmail of tax farmers? And would he deliver himself to the caprices of a sovereign who might prefer the easiness of borrowing to the rigorousness of a strict budget? He was circumspect in his borrowings. Subscribers were hesitant; interest rose from 5.5 percent in 1672 to 7.8 percent by 1674. In order to "cultivate credit," he explained to the king, public opinion must be convinced of the healthy state of government finances: rapid reimbursement was essential.[2] Under no circumstances should there be recourse to the old system of undetermined *rentes,* reimbursable at the will of the king. Colbert's dislike was doubly justified. On the one hand, the discontent of the *rentiers* in the case of tardy payments and low interest was a source of political unrest: The Fronde was still in everyone's memory. On the other hand, the tying up of capital by the *rentes* discouraged investments in industry and commerce.

The minister, thus, tried to have recourse to short-term borrowing by instituting a central savings bank called the *Caisse des emprunts* in 1674. The bank issued, in return for private deposits, promissory notes similar to our savings

[1]August 9, 1682, Pierre Clément, *Lettres, instructions, et mémoires de Colbert,* vol. 2.

[2]Letter to the king, May 22, 1674.

bonds, which could be cashed with short notice. These notes, which paid 5 percent interest, were accepted by the government as a means of payment, and thus passed for money in the eyes of the public. In short, it was a matter of the creation of a short-term floating debt. To escape the dictates of the financial class, Colbert opened the savings bank to the public: Anyone could deposit his money there and withdraw it upon simple notice. The institution, well-managed, was useful, but it was too contrary to the habits of the treasury and the French. Paris was very unlike Amsterdam. An institution of this type must have sufficient liquid assets at all times, and by 1680 the *Caisse* could not reimburse its depositors, short of bringing on what Colbert bitterly called "universal bankruptcy."

Colbert was then forced to turn to the financiers he had treated so roughly after Fouquet's fall. He hoped these grave compromises would only be provisional. But the years passed and the deficit grew. It was with genuine despair that the minister saw himself obliged to dismantle his own reforms.

In the same year that he created the *Caisse des emprunts,* he accepted a small departure from his monetary principles and resorted to issuing devalued coins. A proclamation announced the minting of silver coins in denominations of two, three, and four sols, whose real value was 80 percent of face value. The minting of money, which had been put under government control in 1666, was farmed out again. It was farmed by Lyonnais financiers, who realized an illicit profit. The financial scandal tarnished Colbert's own entourage. The Lyonnais minted coins in greater numbers than authorized, and of inadequate weights. Not only did the minting have to cease and the money be reduced to its true value, but it became known that the fraud had been abetted by two of Colbert's close collaborators. The Italian Bellinzani, one of his principal aides for industrial affairs, was accused of having received a bribe of 350,000 livres from the Lyonnais. In turn, Bellinzani accused Nicolas Desmarets, Colbert's nephew, of having kept five-eighths of the gratuity for himself.

We have seen that a reduction in the number of public offices for sale was an essential element in Colbert's political plans. Until the war with Holland, he had regularly issued edicts providing for the repurchase of those offices. After William of Orange succeeded in forming a European coalition against France, Louis XIV signed a proclamation that suppressed the edicts "in consideration of the prodigious expenditures to which we have been driven in order to carry on the present war." Not only was the repurchasing of existing public offices dropped, but new offices were created. Bellinzani and Desmarets showed great ingenuity in devising them. Thus, curious officials came into being: measurers of grains and liquids and sellers of seafood, pigs, and chickens. The city of Paris found twenty-four new royal fowlmongers and wild-game butchers bestowed on it without having asked for them. The discouraged corporations bought up these offices. The civil servants in the finance department had too many problems to manage by themselves. The tax farmers and the financiers had their revenge. They rejoiced at assuming their profitable roles as intermediaries again. A rascal such as Berrier, formerly in the service of Mazarin and Fouquet, now frequented the comptroller general's office once more.

As France returned little by little to Fouquet's practices, the unfortunate Fouquet experienced an improvement in the dreadful conditions of his detention at Fort Pignerol. In 1671, a prisoner of note was sent to that same fort: the duc de Lauzun, La Grande Mademoiselle's beloved. In 1675 Lauzun (whose quarters were directly below Fouquet's) managed, with his valet's help, to visit the ex-superintendant by crawling up the chimney flue.[3] The adventurer brought Fouquet up to date on events of the recent years. Around the same time, Fouquet finally obtained permission to receive a letter from his wife; he could, in turn, send her two letters a year, subject to censorship. His health was terrible.

In 1677 the two prisoners were allowed to see each other freely. In the spring of 1679, Fouquet witnessed the arrival of his wife and children, who had been permitted to live in the sinister dungeon. Was the clemency shown to Fouquet a cover for La Grande Mademoiselle's being blackmailed, as has been supposed? Eventually she obtained Lauzun's release, but only by bequeathing her lands to the duc du Maine, Louis's son by Mme de Montespan, whom he had made legitimate. Or it may be that Colbert and Louvois still feared Fouquet might return to prominence, or that the king might pardon him. One doesn't know. In any case, in early 1680 Paris expected Fouquet's liberation at any moment; but on March 23, the unfortunate man, weakened by illness and suffering, died of "apoplexy."

Court life contrasted scandalously with the "misery of the people," of which Colbert reminded the king more than once. On July 31, 1675, Mme de Sévigné passed this "little story" on to her daughter: "A poor laceseller, in the Saint-Marceau district, was charged ten ecus in occupation-taxes. He did not have the money. He was pressed again and again. He asked for more time; it was refused him. They took his bed and bowl away from him. When he realized the shape he was in, madness seized his heart; he cut the throats of three children who were in his room. His wife saved the fourth and fled. The poor man is in the Châtelet and will hang in one or two days' time." In the same letter the marquise described the pleasures of the court, which were "painful in their quantity."

War and festivities were costing the nobility dearly, and many were penniless or bankrupt. They did anything for money. Gambling was all the rage at court. One day the queen was so absorbed in it that she forgot Mass, and lost 20,000

[3]Cf. Georges Bordonove, *Fouquet, coupable ou victime?*

ecus before noon. The king said to her, "Madame, let's see what that adds up to in a year." On Christmas Day, 1678, Mme de Montespan lost 700,000 ecus. As for Monsieur, the king's brother, he had to pawn his jewelry.

Louis's reaction was strange. He backed Colbert when the latter outlawed gaming academies and games of basset in private homes; but there was gambling in his suite at Versailles every day, between comedies, concerts, and suppers on the water. Gambling became an efficient means of subjugating a nobility discouraged by the expenses life at court demanded. Financial deals and schemes were in vogue. Courtiers became "advisors," and used their influence or their connections in return for bribes.

Louis XIV would not give up the pomp of his court, the magnificence of Versailles, and the continual buildup of his formidable army for anything in the world. By 1680 Colbert could see that despite two years of peace, the financial situation was as bad as ever. There could be no more "special measures," no further imposition on a population bled dry; the conquered countries had given all they could give; the *Caisse des emprunts* could no longer redeem its bonds. The government was powerless to increase its income. There would have to be a decrease in spending, and Louis XIV had no desire to do that. Exasperated, Colbert drafted a warning to the king that showed his immense bitterness.

Concerning expenditures, though it is none of my business, I only beg Your Majesty to permit me to tell you that in war and in peace you have never once consulted your budget to determine your expenditures, which is so extraordinary that surely there is no precedent for it.

If you would only come and compare the present with the past years, for the twenty years that I have had the honor of serving you, you would discover that though income has increased greatly, expenses have greatly exceeded the income, and that might induce Your Majesty to moderate or cut back on excesses, and set a better relationship between income and expenditures.

I am aware, Sire, that the role I am playing here is unpleasant, but in Your Majesty's service, duties are diverse. Some bring only pleasure, based as they are on expenditures;[4] but the one Your Majesty has honored me with has the misfortune of yielding anything pleasant only with difficulty, since proposed expenses have no limits; but I must take consolation from always doing my best.

Once again I beg Your Majesty to reflect seriously on all I have just set forth.[5]

[4]That is to say, the duties of Louvois.

[5]Seignelay preserved the undated draft of his father's note.

On May 2, 1680, Louis wrote his minister: "You are right to be working to establish credit; I hope you reach your goal in a short time."[6] It was not that the king was unaware of the broad outlines of Colbert's financial doctrine, but he rejected it instinctively. To him, his minister was no more than a purveyor of money, just as Fouquet had been.

The king's lavishness was not the only reason for the profound cracks in Colbert's financial structure. It was also the mercantilist policy that was at fault. An abundance of money determined the rate of exchange abroad. The rate of exchange was the infallible sign of a negative balance of payments. And throughout Louis's entire reign, French money was depreciated on the London and Amsterdam markets. According to Savary, for an ecu worth three livres, one should receive 120 Dutch pennies in 1675, but one received only 107. This constantly unfavorable rate of exchange was perhaps, as Henri Hauser claims, "the definitive explanation of Colbert's failure, of France's ruin, and of final defeat."[7]

MERCANTILISM ON THE WANE

The industrial effort was still being sustained by the will of a single man. As long as Colbert was in power, the factories were more or less kept going. But their subsidies were considerably reduced or even canceled during the war. Thus, the royal tapestry works at Beauvais, which had received 175,000 livres between 1665 and 1673 in the form of subsidies and commissions, received nothing from 1674 to 1678. Irritated by being forced to neglect his industrial program, the minister fulminated against "the idleness of the populace" and hardened his position with respect to skilled workers. In 1682 he warned: Workers who left the kingdom would be sentenced to death.

The improvement of the economy was obstinately pursued. Despite the war, he had Dutchmen drain the marshes of Dauphiné.

Domestic trade, which Colbert so wanted to revive, stagnated. Roads were still inadequate, which meant trade fairs were still required, and they were too few in number. Thus, in 1681 the mayor of Bourges begged Colbert to reopen his city's trade fairs. "The province of Berry has a large stock of sheep, but the lack of sales is ruining everyone, and thus we are poor in the midst of abundance," lamented the mayor. Trade was in the hands of foreigners, who carried raw materials away cheaply and sold back manufactured goods dearly. And when the clothiers of Berry tried to take their own goods out of the province, the costs of transportation and storage ate up their profits in advance.

[6]Unpublished handwritten letter from the Louvre.

[7]Henri Hauser, *Les origines historiques des problèmes économiques actuels.*

The battle for foreign trade was far from being won. A few colonial conflicts with Holland somewhat prolonged the naval war after the Treaty of Nijmegen was signed. The Dutch Republic had been weakened by its terrible ordeal, but it had not been beaten. The banking and commercial power of Amsterdam was still intact. The dangerous English economic rivalry grew. To combat foreign competition, Colbert maintained his maritime policy, cost what it might. The war dealt a serious blow to the system of recruitment by classes. English admirals complained that the French fleet was too slow. To avoid their reproaches, Colbert's agents returned temporarily to the harshness of the press-gang system, despite official avowal of voluntary service. Along France's coasts and waterways, recalcitrant sailors were threatened with death. Sea battles were often fatal. Colbert quickly organized relief for wounded sailors and for widows. Two hospitals were constructed in Rochefort and Toulon. Crippled soldiers were fed and supported for life. A whole series of financial measures was decided upon, including the establishment of the Invalides Hospital and the Seamen's Fund, to help the injured or the families of those missing.

The remarkable expansion of ports and naval yards was pursued with care, despite financial problems. The fortifications of Rochefort were begun in 1674. Terron began to build a road from Royan to Bordeaux in 1677. The docks at Brest were continued from the plans for fortification Vauban drew up in 1680. In 1665 Brest had had only 50 inhabitants; there were 6,000 in 1681.

In 1677 a fire destroyed part of the yards at Toulon. Vauban offered Colbert new plans. He wrote to the minister: "The size of the undertaking and the cost of the work should not shock you, since it is the best port situated in the finest roadstead. As for the expense, I could put it this way: It is like lending the money at interest, nothing more." Unable to resist such an argument where naval affairs were concerned, Colbert accepted Vauban's estimates. The works, quickly executed, were admirable. The port of Le Havre was improved. Vauban worked miracles at Dunkirk. Everywhere, the dockyards were busy. Thus, the port of La Rochelle, which had sheltered only thirty-two aging vessels in 1664, had ninety-two in 1682, of which fifty-three were of French construction. The organization of schools was also being perfected. The naval gunnery school received permanent statutes in 1676. Schools of hydrography were more efficient than ever and were open to a greater number of students.

Since this immense activity was in the hands of a limited number of agents, supervision was irregular. There was occasional negligence or misconduct: Louvois took a malicious pleasure in pointing them out through perfidious allusions that deeply wounded Colbert and Seignelay. Louis XIV's unexpected visit to Dunkirk rewarded the efforts of so many years. Colbert had never stopped trying to show the king a port and its ships. In 1678 the king's arrival was proclaimed in Toulon and Brest. The intendants hastened to make ready, but he did not come. In 1680, Louis inspected Vauban's fortifications at Dunkirk. He saw ships in the middle of maneuver. He seems to have been all the more struck by it because it was unrehearsed. Intrigued, he observed this hitherto unknown world for several days. Then, on July 29, he sent Colbert a rather startling letter:

I wanted to see everything before I wrote. I was very pleased with the work on the port, and with the ship, which I examined thoroughly. Its condition is a tribute to the chevalier de Lhéry.[8] I told your son to inform you how things are. I will now understand marine dispatches better than I did, for I saw the ship inside and out, and saw it execute every maneuver, in preparation for both combat and for setting sail. I have never seen such fine men as her soldiers and crew. If I ever see a number of my ships together, I will be greatly pleased. The naval works are surprising, and I had not imagined them thus; in short, I am very satisfied.

The war was very hard on Colbert's already fragile colonial policy. In 1673 the West Indies Company sold to various societies and companies its rights to the coasts of Africa. More than three million in debt, it was dissolved the following year with the blessings of Colbert, who was powerless to help it. The minister established the Company of Senegal by guaranteeing it exclusive rights to the slave trade. The company transported 800 Blacks a year, and later 2,000 a year, to the Antilles.[9]

Toward the end of the war, French naval forces seized the island of Gorea, between Gambia and Senegal. The leader of the squadron, du Casse, strengthened the coastal defenses and managed to drive the Dutch out of an important fortress near Cape Blanco. The Treaty of Nijmegen confirmed the new French possessions, but the Dutch fomented revolts against the French. The warehouses in the settlements where du Casse visited were set on fire. The officer, pursued by a throng of Blacks, escaped by swimming, although a number of his companions were killed. The French returned in force and put down the revolt harshly.

In the Antilles, Admiral d'Estrees had captured Cayenne, capital of Guyana, from the Dutch, as well as the island of Tobago: The Treaty of Nijmegen recognized both conquests. Colbert's determination to prevent the Dutch from trading in the

---

[8] It was the chevalier Henri Cauchon de Lhéry who had the honor of having the king visit the ship *Entreprenant*. It had on board 374 men, including officers and 100 soldiers. (Charles de La Roncière, *Histoire de la marine française,* p. 336n.)

[9] The Guinea Company, founded in 1675, two years after the Senegal Company, did not last. The Senegal Company took over its rights. Let us note that with respect to Atlantic trade, the Pyrenees Company was created to furnish wood to the navy. It ended as obscurely as it began.

region harmed the Dutch Republic, but harmed French industry as well. The minister stated in 1680: "The exclusion of the Dutch from trade in the islands deprives them of four million pounds of sugar a year, which they used to send to this kingdom." Since the Dutch were no longer buying sugar in the Antilles, the mother country's refiners suddenly were oversupplied with raw sugar and could not adjust to the drop in prices, which might, after all, have permitted wider distribution. The concept of a consumer society was still a long way off. From La Rochelle, Nantes, and Saint-Malo, a few ships secretly carried raw sugar to Amsterdam. The minister officially forbade the export of French sugar in 1682, and the result was paradoxical: He asked the intendant of the Caribbean islands to reduce the area planted in sugar cane (formerly encouraged) and to plant mulberries instead. At the same time, the islanders at last received permission to refine their own sugar. There can be no doubt that the requirements of mercantilism brought on a partial failure of Colbert's policies on sugar.

By 1673, Colbert had realized: "His Majesty cannot give any aid to Canada this year, because of the great and prodigious expenditures caused by the upkeep of over 200,000 men and 100 ships." The shipments of soldiers and girls to build up the population were stopped. There were barely 10,000 French subjects in Canada by 1681. The Ursuline convent in Quebec was given a subsidy to convert and instruct young savages to be future brides for the colonists. Despite the war, trade between Canada and the Antilles was encouraged. To protect private interests, Colbert forbade the governor and the intendant to engage in any trade themselves, directly or through agents: "It is impossible," he wrote to the governor, Frontenac, "for the inhabitants to be persuaded that you will maintain the equality of justice and protection that you should, as long as they see that certain persons who have privileged access to you are involved in commerce."

The authoritarian and difficult Governor Frontenac got along very well with the explorer La Salle. In 1674 La Salle reached Paris with a letter of introduction from Frontenac. The explorer was knighted and received the right to keep a garrison and to clear the lands around Quebec. Louis XIV and Colbert wanted above all to hold the Great Lakes, while La Salle wanted to go south to the Gulf of Mexico. In April of 1677, the minister refused permission to another explorer, Louis Jolliet, "to go and settle in the land of Illinois with twenty men. We must multiply the inhabitants of Canada before thinking of other places."

When La Salle returned to France in November of 1677, he obtained, with difficulty, an audience with Colbert. According to La Salle, who was loquacious and prone to exaggeration, the minister treated him as a visionary and as a madman ready for the asylum. The Parisians doted on the explorer and his Indian stories. After a year, he was presented to Louis. The king was taken with him. In 1679 La Salle, with exceptional courage, left to explore the vast region between the

Great Lakes and the Gulf of Mexico. He first followed the course of the Illinois River, which he named the Seignelay River. He learned that the Mississippi was navigable; he named that already famous river the Colbert River. After returning to the Great Lakes, he continued his explorations and descended the Mississippi in 1682. On April 9 of that year, La Salle, wearing a gold-trimmed scarlet suit, claimed "the land of Louisiana, near the three mouths of the Colbert River, in the Gulf of Mexico." The French court did not receive proof of his adventures until 1684; Colbert would die without ever knowing of it.

The French East India Company remained active throughout Louis's entire reign, thanks largely to the courage and perseverance of a few men of character. Nevertheless, the disappointments were serious. By 1672, the Dutch had driven the French out of their settlements in Ceylon. Two years later Madagascar was abandoned. But the French also established themselves on Bourbon island and Ile de France.* In 1673 Commander Delahaye seized Saint-Thomé (Meliapore) near Madras on the east coast of India. Colbert wrote to the king and told him of the capture, of which he had learned from a shipwrecked Capuchin monk. The city "is of very considerable importance. Your Majesty can easily find it on a map. . . . I believe that if we sent a ship with 150 men and some money and munitions, we could hope that the said M. Delahaye could hold the outpost." Louis replied: "I approve of what you propose about Saint-Thomé. Send off a ship with whatever you think necessary."[10]

Delahaye held out for three years. In 1675, he had to yield to greatly superior Dutch forces in the region. The company, not abandoning hope of establishing itself in India, purchased Pondicherry, which was to form the nucleus of a French colonial empire on the subcontinent. When its stockholders grew impatient, the company drew from its capital an amount sufficient to pay a first dividend of 10 percent. Despite the loss of its monopoly, the company continued its operations.

The Company of the Levant outlived Colbert.[11] In 1681, to restore the confidence of the merchants who feared the numerous and formidable Barbary pirates, Colbert sent Duquesne with several squadrons to drive the pirates back to the North African coasts. The old officer visited Tripoli, Algiers, and Tunis, where his large forces made a strong impression locally.

The North Sea Company was seriously hurt by the war with Holland. Not having access to military escorts, the company did not dare allow its vessels into a territory thick with enemy ships. In 1673 its Bordeaux agency was liquidated,

*Now Réunion and Mauritius respectively.

[10]Unpublished note of May 15, 1673, with a reply from the king.

[11]It was not dissolved until 1690.

followed in 1677 by the large office in La Rochelle. The company struggled on until 1684.

The tragic war, for which Colbert must bear a serious part of the responsibility, had dramatic consequences for Holland, but also for France. The real winner, at least from an economic point of view, was England. Profiting from their neutrality from 1674 on, the English built up their merchant marine, to the detriment of Holland and France. After 1670 the belligerents built ever larger ships.[12] But shallow beds along the Dutch coast meant that ships had to enter their ports by way of canals that were not very deep. Thus, Dutch ships, in order to have access to their ports, had to remain at a lesser tonnage. Little by little, Dutch domination of commerce was replaced by English domination.

Colbert guessed that sooner or later a war with England was inevitable. After his death, the future would prove him right. The mechanism was the same as before: Economic warfare led inevitably to armed conflict. The minister prepared not only the navy but industries as well for the eventuality he feared.

Finally, after having required French lacemakers to imitate Venetian lace, done as needlework, he tried in 1682 to introduce English, or "Malines," lace, done with a spindle. The innovation encountered localized resistance and generalized indifference.

THE PURSUIT OF UNITY

The first condition for attaining unification was, as ever, the creation of a road and river network free of tolls. Riquet, the salt-tax farmer, was still working passionately, at immense cost, to complete the Languedoc canal. Colbert learned that the accounts of the tax farm and those of the canal had been mixed together, and he was furious. He also learned of the harshness of Riquet's agents towards the taxpayers. The relationship between the tax farmer and the minister became unpleasant and tinged with suspicion. One of Colbert's engineers, La Feuille, was sent to oversee the works. Vauban was angry at not having been consulted, and he later criticized the canal, although it was a technical achievement. Riquet died in 1680, one year before it was finished. In 1681, water was let in, and the canal was solemnly inaugurated in the presence of the minister.

The wars slowed work on many other projects, and some were not finished until after Colbert's death. The age of Louis XIV was an age of strong will and limited means. Colbert was no exception. It was too early to break down the multiple frontiers that separated Frenchmen from each other and paralyzed the economy. Thus, in 1682, the minister was obliged to furnish a domestic passport

---

[12]Jacques Godechot, *Histoire de l'Atlantique.*

for the transporters bringing iron for the famous machine of Marly. It specified: "His Majesty expressly forbids all his tax farmers and agents, masters of bridges, tolls, and barriers, to require any payment between Dinan and said port of Marly, on pain of being held disobedient."

The unification of tax structures and laws dealing with commerce was continued. The war, which had curbed many reforms with disastrous effects, had left the arrangements for collection of the salt tax in disorder. After the Treaty of Nijmegen was signed, Colbert had a royal edict promulgated providing for "a collection of all edicts . . . into a single body of ordinances reducing all rights into a single one, and establishing reliable laws, which would procure both profit and relief for our people." His preparatory work would be used by the Revolution, a century later. Along the same lines, the five major tax farms were united in a single General Tax farm, responsible for farming out all indirect taxes (1680).

The ordinance for commerce, dating from 1673, fixed French commercial law for an extended period. The creator of the Napoleonic Code would borrow many of its provisions and would even copy entire passages from it. In 1681 the naval ordinance appeared; it was a legislative masterpiece and was widely admired even by foreigners. Its preamble clearly states its purpose: "To fix the law governing maritime contracts, to regulate the laws of the officers of the Admiralty and the principal duties of seafarers, to establish law enforcement in ports, along coasts, and in roadsteads." Fishing was regulated. The functions of Admiralty courts were at last unified and specified. Let us note, among the many police regulations, that it was forbidden to tie up docks by unloading garbage on them.

After Colbert's death came the Negro Code (1685), concerning the question of slavery. But all the groundwork was due to Colbert. If some of its provisions seem cruel today, it is nonetheless true that the code marks unquestionable humanitarian progress for the time and respects the rights of the family—which was not the case for other colonial powers. It was forbidden to separate husbands, wives, and prepubescent children when slaves were sold or became subject to seizure. Any slave, if ill-fed, ill-clothed, or ill-cared-for by his master, had the right to lodge his complaint with the king's attorney.

For Colbert, there could be no national unity without there being first unified justice. The power of the state was made manifest in its capacity to dispense justice. As we have seen, Chancellor Séguier in effect delegated his powers to Colbert. Pierre Séguier died in early 1672 at eighty-six years of age. Colbert took over his duties for the interim. Rumor had it that the comptroller general would also be appointed chancellor. Le Tellier put forth his own candidacy, but in 1674 the title went instead to the aged d'Aligre, who was already keeper of the seals. Olivier d'Ormesson made this comment: "With the choice of d'Aligre, one sees that M. Colbert is still in charge. Le Tellier had laid claim to the position of chancellor and would have gotten it if Colbert had not expressly opposed it in order to have d'Aligre appointed, having told the king that if M. Le Tellier obtained that office, he could not serve him any longer, for he was opposed to everything Colbert tried to do." The octogenarian d'Aligre was so surprised to be both keeper of the seals and chancellor that, according to Mme de Sévigné, he asked the king, "Sire, is Your Majesty relieving me of the seals?" To which the king answered, "No; sleep in peace, Monsieur Chancellor." And indeed, the marquise added, "They say he is nearly always asleep."

D'Aligre died in 1677 at the age of eighty-five. At that time, Louis was accumulating military victories. He knew what he owed to Le Tellier, who, with more discretion than his son, had taken a leading part in the organization of the army. The king granted him the chancellorship, to Colbert's despair. The new chancellor was already seventy-four years old, but unlike his predecessors, he was determined to fully carry out his duties. Colbert and his former patron were of the same social class and had basically the same concept of the state, the same political reflexes. Hence, the unification of justice on the Parisian model was continued. But as Colbert had foreseen, Le Tellier did his best, in matters of practice, to continually thwart his former aide and his aide's agents. Claude Pellot, First President of the Parlement of Rouen and well known for his friendship and close collaboration with Colbert, had to suffer more than any other from Le Tellier's interference. The chancellor first forbade him to commute death sentences into sentencing to the galleys. Everyone knew Colbert's bias in this kind of sentencing. On another occasion, Pellot was reprimanded for having allowed the Parlement of Rouen to permit the printing of two books, which, according to Le Tellier, was not part of its jurisdiction. The chancellor went so far as to write Colbert's friend these lines: "I feel obliged to tell you that decisions of your parlement are published here that are contrary to the rules of justice." The significant example of Pellot was surely not unique.

ARTS AND SCIENCES

During this last period of his life, Colbert showed some concern with popularization and a relative decentralization of culture. In 1673, for the first time in France and probably in Europe, an art exhibit was opened to the public. Hangings in the courtyard of the Brion palace, an annex of the Palais-Royal, served as backdrop for the academicians' works. The "book" or catalogue for this open-air salon also named the three members of the académie (the Boulongne sisters) and seven engravers.

Literary academies were created in Soissons (1674) and Nîmes (1682). All over France, in leading cities, academies of painting and sculpture were given their letters patent. The minister also wanted to modernize the obsolete teaching practices of the University of Paris. In 1675 he reproached the rector for the poor quality of university teaching: Its students learned some Latin, but knew nothing of "geography, history, and most other sciences that are useful in commerce and in life." Once again, the war delayed reforms still in the planning stage. Nonetheless, even during the conflict, there was an active cultural policy. The hunt for rare books and manuscripts for the king's library was carried on with enthusiasm. In 1676, in the middle of the sea war in the Mediterranean, the minister could be found fretting over the forty-three Hebrew and twenty-two Arabic books captured by a pirate. The naval intendant at Toulon was asked to make every effort to recover them. The creation of the Cabinet of Medallions and Prints, placed in the rue Vivienne near the royal library, dated from 1674. The royal factories, such as the Savonnerie and the Gobelin, began to fulfill royal orders: The abbé Strozzi in Florence virtually ceased his shipments.

All academies were constantly encouraged—and overseen. In 1673 Charles Perrault was elected chancellor of the Académie française. Everyone knew that he represented the minister's eyes and ears. Perrault especially favored the establishment of fixed spellings for the French language, by limiting the influence of Latin and by rationalizing the rules of grammar. There was an obvious political design behind that, linked to the rise of a sense of nationhood. The French had to affirm national independence from universal Latin and from the diverse local dialects.

The king had forced Lully on Colbert. The minister tried, afterwards, to regain control over performances. At Colbert's insistence, Louis granted Henri Guichard, intendant of buildings to the king's brother, a license to build circuses and amphitheaters for the production of "imitations of the ancient games of the Greeks and Romans." What a curious test! Lully waged a four-year struggle and succeeded in preventing the ratification of Guichard's letters patent.

Public spectacle was the king's business and his alone. The staging of his daily life fascinated everyone. In 1682 Mansart, who had just finished the two wings of Versailles, built the Orangerie. Louis moved into the palace for good, although hundreds of workers were still active there. The monarch received ambassadors while seated on a throne of solid silver and dressed in clothing adorned with precious stones. For him, Versailles was both a weapon and an expression of his power. He opened the park gates to the public. His subjects must have been overwhelmed by the spectacle in which so few of them were participants. But from the bottom of his soul, Colbert rejected that concept of power and perhaps even that form of legitimacy as long as he lived. His complaints about the cost of Versailles and royal buildings in general grew. The work on the château of Marly had begun in 1679. The minister's sorrowful and reproachful tone finally irritated Louis.

According to Charles Perrault, First Clerk of Buildings, the king had even blamed Colbert's management for the enormous costs of building at Versailles. One day in 1679, after having visited some of Louvois's fortifications, the king said to Colbert: "I have just seen the most beautiful and best-kept fortifications in the world; but what has most astonished me was the small expense required there. How is it that we are spending frightful sums at Versailles and yet nearly nothing there is finished? There is something here that I do not understand."

Deeply hurt by that reproach, Colbert ordered all future work to be done at a discount. The quality of work suffered so much that the minister often had to return to earlier prices. Perrault had more and more trouble putting up with the difficult character of a man crushed by so many disappointments. Besides that, Colbert wanted his son d'Ormoy to take over Perrault's job little by little. The future author of the famous *Fairy Tales* then decided to withdraw "without outburst or scandal."

The minister instructed his son how to attract the king's attention. "The account you have given me is very good. Keep in mind how important it is for you to please the king and carry out his orders properly. You must have all his orders carried out, and in such a way that he sees that his orders are more promptly executed when he gives them to you than when he gives them to another."[13] But d'Ormoy, less intelligent than Seignelay, caused his father a great deal of worry: "Everything you send me is so sloppy, and you are still giving so little attention to the punctual and exact execution of the orders I give you, that I am beginning to despair of being able to make anything of you."

Some historians have been pleased to describe a "disgrace" suffered by Colbert, a disgrace brought on by d'Ormoy. The term is inaccurate. Louvois's influence was certainly the equal of Colbert's during this period. But nothing in correspondence between Louis and his minister allows one to suspect the least disgrace. On July 24, 1680, the king wrote:

Tell d'Ormoy he can pay me court quite well by working to make progress in every area.

I have only to assure you of my satisfaction with all you are doing, and of my friendship for you.

On August 2, 1680, the king even seems to have wanted to reassure Colbert, to judge by the first sentence of the following letter: "I see that everything is progressing thanks to your diligence and your son's. There is no time to lose, for I will be at Versailles without fail on September 1. I have gotten all your letters, and I have told Seignelay to notify you of what I had to say, for I have little time

[13]Cited by Clément and Mongrédien.

to myself during this trip. Bontemps will be asking for doors and hinges: Have them made."[14] Nor did Colbert fail to profit from the king's good opinion: He asked Louis "to grant d'Ormoy some indulgence that might allow him to outfit a small carriage and maintain it." Louis wrote his answer in the margin: "6,000 livres."

While Versailles shone with a mad brilliance, work on the Louvre was suspended in 1676. The façades were completed, but Colbert never saw the roofs put in place. The magnificent colonnade, planned as the entrance to the king's most beautiful palace, was used to store straw for horses. We may imagine the minister's disappointment; yet he continued to beautify the capital and to pave and widen its streets. Colbert even planned a tree-lined boulevard that would have ringed the city with greenery. The work was begun, but the war ended the project, as it had so many others.

The king's absence from Paris precipitated a development that contained hints of another age. The exercise of power required ever greater competence; the middle class had become indispensable in all of Europe's leading countries. Yet bourgeois subjects were rarely received at Versailles. Shut out of the universe of the court, the Parisians developed the fashion of holding salons, where the middle-class business and administrative elite mingled with the nobility and the elite of the literary and artistic world. Such meetings were unthinkable at Versailles. They laid the groundwork for eighteenth-century thought. Parisians of intelligence and talent began to get into the habit of thinking without the king. In other words, they began to have a presentiment of a universe free of monarchical guardianship. Louis XIV was making an immense mistake. Already, ideas of political freedom, and even of free thought, were being experimented with.

Colbert and Le Tellier were both powerless to contain the avalanche of books printed in Holland, which invaded all the major cities in France. In Bordeaux, the Dutch bookseller Van Esteden was under surveillance by a government agent. It was officially forbidden for "all merchants and other persons of the city of Lyons to traffic in, to sell, or to distribute any book or pamphlet coming from foreign countries before they have been inspected by the lieutenant general of the Seneschalship." All these measures were ineffective. Foreign books had all the attraction of forbidden fruit—to such a degree that certain booksellers in the east of France had books made up with a false foreign imprint. Large numbers of Protestant books, scientific works, lampoons, and pamphlets on politics and the king's private life spread throughout the kingdom.

Colbert did not succeed in containing that invasion. At the same time, the shortage of funds was seriously hampering his campaign of royal propaganda.

---

[14]Unpublished handwritten letter from the king at Lille.

Gratuities granted to the king's flatterers grew smaller. In 1678 Pierre Corneille humbly begged the minister to arrange the renewal of his lost annuity: "My Lord, in the misfortune that has overwhelmed me, these four years, of no longer having a part in the gratuities with which His Majesty honors men of letters, I can have no more just and favorable recourse than to you, My Lord, to whom alone I owe the one I had."[15] The great tragedian received satisfaction only in 1683. His name can be read in a list of gratuities: "To Corneille, in consideration of the various works of poetry that he has composed: 2,000 livres tournois."

The construction of the Observatory was completed in 1683. Astronomers were sent to make observations in Africa or on the island of Saint-Thomé in India. The minister was personally occupied with all forms of scientific research. He had a passion for the dissections of fish made in Brittany by the naturalist La Hire, to whom he wrote: "Arrange things so that none of the fish found on the entire coast of Brittany and Normandy are overlooked, and send me your news often."[16] The purchases of rare plants and animals for the embellishment of the menageries and royal gardens also profited the work of the Academy of Sciences. The brilliant Dutchman Huyghens submitted all of his experiments and discoveries to Colbert. The German Leibniz lived in France for four years, where he often met with Huyghens and other scholars. In 1673 Colbert established a chair of medicine, pharmacology, and surgery at the Botanical Garden. He wanted demonstrations to be given without fee by the garden's professorial staff.

Very interested in the practical applications of recent discoveries, he asked the Academy of Sciences to undertake a treatise on mechanics, "showing all machines in use in France and abroad."[17] Denis Papin, the minister's protégé, began his experiments that would result, in 1691, in the discovery of the "fire machine."

The taste for science became a sort of fad. Duverney gave the dauphin lessons in human anatomy, in the presence of Bossuet. The death of the elephant in the Versailles menagerie in 1681 was a source of entertainment. The whole court wanted to attend the dissection. According to the report in the *Mémoires de l'A-cadémie des Sciences*: "When the king entered, he asked where the anatomist was. Duverney rose up out of the flank of the animal, which had practically swallowed him up." Perrault drafted the description, while La Hire did the sketches.

In 1677 the dauphin visited the Academy of Sciences with Bossuet, the prince de Conti, and a number of young lords from the court. Colbert received him at the head of the assembled academy. The next day, the young prince toured

[15]Clément, *Lettres*, vol. 5, p. 562.

[16]Clément, *Lettres*, vol. 5.

[17]The first volume of the *Recueil des machines* appeared in 1699.

the Observatory, guided by the minister. Louis went to the Academy of Sciences himself in 1681. Colbert showed him the laboratory. The sovereign watched various experiments such as the freezing of water, the reduction of acid salts to neutrality, and the distillation of wine with a spirit lamp. In the assembly hall, the minister presented the publications devoted to the academy's work. The monarch admired the drawings of land and sea creatures and astronomical devices, then gave a speech: "Gentlemen, I have no need to exhort the academy to work; it is working hard enough by itself." The next year, he visited the Observatory, where Cassini's work was explained to him.

This infatuation with experimental science reveals a profound change in mentality: Experiment was imperceptibly replacing dogma. The eighteenth century began, perhaps, around 1680. Louis XIV, a man of intuition, felt the rising magma of repugnant ideas. He tried to dispel this evil through the more and more brutal affirmation of a politico-religious Manichaeanism that aggravated even more the monarchy's isolation.

GOD AND CAESAR

Louis XIV's religious policy during the last years of Colbert's life consisted of an ever more violent imposition of Catholic orthodoxy, while assuring French independence in regard to the Holy See. The great dream of unity, passed down from antiquity, disappeared. The Pope was no longer considered the arbiter of Europe; national states were on the rise. The king of France received his power from God, and the national unity that he represented should be mingled with religious unity. According to Louis's logic and that—it must be emphasized—of the great majority of Frenchmen, all of the sovereign's subjects should profess the Catholic religion. In counterpart, the sacred function of kingship implied that the king exercise an important part of the temporal power of the Church of France.

It goes without saying that these "Gallican" conceptions of the church matched financial requirements, in these difficult times, quite well. According to an ancient custom of indeterminate origin, the *droit de régale,* the king had the right to receive income from certain dioceses, and even to fill ecclesiastic offices on condition that the bishopric had become vacant. In 1673 Louis tried to extend that right to the entire kingdom, and he ordered Colbert to arrange for the next general assembly of the clergy to look upon it favorably. The king's authority then seemed immense. The Church of France easily submitted to the claims of the king. But when Colbert's fiscal edicts applied the *droit de régale* to the dioceses of the south, two Jansenist bishops, Pavillon and Caulet, protested vigorously. Pope Innocent XI decided against Louis in 1678. In 1682, under Bossuet's inspiration, the assembly of the clergy drew up the Declaration of the Four Articles, which supported Louis

XIV, that is to say, the independence of the Gallican Church against the temporal authority of the Pope. Rome won in the end, after the death of the minister.

Even before the war, Louis had attempted to restrict Protestant influence in the kingdom. In 1669 a declaration limited the scope of the Edict of Nantes by declaring forbidden anything not specifically conceded therein. During the war, two Protestants, Turenne and Duquesne, led the army and navy brilliantly. Turenne's presence in particular probably made the king hesitate to use violence against the "so-called reformed religion," as it was then called. The marshal's death in 1675 would unleash intolerance. We may conjecture that Louvois's well-known religious fanaticism had something to do with Turenne's preference for Colbert.

In 1677 Pellison, Fouquet's former agent, who had recently converted, didn't know how to express his gratitude to the king for his return to grace. He proposed the creation of a conversion fund to distribute monetary rewards to the poorer Protestants in exchange for their abjuring their faith. Colbert would willingly have done without this new utilization of public funds in a time of worrisome budget deficits. But he did not dare refuse the proposal, for he knew Louis's feelings and his determination in the matter. When financial persuasion was judged insufficient, scandalous persecutions followed. In 1678 an unfortunate Calvinist gatekeeper in the gardens of the château at Blois was fired. In the following year we find a curious correspondence among Louis XIV, Colbert, and the archbishop of Paris concerning an incident in the Rohan family. On January 26, "at four in the afternoon," the archbishop sent the king the following letter:

> Sire, the duchesse de Verneuil, the duc de Sully, her son, and part of her family of the house of Rohan have come to the diocese to inform me that Mme de Coachin is extremely ill, that Father Chaussemet has heard her confession, that Our Lord's body was given her from the hand of her priest, and that afterward the duchesse de Rohan, her mother, went to her bedside and made every effort to pervert her by telling her to leave her religion and its errors, and that when the duc de Rohan, her son, was opposed to this violence, she exploded into rage against him with a thousand insults, she struck him (in which claim he remains constant) and finally they have asked my advice on what they should do in such an extraordinary and dangerous situation. . . .
>
> In the end, Sire, we judged it best . . . to inform Your Majesty, so that you might have the kindness (if you think it proper) to send an order and a representative to give the sick woman protection and to prevent Mme her mother from overturning the good disposition to which she now stands.

Louis XIV replied:

I am sending Colbert, who is in Paris, an order to go see Mme de Rohan and to tell her on my behalf that I am astonished that she can act as she is doing toward her daughter, and to beg her on my behalf not to continue in this scheme, and finally, to tell her that he has orders to prevent her, by whatever means necessary, from doing anything contrary to my desire, which is to allow the sick woman to live or die in peace within our religion which she has professed until this time. I am telling him to discuss with you what needs to be done if there is no hurry, and otherwise he is to execute my orders and give whatever orders are necessary to separate Mme de Rohan from her daughter, even using force if necessary; as for you, I think you should go there if it is necessary and do the duty of a good archbishop at that meeting, if the illness and excitement continue. I think you would do better not to come tomorrow, but to stay in Paris and do your duty in such an important matter. You may come Sunday if you think best, and give me a full account.

By the same messenger, he wrote Colbert:

I am sending a copy of the letter I am writing the archbishop in reply to his letter informing me of what Mme de Rohan is doing to Mme de Coachin.

I am telling him what I am ordering you to do, and you will execute in exact detail what the letter contains. If it is necessary for you to remain in the house on my behalf, and if you feel obliged to do more, I order you to, for too much cannot be done in a matter of such importance.[18]

The year 1680 marked the beginning of the waning of Colbert's influence. Louvois's arrogance suited the unlimited pride of the conqueror king better than did Colbert's melancholy: Louvois had won his war—the military war—while Colbert knew he had lost his—the economic war. Even as Colbert made preparations for a second economic battle with England, Louis XIV and Louvois exercised an especially aggressive policy toward Germany. This policy of annexations[19] (called "reunifications"), furthermore, provoked England's later entry into the war, which Colbert had so feared. But in the meantime the king, at the summit of his glory, allowed no disagreement.

The refusal of many Protestants to convert seemed to him to be an insult to his royalty. Louvois instituted the terrible *dragonnades,* in the course of which soldiers forced conversions by pillage and torture. The results were startling: 37,000 conversions in a few weeks. Colbert agreed to back measures he would have rejected before. The Protestants played an important role in the navy, the great companies, and industry. He could no longer withstand the stupid wave of

[18]This correspondence is unpublished.

[19]The independent republic of Strasbourg was occupied in 1681.

indiscriminate exclusions. The intendants received a letter from the minister denying them the right to employ Protestants for the collection of the *taille*. The navy's officers, like the finance officials, were asked to convert if they wished to retain their positions. In July 1680, the minister wrote the intendant at Brest: "His Majesty will wait a month or two longer for the officers of the so-called reformed religion to put themselves in a position to take advantage of the mercy he has kindly agreed to show them, and he will remove those who persevere in their stubbornness."

The example of Duquesne worried Colbert greatly. The old sailor energetically refused to abjure. His departure would be a catastrophe for the navy. Duquesne was complaining of not having been promoted to the supreme rank of admiral of the Levant and marshal of France. Colbert suggested that his obstinacy prevented the king from rewarding him according to his merits. The officer persisted. Colbert sent Bossuet to him, who, for two hours, tried in vain to convince Duquesne that the path to salvation lay in the Catholic church alone. On February 20, 1680, Duquesne sent Colbert a very fine letter that deserves to be quoted in full:

My lord, I have received the letter with which you honored me on the first of this month, where you tell me that if it were not for the exclusions of which I myself am the cause, I would receive rewards from the king greater than my claims.

I was of the belief that after I had expounded the principal articles of my religion to the bishop of Condom, and he had approved them as being Christian doctrine and in conformity with good morals, the only defect he found therein being that I do not believe quite enough in them, that should not, it seems to me, have subjected me to such exclusions, and without injury to the respect I owe you, one might say that offense has been taken as well as given here; and since it is the Lord's commandment to render unto Caesar what is Caesar's and unto God what is God's, Caesar will surely not take it amiss if, in rendering him scrupulously what is due him, one also renders unto God what is His. And you, My Lord, who are so eager for the king's glory, please consider that nothing is more capable of increasing it and of making his generosity known throughout the globe, than the excess of grace His Majesty shows those who serve him well, and that very fact fortifies the zeal his subjects show in his service.

I am, with much respect, My Lord, your very humble and very obedient servant.

DUQUESNE

Colbert managed, all the same, to convince Louis to grant the old and inflexible officer the title of marquis and a gift of land. At the same time, however, Protestants began to be excluded from supplying naval yards and from piloting ships. Frightened, Colbert and Seignelay asked the naval intendant at Rochefort "to calm the spirits of the so-called reformed, without any new measures against them, so as to keep them from going to foreign countries."

The time was long gone when Colbert could ask the bishop of Amiens to "curb the zeal" of a "good monk" who was trying to convert Van Rohais and his men. In 1682 the minister wrote the intendant of Amiens: "I entreat you to employ at once any means you think able to convert said Van Rohais and his family."

Political reasons were probably not the only explanation of Louis's animosity. Terrible events had taken place, and they had made his faith more rigid. The *Affaire des poisons* had raised the specter of Satan. Mme de Montespan had given place to Mme de Maintenon, a fanatical ex-Huguenot. Colbert, who remained a close confidant of the king until the end of his days, tried, with all his wisdom and all his strength, to save his ally, the king's former mistress.

CHAPTER 17

The Affaire des poisons

THE BEAUTIFUL BALANCE of classical art, the apparent orderliness of society and its laws, and the dazzling glory of a triumphant monarchy brilliantly masked an ill-contained evolution in ideology, an unconscious transition, and contradictory aspirations, which were still unrecognized. Social and even mental structures from the Middle Ages persisted. And yet didn't the ineradicable nostalgia for the Classical world secretly proclaim a rejection of the mystical revelation?

The confusion in religious faith best indicates the profound complexity of the century. Simultaneously, a clear decline in religious feeling was present with admirable outbursts of mysticism, mixed with a paganism full of vitality and gross superstition. One prayed to God with exaltation and feared the devil. The Mass pleased God; magic pacified Satan. Louis XIV's contemporaries often considered, with surprising ease, that the two cults were complementary.

Behind the luminous decor of the great reign, there swarmed a world of sorcerers, of criminal seers and healers, and of alchemists in quest of the philosopher's stone—that is to say, more simply, a world of shams. Ignorance of medicine, a bewildering trait in an age so open to science, encouraged belief in remedies that were more like sympathetic magic than medicine. Mme de Sévigné tells us that Mme de Lafayette took "bouillon of viper, which gives her new strength before your very eyes." Georges Mongrédien[1] has pointed out in the pharmacopaia of Charas (approved by d'Acchino, one of the highest medical authorities of the time) the following remedies: peacock droppings for epilepsy, frog sperm for vomiting, salts of louse or earthworm for gout, bee ashes to restore hair, and ant oil to improve deafness.

Doctors were still unable to detect traces of poison in autopsies. The knowledge that one could eliminate enemies without consequences was a great temptation. Hired killers, who surrounded their crimes with dreadful or comical shows of witchcraft, were gradually unmasked by La Reynie. Some of this filth even

[1]Georges Mongrédien, *La vie quotidienne sous Louis XIV.*

spattered the royal court. Criminals could worm their way into Versailles with the help of bribed servants. Certain important personnages consulted fortune-telling sorceresses. Lovers readily had philters concocted for their use. Where then did curiosity leave off, and where did crime begin?

What is called the *Affaire des poisons* had several stages. Colbert was involved more than once, and in more than one capacity. Let us consider the stages of this dark business in the order in which they became known to the minister.

THE BRINVILLIERS WOMAN

With the discovery in 1672 of the crimes of the marquise de Brinvilliers, the public's poisoning phobia began. Henriette d'Orléans, known as "Madame," died in June of 1671, just after her return from England, where she had succeeded in getting her brother Charles II to sign the treaty of Dover. Everything pointed to death by appendicitis, but many people, including Charles II, came to think that Madame had been poisoned.

In the meantime, the marquise de Brinvilliers, daughter of Antoine Dreux d'Aubray, civil lieutenant of Paris, had killed her father and two brothers by means of poison, because they had been keeping her from seeing her many lovers freely. Her husband was sometimes administered poison but received antidotes from sympathetic lovers: He managed to survive this rough treatment. It is possible that the marquise used the same means for other murders. The discovery of compromising papers in a box at the time of the natural death of her lover and accomplice, Sainte-Croix, an occasional alchemist, caused the royal police to begin surveillance.

Mme de Brinvilliers fled to England. Colbert first thought the English police would lend him assistance. But the English magistrates were not of that opinion. Charles II, who did not dare contradict them, allowed the French ambassador himself—then Charles de Croissy, Colbert's brother—to try to arrest the marquise with French police. Colbert thought that would be a political blunder, and wrote his brother to tell him so in November 1672: "It is certain that the people, being easily stirred up against the French, would not suffer our officers to make a capture of that importance in the city of London."

Louis XIV once more asked for her extradition, and Charles again refused. The marquise learned she was in danger, fled from London, and changed her place of residence often. Three years later, Louvois learned that Mme de Brinvilliers was in a convent in Liège. The city was then occupied by French troops. Louvois quickly had her arrested and brought to Paris.

Her trial stirred up considerable public reaction and created an embarrassment for Colbert. The marquise sent notes from prison to one of her former lovers,

Reich de Penautier, treasurer of the Estates of Languedoc and an official collector of the tax on the clergy. Penautier, already under suspicion, was arrested on June 15, 1676. The man was one of Colbert's most intelligent agents and a highly efficient tax collector. The minister left no papers proving that he intervened on Penautier's behalf, but according to the testimony of Mme de Sévigné, and later that of Saint-Simon, it seems certain Colbert and Cardinal de Bonzi, a principal religious leader in Languedoc, gave the prisoner total support. It seems likely, furthermore, that Mme de Brinvilliers meant to compromise a man to whom she had formerly lent money and whose high position would embarrass the government. The marquise was executed in 1676, and Penautier was freed eleven months later, nothing having been proved against him.

There is no denying that Louis XIV wished to cleanse the kingdom of that criminal element with complete justice and regardless of class distinctions. From his camp at Valenciennes, he ordered Colbert to contact the First President and the attorney general and inform them in his name "that they are to do what is expected of men of their stature." The king then had no idea how close the sordidness was to his own royal person.

THE VOISIN WOMAN

In September 1677, an unsigned note describing a plot to poison the king and the dauphin was found in a church in Paris. Elsewhere the father confessors of Notre-Dame, without giving names, informed the police of the existence of a band of evildoers, occasional sorcerers, experts on poisons and counterfeiting. La Reynie succeeded in hauling in several of the criminals by having the fortune-tellers' milieu infiltrated. The arrest of Marie Bosse, on January 4, 1679, was quickly followed by that of the magician Lesage (who had already done time in the galleys); that of the woman known as La Filastre; and above all, those of the famous Voisin woman and her horrible accomplice, the abbé Guibourg. Black Masses, sacrifices of aborted or abandoned children, poisons, magical spells using consecrated wafers, were mingled with inoffensive fortune-telling consultations to which important personages came, who were complacently named by the fortune-tellers. These terrifying revelations, along with a plan for regicide, would little by little transform a simple criminal case into an affair of state.

On March 8, 1679, counseled by Louvois, Louis XIV created a special court called the Arsenal Commission, whose decisions would be without appeal and whose proceedings would be secret. The administrative confusion characteristic of the period made it difficult to ascertain what the official duties of Le Tellier and Colbert were in the affair. The letters patent creating the commission were signed by the king on April 7 and were countersigned by Colbert, who had, as part of his jurisdiction, the department of Paris. But the chief of justice was then Le Tellier. It was his son Louvois who was responsible for administering the whole affair. The parlement, furious at having had such an important matter removed from its jurisdiction, protested in vain to the king.

Marie Bosse and several other accomplices were quickly sentenced. Lesage and the Voisin woman began to name important names. Lesage had previously mentioned Mme de Montespan. The Voisin woman contradicted him, but pointed the finger at other leading figures, such as the marshal of Luxembourg, the comtesse de Soissons, and her sister, the duchesse de Bouillon (of the Mancini family), the marquise d'Alluye (former mistress of Fouquet), and Mme de Polignac.

We should note here Louvois's curious visit to Lesage, widely criticized by his contemporaries. He had no compunction about going in person to visit Lesage in the prison of Vincennes. We may never know what the two men said in private, but the next day Louvois wrote to Louis: "I went yesterday morning and spoke to him along the lines M. de la Reynie wanted, letting him hope that His Majesty would be clement provided he made the statements required to make known to the law everything that was done with respect to poisons."

And it has been shown that these magicians, imprisoned in different places, benefited from a network of accomplices who informed them thoroughly of the unfolding of the inquiry. It is quite possible, then, that the Voisin woman already knew what Louvois had promised Lesage when she decided to name names.

La Reynie prosecuted the case with admirable strictness and integrity. He had, furthermore, received precise verbal orders from the king, which he noted in his papers on December 27, 1679.

His Majesty commended justice and our duty to us in extremely strong and precise terms, emphasizing that he desired us to penetrate as deeply as possible, in the name of the public welfare, the unhappy trade of poisoning, so as to have it out by the roots, if that were possible. He ordered us to execute exact justice, without any distinction of person, status, or sex. And His Majesty told us this in such clear and vivid terms, and at the same time with such benevolence, that it is impossible to doubt his intentions in this respect and not to understand with what spirit of justice he wishes the search to be made.

On January 23, 1680, the Arsenal Commission—more commonly known as the *chambre ardente,* after former courts of the Middle Ages—ordered the arrests of the comtesse de Soissons, of her friend the marquise d'Alluye, of Mme de Polignac, and of the marshal of Luxembourg. While the marshal refused to hide from justice (and he was eventually acquitted), the three women hastily fled. The king probably aided his former mistress, the comtesse de Soissons, in her flight.

The duchesse de Bouillon, who had been accused of trying to poison her husband with her lover's help, appeared in court on both men's arms. The aristocracy was indignant. The upper middle class was also involved, but generally profited from relationships with members of the commission. Public opinion was bewildered. Mme de Sévigné wrote that "there is hardly a precedent for such a scandal in a Christian court."

Louvois suspended the trial from January 25 to February 15. On February 22, the Voisin woman died at the stake. On the twenty-fourth, the commission's charge was extended to include "sacrilege, blasphemy, profanations, and the manufacturing and display of counterfeit money."

MME DE MONTESPAN

On May 18, 1680, Bussy-Rabutin reported this incident: "The day the king left Saint-Germain, as he was getting into his carriage with the queen, he had hard words with Mme de Montespan concerning suspicions with which she was still charged, and which were harming His Majesty. The king spoke politely at first, but when she answered very sharply, His Majesty grew angry."

On May 25, Mme de Sévigné added this story: "There was a big quarrel the other day between the king and Mme de Montespan. M. Colbert worked for a reconciliation, and managed, with difficulty, to have the king take his midnight supper as usual, but only on the condition that everyone would be admitted." In other words, the king agreed to see Mme de Montespan again after the great dispute, but refused to be alone with her. The king's mistress had already been named by Lesage, but it was known that the Voisin woman had denied his story. The veritable attacks of the prisoners against the king's mistress had not yet begun at that precise date.

Colbert had a good reason to defend Montespan. His third daughter, Marie-Anne, was engaged on February 13, 1679, to Louis de Rochechouart, duc de Mortemart, Vivonne's son and thus the nephew of the king's mistress. Colbert had reason to hope, for his daughter's sake, that Mme de Montespan would retain the king's favor.

Besides, Mme de Montespan offered Colbert the immense advantage of not mixing into policy and of not trying to influence the king on public or national matters. That was not the case with Mme de Maintenon, whose moral and intellectual power over the king grew stronger day by day. Colbert probably did not hide his exasperation at the dangerous influence the beautiful Widow Scarron had on the king's religious policies. Stupidly, Mme de Maintenon wrote to her friend

Mme de Saint-Géran that "M. Colbert thinks only of his finances and never of religion."

The Widow Scarron had embarked on her fortune when she was given the king's and Montespan's children to raise. In 1674 Louis allowed her to buy the domain of Maintenon, made her marquise of the same name, and granted her an income of 10,000 livres a year. It was the payment of a simple debt of gratitude; Mme de Montespan's standing was then indisputable.

In 1675 Bossuet, indignant at the official character the king's adultery had assumed, scolded the king's mistress severely. Tears, remorse, religious fervor, and threatened separation gave way to the reconciliation of the lovers and a new birth quickly followed. The following year, Mme de Montespan, "a triumphant beauty to parade before ambassadors," as Mme de Sévigné put it, and a marvelous living advertisement for Colbert's royal factories, appeared at court "dressed all in French lace, her hair in a thousand ringlets." The king was tiring of her jealousy, her extravagances, and her character. He was frequently unfaithful to her. But she still knew how to conquer the heart of the king. Mme de Sévigné said it best, on June 11, 1677 to her daughter: "Ah, my daughter, what a triumph at Versailles! What a surfeit of pride! How solidly she is established, how like the duchesse de Valentinois![2] How she is relished again even after distraction and absence! What a taking of possession anew! I was in the room for an hour. She was in bed, adorned and coiffed, resting up for the midnight supper."

In May 1678, Louis XIV was worried by the presence of M. de Montespan, who had never accepted his misfortune, and showed it in a thousand foolish ways. Though still on campaign, the king wrote to Colbert: "I forgot to tell you when I left that, M. de Montespan being in Paris, it would be well to watch how he acts. He's a fool capable of doing something outrageous. Therefore, I would like for you to have him watched: what he does, who he spends time with, what he says; in short, be as well-informed as you can of what he does, and when anything that seems important to you arises, you are to let me know."

These are the words of a man who prizes his mistress. In the same year, Colbert had to outfit racing boats for Mme de Montespan! At a time when it was necessary to prepare the navy for a future war with England and the other European naval powers, Colbert had to equip the boats at Le Havre and to raise crews at La Rochelle in order to serve the private interests of the king's mistress.

Yet Louis's infidelities continued. The ravishing Mlle de Fontanges particularly worried Mme de Montespan, who succeeded, all the same, in getting herself named superintendant of the queen's household in April of 1679. And the king

---

[2]Title of Diane de Poitiers, the triumphant mistress of Henry II as Mme de Montespan was of Louis XIV.

was more and more attracted by the efficient and dignified charm of Mme de Maintenon.

In July 1680, Abbé Guibourg, the sinister assistant to the Voisin woman, stated that he had said Mass in a château near Montlhéry over the belly of a woman he did not know, at the request of Leroy, governor of the pages of the small stable. All through the summer of 1680, Mme de Montespan was accused by name by several prisoners. La Reynie took those accusations seriously. He established that Mlle des Œuillets, the mistress's chambermaid, had been living in the home of Leroy. It was strange that two sorceresses, La Vertemart and La Filastre, had tried to find positions, one in Mme de Montespan's retinue and the other with Mlle de Fontanges. The daughter of the Voisin woman accused the king's mistress in great detail.

The prisoners even suggested that Mme de Montespan was implicated in the business of the famous poisoned petition that the Voisin woman was supposed to have tried to hand the king. On August 2, 1680, Louis XIV, frightened by La Reynie's revelations, transformed an already secret trial into an ultrasecret trial in La Reynie's hands alone, under Louvois's authority. On the same day, La Filastre testified that "Prior Guibourg, priest of Saint-Denis, had told her he had worked for Montespan as well as for a man who had some resentment against M. Colbert." Still according to the prisoner, Mme de Vivonne, who was Mme de Montespan's sister-in-law (and her enemy), had requested "along with freedom and reinstatement for M. Fouquet, death for Colbert." It is a fact that La Reynie would later find a document in which 1,000 livres were promised Guibourg in 1675 by a certain d'Amy, an official in the finance office in Provence, who had had differences with the minister. Guibourg furnished drugs to d'Amy. Could they have been administered to Colbert? If so, they would no doubt explain the minister's terrible stomach pains.

Louis XIV, horrified by La Filastre's new statements, decided to suspend the trial entirely during his absence upon the occasion of the dauphin's marriage. He wanted to conduct the matter himself, when he returned. The daughter of the Voisin woman took the stand and once more accused the king's mistress. But her testimony was contradictory. On August 13 she said she had never seen Mme de Montespan. On the twentieth she said she had seen her, and had spoken with her through her carriage door, while giving her a powder. On the twenty-second, she formally accused Mme de Montespan of having participated in a Black Mass where a child had been killed. La Filastre, under torture,[3] repeated her earlier statements. Her confession was heard before her execution, and she afterward asked

---

[3]Shocking as it may seem to us, torture was generally practiced in Europe, even in Holland.

to speak to La Reynie in order to withdraw her accusations against Mme de Montespan.

But the priest Guibourg then accused the king's mistress in his turn. He claimed to have said Mass over the body of Mme de Montespan, who had brought a letter of hers addressed to the devil, in which she asked that the queen be sterile and renounced, that the dauphin grant her his affection, and that she, the mistress of the king, should become his wife and be named to the council. This web of absurdities discredited the prisoners' statements, it is true. The Voisin woman and La Filastre had both separately accused Mme de Montespan of having tried to poison Mlle de Fontanges with cloth and gloves.

La Reynie was probably very embarrassed when the king asked him for his advice. The characters of the witnesses and the contradictions in their testimony were points in Montespan's favor. Lax surveillance might have allowed secret arrangements for simultaneous accusations that could transform the criminal case into an affair of state that the king would want to suppress. But La Reynie had come across the transcripts of the 1668 interrogations in the châtelet of Mariette, a priest of Saint-Sauveur, and Lesage. They showed that both men had referred to Mme de Montespan at that early date. According to the two men, she had had the Gospel of the Kings read over her head and had made Mariette, during the Mass, pass her herbs and powders in the chalice in order to make a conquest of the king and to drive away Louise de La Vallière. With reason, La Reynie thought all of that was "of considerable weight," because it had been said "before the period of suspicion."[4]

On October 1, 1680, a frightened Louis suspended the deliberations of the special tribunal and ordered La Reynie to go on with his investigation in secret. On November 19, Louis granted Mme de Montespan a gift of 50,000 livres "as a reward, in consideration of her services." Despite the opinions of some historians, this gift does not seem to us sufficient proof that the king was convinced of his mistress's innocence: Otherwise, why, over the following months, would Colbert— with the collaboration of a well-known criminal lawyer—prepare a large file for the king's use in exculpating Mme de Montespan? The royal grant seems more like a farewell present.

Mme de Montespan gave Louis seven children, of whom three died young and four lived.[5] Louis XIV had them declared legitimate and seemed to show them special affection. The scandal of an official legal proceeding against their mother could damage the royal house in the eyes of France and all of Europe.

[4]Quoted in Georges Mongrédien, *Mme de Montespan et L'affaire des poisons*.

[5]The duc du Maine (1670), the comte de Toulouse (1678), Mlle de Nantes, and the second Mlle de Blois.

Louvois, who didn't hide his suspicions, nevertheless agreed with Colbert on this point. Early in 1681, Colbert decided to devote every effort to removing the affair from its current impasse. The minister was familiar with all the transcripts of the interrogations, which La Reynie had sent him faithfully.[6] He went over them one by one, making two summaries of each for himself and noting some comments in the margins.[7] At the top of one of his summaries, Colbert wrote this analysis in his cramped, difficult hand:

> Summary of the great affair.
>
> Three kinds of crimes divided by three distinct periods are involved.
>
> The first, set forth by Lesage in 1667 and 1668: impieties, Mariette's ceremonies at Saint-Germain.
>
> The second, in the following year, abominations, Masses . . . sacrifices of children whose throats were cut.
>
> The third: attempt on the king's person, by poison.

The minister's orderly mind thus accurately outlined the scale, so to speak, of the presumed crimes, whose seriousness increased with time.

Colbert was well aware of the statements made by Lesage and Mariette concerning Mme de Montespan's visit to them in 1667 and 1668. He noted at length—in a hurried script full of abbreviations—these events, which were evidently highly embarrassing. "She went, Mass was said, two pigeon hearts passed around in the chalice, the following Sunday . . . secret conjuring, Gospel of the Kings placed in the same box with a small piece of paper inscribed Lucifer's host." The testimony of Lesage and Mariette in 1680 confirmed the accusations concerning that time when the favor in which Louise de La Vallière was held could still get in the way of Mme de Montespan.

Colbert wrote on November 10, 1680, that Mariette "said the same things as Lesage . . . beginning with his seeing M[8] with the Voisin woman at the end of 1667 and the beginning of 1668. . . . When he was confronted, he varied somewhat . . . but in the end he stood by nearly everything."

---

[6]We remain surprised by the lightness of the work (recently reedited) by Frantz Funk-Brentano (*Le drame des poisons*), which, incidentally, seems well documented. The author claims that Colbert only followed the affair from afar, which is completely belied by the minister's papers. On the other hand, the author authoritatively condemns Mme de Montespan without definitive proof.

[7]These documents are unpublished.

[8]Colbert's abbreviation for Mme de Montespan.

The transcripts bearing on the other two "crimes" showed contradictions and implausibilities that would be of much greater use for an eventual defense of Mme de Montespan.

In February 1681, after his long and detailed study of the transcripts, Colbert called on the lawyer Claude Duplessis for an opinion on two separate points. First, Mme de Montespan's legal innocence had to be shown. Second, it was necessary to examine the value or the usefulness of the investigation then under way.

In reply to the first question, Duplessis sent the minister an extremely long report in which he showed the lack of any substantial proof. Furthermore, he brought out the serious contradictions in the prisoners' testimony, which seemed itself sufficient to remove all traces of suspicion.[9] It is, however, significant that Duplessis never mentions the participation of Mme de Montespan in the "impieties" at Saint-Germain in 1667 and 1668. Was Colbert careful not to give him the excerpted testimony from Lesage and Mariette? Or did the two men agree to expunge it?

On February 26, Duplessis wrote in confidence to the minister, "Please note the remark at the beginning, because it could furnish evidence against many things that seem well-established." He may have been referring to the relations between Mme de Montespan and the sorcerers, who were supposed to have given her "love-powders" at sacrilegious ceremonies. The celebration of Black Masses that were supposed to have been said over the belly of the king's mistress, at the height of her glory, seemed very improbable. She was then under discreet surveillance or, at least, was rarely alone. Mlle des Œuillets, accused of having served as a go-between, had left the service of Mme de Montespan in 1677. And the accusation of her having wanted to kill the king by means of a poisoned petition to be given him by the Voisin woman, was really absurd. Why would the Voisin woman and her accomplice, La Trianon, have had such trouble reaching the king if Louis's own mistress was in league with them? And why would Mme de Montespan have wanted to kill the lover from whom she obtained all her favors? Louvois should never have promised Lesage his safety in return for interesting information.

After having minutely examined the transcripts and the recommendation of Duplessis, Colbert wrote a lengthy "argument against the calumnious acts imputed to Mme de Montespan." In all probability, this memorandum was intended for Louis XIV. Colbert begins with these lines: "There are four[10] prisoners whose testimony and declarations are to be discussed in connection with the matter, to

---

[9]The correspondence between Colbert and Duplessis is found among the personal papers of the minister and has been published in Pierre Clément, *Lettres, instructions, et mémoires de Colbert,* vol. 6.

[10]Colbert said "four" prisoners, but names five.

wit: the daughter of the Voisin woman, the priest known as Guibourg, the man called Gallet, La Belliere, and La Filastre. The latter's accusation is so horrible that it collapses of its own weight."[11] Once again we notice that the minister makes no reference to either Lesage or Mariette.

Colbert listed the contradictions and absurdities. Thus, in the story of the famous poisoned petition, the daughter of the Voisin woman claimed that:

her mother stayed at Saint-Germain from Sunday to Thursday without being able to present her petition, and returned very upset about it; and Bertrand, in his testimony of July 25, 1680, says she was unable to present it through negligence and lack of status. On the contrary, according to their so-called confession, nothing could have been easier, for either Mme de Montespan (or else Mlle des Œuillets without her) would have arranged it for them, she would have given them agents who would have been safer and more secret than all these miserable beggar women, or else Mme de Montespan would have herself taken the powder to give it or have it given to the king, as she had a thousand opportunities: The king saw her daily, ate with her often, and had no hesitation in these matters because he never saw anything to make him suspicious; besides, he could never be deceived about that.

But can there be a more confident witness or a better judge of the falsehood of all this calumny than the king himself? His Majesty knows in what fashion Mme de Montespan has lived with him, he has witnessed all her behavior, known her entire character, her total bearing at all times and in all circumstances, and His Majesty's mind, so keen and discerning, has never become aware of anything that might have placed her under the slightest suspicion.

Colbert's argument was very clever: If Mme de Montespan had been guilty, the king would have had to be an imbecile not to notice it. Of course, that was inconceivable. The minister added new evidence based on his knowledge of the private relations between the sovereign and his mistress. When necessary, the style of the argument became lyrical. According to the testimonies, Mme de Montespan had seen the Voisin woman frequently after 1673.

But His Majesty is aware that the little pangs of jealousy that affection might have caused in Mme de Montespan's mind did not begin until 1678, and His Majesty knows in what a calm state of mind Mme de Montespan was living both in 1673 and before, and he knows what attention, attachment, and affection the lady has shown him since, as well as the security and quietness of mind she has always displayed, and that her jealousy since 1678 was due only to strong feelings of affection that have not moved her in the least from

[11]Seignelay preserved his father's handwritten draft.

that same attention and attachment. What! Conceive a plan to poison her master, her benefactor, her king, a person she loves more than her life; to know that one would lose all in losing him, and to support the execution of such a mad enterprise, and yet, while under the sway of these frightful thoughts, to have maintained a peace of mind that only the purest innocence could produce! These things are inconceivable; and His Majesty, who knows Mme de Montespan to the bottom of her soul, will never be persuaded that she has been capable of these abominations.

After having prepared the defense for the king's mistress, Colbert and Duplessis sought to find ways to end an investigation that had proven embarrassing in many respects. Colbert was not displeased to enumerate the blunders in the trial and the inquiry—blunders that he would have been able to avoid had he still been in charge of the justice department. On February 25 he wrote to Duplessis:

It seems to me that one can strongly suspect that the length of the imprisonments, the multiplicity of interrogations, the great number of prisoners— all suspects and accomplices of the same crimes and who were easily able to communicate with each other—gave rise to and facilitated these different accusations, in order that, by implicating important persons in their crimes, they might hinder judgment of their case, put off the sentences they knew they deserved, and perhaps even annul them.

We should then examine whether it was necessary or not to have so many interrogations, to establish a special court for crimes of this sort,[12] to prolong the trial contrary to ordinary judicial procedure, and whether, if the case had been entrusted wholly to the criminal lieutenants, it would not have been more promptly ended and the guilty more surely punished, without all the difficulties we have fallen into, stemming from the aforementioned causes.

To extricate themselves from this "predicament," the minister suggested several solutions. The simplest method would be to sentence the most obviously guilty prisoners, while avoiding, despite the great difficulties, all confrontation with the accusers, then to send the others to prisons or fortresses not far from Paris. Duplessis advised an end to the tortures, summary judgment for those presumed guilty, even if they had not confessed (a singular recommendation coming from a lawyer), the continued incarceration of some of them without trial, and finally the burning of the records of the trial, "because of the execrable impieties and abominable filth therein, whose recollection it is important to avoid." Otherwise, the lawyer found nothing improper about the investigation up to that point.

[12]The establishment of a special court had been suggested by Louvois.

Louis seemed inclined toward Colbert's solution. La Reynie, with obstinacy and courage, wanted to continue the trial so that the criminals might not go unpunished. For four days straight, four hours a day, he defended his point of view vigorously before the king, Le Tellier, Louvois, and Colbert. Will we ever know what they said in those long meetings? La Reynie persuaded the king to continue the special tribunal, which took up its work again on May 19, 1681, but had to accept a discontinuation of Mme de Montespan's case. The lieutenant of police soon established, to his chagrin, that under those conditions it was impossible to try her principal accusers, such as Lesage and Guibourg. In essence, Colbert's and Duplessis's plan prevailed. While certain criminals were condemned to death, others died in prison, where they had lived for a more or less long time, chained, under horrible conditions.

Mlle de Fontanges died in June of 1681, probably from pneumonia of tubercular origin. Louis must have been particularly struck by her death, remembering how Mme de Montespan had been accused of trying to poison her young rival. His former mistress knew she was not then under suspicion, but at first she did not understand her new situation. Quite probably Louis was convinced—and I think, justifiably—that Mme de Montespan had for years been giving him "love powders" furnished by the criminals. That conviction was unpleasant enough to put an end to all close or privileged relations with the mother of the royal bastards. But things were not serious enough to bring about a total break, especially since secrecy should be maintained and scandal avoided. Once more, it was Colbert who found himself entrusted with explaining to Mme de Montespan the new nature of her relationship with the king. It was a delicate task. Louis specified it to his minister in these terms:

Before coming to join me, Mme de Montespan sent me a letter from my Grand Cousin, in which she asks me for things I cannot grant her; she has also asked me to give her some reply.[13] I will give her a general one, and call upon you to tell her what my intentions are. I am sending you her letter so that you can know better what she wants, and explain to her more exactly what you are to tell her on my behalf. Go to her, then, and after having given her the letter I am sending her through you, explain to her politely that I always receive the tokens of her affection and confidence with pleasure and am quite unhappy when I am unable to do as she wishes; say that I think I have adequately shown the pleasure I take in showing her favor by granting to Lauzun what I have just granted him;[14] that her new request has surprised me; that there is some

[13]La Grand Mademoiselle.

[14]Allusion to the favors granted Lauzun (including his freedom) following his renunciation of land given him by La Grand Mademoiselle, in favor of the duc du Maine.

hope there will be changes in time, but that presently I am unable to do any more than I have done. Add to that all the polite expressions and compliments that seem required. [15]

Mme de Montespan kept her large apartment at Versailles until 1687. She left court in 1692 to take up residence in the convent of the Ladies of Saint Joseph, where she lived in great piety. Louis XIV waited until La Reynie died, in 1709, before burning the "private acts" of the *Affaire des poisons*. The secret would be kept incredibly well. It seems no one at court ever knew of the accusations brought against the king's powerful mistress. Only La Reynie's, Louvois's, and Colbert's personal papers would reveal the truth about an affair that in fact had been blown out of proportion by a very clumsy investigation.

But at least these unhappy events brought about one valuable decision. In collaboration with La Reynie, Colbert drew up the famous edict against soothsayers and poisoners, published on August 30, 1682: The manufacture and sale of poisons for industrial and medicinal use were regulated. The edict's provisions have been part of French law ever since.

[15]Letter from Louis XIV to Colbert written from Vitry, October 5, 1681.

CHAPTER 18

The Age of Colbert

There are many reasons why great things should not be undertaken,
but they do not fail to produce great effects when sustained.—COLBERT

OLBERT PURSUED HIS MANY ACTIVITIES until, by 1683, he was at the extreme limit of his strength. His illnesses became more and more serious. After 1680, a new remedy, quinine, sometimes helped to overcome high fever. D'Ormoy did not have the intelligence of Seignelay. It was said at court that Louis XIV had complained to his minister of the disproportion between his largesse and certain inadequate services. That reproach, according to contemporary reports, hurt Colbert deeply. The Venetian ambassador, Sebastian Foscarini, would describe the particularly melancholy character of the minister in the last moments of his life (*"melancolico biliosissimo temperamento"*). Yet no difficulty, however great it might be, no disappointment, could vanquish his exceptional political stubbornness.

In the domain of the navy, Colbert organized the naval guards along the lines of the army's corps of cadets. The intendants began to recruit a rather large number of gentlemen for it.

In June of 1683, two months before his death, the minister sent a circular to the intendants, exhorting them to encourage "men of literature" who were studying some specialized branch of science or the history of their province. When he went to the Academy of Painting for the last time, it was to personally award the first prize to a young painter of twenty, Hyacinthe Rigaud.

Louis's nonchalant attitude toward budgetary planning drove the minister to despair. On June 8, he wrote the king from Sceaux. "[Your Majesty] will please note that besides the 5,540,887 livres to which the fixed payments have risen, another 2,266,500 livres are required to cover the payments Your Majesty has ordered or decided to order according to the attached memorandum, and that these expenditures exceed income by 3,600,000 livres, as shown in a memorandum you saw before your departure."[1] On June 13, Louis wrote this reply in the margin: "The size of the expenditures is very painful to me, but some of them are necessary."

[1]Pierre Clément, *Lettres, instructions, et mémoires de Colbert*, vol. 2.

Colbert, discouraged, confessed his helplessness: "With all the diligence and concentration I have been able to apply until now, I have so far been unable to find more than 1,400,000 livres to borrow, which makes it very difficult to cover these expenses." The king's only attempt at consolation was this reply: "I know you are doing everything possible."

Shortly thereafter, the minister wrote: "Financial matters are following their usual course, the intendants are inspecting the *généralités* and giving reports in all their letters, which are full of the people's sufferings." Louis replied: "The suffering gives me great pain. We must do what we can to assist the people. I hope to be able to soon." The king was then on tour, inspecting the fortresses in Franche-Comté. Maria Theresa was with him. The queen's health had changed for the worse. On June 15, Louis wrote to Colbert: "Hurry things along at Versailles, for I may well shorten the trip by a few days." The court was back at Versailles on the twentieth. The queen died ten days later. Colbert was already very ill. Thus, it was Seignelay who found himself in charge of organizing the burial and the ceremonies—and of inquiring into the debts of Maria Theresa.

On August 3, the son of the minister wrote the king: "I am sending Your Majesty the list of the bodies in the vault at Saint-Denis. There is no more room, and someone will have to be put into the Valois vault, which is closest. It seems to me that might fall to the late Monsieur's[2] two wives."[3] The king replied: "I have seen the list you sent me, and since there is no hurry, I will tell you my intentions when you get here."

A little later Seignelay added: "I have inquired into the queen's debts, and from what M. de Visé and M. Bontemps tell me after having questioned the pages, I have learned that the queen didn't owe anything on her usual gambling, but that she owed 14,000 or 15,000 pistoles on the game of cassetta: The boys didn't know precisely if it was the one or the other of the two sums, but now the players themselves can tell us more exactly." Louis wrote in the margin, "Try to get precise details without being cheated." And Seignelay went on to say: "During the trip she [the queen] had borrowed 200 pistoles from Mme de Béthune, 33 from Madame La Nourrice. Her Majesty owed 700 pistoles to Montarsy, jeweler, and 100 to Gauthier, merchant. Mme de Visé having told me that she knew that M. du Vau had lent the queen money at various times, I called him in, and to my surprise he showed me receipts in the queen's own hand, a list of which is attached, adding up to 111,133 livres. I await Your Majesty's orders in reply to this note." Louis, who from all evidence preferred to reply orally, wrote in the margin, "I have nothing more to say to you on this note."

[2]Unpublished handwritten memorandum with the king's replies written in the margin.

[3]Gaston d'Orleans.

On August 8 it came time to choose the bishop who was to officiate at the funeral. Seignelay tried to have the honor given to his brother. If the bishop of Orléans "couldn't do it," he wrote to the king, "my brother, who is young and in good health, would be ready to carry out Your Majesty's orders in that regard." The king replied, "The bishop of Orléans will go to hold the ceremony; otherwise, I would have chosen your brother."[4]

Of course, the court was excited over the question of rank and precedence at the ceremony. Louis decided to follow the precedents set at the time of Anne of Austria's burial. Seignelay went over the records with care and was obliged to disappoint a few ladies who claimed the right to a seat in the official carriages.

On August 17, Colbert signed his last official letter. It was addressed to the intendants, whom Colbert pestered in the most energetic of terms until the last days of his life: "I am obliged to warn you that the king is now having reports made on the inspections of the *généralitiés* in every council meeting; since you have not yet sent me your report on your inspection of your *généralité* if you do not do it at once, it will seem to His Majesty that you have not executed his orders, which I gave you and have often reiterated."[5]

On August 29, the minister was in critical condition. Seignelay wrote to Louis: "Responding to the order Your Majesty kindly gave me to report on my father's health, I shall say that he had a very bad night, that his pain persisted for the better part of the day, and that, weak as he is, if he were to have a fever along with his other ills, his sickness would become quite dangerous, but, thank God, he has had none so far."[6] The king replied in the margin: "I am very concerned about your father's illness, and I am very sorry to hear of the pain he is suffering. I hope he will soon be in as good condition as we all wish him to be. Tell him on my behalf what I have told you."

On September 2, "from Paris, at two in the morning," Seignelay again wrote Louis:

My father's illness has so intensified, Sire, and his weakness is so great, that the doctors, who knew nothing about this disease that they claimed was harmless in the absence of any fever, have now advised that he be given the last rites, which is why I thought well to inform Your Majesty. You will be given precise information on what happens next, and I am persuaded that, on this sad occasion, Your Majesty will permit me to stay here to observe the consequences of this illness.

[4]Unpublished handwritten memorandum, with the king's reply.

[5]Clément, *Lettres,* vol. 2.

[6]Not published in Clément.

Louis replied: "Your father's condition means a great deal to me; stay with him as long as you are needed, and I hope your own pain will not keep you from doing everything possible to comfort and to save him. I still hope God will not see fit to take him from this world, where he is necessary to the health of the state. I wish it with all my heart, both because of my special friendship for him and because of my friendship for you and the entire family."

On the same day, Louis, who by then thought Colbert's death imminent, had the presence of mind to order Seignelay to close the *Caisse des emprunts.* With all the refined politeness of which he was capable, the king ended his letter with these words: "The fall I took, which, thank God, did me little harm, keeps me from writing you this note in my own hand, which shall still not fail to sign it." And despite his sprained wrist, the king signed in his own hand. Thus, the greatest king in Europe apologized to Colbert's son for not having written the letter entirely in his own hand. That proves, in my opinion—if the documents cited above haven't already proved it—that the so-called disgrace of the minister near the end of his life was greatly exaggerated by his contemporaries.[7]

On September 5, the notaries came to the house in the rue Neuve-des-Petits-Champs. Colbert dictated his will. Seignelay was named his universal legatee. There were also various legacies to religious and charitable organizations, such as the Paris hospital called L'Hôtel-Dieu, which he had founded.

On September 6, Colbert died, at the age of sixty-four, after horrible suffering caused by a violent attack of nephritic colic. He had had to be submerged in a bath ten times to make the pain bearable. His body was cut open, and the doctors found "one large stone in one of the urethrae, and others of smaller size in the gall bladder." He was buried by night in his parish church, Saint-Eustache. His contemporaries said that he had to be buried at night for fear of the hostile reactions of the people to a daylight ceremony, for Colbert had been held responsible, despite himself, for all the misfortune of his day.[8]

Pussort and Desmarets very briefly replaced him at the head of the department of finances, while awaiting the nomination of a new comptroller general. The minister's uncle and nephew then carried out the reimbursement of the depositors of the *Caisse des emprunts,* which had been permanently closed on September 9.

Le Tellier and Louvois had their friend and relative Claude Le Pelletier, former provost of the guilds, appointed comptroller general to succeed Colbert.

[7]The Venetian ambassador insisted strongly on this disgrace. Racine spoke of a letter from the king that Colbert, on his deathbed, refused to read. A letter from Mme de Maintenon (probably of doubtful authenticity) mentions the same incident. No primary source refers to that event, however.

[8]Mme Colbert had Coysevox sculpt his monument (the angel is by Toby). It was removed during the Revolution, but was replaced, later, in the Church of Saint-Eustache.

The French have always had a taste for the play on words, and the nomination of Le Pelletier* didn't fail to evoke one. Le Tellier had three lizards on his coat of arms, and Colbert had a serpent. The abbé de Choisy would later say that meant that the lizard had skinned the serpent and that its skin was at the skin trader's.

The Le Tellier clan in fact did acquire a predominant influence. The king awarded Louvois the office of superintendant of buildings, which had been bought from d'Ormoy. In compensation, Louis granted Colbert's son the very large sum of 500,000 livres, or double what Colbert had paid for the office twenty years before. D'Ormoy joined the army. Did Mme Colbert write the king on his behalf? On September 12 Louis sent her a letter of sympathy, which was meant to reassure her where her children's futures were concerned:

> Madame Colbert, I sympathize in your loss, and all the more so because I myself feel the same affliction, since while you have lost a husband who was dear to you, I am mourning a faithful minister with whom I was fully satisfied. His memory will always serve as a strong recommendation, not only for yourself, for your virtue is recommendation enough, but also for all of your family, and you should expect that if Lord Blainville[9] does his duty, as I expect, in his chosen profession, he will feel its effects as much as the rest do. In the meantime, I pray God keep you, Madame Colbert, in His holy care.[10]

Seignelay kept control of the navy, and Croissy, foreign affairs. The Le Telliers may have dominated the government, but they could not drive the Colberts out.

THE TWO CLANS

Once Colbert was dead, Louis felt he had been freed from the burden of a financial theory that he had at first seemed to adopt, but that had weighed upon him for some time. Under Le Pelletier, the department of finance was no longer at loggerheads with the war department and the department of buildings. The new comptroller general abandoned the floating debt policy dear to Colbert and returned to borrowing in order to convert that debt into income. The interest rate, which had been 5 percent in Colbert's day, was set at 5.5 percent. Thus, anyone who did not hold bonds paid the expenses of the operation. A de facto devaluation and the sales of ever-increasing numbers of offices brought in money for the short term.

[9]D'Ormoy's second title.

[10]Clément, *Lettres,* vol. 7.

Pelletier means furrier, or seller of animal skins.

In 1685 the expenses of Versailles reached eleven million livres. The work carried out there under Colbert's direction had cost more than fifty million livres. At Louvois's death in 1690, the total expenditures, including what was spent for the Grand Trianon, the chapel, furnishings, and silverware, added up to 116 million. It is hard for us to imagine the exceptional brilliance of the Hall of Mirrors at that time with its dazzling furnishings. Silver statues, silver planters, silver tables, seats, and stools filled the palace, and the flowerbeds were newly arranged every day.

Around 1688, Louis and his entourage began to tire of Louvois's haughty and violent character. The court took note of Seignelay's high standing with Louis and Mme de Maintenon. Brilliant, eloquent, luxury-loving, the eldest son of Colbert charmed everyone who came near him. He owed his success in large part to his sisters, especially the two elder ones, who were very pious and held in high regard by the king and his morganatic spouse. Saint-Simon later had this to say about Mme de Chevreuse:

> [She] was always in the king's company, whenever ladies were admitted, and he felt the lack whenever she was absent, which almost never happened. Her union with M. de Chevreuse remained intimate throughout their lives; and that of the duc and duchesse de Beauvilliers was the same. Mme de Chevreuse was the sister of Mme de Beauvilliers; they had only one heart and soul; both brothers-in-law were also one, without interruption from the day of their weddings until they died, being always in the same place whenever they could, and taking meals with each other continuously. The closeness and unity of M. Colbert's family set the whole court an example, while they lived, that no others could match, and it contributed greatly to the esteem in which they were held.

The duc de Chevreuse, captain-lieutenant of the light-horse company of the king's guards, became one of Louis's closest advisors, and in the words of Saint-Simon, a "minister incognito."

Seignelay, as well as his brothers-in-law—with whom he was on excellent terms—esteemed and admired Fénelon, by then the leading ecclesiastical figure at court. That prelate's calls for kindness and tolerance toward the Protestants even touched Mme de Maintenon somewhat, who was moved by the horrors of their repression. Le Tellier died in 1685, after having drafted the revocation of the Edict of Nantes. That revocation was a catastrophe for industry, trade, shipping, and even for French foreign policy. Large numbers of industrialists, skilled workers, great businessmen who had once helped Colbert to establish trading companies, naval officers, and sailors fled the objectionable reign of terror led by Louvois and took refuge in Holland or England. The Protestant countries set up underground railways to aid these escapes and to prepare hiding places. Seignelay expressed his dismay in a letter to Fénelon, and begged him to intervene at court. He himself used all his influence to soften the repressions and to persuade seamen to stay in France.

Duquesne went to sea for the last time in 1684. Seignelay sent him to punish Genoa, allied with the Spanish. News of the revocation of the Edict of Nantes in 1685 came as no surprise to him; the seventy-five year old officer requested and received his discharge. In recognition of his services, he was exempted from the obligations imposed by the edict of revocation. But the old sailor was greatly saddened by having to separate from his eldest son. Commander Henri Duquesne, as intractable as his father, went into exile in Switzerland. Duquesne died three years later.

Louis's religious policy was an inducement for Protestant countries to create an anti-French alliance. The king of England, Charles II, died in 1685. His brother, the duke of York, succeeded him as James II. The new king was Catholic. The Tory and Whig factions worked together in secret to bring James's daughter Mary, wife of William of Orange, to the throne. In November 1688, William landed in England with a small army. Janes II, frightened, fled to France, but Catholic Ireland rebelled in his favor. To Louvois's great irritation, Seignelay was entrusted with Irish affairs.

Colbert's son was a remarkable minister of the navy. In February 1689, Tourville, at the head of a well-equipped fleet, won engagements that allowed James II to enter Dublin in triumph. In London, William and Mary were proclaimed king and queen of England. With his usual intelligence, William began to arrange for a new coalition against France.

Seignelay wanted to deal the English navy a decisive blow without delay. Louis prevented it. In August he wrote to Seignelay, "Do everything with prudence, patience, and wisdom. And don't rush into anything we might regret. . . . You have nothing to fear from your absence; be assured that I am very pleased with you." Despite his youth, Seignelay was named minister of state. By not following his advice, hadn't the king committed a grave error? France had perhaps lost its last chance to become a dominant naval power.

The treasury was exhausted; industry and trade were in jeopardy; Le Pelletier abandoned his post. And France had to face nearly all of Europe alone. Early in 1689, Mme de Maintenon wrote to her friend Mme de Saint-Géran, "I still think that if M. Colbert had lived, none of this would have happened."

In July of 1690, William attacked Ireland and forced James II to flee to France, while Louis's armies crushed the allies at Fleurus. On November 3, Seignelay died prematurely, covered with debts, exhausted by work and pleasures. Mme de Sévigné made this comment: "What youth! What high fortune! What a situation in life! His happiness was complete; it seems to us that it is Splendor itself that is dead." The young minister's death was a great political misfortune. His successor, Pontchartrain, failed to grasp the strategic and political importance of mastery of the seas, and he got along poorly with his principal co-worker, Bonrepaus, the intendant general. Two years after Seignelay's death, the French fleet was decimated by the Anglo-Dutch fleet. What would be called the "disaster of La Hougue" marked the beginning of England's hegemony in Europe.

In the course of that difficult conflict, three of Colbert's sons died in combat. Antoine-Martin Colbert, commandant de Boncourt, was killed at Valcourt in 1689. Charles-Edouard Colbert, comte de Sceaux, was mortally wounded in the battle of Fleurus in 1690. The unlucky d'Ormoy died courageously, both legs blown off, at the battle of Hochstett in 1704.

Louvois died in 1690, the same year as Seignelay. The Colbert family was still represented in government until the end of Louis's long reign. The Croissy branch continued in the department of foreign affairs.[11] When Le Pelletier took over the department of finances, the Le Tellier clan presumably rejoiced at his prosecution of Colbert's nephew Nicolas Desmarets, who had been involved—as we have seen—in a suspicious manipulation of the coinage. In 1684 Desmarets was removed from his post. In 1708 the comptroller general, Chamillart, retired, leaving the treasury empty and the kingdom ruined. Louis remembered the days of Colbert and called on Desmarets again. The new comptroller general brought the treasury back to solvency and managed to pay the armies until the treaties of Utrecht were signed.

Today virtually nothing is left of Colbert's principal properties. His widow died in 1687. The furnishings of his Parisian home were sold. In 1720 the Regent bought the property and installed his stables. Later his stables were destroyed. The site of the house was on the rue Colbert, near the Bibliothèque nationale and a few neighboring houses.

Seignelay transformed the château of Sceaux into a luxurious residence where he enjoyed giving magnificent receptions. Colbert's orangery was converted into a suite of rooms, with lacquered decor, for Mme de Seignelay. Mansart built a new orangery, a long building that could be used as a banquet hall in summer and a shelter for delicate plants in the winter. In 1685 the edifice was solemnly inaugurated by a visit from Louis XIV and Mme de Maintenon. Seignelay entertained the king with a pageant, *The Idyll of Peace:* Racine wrote the text, and Lully composed the music. The king and his court then went to the garden, where they found tables already prepared for dinner around a pond.

---

[11]The marquis de Croissy was minister in 1689. His son, the marquis de Torcy, succeeded him in 1696.

In 1699 the property was sold to the duc du Maine, legitimized son of Louis XIV and Mme de Montespan. Each time he traveled to Fontainebleau or returned from there, the king stopped at Sceaux to see his favorite son. After having passed through the hands of the comte d'Eu and the duc de Penthièvre, the château was declared the property of the nation under the Revolution; it was sold in 1798 and demolished by its purchasers. We may still see the handsome groups of animals, sculpted by Coysevox, at the entrance gate; the delightful Pavillion of Aurora that Le Brun decorated and in which Colbert received the Académie française; Seignelay's orangery, restored after having been damaged in the last war; and a few elements of the former gardens, including the magnificent "grand cascades."

The château of Seignelay, in Burgundy, was sacked and burned in 1793.

In 1728 the marquis de Seignelay, Colbert's grandson, sold (in a public sale) the printed books from the minister's famous library. The catalogue listed 18,219 items and filled three small volumes itself. The famous Mainz Bible of 1462, printed on vellum, was sold for 3,005 livres. The representatives of the royal library expressed fears that the manuscripts would be scattered. After lengthy and difficult negotiations, Louis XIV agreed to buy the entire collection for 300,000 livres.[12] The king's agents soon realized that Seignelay had retained certain volumes, which he was selling secretly to individuals. They were seized in the home of Colbert's grandson. There was considerable scandal.

Finally, we may note that what was thought to be Colbert's birthplace, at no. 13 rue Cérès in Rheims, was destroyed by German artillery fire in the First World War.

THE AGE OF COLBERT

Colbert's death had come as a relief to many Frenchmen. Louis may have had some feelings of sorrow, but he also found himself delivered from the frequent recriminations of a minister grown more and more bitter. The peasantry, overwhelmed with taxes, cursed the comptroller general, although he had been the last to allow that misery was inevitable.

Merchants, manufacturers—not all, but a great many—complained of the minister's insistence on rigorous administrative supervision. Most shipbuilders and those involved in sea trade were exasperated by the enforced subscriptions that had financed the great trading companies. The privileged classes could only detest his unconditional commitment to justice.

Then the criticism slowly gave way to nearly unmixed praise, especially in the Revolutionary period and thereafter. The writings of the historian Ernest

[12]That exceptional collection is still found in the Bibliothèque nationale.

Lavisse, especially his famous passage on "Colbert's offer," set him on a pedestal where he remained for a long time. This unremitting praise eventually grew irritating and led to new criticisms, still in vogue, and every bit as exaggerated as the praise had been.

And what became of his vast life's work, of his strenuous effort? His maritime and colonial achievements were the result of his ambition alone. Did Seignelay's death and the catastrophe of La Hougue mark the definite decline of all naval policies? In his *Instructions* to the young dauphin, Fénelon wrote: "Let the Dutch have their profit from their austere frugality and industry, from the risks of having few sailors aboard each ship, from the fine organization that allows them to unite for trade, from their abundance of freight-carrying vessels." On the back of the last page, the duc de Chevreuse added a few lines in which he contradicted his father-in-law's ambitious policies: "A medium-sized navy, not pushed to excess, in proportion to the needs of the state, which should not undertake to make war on the seas alone, against powers that concentrate all their forces there." France renounced the Atlantic for a long time, perhaps forever, despite Louis XIV's interest in the navy.[13] Yet the impetus given by Colbert was so strong, his naval policy so coherent, that it bore fruit despite the indifference of governments and the majority of the French. The improved harbors, the progress in naval training, and the uniformity of the maritime ordinance all represent unqualified successes. His system for protecting seamen continued in use throughout the eighteenth century, and was maintained under the Revolution and the Empire. In 1866 Thiers told the National Assembly, during a debate on Colbert's principles: "I will not hesitate to tell you, gentlemen, that if Colbert's statutes had not already been written, you would write them yourselves." Even today we can trace Colbert's influence on the way the French navy is organized.

Colbert's controlled approach to sea trade has been widely criticized. The failure of all the companies artificially created by the minister seemed to prove, in a very Manichaean perspective, the harm caused by government intrusion into economics. But Colbert was more pragmatic here than theoretical. Individualism, as it was conceived and practiced by French sea traders of his time, was absolutely no match for foreign competition. Yet the companies succeeded in increasing the volume of trade significantly, even after they were disbanded.

The war with Holland and the revocation of the Edict of Nantes destroyed the North Sea Company. But—as P. J. Charliat notes, for example—in the decade between 1679 and 1689, the French merchant flag appeared more than twenty times in Elsinore (Norway), a frequency never before recorded.[14] The links established with Nordic traders allowed the kingdom to be supplied, and furnished

[13]Jacques Godechot, *Histoire de l'Atlantique.*

[14]P. J. Charliat, *Les relations entre la France et la Norvège à la fin du XVIIᵉ siècle* (1927).

Louis with weapons for the last wars of his reign. The end of the West Indies Company did not lead to the commercial failure of such port cities as Bordeaux and Nantes. The two Atlantic cities experienced intense commercial activity with the Caribbean during the eighteenth century. The East India Company, based in Lorient, continued to prosper after Colbert's death; it was dissolved under Louis XV, once the Treaty of Paris had made official the abandonment of France's colonial pretensions to the profit of England. And yet during the eighteenth century, French colonial expansion had been considerable, especially in India. A glance at the map shows that the French possessions of the eighteenth and even the nineteenth centuries often grew from the seeds first sown by Colbert or by Richelieu before him.

The commercial and industrial policies Colbert had favored were violently criticized after his death and, simultaneously, were carried on in exaggerated forms. Protectionism was denounced by the partisans of free trade, in the name of a sort of international division of labor and in the name of economic cooperation among countries, patterned upon divine creation. In 1701 an economist wrote: "We must renounce M. Colbert's maxim according to which France could get along without the rest of the world. It was contrary to nature and to the decrees of divine Providence." France could not be sufficient unto herself. Another author of the eighteenth century added: "All nations have need of one another."

These free-trade credos implied the abandonment, pure and simple, of all commercial ambitions for France. As early as 1692, the economist Bélesbat addressed a report to Louis XIV explaining that Holland needed France, a rich and productive country that could feed the Dutch. France, by nature not very interested in business, could in exchange persuade the more commercially minded Dutch to assume the responsibility of exporting and importing in her stead.

Still it is worth mentioning that in practice no one dared apply liberal ideas to their fullest extent. Foreign competition caused fear. Regulation was accepted as dogma, was often even demanded. In the eighteenth century, there was still a strong belief that only perfection in manufacturing could reestablish the balance of trade. The department of industrial inspectors had fourteen inspectors in 1669, twenty-one in 1671, thirty-eight in 1715, and sixty-four by 1754. The regulations grew ever more precise. The increase in the number of inspectors, along with the proliferation of offices, led to nit-picking and an increase in the amount of administrative red tape.

It is commonly said in our time that Colbert's industrial creations did not survive their author and that eighteenth-century industry was born just as that of the seventeenth-century had been, with no links to what had come before. That statement seems inadequate. It is true that many businesses had to shut down late in Louis's reign, for lack of government support. Van Robais was given special treatment. The Dutch industrialist was only able to pay his workers thanks to two remissions of his taxes in 1705. The Protestant exodus and the excesses of post-Colbertian regulation contributed in large part to the industrial and commercial decline of the first decades after the minister's death.

After a period of stagnation, the tenacious policies of the minister finally showed results. Colbert, whatever one may think, had put French industry on the map. Well-to-do families were beginning to buy cloth from Elbeuf or Rouen rather than from the Netherlands. In Languedoc, the factories Colbert had set up artificially to export cloth to the East were barely able after the minister's death to send off 700 or 800 bolts of fine cloth per year. But their production procedures continued to be perfected, while the Dutch were beginning to dilute their dyes. Levantine buyers returned to French trade: In 1698 the Languedoc manufacturers exported 3,200 bolts of fine cloth, not counting ordinary material.[15] This success increases the validity of the dogma of Colbertism. The factories that produced mirrors, furniture, or rugs, the forges, the paper mills, the woolen mills, and the silk mills owed a great deal to the energy of a man who, according to the German economist List, "had the courage to undertake, entirely alone, a piece of work that England did not complete without three centuries of effort and three revolutions."

Indeed, Colbert cannot be judged without taking into account his isolation in his attempt to apply the "grand design." What was involved was not just specific policies, whether good or bad, but a concept of government. Without any doubt, the man wanted economic greatness for France, despite many of the French, who were little inclined to the sea and little attracted by industry or commerce. His policy of full employment was also a struggle against poverty: That is very often forgotten.

Colbert forced the French to make a sustained effort without precedent in their history, in an area where other nations were proving more ambitious and more enterprising. Was government intervention a brake or a spur? An economic policy based on government subsidies—even if they are provisional—is dangerous, because too much depends on the state of the government's own finances, as the crisis that followed Colbert's death proved. Frequent rescues by a protective state kill the spirit of enterprise. But here as elsewhere Colbert was more of a pragmatist than a theoretician. The state's presence made up for the startling lack of any coordination among private enterprises, such as those in England or in the United Provinces—and even in England, the will of the government also played a determining role. We may find it regrettable, but in France, great industrial progress has often, if not always, resulted from a political desire by the government or the

[15]Prosper Boissonnade, "Colbert, son système, et les enterprises industrielles d'état en Languedoc (1661–1683)."

state. The state's withdrawal from industry strongly risks leading to the end of industry pure and simple.

The protectionism by degrees and by stages that Colbert arranged derived its justification from the historical context. Closing the customs boundaries forced the French to fill their needs locally, hence they had to build factories and increase production. An economic war declared by a country that kept salaries low could encourage the protection of national production and encourage full employment as well. But his preoccupation with the very real problem of scarce currency led Colbert to practice an export policy whose aggressiveness hurt France's economy and foreign relations in the long run. That goods of high quality were required for the export trade is not to be doubted; but Colbert understood regulation as terrorism, and that was probably his greatest economic mistake. Finally, his inflexible mercantilism contributed greatly to bringing on the war with Holland, a disastrous war if there ever was one.

Colbert was not, strictly speaking, an innovator. His economic theories were those of his times. His concept of finance alone seemed new in his day. His analysis was lucid. Yet he could not avoid the same failures that, after him, a Law or a Turgot would undergo. How could new financial habits be imposed within a system where taxation was based on inequality, the budget depended on the king's pleasure, and the immaturity of the banking system hindered borrowing?[16]

Colbert's devotion to the common good was undeniable: His nepotism and personal cupidity should not obscure his rigorous professional sense and his lofty concept of the state. But here again, his policies were considerably limited by his own contradictions, which were those of the age as well. Colbert's ambitions for France as a nation were indistinguishable from his passion for the state and his devotion to the king. Yet the relationship between king and state was confused. The monarch was the nation's sovereign, but he was also the head and protector of a feudal hierarchy that the state wanted to supplant. Such a man as Vauban let himself be misled. But in 1707, the king had the "Plan for a Royal Tithe" seized, a plan in which Vauban advocated a graduated tax on the income of all subjects. The old marshal died shortly thereafter, overcome with sorrow. The concept of the state as dispenser of justice, which he had seen grow stronger, should lead, according to him, to a new social order with the unprecedented notion of the pursuit of happiness as one of its elements.

Colbert, more clever or a better politician, strengthened the judicial and unifying roles of the state without violating Louis XIV's natural caution. The frequent reproaches that Colbert helped to strengthen the tyranny of the state

---

[16]The Bank of London was founded in 1694, in imitation of the Bank of Amsterdam. Paris was not able to consider such an establishment.

border on anachronism. The relationship between the state and the nation in contemporary France are not to be likened to those between the state and the nation under Louis XIV. The idea of a *patrie,* a fatherland, was still vague. National unity in politics and economics barely existed. The king alone represented the unity of the realm. His profound weakness and the nature of his contracts with the French people kept him from breaking down barriers. And when Colbert tried to bring about centralization—on a much smaller scale than in France today—it was Louis himself who, from caution or from mistrust of the state, intervened more than once.

The French nation is not a mere accident of history; it is also the creation of the unifying action of the state. In Louis XIV's time, only a powerful state had the means to guarantee efficiency and longevity to any ambitious and coherent policy, especially in the judicial arena. The great weight of privilege and habit was constantly opposed to any real application of basic reforms. Despite the power he wielded, and despite his strength of will, Colbert had to give up his attempt to draw up surveys that would have allowed a fairer distribution of the tax burden. But it would be wrong to say nothing is left of his work in this area. The civil ordinance of 1667 served as a model for the civil procedure in the Napoleonic Code, and the codification of Parisian customary law, encouraged by Colbert and, in his turn, Le Tellier, was the essential source of the Napoleonic Code itself.

The cultural policy of Louis's minister was prestigious. His most worthy act, perhaps, was to make Paris a scientific capital. It is a shame it did not remain one.

His will and his ambitions for France were such that they left their mark on France for a long time, in some cases down to the present day. In the world of politics or history, character and clear-sightedness matter more than elsewhere. Colbert lacked neither. And his intense perseverance was also a form of hope.

BIBLIOGRAPHY

INDEX

BIBLIOGRAPHY

MANUSCRIPT SOURCES

Archives of the Luynes family (Colbert: boxes 1–4).

GENERAL WORKS
ON THE SEVENTEENTH CENTURY

Ashley, Maurice. *Le Grand Siècle*. Paris: Fayard, 1972.

Champollion-Figeac, Jacques Joseph. *Documents historiques inédits*. Paris, 1841–48.

———. *Œuvres de Louis XIV: Mémoires*. Paris, 1860.

Choisy, François Timoléon, abbé de. *Mémoires pour servir à l'histoire de Louis XIV*. Paris, 1888.

Erlanger, Philippe. *Louis XIV au jour le jour*. Paris, 1968.

Gaillardin, Casimir. *Histoire du règne de Louis XIV*. 6 vols. Paris, 1871–76.

Gaxotte, Pierre. *Louis XIV*. Paris, 1974.

Goubert, Pierre. *Louis XIV et vingt millions de Français*. Paris: Fayard, 1966.

———. *Cent mille provinciaux au XVIIe siècle*. Paris, 1968.

Mandrou, Robert. *Louis XIV en son temps*. In the *Peuples et civilisations* series. Paris: Presses Universitaires de France, 1973.

Normand, Charles. *La bourgeoisie au XVIIe siècle*. Paris, 1908.

BIBLIOGRAPHY

Plattard, Jean. *Un Ètudiant écossais en France en 1665–1666: Journal de voyage de Sir John Lauder*. Paris, 1935.

Saint-Maurice, marquis de. *Lettres sur la cour de Louis XIV, 1667–70*. Paris: 1910.

Seignobos, Charles. *Essai d'une histoire comparée des peuples de l'Europe*. In the *Peuples et civilisations* series. Paris: Presses Universitaires de France, 1947.

Sévigné, Marie de Rabutin-Chantal, marquise de. *Correspondance*. Edited by Roger Duchêne. Paris: Bibliothèque de la Pléiade, 1978.

For documentation more specifically concerning government and administration in the seventeenth century, I have consulted these works in particular:

Chéruel, Pierre Adolphe. *De l'administration de Louis XIV, 1661–1672, d'après les Mémoires inédits d'Olivier d'Ormesson*. Paris, 1850.

Depping, G. C. *Correspondance administrative sous le règne de Louis XIV*. Paris, 1850–55.

Esmonin, Edmond. *Etudes sur la France des XVIIe et XVIIIe siècles*. Paris, 1964.

O'Reilly, E. M. J. J. *Mémoires sur la vie privée et publique de Claude Pellot*. Paris, 1882.

Pellot, Claude. *Notes du premier président Pellot sur la Normandie*. Paris, 1915.

I have also used these titles from Hachette's *La vie quotidienne* series:

Bercé, Yves-Marie. *La vie quotidienne dans l'Aquitaine du XVIIe siècle*. Paris, 1978.

Mongrédien, Georges. *La Vie quotidienne sous Louis XIV*. Paris, 1948.

Wilhelm, Jacques. *La Vie quotidienne des Parisiens au temps du Roi-Soleil, 1660–1715*. Paris, 1977.

Among the works published by Hachette, *La France au temps du Louis XIV* (1966), of multiple authorship, and especially the parts contributed by Jean Meuvret, should be mentioned.

GENERAL WORKS ON COLBERT

The basic source is still the work of Pierre Clément. His first publication was the *Histoire de la vie et de l'administration de Colbert, contrôleur général des finances . . . précédée d'une étude historique sur Nicolas Fouquet* (Paris, 1846).[1] Between 1861 and 1882, the seven volumes of Clément's best-known work appeared, under the general title of *Lettres, instructions, et mémoires de Colbert*. Each volume includes an introduction.

[1]It seems useful to point out to historians an error by Clément on p. 91 of the 1846 edition. Clément cites a fragment of a letter from Colbert to Mazarin, dated June 16, 1657, in which Colbert seems favorably inclined toward Fouquet: "The attorney general, having always served Your Eminence well," Colbert appears to be arguing. The hand-written draft of the entire letter (preserved in the family archives) shows, however, that "the said attorney general" is not Fouquet but Regnaudin, attorney general of the Grand Council.

Vol. I: *1650–1661.*

Vol. II (in two parts): *Finances, impôts, monnaies—Industrie, commerce.*

Vol. III (in two parts): *Marine et galères—Instructions au Marquis de Seignelay—*
        Colonies.

Vol. IV: *Administration provinciale—Agriculture, forêts, haras—Canal du*
        Languedoc, routes, canaux et mines.

Vol. V: *Fortifications—Sciences—Lettres—Beaux-arts, bâtiments.*

Vol. VI: *Justice et Police—Affaires religieuses—Affaires diverses.*

Vol. VII: *Lettres privées.*

An eighth volume, *Errata général et tableau analytique,* was done by Pierre de Brotonne and Jean de Boislisle.

Since Clément, there have been few (or perhaps no) studies of Colbert of the same scope. We might mention:

Dussieux, Louis-Etienne. *Etude biographique sur Colbert.* Paris, 1886.

Farrère, Claude. *Jean-Baptiste Colbert.* Paris, 1954.

Mongrédien, Georges. *Colbert, 1619–1683.* Paris, 1963.

Neymarck, Alfred. *Colbert et son temps.* Paris, 1877.

Where the minister's administrative methods are of particular concern, these works may be of interest:

Boissonnade, Prosper. *Colbert: Le triomphe de l'étatisme, la fondation de la suprématie industrielle en France, la dictature du travail.* Paris, 1932.

Clément, Pierre. *La Provence et Colbert, d'après les documents inédits.* Toulon, 1862.

Colbert de Croissy, Charles. "Rapport au roi et mémoire sur le clergé, la noblesse, la justice et les finances du Poitou, 1665." *Revue historique de la noblesse* 2 (1865).

And for anecdotal history:

Des Gachons, Jacques. *Gens de France au labeur.* Paris, 1929.

Héron de Villefosse, René. "Jean-Baptiste Colbert, Rémois au gouvernail de la France du Grand Siècle." In *La Champagne économique.* Reims, 1956.

Villetard, Abbé Henri. *Colbertina—le tricentenaire de Colbert à Seignelay.* Paris, 1921.

A SUMMARY BIBLIOGRAPHY ON
ECONOMIC HISTORY

I would like to thank Professor Jean Domarchi, who very kindly helped me with the bibliography and with the understanding of certain technical aspects of economics in Colbert's time.

Bacquié, Franc. "Un siècle de l'histoire de l'industrie: Les inspecteurs des manufactures sous l'Ancien Régime." In *Mémoires et documents pour servir à l'histoire du commerce et de l'industrie,* 11th ser. 1927.

BIBLIOGRAPHY

Bloch, Marc. *Esquisse d'une histoire monétaire de l'Europe.* Paris: Cahiers des Annales, 1954.

———. *Aspects économiques du règne de Louis XIV.* Paris: Cours de Sorbonne, Centre de Documentation Universitaire, 1939.

Boissonnade, Prosper. "Colbert, son système, et les entreprises industrielles d'état en Languedoc (1661–1683)." *Annales du Midi,* 1902.

———. "La production et le commerce des céréales, des vins et des eaux-de-vie en Languedoc dans la seconde moitié du XVIIe siècle." *Annales du Midi,* 1905.

———. "La restauration et le développement de l'industrie en Languedoc au temps de Colbert." *Annales du Midi,* 1906.

Bondois, Paul. *Colbert et l'industrie de la dentelle.* Poitiers, 1926.

Bouvier, Jean, and Henri Germain-Martin. *Finances et financiers de l'ancien régime.* Paris: Presses Universitaires de France, 1969.

Braudel, Fernand. *Civilisation matérielle et capitalisme, XVe–XVIIIe siècle.* Paris, 1967.

Cole, Charles. *Colbert and a Century of French Mercantilism.* 2 vols. New York, 1939.

Dienne, Comte Edouard de. *Histoire du dessèchement des lacs et marais en France avant 1789.* Paris, 1891.

Gueneau, L. *L'organisation du travail (industrie et commerce) à Nevers, XVIIe et XVIIIe siècles.* Paris, 1919.

Hauser, Henri. *Les origines historiques des problèmes économiques actuels.* Paris, 1930.

———. *Les débuts du capitalisme.* Paris, 1927.

———. *La Prépondérance espagnole, 1539–1660.* Paris, 1940.

———. *La pensée et l'action économique du Cardinal de Richelieu.* Paris, 1944.

Heckscher, Eli. *Mercantilism.* London, 1955.

Huvelin, Paul-Louis. *Essai historique sur les droits des marchés et des foires.* Paris, 1897.

Luthy, Herbert. *La banque protestante en France, de la révocation de l'Edit de Nantes à la Révolution.* Paris, 1959.

Meuvret, Jean. *Etudes d'histoire économique.* Paris, 1971.

Renaudet, H. *Etudes sur la France du temps de Louis XIV.* Paris: Cours de Sorbonne, Centre de Documentation Universitaire, 1940.

Toubeau, Jean. *Mémoire adressé par ordre de Messieurs les maires et échevins de la ville de Bourges pour le rétablissement des foires dans leur ville.* 1681.

On the history of the Netherlands in the seventeenth century:

Braure, Maurice. *Histoire des Pays-Bas.* Paris: Presses Universitaires de France, collection "Que sais-je?" 1951.

Pomponne, Simon Arnauld, marquis de. *Relation de mon ambassade en Hollande.* Edited by Herbert H. Rowen. Utrecht, 1955.

Wilson, Charles. *La République hollandaise des Provinces-Unies.* Paris, 1968.

Bibliography

Zumthor, Paul. *La vie quotidienne en Hollande au temps de Rembrandt*. Paris: Hachette, 1960.

Concerning naval affairs, including commercial shipping and colonization:

Asher, Eugene L. *The Resistance to the Maritime Classes: The Survival of Feudalism in the France of Colbert*. Berkeley, 1960.

Boissonnade, Prosper. *Colbert et la souscription aux actions de la Compagnie des Indes, spécialement au Poitou (1664–1668)*. Poitiers, 1908.

———. *Histoire des premiers essais de relations directes entre la France et l'Etat prussien pendant le règne de Louis XIV*. Paris, 1912.

———. *La marine marchande, le port, et les armateurs de La Rochelle à l'époque de Colbert (1662–1683)*. Paris, 1923.

———., and P. Charliat. *Colbert et la Compagnie de commerce du Nord*. Paris, 1930.

Bondois, Paul. "Colbert et la question du sucre: La rivalité franco-hollandaise." *Revue d'histoire économique et sociale*, 1923.

Cangardel, Henri. *De J.-B. Colbert au paquebot "Normandie": Etudes et souvenirs maritimes*. Paris, 1957.

Carré, Henri. *Duquesne et la marine royale de Richelieu à Colbert*. Paris, 1950.

Cordier, L. *Les compagnies à charte et la politique coloniale sous le ministère de Colbert*. Paris, 1906; reprint ed. Geneva, 1976.

Crisenoy, de. *Les Ordonnances de Colbert et l'inscription maritime*. Paris, 1862.

———. *Le personnel de la marine militaire et les classes maritimes sous Colbert et Seignelay*. Paris, 1864.

Dainville, de. "Les relations commerciales de Bordeaux avec les villes Hanséatiques au XVIIe et au XVIIIe siècle." In *Mémoires et documents pour servir à l'histoire du commerce et du industrie*, 4th ser. 1916.

Ducasse, Baron Robert. *L'Amiral Ducasse, chevalier de la Toison d'or (1646–1715): Etude sur la France maritime et coloniale (règne de Louis XIV)*. Paris, 1876.

Godechot, Jacques, *Histoire de l'Atlantique*. Paris, 1947.

Higounet, Charles, comp. *Histoire de Bordeaux*. Bordeaux, 1966.

Howe, Sonia. *Les grand navigateurs à la recherche des épices*. Paris, 1939.

Jal, Auguste. *Abraham Duquesne et la marine de son temps*. Paris, 1873.

La Roncière, Charles de. *Histoire de la marine française*. Vols. 4, 5. Paris, 1899–1920.

———. *Cavelier de la Salle: Explorateur de la Nouvelle-France, père de la Louisiane*. Tours, 1943.

Lévy-Bruhl, Henri. "La noblesse de France et le commerce." *Revue d'histoire moderne*, May–July 1933.

Masson, Pierre. *Les Ports francs d'autrefois et d'aujourd'hui*. Paris, 1904.

Pauliat, Louis. *Madagascar sous Louis XIV: Louis XIV et la Compagnie des Indes orientales de 1664*. Paris, 1886.

Varillon, Pierre. *Coureurs de mer sous les étoiles*. Paris, 1961.

BIBLIOGRAPHY

COLBERT'S FAMILY AND CHILDHOOD

Bourgeon, Jean-Louis. *Les Colbert avant Colbert: Destin d'une famille marchande.* Paris: Presses Universitaires de France, 1963.

MAZARIN'S AGENT

Cosnac, Comte Gabriel-Jules de. *Mazarin et Colbert.* Paris, 1892.

THE FOUQUET AFFAIR

Bertin, Claude, ed. *Les grands commis, Jacques Coeur, Fouquet.* Vol. 14 of *Les grands procès de l'histoire de France.* Paris, 1968.

Boislisle, Jean de. *Mémoriaux du Conseil de 1661.* Paris, 1907.

Bordonove, Georges. *Foucquet, coupable ou victime?* Paris, 1975.

Chergé, Charles de. "François de Neuchèze, vice-amiral, intendant général de la marine de France, sa correspondance avec Louis XIV, Colbert, etc." In *Mémoires de la Société des Antiquiaires de l'Ouest.* Poitiers, 1854.

Chéruel, Pierre Adolphe. *Mémoires sur la vie publique et privée de Fouquet.* Paris, 1862.

Depping, G. *Barthélemy Herwarth, contrôleur général des finances (1607–1676).* Paris, 1879.

Lair, Jules-Auguste. *Nicolas Foucquet: procureur général, surintendant des finances, ministre d'état de Louis XIV.* Paris, 1890.

La Roncière, Charles de. *Le vrai crime du Surintendant Fouquet.* Paris: Fifty-second Congress of the Society of Scholars of the Sorbonne, 1924.

Mongrédien, Georges. *L'affaire Fouquet.* Paris, 1956.

Morand, Paul. *Fouquet, ou le soleil offusqué.* Paris, 1973.

CULTURAL POLICIES

Alazard, Jean. *L'Abbé Luigi Strozzi, correspondant artistique de Mazarin, de Colbert, de Louvois, et de La Teulière.* Paris, 1924.

Soriano, Marc. *Le Dossier Perrault.* Paris, 1972.

The remarkable catalogue of the exhibit entitled "Collections de Louis XIV, Orangerie des Tuileries," held in 1977, should be mentioned.

THE AFFAIRE DES POISONS

Clément, Pierre. *La police sous Louis XIV.* Paris, 1866.

———. *Madame de Montespan et Louis XIV.* Paris, 1868.

Funck-Brentano, Frantz. *Le drame des poisons.* Paris, 1928.

Lemoine, J. *L'enigme Montespan.* Blois, 1935.

Mongrédien, Georges. *Mme de Montespan et l'affaire des poisons.* Paris, 1953.

AFTER COLBERT

Clément, Pierre. *Le gouvernement de Louis XIV, ou la cour, l'administration, les finances de 1683 à 1689.* Paris, 1848.

Bibliography

Schatz, P. A., and R. Caillemer. *Le mercantilisme libéral à la fin du XVIIe siècle: Les idées politiques et économiques de M. de Bélesbat.* Paris, 1906.

Serruys, Jean. *De Colbert au Marché commun.* Paris, 1970.

Other important figures are treated in:

Eriau, Chanoine Jean-Baptiste. *La Madeleine française: Louise de la Vallière, dans sa famille, à la cour, au Carmel.* Paris, 1961.

Parent, Michel. *Vauban.* Paris, 1971.

Rebelliau, Alfred. *Vauban.* Paris, 1962.

I have also made use of the bulletins of *Lettres autographes et documents historiques* published by the house of Charavay, and the catalogues of autographs and historical documents sold under the auspices of Maître Dominique Vincent in Paris and of Maîtres J.P. Chapelle, P. Perrin, and D. Fromantin in Versailles.

Index

Académie française, 123–24, 227, 244
Academy of Music, 125
Academy of Sciences, 126, 128, 180, 247–48
Affaire des poisons, 252–66
Aides, 25, 38, 54, 94
Alexander VII, Pope (r. 1655–67), 41, 59
Ancien régime, 3, 91, 93–94, 231
Anne of Austria (queen regent of France, 1643–61), 11, 13, 15, 26, 39, 47, 50; and Mazarin, 41–42; and the Fronde, 52; diminishing influence of, 57; and the fall of Fouquet, 60, 62–63, 65, 69; death of, 83–84, 269
Arsenal Commission, 255–56
Artagnan, Charles de Batz-Castelmore d', 66, 68, 98, 101
Ashley, Maurice, 128
Assérac, marquise d', 46–47, 49, 54

Baluze, Etienne, 224–25
Barbary pirates, 173, 177, 240
Beaufort, François de Vendôme, duc de, 175, 177
Beauvilliers, duc de. *See* Saint-Aignan
Beauvilliers, duchesse de. *See* Saint-Aignan
Bernini, Giovanni Lorenzo, 109–10, 125
Bibliothèque Mazarine, 23
Black Masses, 255; and Mme de Montespan, 259–60, 262
Blois, Mlle de (daughter of Louis XIV and Louise de La Vallière), 84, 216, 220, 229
Boileau, Nicolas, 110, 116, 227
Bosse, Marie, involved in *Affaire des poisons,* 255–56

Bouillon, duchesse de. *See* Mancini, Marie
Boulle, André Charles, 120
Boullongne, Geneviève de, 125
Boullongne, Madeleine de, 125
Brandenburg, Elector of, 202, 204
Braudel, Fernand, 162, 171
Brienne, comte de, 57, 65, 68
Brinvilliers, Marie Madeleine, marquise de, 254–55
Brissac, duc de, 49
Broussel, Pierre, 11
Bussy, Roger de Rabutin, comte de, 257; letters from Mme de Sévigné, 205, 222

Cabinet du Roi, 119
Caisse des emprunts, 232–33, 235, 270
Calvin, John, 224
Calvinism, 139, 141
Canada, 55, 171, 183, 190–93, 239–40
Capitalism, 3; in United Provinces, 145
Cartier, Jacques, 183
Catholicism: in Holland, 141, 144–45; and Louis XIV, 76, 248; in French colonies, 186
Chapelain, Jean, 6, 114–16
Charlemagne, 95
Charles I (king of England, r. 1625–49), 135–36
Charles II (king of England, r. 1660–85), 58, 136, 146, 203; joins France against Dutch, 201; receives subsidies from Louis XIV, 202, 210; makes peace with Holland, 209; opposition at home, 216; death of, 273
Charles V (Holy Roman Emperor, r. 1519–56), 5, 58, 146

Chaulnes, duc de, 87, 214

Chevreuse, Charles Honoré d'Albert, duc de, 87–88, 122–23, 210, 222, 272, 276

Chevreuse, Marie-Thérèse, duchesse de (Colbert's daughter), 87–88, 213, 221, 272

Chevreuse, Marie de Rohan-Montbazon, duchesse de, 13, 43, 62, 85, 87, 210

Choisy, Abbé de, 62, 65, 271

Christina (queen of Sweden, r. 1632–54), 42

Church of France, the, 248

Clerville, chevalier de, 175–76, 199

Code Louis, 104

Code Michaud (1629), 132

Colbert, Antoine Martin (son of Jean-Baptiste), 223, 274

Colbert, Charles. See Croissy

Colbert, Edouard-François, comte de Maulévrier (brother of Jean-Baptiste), 17, 221

Colbert, Gérard I, 2

Colbert, Gérard II, 5

Colbert, Gérard III, 3

Colbert, Henriette. See Saint-Aignan

Colbert, Jacques-Nicolas (son of Jean-Baptiste), 223

Colbert, Jean-Baptiste: ancestry in Rheims, 1–3; birth and early childhood, 5; financial training, 6; and the tax farmers, 7, 67, 79, 100, 102, 119, 137, 241–42; first government post, 8; influence of Richelieu on, 8, 12–13, 21, 39, 77–78, 171; joins Le Tellier's staff, 9; marriage, 9; and the Fronde, 11; clash with Mazarin, 12; first meeting with Fouquet, 13; as Mazarin's agent, 15, 21–34, 40–44, 50, 52; devotion to those he served, 15, 74; service to Mazarin in exile, 16–19; rivalry with Fouquet, 18–19, 33, 39–40, 43–45, 51–53, 59; nepotism, 19, 88, 279; cultural policies and the arts, 28, 112–15, 121, 128, 243; increase of personal fortune under Mazarin, 30–33; personal library, 32, 224–25, 275; financial policies, 39, 51, 77, 128, 145, 231–33, 236; and Louvois, 48, 79, 81, 180, 222, 237, 270; and taxation, 50, 94–95, 231–32, 241–42; judicial policies, 51, 91–92, 96, 103–5, 242, 279; and the unification of weights and measures, 52; protectionist policies, 58, 146–47, 149, 279; plots the fall of Fouquet, 59–71, 90; and the Royal Council of Finance, 70, 78; rise to power under Louis XIV, 73–78; relationship with the king, 74, 80–82, 89; political convictions, 75; and the pursuit of national unity, 75, 92; and the king's expenditures, 76, 234–35, 267; as secretary of state for the king's household, 78; as superintendant of buildings, 78, 107–8, 113, 198; as secretary of the navy, 78, 198, 267; patriotism, 80; and Mme de Montespan, 85, 198–99, 202, 212, 257, 262–65; as royal treasurer, 102; acquisitions for the royal collections, 117–18, 120, 244; and the Académie française, 123; and science, 125–28; and mercantilism, 130, 135, 143, 147, 156, 236, 239, 279; industrial and commercial policies, 152, 164–69, 194, 242, 277–78; and transportation, 157–59; maritime policies, 172–73, 176, 181, 237, 242, 276; and Protestants, 173; colonial policies, 183, 189–93, 238–40, 277; and trading companies, 185–86; as comptroller of finances, 199; growing friction with Louis XIV, 212, 235, 244; personal fortune, 219, 225; illness, 219, 267–68; last years, 220, 267; at Sceaux, 226–29; and the slave trade, 238, 242; and the Napoleonic Code, 242, 280; waning influence, 250; and the *Affaire des poisons*, 255–66; death of, 270

Index

Colbert, Jean-Baptiste, marquis de Seignelay. *See* Seignelay

Colbert, Jehan V (grandfather of Jean-Baptiste), 3–4

Colbert, Jehan VI, 4, 5

Colbert, Jules-Armand, marquis d'Ormoy and de Blainville (son of Jean-Baptiste), 223, 245–46, 267, 271, 274

Colbert, Louis (son of Jean-Baptiste), 223

Colbert, Marie (Mrs. Jean-Baptiste), 9, 44, 87; raises Louis XIV's children by Louise de La Vallière, 84, 220; friend to Mme de Montespan, 213, 228, 271

Colbert, Marie-Anne. *See* Mortemart

Colbert, Marie Bachelier (grandmother of Jean-Baptiste), 4

Colbert, Marie-Thérèse. *See* Chevreuse

Colbert, Nicolas (father of Jean-Baptiste), 4–8, 30, 39, 71

Colbert, Abbé Nicolas, bishop of Auxerre and bishop of Luçon (brother of Jean-Baptiste), 17, 31, 88, 117, 183, 221

Colbert, Oudard I, 2–3

Colbert, Oudard II, 3–7

Colbert de Saint-Pouange, 4, 6, 7, 8, 9

Colbert de Villacerf, 4, 6

Colbert du Terron (cousin of Jean-Baptiste), 31; and the fall of Fouquet, 61–64, 71; and naval affairs, 89, 175–76; and Seignelay, 181; and the North Sea Company, 195

Collège des Quatre-Nations, 23, 118

Company of the Levant, 188, 240

Company of Senegal, 238

Condé, Louis II de Bourbon, prince de ("the Great Condé"), 59; and the Fronde, 11, 15; allied with Spain, 30, 40, 43, 48; reconciled with Louis XIV, 54; and the arrest of Fouquet, 68; in war with Holland, 200–201, 205, 213; and Louvois, 210

Conservatory of Machines, Arts, and Trades, 127

Conti, Armand de Bourbon, prince de, 15, 48

Conti, prince de (son), 220–21, 229, 247

Coquebert, Marie, 2

Corneille, Pierre, 116, 247

Council of State, revival of, 30, 95

Council of Trade, 164, 184

Coysevox, Antoine, 120, 227, 275

Creoles, 189

Crequi, marquis de, 61, 63, 71

Croissy, Charles Colbert, marquis de (brother of Jean-Baptiste), 31, 32, 59, 88, 96, 155; ambassador to England, 181, 219; negotiates marriage of dauphin, 221; and *Affaire des poisons,* 254; after the death of Colbert, 271, 274

Cromwell, Oliver, Lord Protector of England (1653–58), 48, 136, 146, 149

Damville, duc de, 23

Dati, Carlo, 116

Dauphin. *See* Louis de France, the Grand Dauphin

Declaration of the Four Articles, 248

Defoe, Daniel, 137

Delorme, Marion, 44

Descartes, René, 126

Deslandes, governor of Concarneau, 47, 49, 54

Desmarets, Nicolas, 221, 233, 270, 274

d'Estrées, Gabrielle, 172

d'Estrées, Jean, 177, 201, 205, 214, 238

De Witt, Cornelius, 202

De Witt, Jan, 140–41, 148, 186, 193–95; and the war with France, 200, 202

Diderot, Denis, 128

d'Orbay, François, 110, 111

d'Ormesson, Oliver, 88, 98, 100–101, 242

Duplessis, Claude, 262, 264–65

Duquesne, Marquis Abraham, 63, 71, 175, 177–78, 193, 214–15; and the Barbary pirates, 240; refuses to renounce Protestantism, 249,

Index

Duquesne, Marquis Abraham (*cont.*) 251
Duquesne, Henri, 273
Dutch India Company, 207

East Indies Company (French), 185, 240, 276–77
Edict of Nantes, 76, 249; revoked by Le Tellier, 272–73; effect of revocation, 276
Elizabeth I (queen of England, r. 1558–1603), 77, 135, 154
Enghien, duc d', 59
England, mercantilism in, 135–36; and the Dutch, 146–47; naval assistance to France, 201; peace with Holland, 209
Estates General, 52–53, 68

Febvre, Lucien, 35
Feudalism, 31, 37–39, 75, 76, 91, 161, 279
Fontanges, Marie Adélaide de Scorailles de Roussilhe, duchesse de (mistress of Louis XIV), 258–59, 265
Foscarini, Sebastien, 267
Foucault, Nicolas, 98, 101
Fouquet, Basile, 18, 40, 49
Fouquet, Nicolas, 7, 18–19, 35; first meeting with Colbert, 13; and the Fronde, 14, 40, 52, 99; named attorney general, 15; becomes superintendant, 19, 39; rivalry with Colbert, 33, 39–40, 43–45, 51–53, 59; builds Vaux-le-Vicomte, 35; marriage to Maria-Magdalena of Castille (1651), 35; at zenith of his power, 35–36, 43; financial practices, 38, 51, 60, 99; personal qualities, 38–39; his *Defenses*, 39, 44, 99; relations with Mazarin worsen, 44–47; and the plan of Saint-Mandé, 46–49, 52–55, 61–64, 71, 99; sole superintendant of finances, 50; intercepts Colbert's correspondence, 50–51; appointed to the High Council, 57; and foreign affairs, 57–59; the fall of, 59–71; the fete at Vaux-le-

Vicomte, 64; arrest of, 66–71; imprisonment, 98; trial, 99; sentenced, 101; death of, 101; personal art collections, 114, 117–18; personal trade with the colonies, 183
France: during the Fronde, 11–19; war with Austria, 23; war with Spain, 24, 38, 48, 146; remnants of feudalism in seventeenth century, 31; system of public finance, 35–36; assistance to Portugal, 58; alliance with United Provinces, 58; protection of commercial interests, 58; and mercantilism, 129–35; economic war with United Provinces, 129–35, 143, 149–50, 279; enters Anglo-Dutch war, 148, 150; agriculture, 153–56; poor transportation, 156–59; economic conditions, 162–64; backwardness in maritime matters, 171; North American colonies of, 189–93, 239–40; banking system, 194; war with Holland, 198–201; shaky alliance with England, 201–2; retreat from Holland, 205; and the Treaty of Nijmegen, 217–18; stagnation of domestic trade, 236; isolation in Europe, 273; industrial progress, 278–79
Franche-Comté, 26, 212, 217
Francis I (king of France, r. 1515–47), 35, 77, 94, 183
French Revolution, 39, 242, 275, 276
Fronde, the, 9, 11–19, 40, 42, 52, 62; and Mazarin, 22–23, 37; and Fouquet, 36, 46–47, 99; effect on Louis XIV, 73, 76; and the intendants, 95; lingering memory of, 210, 232

Gabelle, 54, 94
Galilei, Galileo, 126–27
Girardin, Claude, 225
Gobelin tapestry works, 109, 113, 120, 133, 164, 170, 225, 244
Goubert, Pierre, 37, 143
Gourville (ally of Fouquet), 47, 51, 52, 54

Index

Grand Jours, 50, 101–2

La Grande Mademoiselle (Anne Marie Louise d'Orlean, duchesse de Montpensier), 86, 222, 234, 265

Grotius, Hugo, 196

Guibourg, Abbé, involved in *Affaire des poisons*, 255, 259, 263

Guilds, 139, 163

Guise, duc de, 24, 27–28, 31, 100

Hauser, Henri, 130–31, 144, 163, 167, 194, 236

Henri IV (king of France, r. 1589–1610), 4, 108, 120, 132, 183; influence on Louis XIV, 73, 77

Henrietta of France (Queen Consort of Charles I of England), 135

Hercule gaulois (Puget), 114, 227

Herwarth, Barthélemy, 38, 186; eclipsed by Colbert, 45, 49–50, 59, 66, 69–70, 78

High Council, 65, 73, 77

Holland. *See* United Provinces

Huxelles, Mme d', 62, 63, 64

Huyghens, Christian, 127–28, 180, 247

Innocent XI, Pope (r. 1676–89), 248

Intendants, 11; and Colbert's policies, 95–97, 151, 158, 224, 267; Colbert's last letter to, 269

Iroquois, 191–93

Jacobinism, 39

James I (king of England, r. 1603–25), 135

James II (king of England, r. 1685–88; earlier, duke of York), 216, 273

Jansenism and Jansenists, 41, 248

Jesuits, 127, 141, 190, 192–93

John II Casimir (king of Poland, r. 1648–68), 59

Jolliet, Louis, 239

Journal des savants, 127

Juan of Austria, 43, 48

La Bruyere, Jean de, 153

Laffemas, Barthélemy de, 132–34, 155, 162

La Filastre, involved in *Affaire des poisons*, 255, 259, 260, 263

La Fontaine, Jean de, 49, 116, 137

Lamoignon, First President of the Parlement of Paris, 99, 101, 104

Langlade (ally of Fouquet), 47

La Quintinie, Jean de, 113, 227

La Reynie, Nicolas Gabriel de, 95, 108, 116, 211, 254; and *Affaire des poisons*, 255–56, 259–61, 265–66

La Rochefoucauld, François, duc de, 47

La Salle, Robert Cavelier, sieur de, 192–93, 239–40

Lauzun, Antoine Nompar de Caumont, duc de, 84, 86, 234, 265

La Vallière, Louise de La Baume le Blanc de, 64, 177; children by Louis XIV, 83–84, 87, 220; retires to convent, 84, 220; rivalry with Mme de Montespan and *Affaire des poisons*, 260–61

Lavisse, Ernest, 275

Le Brun, Charles: work at Vaux-le-Vicomte, 54, 64, 225; at the Louvre, 110; as King's First Painter, 113–14, 120, 122, 124–25; work at Versailles, 198; and the Temple of Aurora at Sceaux, 227, 275

Leibniz, Baron Gottfried Wilhelm, 247

Le Nôtre, André, 43, 54; and Paris, 108; and Versailles, 111, 113, 121; and the chateau at Clagny, 213; and Sceaux, 227

Leopold I (Holy Roman Emperor, r. 1658–1705), 59, 202

Le Pelletier, Claude, 270–71, 273–74

Lesage (magician involved in *Affaire des poisons*), 255–57, 260–63

Le Songe de Vaux (La Fontaine), 49

Le Tellier, Claude, 4, 9

Le Tellier, Michel, 4, 8, 9, 12, 16, 17, 25, 48, 53; on High Council, 65, 77; helps Colbert become intendant of finances, 59; and the fall of Fouquet, 65, 68, 101; rival of Colbert, 180, 182, 200, 242–43, 270; chancellor of France, 221, 243; and *Affaire des poisons*, 255–56, 265; death of,

Index

Le Tellier, Michel (*cont.*)
272; and the Napoleonic Code,
280
Le Tellier, François Michel. *See* Louvois
Le Vau, François, 175
Le Vau, Louis, architect, 43, 54; and
the Louvre, 109–10; and Ver-
sailles, 111, 113
Lhéry, Henri Cauchon, chevalier de,
238
Lionne, Hugues de, 14, 44, 172, 188;
on the High Council, 65, 77
"Little academy," the, 115, 119
Longueville, Anne Geneviève, duchesse
de, 86
Longueville, duc de, 15, 201
Long Vestu, 2–4, 171, 185
Lorraine, chevalier de, 85–86
Louis XI (king of France, r. 1461–83),
75, 92
Louis XII (king of France, r. 1498–
1515), 128
Louis XIII (king of France, r. 1610–
43), 8, 91
Louis XIV (king of France, r. 1643–
1715), flight from Paris during
the Fronde, 11; and Cardinal
Mazarin, 19, 41, 50–51; crowned
at Rheims (1654), 39; and the
siege of Arras, 40; disbands parle-
mentary assembly, 41; and Fouquet, 48, 50, 59–60, 62, 66–68;
first visits to Vaux-le-Vicomte,
50, 54; marriage to Maria Theresa of Spain, 50–51; and Marie
Mancini, 51; and creation of the
High Council, 57; interest in foreign affairs, 57; subsidies to
Charles II of England, 58, 202,
210; *Memoirs* of, 62, 160, 172;
and Louise de La Vallière, 64, 83;
and the fete at Vaux-le-Vicomte
(August 1661), 64; and public
finance, 67, 69; personal qualities, 73–75; Catholicism, 76,
248; as a military leader, 76; and
Mme de Montespan, 84–85, 211;
and the nobility, 89; and the
French judicial system, 91–92,
97, 103; restricts role of intendants, 95; and Versailles, 107–8,
111–12, 198–99, 201–2, 208,
211, 244, 246; acquisition of
Fouquet's collections, 114, 118;
and the arts, 121, 125; prepares
for war with Spain (1666), 147;
invades Holland, 150, 197; unin-
terested in naval affairs, 172; and
trading companies, 186; refuses
to retract protectionist measures
against Dutch, 196; refuses
Dutch peace proposal, 202; intox-
icated by the war, 212; growing
friction with Colbert, 212, 235,
244; punishes revolt in Brittany,
213–14; entertained at Sceaux,
228–29; lavishness, 236, 267;
seeks independence from Papal
authority, 248–49; and Protestants, 249–252, 273; and *Affaire
des poisons,* 255–66; and Mme de
Maintenon, 257–58; and Seignelay, 272
Louis de France, the Grand Dauphin,
221, 228, 247, 259
Louvois, François Michel Le Tellier,
marquis de, 4, 48, 79–80, 88,
134, 182; named secretary of war
and chancellor of the royal ordinances, 81; rival of Colbert, 180,
222, 237, 270; in war with
Dutch, 197; growing influence
of, 198, 245, 250; and Vauban,
200; temperament, 210; plot
against Pomponne, 221; and
Affaire des poisons, 255–57, 259,
261–62, 265–66; becomes superintendant of buildings after Colbert, 271; repression of
Protestants, 272; death of, 274
Louvre, designs for, 109–10; royal
library located in, 118; workshops
in, 120–21; Royal Academy of
Painting and Sculpture in, 124;
Galileo resides in, 127; work on
suspended, 246
Lully, Jean Baptiste, 125, 212, 244,
274
Luxembourg, François Henri de
Montorency-Bouteville, marshal
of, 256
Luynes, duc de, 88, 186

Index

Maine, Louis Auguste de Bourbon, duc de, 234, 274

Maintenon, Françoise d'Aubigné, marquise de, 252, 257–59

Maîtres des requêtes, 13, 42, 104; and the fall of Fouquet, 65, 67, 69; and Colbert, 95–96, 98, 151, 160; and trial of Fouquet, 99; and the Church, 161

Mancini, Alphonse, 29

Mancini, Marie (later duchess de Bouillon), 51, 83; and *Affaire des poisons,* 256–57

Mancini, Olympia (comtesse de Soissons), 29

Mancini, Philippe, duc de Nevers, 29, 85

Mansart, Jules Hardouin, 244, 274

Maria Theresa of Spain (queen of Louis XIV), 50–51, 54, 58, 147, 268

Martinozzi, Laura, 29

Mary II (queen of England, r. 1689–94 with William III), 216, 273

Mary Stuart (Mary, Queen of Scots; r. 1542–67), 135

Matignon, Mlle de (second wife of Seignelay), 222

Mazarin, Jules, Cardinal, 8; during the Fronde, 11, 37; clash with Colbert, 12–13; exile in Germany, 15–19; and Fouquet, 18–19, 39, 43, 47, 49, 52; return to Paris, 19; personal fortune, 22–23; questionable financial practices, 24–28, 38, 99; favors to Colbert, 30–32; political mentor of Louis XIV, 41; begins to distrust Fouquet, 44; and the "grand design," 45; negotiates marriage of Louis XIV, 50–51; death of, 55; influence on Colbert, 75; and the navy, 172; and trading companies, 186

Mazarini, Pierre, 29

Mercantilism, 130–36, 144–47, 156, 183, 193, 236, 239

Middle Ages, 91, 126

Mignard, Pierre, 122, 124, 225

Modena, duke of, 42

Molière (Jean Baptiste Poquelin), 111, 116, 121, 122, 212

Mongrédien, Georges, 22, 65, 253

Montespan, Françoise Athénaïs Rochechouart, marquise de; begins affair with Louis XIV, 84; alliance with Colbert, 85, 198–99, 212; at Versailles, 202, 209, 266; at Clagny 211–12; at Sceaux, 229; mother of the duc du Maine, 274; waning of the king's interest in, 252, 259; and *Affaire des poisons,* 256–66; leaves court for convent, 266

Montespan, Louis Henri, marquis de, 212, 258

Mortemart, Marie-Anne, duchesse de (Colbert's daughter), 222, 257

Napoleonic Code, 242, 280

Navigation Act of 1651, 146

Negro Code (1685), 242

Neuchèze (commander of the French royal navy), 47, 52, 60, 63, 71

Noblesse de robe, 4

North Sea Company, 194–95, 240, 276

Noyers, Sublet de, 7–8

Octroi, 80

Orleans, Gaston Jean Baptiste, duc d', 14–15, 50, 52, 54, 86n, 121

Orleans, Henrietta of England, duchesse d', 254

Orleans, Philippe I, duc d' ("Monsieur"), 85–86

Papin, Denis, 247

Paris: early seventeenth century financial center, 6; during the Fronde, 11, 15, 18; administration and renewal of under Colbert, 107–10; Tuileries, 108, 109, 110, 112, 116; Champs-Elysées, 108; Observatory, 110, 247; effect of the king's prolonged absence from, 246

Parlement of Paris, 11, 41, 48, 99, 105; ratifies trading-company charters, 185; and the war with Holland, 201

Partis and *partisans,* 6, 7, 37, 50, 94–95

Index

Patin, Gui, 81, 89

Pellison (agent of Fouquet), 47, 53, 65, 98, 249

Pellot, Claude, 97–98, 195, 243

The Perfect Merchant (Savary), 152, 167

Perrault, Charles, 110, 111, 116, 124, 126, 210; author of *Fairy Tales*, 114, 245; and the "little academy," 115; at Sceaux, 228; memory of Colbert, 231; chancellor of the Académie française, 244

Perrault, Claude, 108, 110, 115, 127, 226

Perrot, Nicolas, 193

Petitière, Mme de la, 164, 167

Philip IV (king of Spain, r. 1621–65), 40, 50, 58

Plan of Saint-Mandé. *See* Fouquet

Plessis-Bellière, marquise du, 46–47, 61, 65, 68

Poland, 59, 80, 154

Polignac, Mme de, involved in *Affaire des poisons*, 256

Pomereu, Mme de (follower of Cardinal de Retz), 42

Pomponne, Simon Arnauld, marquis de, 99, 148, 195–96, 203–4, 215, 221

Portugal, 58

Protestants, 42, 76, 194; Colbert's protection of, 173; excluded from New World charters, 183; repression of, 249, 252, 272–73; forced conversion of, 250–51; exodus from France, 278

Pussort, Marie, 4, 7

Pussort (uncle of Colbert), 103–5, 270

Quinault, Philippe, 212; *Poem of Sceaux*, 228

Racine, Jean, 116, 121, 122–23, 212, 223; invited to Sceaux, 227; his *Phèdre* performed at Sceaux, 229; and *The Idyll of Peace* at Sceaux, 274

Ratabon, Antoine de, 107

Rentes and *rentiers*, 100–101, 232

Retz, Jean François Paul de Gondi, cardinal de, 40–43, 47, 59, 76

Richelieu, Armand Jean du Plessis, Cardinal: influence on Colbert, 6, 7, 8, 11–13, 21, 39, 77–78, 171; and financiers, 37; Académie française founded by, 123; and the "grand design," 129; protectionist policies of, 132; and the Dutch, 137–38, 146; naval policies of, 171–72, 176

Rigaud, Hyacinthe, 267

Robert, Nicolas, 121

Rohan, chevalier de, 210–11

Royal Academy of Painting and Sculpture, 124, 267

Russell, Bertrand, 126

Ruyter, Admiral Michel Adriaanszoon de, 140, 148, 202, 205, 207, 215

Saint-Aignan, comte de (later duc de Beauvilliers), 87, 123, 221

Saint-Aignan, Henriette, comtesse de (later duchesse de Beauvilliers; Colbert's daughter), 87, 88, 221, 272

Saint-Maurice, marquis de (ambassador from Savoy), 81, 83, 89, 149, 177

Savary, Jacques, 152, 167, 236

Savonnerie tapestry works, 120, 133, 164, 225, 244

Sceaux. See Colbert, Jean-Baptiste, *and* Seignelay

Séguier, Pierre, duc de Villemor: as Chancellor of France, 50, 65, 96, 99, 186; death of, 124, 242

Seignelay, Jean-Baptiste Colbert, marquis de, 88–89, 109, 245, 267–72; personal qualities, 180; assistant to his father, 181–82, 199, 200, 213, 216; first marriage, 222; second marriage, 222; and Louvois, 237; arranges for burial of Queen Maria Theresa, 268–69; at the death of his father, 270; as head of the naval department, 271; high standing with Louis XIV, 272; entertains king at Sceaux, 274; death of, 273, 276

Seignobos, Charles, 184

Index

Servien, Abel, 14, 18, 25, 36, 38, 49

Sévigné, Marie de Rabutin-Chantal, marquise de, 84, 93, 101, 145; describes Mme Colbert, 87; describes Colbert, 89; on the trial of Fouquet, 99; on the war with Holland, 201, 205; describes Clagny, 213; describes an evening at Colbert's home, 220; on the death of Mme Seignelay, 222; on the chateau of Seignelay, 226; describes tax on the poor, 234; and Colbert, 255; on *Affaire des poisons,* 257; on Mme de Montespan, 258; on the death of Seignelay, 273

Soissons, Olympia Mancini, comtesse de, 29, 253

Spain: power in Europe, 146; French workers in, 166; alliance with Holland, 198, 208; and the Treaty of Nijmegen, 217

Spanish Netherlands, 138, 205

Strozzi, Abbé, 119–20, 244

Sully, Maximilien de Béthune, duc de, 154–55, 183

Sweden, 204, 206, 213

Taille, 94, 97, 102, 231–32

Taxes and taxation: and the peasants, 37, 275; obstacles to collection of, 50; feudal legacy, 92–94; abuses, 94–95; Colbert's theory of, 231–32, 280

Tax farmers and tax farming, 2, 6, 7, 37; and the Fronde, 14; and Fouquet, 38, 54, 66, 98, 122; and Colbert, 67, 79, 102, 119, 137; and Louis XIV, 145, 242; under Mazarin, 232; revenge on Colbert, 234; and the beginnings of unified tax structure, 242

Temple of Aurora (at Sceaux), 227–28

Thirty Years' War, 6

Treaty of Aix-la-Chapelle, 149

Treaty of the Hague, 149

Treaty of Nijmegen, 198, 216–17, 237–38, 242

Treaty of Paris, 277

Treaty of the Pyrenees, 58, 114

Treaty of Westphalia, 58

Trécesson, Mlle de (mistress of Fouquet), 49

Tresmitten, Henri, 195

Trésoriers de l'epargne, 24–25, 102

Tubeuf, Jacques, 19

Turenne, Henri de La Tour d'Auvergne, vicomte de: defeated at Valenciennes, 30, 43; victory at the Dunes, 48; and the fall of Fouquet, 68, 101; and the war with Holland, 200, 205, 249; and Louvois, 210; death of, 213

United Provinces: financial ascendancy of, 5; prosperity irritates France, 136, 137, 141–42, 145–46, 184; size of fleet, 136; seventeenth-century life in, 139–45; religious tolerance, 141; shipbuilding, 142; economic war with France, 143, 149–50, 195, 279; and mercantilism, 144; organized system of public credit, 144–45; Franco-Dutch alliance against Hapsburgs, 58, 146; commercial alliance with Spain, 146; Louis XIV invades, 150; economic crisis, 196; war with France, 197–98; alliance with Spain, 198; hegemony in European trade, 142, 237

Valenciennes, siege of, 30, 43

Van der Meulen, Antoine François, 198

Vauban, Sébastien Le Prestre, Marquis de, 157, 175, 199–200, 203–5, 213, 217, 237, 241

Vaux-le-Vicomte, 35, 43, 45, 49; Mazarin visits, 50; Louis XIV visits, 50, 54; triumphal fete at (August 17, 1661), 64, 228

Ventadour, monseigneur de, archbishop of Bourges, 23

Vendôme, César de Bourbon, duc de, 172, 175, 177

Vermandois, Louis de Bourbon, comte de (son of Louis XIV and Louise de La Vallière), 84, 177, 220, 229

Versailles, 107, 108, 110, 218; construction under Louis XIV, 111–
12, 198–99, 202–3; cost of, 111,
112, 199, 245, 271–72; menagerie at, 121, 126; Hall of Mirrors
at, 218, 272; Orangerie at, 244
Villacerf, Lord, 4, 6
Vivonne, duc de, 177, 214, 257
Voisin woman, the (Catherine
Deshayes Monvoisin), 255–57,
260–62

War of Devolution, 148, 174
West Indies Company (French), 185,
189, 195, 238, 276–77

Widow Scarron. *See* Maintenon
William III (stadtholder of Holland,
1672–1702, and king of England, r. 1689–1702), 145; at war
with France, 197, 200, 202–3,
206, 208; marries Mary, princess
of England, 216; victorious, 217;
and the European coalition, 233;
and the overthrow of James II,
273
Witches and witchcraft, 97–98, 253

York, duke of (later James II of England), 201, 203, 216, 273